T0311286

PRISONER
OF THE
VAMPIRES
OF MARS

....

Gustave Le Rouge

Translated by David Beus and Brian Evenson
Introduction by William Ambler

UNIVERSITY OF NEBRASKA PRESS | LINCOLN AND LONDON

Library of Congress Cataloging-in-Publication Data
Le Rouge, Gustave, 1867–1938.
[Novels. Selections. English]
Prisoner of the vampires of Mars / Gustave Le Rouge;
translated by David Beus and Brian Evenson;
introduction by William Ambler.
pages   cm. — (Bison frontiers of imagination)
ISBN 978-0-8032-1896-3 (pbk.: alk. paper)
ISBN 978-0-8032-7713-7 (epub)
ISBN 978-0-8032-7714-4 (mobi)
ISBN 978-0-8032-7715-1 (pdf)
I. Beus, David, 1966– translator. II. Evenson,
Brian, 1966– translator. III. Le Rouge,
Gustave, 1867–1938. Prisonnier de la planète
Mars. English. IV. Le Rouge, Gustave, 1867–1938.
Guerre des vampires. English. V. Title.
PQ2623.E58A2 2015
843'.912—dc23
2014043899

Set in Fournier by M. Scheer.
Designed by N. Putens.

CONTENTS

Introduction by William Ambler ix

....

THE PRISONER OF
THE PLANET MARS

....

PART ONE

I.	A Mysterious Message	5
II.	Ralph Pitcher's Home	14
III.	Missing	31
IV.	Yarmouth Street	34
V.	The Castle of Energy	41
VI.	Marvels	50
VII.	The Catastrophe	58
VIII.	The Awakening	63

PART TWO

I.	The Wilderness	75
II.	Dead from Joy	82
III.	The Conquest of Fire	92

IV.	The White Beast	99
V.	The Vampire	107
VI.	Captain Wad's Experiment	112
VII.	The Martian Village	129
VIII.	Public Festivities	135
IX.	War with the Idols	140
X.	Nocturnal Battle	147
XI.	Explorations	155
XII.	Progress	161
XIII.	The Crystal Mountain	164
XIV.	The Photographs	173
XV.	"RO-BERT DAR-VEL"	178
XVI.	Darkness	188
	Translator's Note	191

THE WAR OF THE VAMPIRES

PART ONE: THE INVISIBLES

I.	Zarouk	197
II.	The Villa des Lentisques	207
III.	A Meal Worthy of Lucullus	219
IV.	The Invisible Being	229
V.	The Catastrophe	237
VI.	A Strange Meteorite	250
VII.	A Potent Cure	260

PART TWO: THE MARTIAN MYSTERY

I.	Robert Darvel's Tale	269
II.	After the Victory	286
III.	The Aerophytes	298
IV.	The Glass Tower	308
V.	Arsenals and Catacombs	321
VI.	The Opal Helmet	336
VII.	The Isle of Death	349
VIII.	The Road Home	364

PART THREE: THE LAST OF THE VAMPIRES

I.	Nocturnal Phantasms	375
II.	The Pursuit	381
III.	Explanations	393

INTRODUCTION | *William Ambler*

> I am calling forth formidable powers.
> Gustave Le Rouge, *Prisoner of the Vampires of Mars*

It's well established that science fiction is a genre that spent many years wandering in the wilderness of ill-repute. Long cast as the undiscriminating purveyors and consumers of adolescent power fantasies and the exploits of bug-eyed monsters, its enthusiasts always found themselves seated around the kids' table at the literary banquet, popularity serving as cold comfort in the face of critical indifference or — worse yet — derision. Such treatment engendered a number of coping mechanisms. Some ran for the shelter of more respectable terms like "fabulist" or "magic realist." Others chose to hang their hat on the predictive qualities of the genre: "Arthur C. Clarke anticipated the satellite belt! William Gibson envisioned cyberspace!" Much of this defensiveness is falling away as the genre is incorporated into the literary canon, but it is still invigorating to encounter a volume like Gustave Le Rouge's *Prisoner of the Vampires of Mars* and find oneself reminded of the true beating heart that kept the genre alive for so long in the face of widespread scorn: the breathless voice of the creator saying, "Look at this thing that I've made — you'll not find another quite like it anywhere."

Le Rouge was himself a unique character. He was that rare anticapitalist relentlessly dedicated to putting his (lack of) money where his mouth was. He composed dozens of works in virtually every genre imaginable, many of them going through a number of translations and selling in the hundreds of thousands, but was known to brag about signing over the rights for a pittance up front and eschewing the enormous riches he stood to accrue through royalties. It's no accident that his first science fiction novel was titled *The Billionaires' Conspiracy* and concerned a plot for world domination hatched by a group of American industrialists. His preferred role was that of the decadent, absinthe-ingesting man of letters and friend to such figures as Paul Verlaine and one-armed Swiss Renaissance man Blaise Cendrars.

Le Rouge was certainly a follower to some degree of the emerging genre of science fiction: his second SF novel, *The Submarine "Jules Verne,"* has a distinct whiff of fan fiction, and *Prisoner* includes an extended . . . homage to the Eloi/Morlocks dynamic from Wells's *The Time Machine*. One of the things that grants *Prisoner* its enormous charm is Le Rouge's willingness to bring past, present, and future crashing together with a relentless sense of energy and discovery. The result feels like a (delightfully) overstuffed greatest-hits compilation that manages to pull simultaneously from the past and future of an artist's oeuvre.

The reader is served notice quite early that Le Rouge will spare no opportunity to provide a concept or incident of interest. Our hero, engineer Robert Darvel, has just returned to the British Isles after a disastrous attempt to communicate with the red planet by carving enormous symbols into the black soil of Siberia. He meets for drinks with his friend, rare bird dealer Ralph Pitcher. Pitcher, it turns out, has enjoyed fortunes quite the opposite of Darvel's, having recently come into a significant sum of money. Has he won the lottery? Inherited the estate of a dowager aunt? Made a sound business investment? Oh, you're no fun. The answer—of course—is that he was captured by Thugs on an expedition in the remote valleys of Nepal and came across a great horde of treasure while making his escape. In the process, he learned one of the most important rules for participants in an adventure story: always be the *second* one to approach the enormous bejeweled idol.

Darvel soon finds himself involved in the supernatural when he is enjoined by a mysterious Brahmin to travel east, there to begin construction of a machine designed to focus the willpower of thousands of mystics into a propellant capable of transporting a man to Mars. Early science fiction authors had a pretty clear field for devising methods of interplanetary travel, and here Le Rouge combines the simplicity of Edwin L. Arnold's *Gulliver of Mars* (magic carpet) and Burroughs's *A Princess of Mars* (astral projection/"he fell asleep in a cave and woke up on Mars and stop asking so many questions!") with a patina of Vernian technology. The science is, of course, all hogwash, and Le Rouge is sure to provide a lot of detail while leaving the connective tissue vague—ultimately it serves the same purpose as the blinking lights and foaming beakers that surround the mad scientist in any low-budget horror film. Darvel is eventually betrayed by his benefactor and rocketed to Mars by himself in a sort of bulbous metal coffin at the speed of thought (half the speed of light, it turns out).

Once Darvel arrives on the red planet, Le Rouge unleashes a torrent of incidents that echo through the genre. A line can be traced from a typical description of an environment—"vegetation, colored blood, gold, and rust and illuminated by the magical, phosphorescent glow of the two moons. . . . In this golden forest, the blue and white trees were like ghosts sadly waving their arms"—through countless paperback and magazine covers, prog rock album art, and the CGI environments in a film like *Avatar*. There's the aforementioned recasting of the Eloi/Morlock dynamic from *The Time Machine*, this time with Darvel liberating a race of hapless humanoids from the bat-winged Erloor and a race of burrowing mole creatures (note how quickly Darvel progresses from colonialist warrior-savior to harried administrator—he's as restless as his creator). When he arrives at the nesting place of the oft-invisible vampires of the title, we find ourselves in the middle of one of the central tropes of the Dying Earth subgenre, in which the characters we follow play out their conflicts against a backdrop composed of the ruins of unfathomably ancient and advanced civilizations, seen again as recently as Ridley Scott's *Prometheus*. Darvel's discovery of the force that bedevils the vampires—too good to spoil here—is a reveal that cries out to be depicted in a color-soaked double splash page by Jack Kirby, our hero's horrified visage pinned in the corner.

For the duration of his exile on Mars, a group of Darvel's friends and compatriots are attempting to effect his return, including Ralph Pitcher and Darvel's ex-fiancée, billionaire heiress Alberte Teramond (one presumes she is spared Le Rouge's customary scorn due to a combination of her status as mere inheritor of wealth and a born storyteller's instinct to let nothing besmirch a good love interest). When Darvel finds himself back on Earth—via exploding volcano—he relays much of his adventures with the vampires to his friends. Le Rouge thus observes one of the central tenets of early science fiction and horror novels: conveying events via omniscient narrator is all well and good, but nothing beats a mysterious manuscript or a tale told over brandy and cigars in the library. But wait! There's more! Several of the vampires have followed our hero back to Earth, and a final battle for the fate of humanity is in the offing. These creatures, with their pendulous red lips, mouths full of fangs, and ability to strike from a cloak of invisibility, exude a primordial malevolence of a piece with the various tentacled and gilled creatures that would populate the work of Lovecraft and others in the decades to come. They're a harbinger of the sort of "gibbering horror" mere humans will feel when unfathomable beings turn their baleful—or merely hungry—attentions our way.

When I imagine Gustave Le Rouge composing *Prisoner of the Vampires of Mars*, I don't see a man filling a stack of blank pages with script. I picture a mad engineer scurrying through a scrap yard piled high with technologies contemporary, ancient, and yet to be conceived. He's building a spaceship, but it's like no spaceship you've ever seen. Sleek metal abuts wood, which gives way to a colorful mosaic of stone. The warp drive appears to run on gears and steam. The passenger brave enough to step onboard is confronted with a riot of tunnels and chambers. Some tunnels are laid out with precision; others dip and curve for no apparent reason. This one dead-ends; that one grows dark and . . . slimy . . . best to turn back. In the chamber to the left, a young man adjusts a series of knobs on a sleek metal cabinet; to the right, an ancient, wizened man inscribes a stone floor with chalk symbols. It seems that any attempt at ignition should find the whole left shuddering on the launch pad. And yet . . . it works. Each bit counterbalances the next in perfect synchronicity, and achieving escape velocity is a virtual afterthought. I envy you your first trip. Enjoy the ride.

PRISONER OF THE VAMPIRES OF MARS

THE PRISONER OF
THE PLANET MARS

PART ONE

I

....

A Mysterious Message

"Has no one asked for me, Mrs. Hobson?"

"No one."

"Has no letter come for me?"

"Not a one."

Mrs. Hobson, the proprietress of the Royal Arms of Scotland, was not, by nature, talkative. Despite her interlocutor's desire to engage her in conversation, she let him know, with a sharp, purposeful gesture, that she had no interest in wasting time on idle chatter.

Stationed behind her counter, framed by pewter tankards, enormous sides of rare roast beef, pots of preserves, and small jars of pickles, she was passing the time before tea in earnestly counting her morning receipts, placing the shillings and sixpence that filled her till into equal piles.

At the other end of the room, which was nearly empty at this particular moment, thick steam rose from the thoroughly soaked clothes of a young man of elegant appearance seated next to a large coal fire.

From time to time he got up, went to the window and, through panes streaming with water, contemplated the view over the quays of the Thames, where hundreds of black steamers, lined up under the smoke-colored sky, displayed their sad profiles in the yellowish fog.

When the young man had had a good look at the piles of coal stretching as far as the eye could see — coal that would disappear into the docks, into the comings and goings of the wheezing locomotives coupled to interminable trains loaded with casks and blocks of stone — he sat down again dejectedly and half-closed his eyes, numbed by the humid heat of the room, his brain aching from the incessant roar of the steamers.

He was a young man of about thirty, with curly blond hair and beard, a noble profile, and bright blue eyes. It was evident from his appearance that he was one of those high-strung types who abhor idleness and rush into things without due consideration.

The fog grew thicker and the landscape more hazy. The locomotives and steamers had become blurred together and the electric lamps were beginning to cast their white stains onto this blotting-paper décor when the bell at the front door jingled.

A newcomer abruptly entered the inn. Despite his heavy suede-lined coat and long gaiters, he was covered with mud and soaked to the bone. His boots squished like sponges and large puddles formed beneath his feet.

"Is that you, my dear Pitcher?"

"How are you, Master Darvel?"

Mr. Pitcher, unintimidated by Mrs. Hobson's peevish expression, pushed back his hood, revealing a bright, ruddy face, cheerful and good-natured, to which not even his bushy red Kitchener mustache could give a bellicose air.

With his fat red fingers bedecked with rings, his paunch shaped like a cask of March beer, and the tiger claws mounted on his watch chain, Mr. Pitcher looked to be one of the most inoffensive inhabitants of the United Kingdom.

He sat down quite out of breath, mopped his forehead, and ordered a glass of mulled port with the grave expression of a prudent man taking precautions against bronchitis.

"Still the same old Pitcher," said Robert Darvel, smiling.

"Yes indeed, Robert."

"How's the bird business?"

"So-so. When I bumped into you yesterday in Drury Lane, I had just completed a deal for a shipment of storks and flamingos with an officer back from the Sudan. And, on my honor, it's disgraceful!"

The large man had stood up, seized by sudden indignation.

"Believe it or not, Robert," he exclaimed, "ten years from now there will be no more wild-bird trade. Mind you, I'm not talking about ostrich feathers. There are still plenty of those, thanks to the farms at the Cape where they raise ostriches like ducks. But the beautiful birds of the virgin forest, the monals, egrets, lyrebirds, birds of paradise, all of these will be nothing more than a legend before long."

"And why is that, my old friend?" said Robert, smiling a little at his indignation.

"Why?" said the other, with growing fury. "Because we are slaughtering, massacring them all. Some men go so far as to run electric wires to the edge of the watering holes where they drink. Yes sir, I have seen three thousand swallows electrocuted in one day through this barbaric practice, and for what? To adorn hats!"

"There are worse ways they could be used."

Ralph Pitcher wasn't listening. His face purple with rage, he continued to rant, punctuating his argument by pounding his fist on the table.

"Yes," he groaned, with a touch of emotion in his voice, "we are exterminating birds, large and small, without mercy. Wherever the railroad and the electric light spread, it's a massacre. Even migratory birds—swans, wild ducks, even albatrosses—are not spared. Do you know that at certain times of the year, lighthouse keepers find hundreds of birds at the foot of their granite towers, birds who, fascinated by the glow of these mighty lamps visible from fifty miles away, smash their skulls against the thick glass of the lantern?"

"Now wait a minute," interrupted Robert Darvel, when Pitcher stopped to catch his breath and, at the same time, knock back a drink. "I don't see why you are so upset. As a naturalist and a hunter, you are by profession the natural enemy of all game, furred or feathered."

"Let me . . ."

"And when I joined you on the steppes of Turkistan and in the jungles of Bengal, you were waging a merciless war against them. What's more, I never recall without a vivid sense of pleasure mornings when we lay in wait among reeds still wet with dew, or our mad charges through forests where we were often obliged to camp and from which we returned laden with slaughtered game."

Pitcher had suddenly grown melancholy.

"Yes," he said, "but in our expeditions we did not employ those blasted machines that systematically destroy an entire breed. We hunted the exotic birds of the forest honestly, rifle in hand, respecting the brood and waging a determined war against snakes and beasts of prey."

"That's the truth!"

"So, it seems you have achieved some success. I saw your picture in the *Daily Telegraph* and the photograph of your facility in Siberia . . . You must be wealthy now."

"My poor friend, you couldn't be more wrong! I am utterly beggared."

"But what about your inventions?"

"Sold for a crust of bread to American interests."

"And your marriage to Teramond's daughter?"

"Called off."

The naturalist opened his eyes wide with amazement.

"How did all of this happen?" he asked, calmly lighting a cigar and leaning forward the better to hear.

"Oh! It was easy. Let me explain. I had made some money from my inventions: my lightweight engine for airships and my alcohol boiler for high-speed steamships. It was then that I made the acquaintance of Teramond the banker and was introduced to his charming daughter, Alberte. She was kind enough to look favorably on my advances. Her father, who saw an opportunity to make a fortune through my patents, did not at first appear hostile to this planned union. Everything was going fine when one day in Whitechapel I bumped into a Mr. Bolensky, a Polish refugee and first-rate astronomer whom I had met before in Paris. He had a firm conviction that every planet is inhabited by beings like us and he supported this opinion with a multitude of proofs. All his research had been focused on methods of entering into communication with the inhabitants of the planets closest to us. He was able to infect me with his enthusiasm and, after eight days of discussion and consultation, we reached an agreement. We decided (and you must have already learned this from the newspapers) that, bypassing the moon, which the majority of astronomers recognize to be a dead planet, we would target Mars, the red planet that medieval astrologers believed to presage wars and natural disasters. Following an idea mentioned by several experts that had never yet been put into practice, we resolved to construct, in a perfectly level place, some elementary geometrical figure, big enough to be clearly visible to Martian astronomers."

"Why a geometrical figure?"

"The laws of this science are no doubt the same throughout the universe. The numerals and letters of the alphabet are conventional. Triangles, circles, and the laws that govern them must, on the contrary, be known to Martian scientists, no matter how limited their scientific development."

"I still don't see how, even if the Martians understand geometry, you could have communicated with them."

Robert shrugged his shoulders, smiling.

"But that's only the beginning. Assume they responded to my signals with similar signals, right away I would make others. I would write next to each figure its name, and the Martians would do the same. There you have the rudiments of an alphabet that would be easy to complete with the help of very simple drawings, always accompanied by their names. After several months of work, it would be simple to communicate fluently. From here, you can envision the marvelous results. We would soon be initiated into the history, discoveries, and even the literature of these newfound brothers who themselves are perhaps stretching their arms out to us across the abyss of the firmament. And we wouldn't have stopped there: I already had plans for a giant camera. We would soon have possessed portraits of kings, queens, great men, and the most fashionable inhabitants of our sister planet."

"Who knows?" murmured Pitcher optimistically. "Perhaps you would have found some customers for me."

"Why not?" exclaimed Robert passionately. "Nothing is impossible in this sequence of events . . . But consider what enormous benefits I would procure for all humanity. We would benefit at little expense, I can tell you, from the intellectual work accumulated by thousands of generations. The solution to the social question, unlimited longevity — the Martians may know all about these things. The success of my experiment would have been an incalculable blessing for all."

"Pardon me!" said Pitcher, who admired his friend's enthusiasm without sharing it. "But what if the Martians are still in a savage state? What if they are cruel beings . . ."

"An excellent objection. In that case, we would have been the ones to civilize them by letting them profit from our knowledge."

"Such noble intentions . . . But enough of this, how did it all turn out?"

"Very badly. My associate and I left for Siberia. At first, everything went quite well. My associate, Mr. Bolensky, who had previously been exiled from Poland, obtained a pardon. The Russian government granted the necessary authorizations. Arriving in Stretensk on the Trans-Siberian railroad, we acquired workers and supplies and then continued to the north until we reached a perfectly flat steppe where we laid out, over several leagues, our geometric figures. The lines were simply drawn, thirty meters to a side, with chalky rocks whose white hue stood out boldly on the black soil of the steppe. At night, powerful electric lights reproduced our signals."

"That must have cost a fortune," interrupted Pitcher.

"When we had finished the circle, the triangle, and the geometric figure that accompanies the demonstration of the theorem of the square of the hypotenuse — which we had chosen as characteristic and easily visible — my funds were seriously depleted; but I was full of hope. From our camp, in the shade of a small wood, we could survey our work. The camp formed a little village that was quite picturesque with its thatched earthen huts and open-air kitchens. I hunted gray bear and fox, fished for sturgeon and salmon, accompanied by Ostyaks outfitted in nettle-thread shirts and fish-skin vests — good men, a bit slovenly, but ready to follow me to the ends of the earth for a packet of tobacco or a flask of rum. I grew accustomed to this pastoral life. Siberia in the summer, with its green forests teeming with game, is a charming place. The inhabitants of Mars, however, gave no sign of life.

"We had made the acquaintance of a prominent Russian landowner, worth several million rubles, who had warmly embraced our ideas and was going to finance us. In his opinion, our figures were much too small; he meant to redraw them, on a much larger scale, and to secure from the emperor several *sotnias*[1] of Cossacks to guard them. Then everything fell apart. Mr. Bolensky, whose certificate of amnesty had not been recorded, was unexpectedly arrested and sent to the penal colony on Sakhalin Island. I too was imprisoned for a time and had great difficulty proving my innocence. When I returned to the camp, I found it had been completely destroyed by

1   A sotnia is a squadron of soldiers.

a band of marauding Khoungouses.[2] The scoundrels had taken everything: weapons, instruments, rations, and munitions, including the beautiful telescope that would have allowed us to see the Martians' signals.

"My geometric designs had already been transformed into sturdy and convenient roads, used by merchants trading in tea and salt fish. As for the Siberian laborers and Asiatic hunters of my escort, needless to say they had dispersed, no doubt after collecting their share of the booty . . . I went to find the Russian landowner who had been going to finance us. He coolly showed me the door, assuring me that he was too devoted to His Majesty, the "Little Father" Tsar Nicolas, to maintain any relationship with a nihilist such as myself."

"Now that's what you call bad luck," said Pitcher, who had lit a second cigar and ordered a rum toddy. "But how did you get out of this mess?"

"I'm not out of it. I had a little money left, luckily. I hurriedly took the train, and here I am. I have enough to live on for a month in London. Between now and then I must make some discovery, otherwise I don't know what will become of me."

"If I were you, I would go to Mr. Teramond. I'm certain he would happily advance you some funds."

"How wrong you are, my poor friend! After I disembarked in London, my first visit was to the banker, whom I already considered my future father-in-law. He knew about some of my setbacks, and his welcome, as a result, was rather cold. To tell the truth, he was barely civil to me.

"'Dear Sir,' he said to me, with the heavy-handed irony of a practical man who has pulled himself up 'by his bootstraps,' as they say, and who understands the value of money, 'my limited resources do not permit me to jump into endeavors as grandiose as yours. I have great admiration for you, of course; you are brilliantly gifted; you will be the pride of your country. But to communicate with other planets, you need at least a billion or two. Go to Chicago, that's what I recommend.'

"I didn't stoop to respond to this lout. I left without a word and in some distress, not because of the missed opportunity — money means nothing to me, thank God! . . . But Miss Alberte has such tender blue

----

2   The Khoungouses are brigands of the steppes

eyes, such a mysterious smile, such beautiful hair, dark yet shiny as new copper . . ."

"Enough of this description, let's get to the point."

"Oh, that's about the sum of it. Only, as I turned around before passing through the gilded gate of the house for the last time, I glimpsed the lovely profile of Miss Alberte through a second-story window. We waved sadly to each other and I left in despair. But from the look she gave me I understood that the poor child is merely submitting to the will of a tyrannical father."

"Everything will work out," said Pitcher. "I wager that in less than a month you'll have made some brilliant discovery that you'll sell for a king's ransom. Then you'll be back in her father's good graces."

The conversation between the two friends had reached this point when they heard the weak, cracked sound of the doorbell.

A dirty, ragged urchin, shivering under an old sailor's sweater, entered and advanced warily to the counter where Mrs. Hobson was enthroned.

"What have you come for, little devil?" she asked.

"I've got a letter to give to this gentleman," said the curious little boy with an important air, conspicuously pointing his finger at Robert Darvel.

At the same time he pulled from his pocket a crumpled missive on which his filthy thumb had imprinted in black an extra postmark. Then he disappeared, slamming the door with a crash, leaving no time for anyone to question him.

Mrs. Hobson, after shrugging her shoulders at this scandalous behavior, returned to counting her money.

"A strange message," said Pitcher guardedly.

"A strange messenger, rather," said Robert, laughing heartily. "I don't know anyone likely to write to me."

"Now that's suspicious."

"I'll find out this very instant."

Robert opened the letter and read out loud:

Sir,

I have made a point of keeping apprised of your work and your travels. I have an interesting proposition to put before you. Please come see me this evening, around ten o'clock, in the apartment where I reside at 15 Yarmouth Street. Ask for Mr. Ardavena.

Please accept my greetings and the expression of my devotion, and, above all, do not miss the appointment that I have set, which is, for you as well as for me, of the utmost importance.

"That's odd," murmured Robert. "I rack my brains to determine who this strange and laconic correspondent might be, but in vain. In addition, look at this mysterious handwriting. Compared to the letter, the envelope is practically a masterpiece of calligraphy. And this brusque and awkward style . . ."

"Yes, you'd think these lines had been written by a child who barely knows how to form his letters and looked every word up in a dictionary."

"Bah! It's probably much simpler than you imagine. It's just some rich foreigner, some industrialist or eccentric, who wants to employ me in one of his factories or purchase my future discoveries."

"Yes, perhaps you're right."

"If that's the case, you'll have to admit that luck is with me. I was already wondering what was to become of me."

Mrs. Hobson had lit the lamps, for the fog had grown so dense that it was impossible to make anything out.

"It is only four o'clock," said Ralph Pitcher. "If you will do me the honor of accepting my invitation, we shall dine together with my mother this evening."

"Agreed," said Robert Darvel. "This fog is oppressive. I'd be delighted, before going to my mysterious rendezvous, to spend a fine evening discussing science and natural history with a friend I haven't seen in many years."

II

....

Ralph Pitcher's Home

Not far from the tavern, on a dark street that led to the quays, Ralph Pitcher inhabited a low, narrow shop bursting with stuffed animals, books, and minerals. Birds of prey and lizards hung from the ceiling. Robert noticed, on a workbench littered with pliers, scalpels, and rolls of brass wire, a compartment box filled with glass eyes of every conceivable size and color. A strange odor permeated this cramped cubbyhole, whose single gas lamp projected the twisted shadows of wading-birds and reptiles onto the walls.

Robert was presented to Mrs. Pitcher, a little old lady with a narrow, angular profile and a sharp chin. She was so wizened and yellow that, with her bright blackbird's eyes, she looked like a strange bird stuffed and mounted on iron wires that had by some procedure been brought to life and given movement. Her small, clawlike hands, which moved restlessly and almost mechanically, completed the illusion.

Mrs. Pitcher greeted her son's friend cordially, and soon places were set on a bright white tablecloth in the back room: dark beer foamed in stoneware jugs, water for tea sang in the kettle. An ample slab of smoked salmon, the first sacrifice to the table-companions' appetite, soon made way for a Scottish mutton pie and other substantial fare.

The two friends dined happily, reminiscing about their hunts and adventures and dreaming up countless future projects.

After dessert had been cleared, Mrs. Pitcher promptly brought hot water and whiskey for toddies as well as some blond tobacco in a bulbous, gilded Dutch pot that, despite its oddity, was quite pleasant to look at.

The ceramic stove, stuffed to the gills, roared majestically, drowning out the bellowing foghorns and the screeching whistles of locomotives in the distant evening mist.

There prevailed in the small room an atmosphere of warmth, of untroubled ease and convivial good nature, that lifted Robert's spirits.

The future looked rosy. He smiled as he watched his friend Pitcher, who had just lit a long meerschaum pipe and was blowing out enormous plumes of smoke and blinking his eyes with a beatific expression.

As he looked at him more closely, Robert found that, with his brick-red complexion and slightly skewed eyebrows, he resembled the solemn, rigid figures painted on ancient Egyptian tombs.

He let his mind drift, imagining Ralph as a descendant of those generations of embalmers who had preserved in pitch and odoriferous gums the millions of ibises, crocodiles, and wasps that one still finds today carefully aligned in underground crypts.

This extravagant thought amused Pitcher very much.

"Humph," he chuckled, "the breed must have greatly degenerated from the Egyptians — who were sacred personages, priests of sorts — down to me, a poor taxidermist who isn't embarrassed to restore the appearance of life to a Dutch canary or many an old lady's favorite lapdog . . ."

The naturalist fell silent. Then his thoughts turned abruptly in a new direction:

"By the way," he said suddenly, and a little sheepishly, "I've been meaning to say . . . You must be short of money. If, until something comes your way, you would accept . . . If, for example, fifty or a hundred pounds . . ."

"That's very kind of you," murmured Robert, truly touched by the graciousness of the offer. "Honestly, I don't need anything right now. If ever I found myself in real need, I wouldn't hesitate to come to you. You are a true friend, Ralph, an excellent friend . . ."

"Oh well," replied the other with a frown of discontent. "It would have made me happy and not caused me any difficulty. After my last expedition, I'm rich enough to give up taxidermy whenever I choose."

"But I thought . . ." the engineer objected.

"Yes, it's true. At the time of our hunting parties in the jungle I wasn't doing so well. This all changed in a single night."

"In a single night?" repeated Robert, surprised.

"Yes. But that's right, I haven't told you about it. The story is quite extraordinary in its own right . . .

"Not long after we last parted, I met a former naval officer named Slud, whose taste for hunting and adventure had led him to resign his commission.

"I have never known anyone as tireless and skillful as this unfortunate boy. We instantly became inseparable companions.

"Slud was marvelously well acquainted with the entire Indian side of the Himalayas, where he had hunted tiger, elephant, and wild yak.

"He gave me such enthusiastic descriptions of new animals, yet to be classified, living in the rugged gorges of Nepal, that I decided to undertake an expedition with him into those wild lands.

"I'll pass over the usual ups and downs of this sort of journey—bivouacs in those ruined temples that Kipling has described so well, the crossing of seemingly never-ending green marshland, encounters with beasts and reptiles and, what was worse, Thug assassins—all the venerable enchantments of this ancient Hindu world on which, as if on a block of granite, the British leopard blunts or breaks its steel teeth, no matter what anyone has claimed.

"But to get to the point:

"Roughly three weeks after leaving the southern jungles, we entered a forest of black cedar that seemed to have no end.

"Not until we had marched for two days did we discover, at nightfall, an avenue of gigantic stone elephants, at the far end of which rose the cupolas of a temple. We thought we had arrived at one of those ruins that stretch over several square kilometers and have been abandoned for centuries, like Angkor or Elephanta.

"We were greatly surprised to discern, above the domes and minarets, the bell tower of a church built in the style of the eighteenth century, complete with a lightning rod and gilded weathervane.

"We expected that the missionaries who had taken up residence there would surely treat us hospitably, and we rashly advanced.

"But, as we crossed the threshold of the first courtyard, a troop of men with shaved heads and long ash-gray robes fell upon us. Despite our vehement protests, we were bound and gagged.

"The strongest of our assailants placed us on their shoulders. We were carried through a complex maze of corridors and stairways to a large, ill-lit room and dumped unceremoniously onto a bedding of corn straw.

"One of the shaved-headed men cut our bonds and removed the woolen cloths that gagged us. Another left us a calabash of boiled rice and a jug of water. Then the massive door groaned on its hinges and we heard the bars and locks being made secure.

"This all happened so quickly that we were dazed for some time.

"Slud was the first to break the silence; he had, as they say, been through this before.

"'Isn't this nice, my unfortunate Pitcher,' he said to me sarcastically. 'Now our food and lodging are assured for some time, wouldn't you say?'

"'I am in no mood to laugh, Master Slud,' I answered crossly. 'Assuming these wretches release us soon — which is not a given — they will certainly not return our arms, nor our pelts, nor any of the rest of our equipment . . . It's hopeless . . .'

"Slud seemed bothered by my chagrin.

"'A little more fortitude, my dear Pitcher, for hell's sake,' he muttered. 'These people can't be too bad, since they're feeding us. These are Buddhists who, by definition, abhor the shedding of blood. That's already one reassuring piece of information . . .'

"'Buddhists? What about the bell tower with its cross and weathervane?'

"'The temple, which has stood here for at least two thousand years, was built by Brahmins. In the eighteenth century, Jesuit missionaries, very numerous at the time, chased out the Brahmins and built the church and, in turn, they gave way to the Buddhists . . .'

"Slud continued to try to comfort me with all sorts of specious arguments and, after sharing our portion of rice like brothers — we were dying of hunger — we studied the layout of our prison before the sun had completely set.

"It was a semicircular room, from which we concluded that it must occupy a half-story of a tower. A single chink placed high in the wall let in some light but left the two corners of the room in darkness. Along with the corn straw that served as our bed, the only furnishings were a wooden stool and some blankets. The walls were six feet thick, the door massive, and we possessed absolutely no tool that would be of any use in our predicament.

"We put off for the time being any attempt at escape and slept that night the sleep of the weary.

"The next miserable day brought neither food nor news. In the evening, a bonze with long ears and a smile of beatific idiocy brought us our rations and left without deigning to answer Slud's queries, although Slud spoke the dialect of this part of India sufficiently well to question him.

"The following days slipped by in the same way, bringing no change to our wretched condition. We slid, little by little, into profound discouragement.

"Every day, at regular intervals, the noise of bells and drums announced the celebration of Buddhist rites.

"Our not knowing the reasons behind our inexplicable detention drove Slud into veritable outbursts of rage. We fell prey to the forced idleness of captives, that restless indolence that is one of the worst forms of torture. Melancholy was beginning to consume us.

"'This cannot go on,' Slud said to me one evening. 'We must try something . . .'

"'What?' I asked mournfully.

"'I don't know. But anything is preferable to this ignominious captivity. Better to die fighting than to rot in this hole.'

"I agreed with Slud, and we set about devising a plan.

"'There's only one way,' I declared. 'Wait until dark, stun the bonze with the long ears—and I mean stun not kill—then make our way to the top of the tower and from there let ourselves down.'

"Slud approved of my idea, in particular because he couldn't see any other practical way out. As we waited impatiently for nightfall, we busied ourselves by braiding, from our blankets, a strong rope capable of supporting the weight of both of our bodies. We tested its strength by pulling on it with all our might.

"We were horribly tense. A storm gathering slowly above the buildings of the monastery only increased our agitation.

"The air that came through the single window of our prison was blistering, as if disgorged from the fiery maw of an oven. Our only consolation was the thought that the storm might assist our plans.

"We awaited the bonze's daily visit in anguish. The hours passed pitilessly slowly.

"Our nerves were stretched thin when we finally heard the grinding of locks and bars.

"The bonze entered, smiling, as always, that same idiotic, complacent smile that drove me mad.

"He leaned down to put the calabash of rice and the jug on the ground.

"At that moment, Slud swung the wooden stool down on his shaved head. There was the dull sound of smashed flesh, of crushed bones. The bonze slid to the ground, unconscious, without a cry.

"We didn't stop to see whether he was dead or alive.

"Without a word, we took his keys and locked him in our cage.

"It was now completely dark. We began to ascend the stairs and climbed two dozen or more without incident.

"We were just emerging onto the rooftop when Slud, who was in front, noticed in a flash of lightning another bonze, completely motionless, crouching near the sculpted lotus crenellations.

"We beat a hasty retreat.

"We were desperate.

"Slud clenched his fists in rage and acted as though he would throw the still-motionless monk from the top of the tower. I was afraid he might actually do it.

"Then, before I could hold him back, he was off. He crept quietly across the rooftop toward the bonze.

"I followed, ready to come to his defense.

"Just then, a great, silent flash of lightning tore the sky, revealing the face of our enemy clenched in an ecstatic grin.

"He was doubtless in one of those semi-cataleptic states into which these sorts of ascetics often put themselves.

"I exhaled.

"We wouldn't have to resort to violence. Simply not awakening the sleeper would be enough.

"Slud, calmer now, agreed with me, and we immediately set to work.

"I uncoiled our rope, which I carried around my waist, and attached it firmly to one of the sculpted crenellations. Then we began our descent.

"I asked to go first. I knew Slud suffered from vertigo, and his unease was heightened still further by the pouring rain. The weight of my body would augment the tension on the rope and keep it from swaying too much, assuring an easier descent for my companion.

"Another cause for concern was what we might find at the foot of the tower: a moat, an interior courtyard, the roof of a temple? We couldn't see anything in the darkness. The light from the intermittent lightning showed us only a jumble of mismatched buildings.

"At first, everything went well. Following my advice, Slud descended with his eyes shut and was glad to have taken this precaution.

"But, suddenly, I let out a terrible cry.

"I had reached the end of the rope! Beneath me my feet dangled in the air. I had almost slipped into the abyss!

"'The rope is too short,' I murmured, in a voice choked with anxiety.

"'How much?' stammered Slud.

"'I don't know . . . Far too much to let ourselves drop.'

"At that moment a great burst of thunder resounded, shattering what little remained of our composure.

"I heard, above me, Slud's plaintive voice:

"'I'm feeling dizzy,' he stammered. 'My head's spinning . . .

"'I'm letting go of the rope . . .

"'It's better this way.

"'I'm going to let go! . . . I can't help it . . .'

"'In God's name, my dear Slud, don't do that!' I yelled. 'I beg you, be brave.'

"'I can't,' he said.

"His voice was hoarse.

"I heard his teeth chattering. I felt the shuddering of the rope, agitated by his shaking hands. There were several seconds of unbearable anguish. I was at the end of my strength. I felt my wrists growing numb. I too was tempted to let go, to drop into the shadowy abyss, to let myself fall to my death.

"You live an entire existence in such moments.

"I have often wondered why my hair didn't turn white all at once during those horrific moments we spent on the side of the old Buddhist tower carved with grimacing monsters . . ."

"What did you do?" interrupted the engineer impatiently, caught up in the storyteller's emotion.

After a moment of silence, Ralph Pitcher continued:

"I was going to let myself drop when a desperate, half-mad idea came to me.

"'Listen,' I said to Slud. 'There is one final chance.'

"'What is it?'

"'I'm going back up. I'm going back to our cell.

"'There are some more blankets. I am going to cut them into strips and make another rope.'

"'But that's mad!' rasped the unfortunate man.

"'What about me?

"'Do you think I can hold on a minute longer?

"'When you return — if you manage to return — you won't find me here.

"'I will have let go!'

"And then he added, in a tone I will never forget:

"'It's better this way, in any case. You are right, Ralph. Let me die.'

"'I won't accept that!' I shouted, overcome with anger.

"'I will not escape alone, I promise you!

"'Let's go, Slud, climb up five or six meters.'

"'What for?'

"'Don't you see? I'm going to tie you firmly to the rope with the rope itself!

"'Don't say anything, just follow my orders!

"'This way you can await my return.'

"Slud pulled himself several meters higher, as I had asked, but with great difficulty. I feared that he might tumble into me and drag me into the abyss. But the glimmer of hope he could now see gave him the strength to master his nerves.

"As soon as I felt it was long enough, I cut the rope below me.

"With the length thus obtained, I tied Slud securely under his arms to the principal rope. Then, placing my foot on his shoulder, I began to climb back up in such a state of violent overexcitement that I no longer felt tired, no longer noticed the granite monsters leaning out toward me, observing me with their hideous demonic faces.

"However, as I reached the top of the tower, something terrible happened.

"I found myself face to face with the bonze, now completely awake.

"He was, I think, just as frightened as I was, seeing a man rise abruptly at his side as if he had been brought there by a thunderclap.

"I didn't give him the chance to recover from his astonishment.

"I leapt for his throat, knocked him down, and half-strangled him. The suddenness of my attack was so successful that he only let out a sort of groan. I finished him off with a blow that would have felled an ox. My path was clear.

"I rushed toward the cell that had served as our prison, so elated, so proud of my triumph that I was roaring with nervous laughter. I am certain that at that moment I was within an inch of madness . . .

"But a horrible disappointment awaited me: in my elation, in my delirious joy, *it hadn't occurred to me that it was Slud who had the key!*

"This time my strength of purpose failed me. I collapsed on the steps of the stairway; all my energy had vanished. I was no longer able to string two thoughts together. I was delirious. For an instant I even forgot about poor Slud whom I had tied just above the abyss and who, without me, could neither climb up nor descend.

"Then I burst into tears. At that moment, a child would have had the better of me.

"I lay on the stones for quite some time, utterly and completely devastated.

"It was the thought of Slud, whom I could not forsake, that gave me the courage to continue the fight.

"I wiped away my tears and, seated on the stone step, began to look for some impossible means of salvation, like a schoolboy struggling with an unsolvable problem.

"But suddenly I let out a cry—no, a howl of joy. I had found it. And it was ever so simple! How had I not thought of it before?

"I climbed hurriedly back up to the roof of the tower.

"I made my way to the bonze whom I had just reduced to such a pitiful state. I began by gagging him to remove any possibility that he might cry for help if he ever showed the slightest sign of waking up. Then I relieved him of his long ash-gray robe, a sort of tunic he wore underneath it, and a bit of a blanket that he used as a coat. I left him as naked as the day he was born.

"With all of these materials, I set to work. I needed a rope, and the bonze was going to provide it. I had in my hands a supply of excellent cloth whose sturdiness I recognized at once.

"I forgot to tell you that I had taken a knife from the bonze who served as our jailor, which I had already used to cut through the rope so I could secure Slud. I began at once to cut the ash-gray robe into long strips, which I knotted end to end.

"I worked feverishly, with inconceivable speed, in the light provided by flashes of lightning. One moment I saw the cock on the bell tower, which I noticed was now right in front of me, illumined by a sort of dazzling halo.

"At almost the same time, an awful wailing rose from the depths of the void.

"It was Slud, calling for help.

"In my haste, I had not tied the rope tightly enough. Under the weight of his body, the knots were coming undone little by little, and he felt them slowly slipping.

"I had no way of knowing this, but I was no less panicked by this lugubrious call that prudence forbade me to answer. I raced with inconceivable ardor, the rope lengthening visibly under my restless fingers.

"Finally it was ready. I coiled it around my waist and let myself down the length of the old rope, fretting that some unforeseeable mishap had befallen Slud.

"I got there in the nick of time.

"The length of rope had come completely untied.

"Slud was holding on only with clenched fingers. I tied the new rope to the old one a little above him, and our perilous descent began again.

"'You made quite a mistake by going back up,' Slud suddenly told me.

"'What do you mean?'

"'I should have thought of it earlier: our clothes would have been enough to lengthen the rope . . .'

"At the very moment he said these words, my feet touched the wet, grassy ground.

"'Bah,' I laughed. 'What's done is done. I think we've finally made it.'

"A moment later he stood at my side. We embraced with delight, drunk with joy. And yet we were far from safe.

"The flashes of lightning showed us that the spot where we had landed—miraculously, I should say—was a sort of wet, marshy trench, situated between the foundations of the tower and those of the Jesuit church. At either end it was closed off with strong grates and must surely have linked to the canals that surrounded the temple, as one sees in many edifices of this type.

"We realized that we were hardly farther along than we had been before leaving our prison cell.

"It was Slud—now that he had been saved from the torments of vertigo he had recovered his wits and all his perceptive lucidity—who discovered, half hidden by a cluster of water lilies, an arched opening through which it appeared we might be able to walk if we bent down a little.

"'This is our salvation,' he declared. 'We are certain, by hiding here, first to avoid being discovered and then to reach, almost without fail, the open air.'

"'But,' I objected timidly, 'what if we get lost in endless tunnels . . .'

"He shrugged his shoulders impatiently.

"'That isn't a tunnel,' he said. 'It's the entrance to a sewer. There must be an exit to the outside.

"'Anyway, let's give it a try.'

"I made no further reply. We went beneath the low arch.

"I had yielded without much resistance because I counted on the darkness to put a stop to this ill-advised march. This hope was thoroughly dashed.

"We hadn't taken two steps when I let out a cry of amazement. As far as the eye could see, the walls, floor, and vault of the tunnel were lit by a greenish glow, a sort of very faint phosphorescence.

"Slud exulted noisily:

"'I wasn't expecting this,' he cried, 'but it's most propitious. Do you know where this light comes from?'

"'Indeed I don't,' I humbly admitted.

"'Whatever you do, don't chalk it up to some miracle of Sakyamuni! These are quite simply phosphorescent animalcules, the lighting of the future.'

"He was trembling with excitement.

"'Edgar Allan Poe has already imagined this,' he continued, 'when, in "The Fall of the House of Usher," one of his finest stories, he tells of that incomprehensible light bathing the walls of the tunnel.

"'Now, luminous microbes — very common, moreover, especially in these latitudes — are perfectly described, classified, and catalogued.

"'Every respectable laboratory possesses several jarsful.'

"I admit that I was amazed. We continued walking in this fantastical light, which dimmed in some spots only to shine even brighter a little further on.

"Slud observed with some surprise that the ground was rising and the tunnel seemed to be growing larger as we advanced.

"After about a hundred steps we could walk without bending over. A little further, we came to a crossroads of sorts; the tunnel branched off in two directions, one descending, the other ascending. We had no idea which one to choose. It was Slud, as usual, who decisively settled the question:

"The descending tunnel,' he announced, 'would more likely than not only lead us to some pool filled with crocodiles and water snakes: we have to take the other.'

"I followed him without objection; Slud had such an influence over me that I rarely disagreed with his opinion. But after a very short time, we found to our misfortune that the phosphorescence began to dim and then disappeared completely. The luminous animalcules apparently needed the warm moisture of the depths.

"Groping along the walls, placing one foot just in front of the other — with tales of secret dungeons running through my mind — we continued a little farther.

"Slud was upset. He grumbled about the magical source of light, so convenient at first, that had suddenly abandoned us. I sensed he was about to turn back.

"'Halt!' he suddenly shouted.

"'Good,' I thought, 'it's about time. We're going to go back the way we came.' I asked out loud:

"'What is it, my dear Slud?'

"'It's impossible to go any further . . . the tunnel doesn't go on. It's a cul-de-sac, a dead end.'

"'So, we're going back?'

"'Not at all . . . Now come help me!'

"I moved closer.

"In the darkness, I felt him place a thick iron ring, icy and rough, into my hand. Then he asked me to pull with all my might.

"And since I groped around somewhat hesitantly:

"'Don't you understand?' he swiftly demanded. 'There must be a secret passage that we have to figure out how to open. The tunnel we have been following would otherwise have no purpose being here. Pull! Pull already!'

"And, to set an example, he had grasped the ring and was pulling with all his might. I added my efforts to his but, at first — seeing how little progress we were making — I thought we were harnessed to a ring that was fastened to the rock. This opinion, timidly expressed, exasperated Slud.

"'Of course the ring is fastened to the rock!' he shouted.

"'That's not hard to see!

"'But you must have never been to a Hindu temple not to know that almost all the secret doors in the crypts are made of stones that swivel and that are so well balanced that a light shove opens them and they close again on their own . . . Now pull!'

"I obeyed, but mostly to satisfy Slud; all we could expect from such a flawed undertaking was that the ring — I could tell it was quite rusty from its roughness — would remain in our hands as we were sent sprawling head over heels.

"Imagine my great surprise when, after a melancholy grinding noise, the rock pivoted abruptly, revealing a narrow, dimly lit opening, just as Slud had predicted.

"We hurriedly went through this miraculously half-open door.

"'What do you think now, eh?' said Slud in a tone of crushing superiority.

"I paid tribute, as always, to my companion's astonishing intuition as we walked through a spacious vault, dimly lit, as before, by a light that seemed to come from somewhere in the distance.

"But it was fated that we would have to go from surprise to surprise. We had hardly taken three steps when we emerged into a vast crypt, a true subterranean cathedral, carved out of the living rock. Battles of gods and monsters from the Mahabharata unfolded in gigantic bas-reliefs on the walls. From the domed vault hung an enormous lantern made of horn, like those from Tibet. It was this that shed the soft, hazy light we had at first perceived. The imperceptible movement that animated it—caused no doubt by invisible currents of air—made great shadows dance across the walls and shiver, crouching, in the darkened corners. We remained silent for a moment. I have never seen a more solemn place than this subterranean sanctuary; I felt as though the crushing weight of the entire mass of the temples, of the entire progression of centuries and generations, was weighing on my head.

"Slud tore me abruptly from this reverie with its feeling of growing dread. With one extended arm, he pointed out a colossal bronze Buddha seated between tall incense burners in a hieratic pose. I then noticed something that had escaped me at first: the god, fifteen to twenty times human size, had large, strangely sparkling pupils.

"'But don't you see?' clamored Slud, frantically. 'They're diamonds, it has diamond eyes!

"'Look at the fiery light they cast with the least movement of the lantern!

"'There's no question about it!

"'I doubt that there exists a third stone as beautiful as these anywhere in the universe!

"'The Koh-i-Noor, the Sancy are nothing but ridiculous pebbles next to these.'

"He was losing his head, gesticulating and capering about.

"'Ha! Ha!' he snickered. 'You bonzes, you are going to pay a pretty compensation for our illegal detention in your tower!'

"'The old Buddha's eyes are ours!

"'And first, I want to give them our names.

"'One will be called the Ralph, the other the Slud. It's as good a way as any to be remembered by posterity.

"'What do you say, my dear Ralph?'

"'I say,' I responded with a composure that stunned him, 'that you've missed something.

"'Look at what the Buddha is holding in his right hand.'

"'Well, by God, it's a lotus!'

"'Not exactly. It's a key, nothing more, nothing less, while the left hand,

27

lower to the ground, rests on a bronze chest that at first I took, because of its size, for a small altar . . .

"'The key, no doubt, opens the chest.

"'We have assuredly laid our hands on one of the secret treasure troves of the Grand Lama, left in the care of the god himself!'

"Slud's joy, after this revelation, knew no bounds.

"'Treasure and diamonds!

"'Hurrah! All is well!

"'Give me the knife, Ralph; I want the glory of detaching them myself.'

"'Do you want me to help?'

"'No need . . . Quick, the knife.'

"I gave it to him and he leapt onto the altar in one bound. There was a terrible rumbling of thunder, but Slud was already climbing the arm, then the shoulder of the god. Standing on its shoulder, he dug at the left eye socket.

"There was a screech of metal.

"'There's one!' he shouted triumphantly, holding up the stone. Then he climbed onto the other shoulder.

"Was it an illusion? It seemed to me that the Buddha had knit his brow. The peaceful smile on his disfigured face now seemed to me full of menace.

"It took some time for Slud to tear out the second eye. But, once he had finished, thunder exploded with such shattering horror that I thought the old temple was collapsing. The lantern danced at the end of its cable; the monstrous images of *devas* and *apsaras*, winged serpents and animal-headed gods, made as if to leave their bas-reliefs and stretched their menacing heads. It looked to me like an angry halo now encircled the august face of the blinded god.

"Slud himself, surprised by the commotion, lost his footing and slipped. If he hadn't caught fast on one of the ornaments of the idol's diadem he would have fallen, would have dashed his skull on the stone floor of the sanctuary. But he only laughed at the accident.

"'I believe,' he declared, 'that the Buddha wants to impress me with his thunderclaps. However, we are not yet even. Now, the treasure!'

"He had placed the diamonds in his pocket and was cautiously climbing down.

"As for me, I was rooted in place, overcome by blind terror augmented by the dancing shadows that appeared to give a quiver of life to the murals. Gongs hanging above the altar repeated the booming thunder and I heard distinctly menacing tones in their bronze voices. A frightful foreboding gripped my heart, and I saw that Slud felt the same thing, for he was no longer laughing, no longer joking.

"He silently took the key from the idol's hand and slid it into the lock. Then, holding with one hand onto a cable dangling from the roof and bracing himself, he set about opening it. The lock clicked dryly and the coffer's lid opened. At the same time, through a cleverly devised mechanism, the god raised his protective hand.

"How can I possibly explain the horrifying catastrophe? The Buddha, with his awful smile, appeared engulfed in an ocean of smoky flames whose blue tongues, like serpents, licked my feet!

"Where Slud had been, a genie with a golden face, a golden torso, was writhing in the midst of the furnace . . .

"I was paralyzed by fear, nailed to the spot, panic-stricken, breathless with horror.

"The booming of an even more violent thunderclap exploded almost within my ears. The brazier had gone out. The golden man stood alone and immobile next to the open coffer.

"For a moment, I was only semiconscious . . .

"When I came to and recovered enough courage to approach the altar to try to understand the awful marvel, I found that the golden man — still motionless — was the unfortunate Slud . . ."

"The thunderbolt had volatized the coffer's gold," murmured the engineer.

"Exactly," replied Ralph Pitcher. "When I reached Slud, when I touched him, he crumbled to dust under my fingers. Beneath the dust, I noticed two large, glowing coals, which were the eyes of the Buddha . . .

"The raised hand of the god had touched the cable of the lightning rod installed no doubt by the Jesuits long ago . . . I don't know who could have devised this diabolical mechanism.

"In the coffer, there was an undamaged lacquered box filled with gems of lesser value and gold bars.

"I had the nerve to flee with these spoils, to reach the secret door, and I managed to escape by following the descending branch of the subterranean canal leading to the jungle.

"It's true that I am rich, but there are times when my wealth weighs on me, when I think of poor Slud's death . . ."

Complete silence greeted the account of this extraordinary adventure, which seemed to leave Ralph Pitcher as devastated as if it had just happened.

Robert Darvel hastened to change the subject.

Impressed by this tale, he left early, but only after agreeing to return the next day and formally pledging to make use of his friend's purse as if it were his own if the need arose.

III

....

Missing

All the following day, Pitcher waited for his friend in vain. He wasn't alarmed at first, but after three days had passed and there had been no news of Robert at his hotel, he began to worry in earnest.

"Robert would have written," he thought. "He was overjoyed to see me. We have been friends for many years and no quarrel has ever cast a shadow over our friendship. Some misfortune must have befallen him."

Pitcher went in to London only two or three times a month, to deliver pieces to connoisseurs and important merchants and to present his manuscripts to prominent scientists, who signed their names in place of his.

Ralph had a noble heart; he didn't hesitate for a moment to leave his birds to search for Robert. He donned a waterproof woolen cape and, armed with a revolver and a heavy walking stick, he set forth.

"It's straight to Yarmouth Street," he said, "to ask in person for the man who signed the letter, this Ardavena, whose name I luckily have not forgotten. Surely I will learn something further there."

After a two-hour dash he finally reached Yarmouth Street and stopped, completely out of breath, before a decrepit carriage gateway whose paint was flaking away. He pounded the iron knocker in vain, even knocked on shutters so rotten that they crumbled beneath his fist.

Upset at the lack of response, he spoke to a fruit seller who had come to see what all the noise was about and who, with her hands on her hips, observed him sardonically.

"My good man," said the woman in a strong Irish accent, "you're wasting your time as well as your efforts. The house has been abandoned for more than a century. Look at it: the tiles are broken, the roof has fallen in. It's a wretched dump, yet it's worth some money."

Hardly satisfied by this information, Pitcher interrogated one after another a grocer, a fishmonger, two policemen, and some street sweepers (to whom he gave a few sixpence) without obtaining any explanation.

He returned very late to his shop, where his mother greeted him coldly.

"Look at how you spend your days," she said. "Your friend is an adventurer—an inventor, for goodness' sake! He found a good business opportunity and he left. He isn't thinking about you at this time of the night. You are truly naïve, son. He'll make out fine, don't you worry."

"I don't see how you can talk like that," said the naturalist. "How can you be sure? What if our friend was attacked by the thugs that prowl Drury Lane?"

"In that case, silly fool, go lodge a complaint with the constable. You would have already done so if you'd paid a little more attention to your old mother's advice."

Pitcher graciously acknowledged he was in the wrong, lit a pipe, and went up to his workshop to continue the dissection of an apteryx from New Zealand that he needed to study the following day.

Over the next few days, he continued his investigation, but neither his natural perspicacity nor the efforts of the most skilled detectives nor even the exertions of firms of private investigators furnished any useful clue as to what might have happened to Robert Darvel.

All Pitcher was able to learn was that the abandoned house at 15 Yarmouth Street, as a result of a complicated lawsuit between French heirs and English heirs living in India, had been sequestered many years before.

A month passed with no news of Robert Darvel's fate.

Pitcher had given up his search; but ever since then, he had been melancholy. Hardly a night passed in which he didn't dream of his missing friend and he reproached himself for not having gone with him. There remained a dark hole in his happiness. Mrs. Pitcher complained bitterly:

"Ever since this Mr. Darvel came to see you, you are a different man," she repeated constantly. "You barely eat any more. It's just what we needed . . .

We used to be so happy, so calm. Now your heart isn't in your work, you're bored, sad . . . Oh, we certainly haven't been lucky."

* * *

Awakening one morning after a night filled with nightmares, Pitcher was petrified to find on his night stand, next to an ink bottle and pen that he was certain he had left in his workshop, a sheet of paper on which were written a few lines signed by Robert Darvel:

"Have no fear for me," said the engineer. *"I'm in the midst of solving a marvelous puzzle. I shall return before long. Above all else, don't worry about me, and do not try to discover the means by which I have been able to deliver this news."*

"Bah!" cried the naturalist when he saw it. "It's a joke: Robert must have climbed in through the window to play this trick on me."

But the window was twenty feet above the ground, and a snarling mastiff that responded to no one but his masters prowled the little garden at night.

The simple Pitcher was genuinely frightened for a time. All the tales of life after death, ghosts, and spiritualism that he had heard or read flooded his memory.

"What will mother say if the house is haunted?"

But he possessed such a wellspring of optimism and openness that he concluded in the end that Robert had assuredly made some new and miraculous invention.

"That Darvel is so clever," he exclaimed, "that he must have invented something extraordinary. It's only natural that he would want to test it out on me first. It must be a device akin to the wireless telegraph."

And Pitcher returned to his workshop to put the finishing touches on the stuffing of a superb lyrebird, destined for the Museum of Edinburgh's natural history collection.

IV

....

Yarmouth Street

It had been dark for a long time already when Robert Darvel turned onto old Yarmouth Street. Not a light burned from the facades of the old mansions, their walls blackened by the passage of time, and the glow of the rare streetlight served only to further deepen the shadows filling the high, majestic doorways. In spite of himself, the young man was moved by the solemnity of these old shuttered lodgings, seemingly asleep in the dust and silence. It seemed to him that the sound of his steps echoed off the cobblestones far behind him. As he passed Pitter Street, a dark alley lined with gardens and closed off by barricades to prevent cabs from entering, it made him think of a London lost in the depths of time: bleak, sealed off, and silent.

He continued on his way. A streetlight's flame agitated by the evening breeze made shadows dance on the street corners. For a moment he thought he saw black spiders, enormous and hairy, running over the walls. A rat leapt from a cellar window and disappeared.

Without knowing why, Robert felt something like anguish clutch at his heart. He had never felt so utterly alone. He was a trespasser, walking through vanished centuries. It was as if he moved through a graveyard of exhausted glories and passions. The pointed roofs acquired malevolent profiles, smiling with the broad laughter of their lead gutters and widening their bulls-eye windows to watch the intruder as he passed. A weathervane creaked softly against its rust.

For perhaps the first time in his adventurous life, he understood the fragility of fate and knew what it was to feel fear. Fear of what? Of the past, of the future, and, perhaps, of himself.

All the inanimate things around him harmonized superbly with his distress and with the mystery of this meeting requested by a stranger.

"No," he told himself aloud, "this is no ordinary business meeting!"

He stopped, surprised by the sound of his own voice. And yet Robert Darvel had visited the ancient ruins of the Siberian wastes, the temples of Hulagu Khan and Timur Lenk, some built on foundations of human skulls. In the deserts of Syria he had entered cadaverous cities inhabited by plague victims and lepers infected with unknown contagions, diseases forgotten since the Middle Ages. He wasn't the sort of man to let himself be overcome by the romantic melancholy of an old London neighborhood with its pointed roofs cut out of a moonlit sky swathed in fog.

"Come now," he told himself, stroking the first-rate revolver—a Colt—in his jacket pocket, "this is an excellent neighborhood. I imagine one could conduct experiments here in perfect peace. After the first good deal I strike, I'll purchase one of these old mansions."

Ten o'clock sounded simultaneously at Saint Paul's Cathedral and the Irish Convent as Robert rapped gently on the door. One of the panels half-opened, then closed behind him so quickly that the young man, without quite knowing how it had happened, found himself in a spacious courtyard overrun by tall grasses, in the middle of which was an old wrought-iron well.

"Mr. Ardavena?" he asked impatiently.

"Please follow me, sir," murmured a rasping voice.

Robert turned around. Next to him, a servant dressed in black had just lit a small lantern. In the reddish glow of its candle, Robert made out an old man with trembling hands who had the look of a cathedral's beadle or a magistrate. His hair and whiskers were white, his lower lip drooped, and he inclined his head obsequiously as he preceded the visitor along a path through the grass. After a cursory examination of this nonentity whose fingers were heavy with rings, Robert followed him without a word.

They first climbed a stairway broad as a street, its crumbling marble steps loosened by the roots of plants growing wild. On the landing, two bronze, Empire-style sphinxes dreamed in pools of verdigris. The rain had washed stripes onto them and, in the gloom, they looked almost like tigers.

The old man opened a door, crossed an antechamber hung with decaying family portraits, raised a leather curtain, and left Robert Darvel alone in a curiously furnished drawing room. Suffocating air emanated from a radiator, and idols with many arms and monstrous heads squatted in the corners on marble pedestals. Censers obscured the air with scented smoke and, here and there, low divans upholstered in black velvet with gold arabesques lay alongside small gueridons encrusted with mother-of-pearl and covered with a variety of curios. On a red lacquer platform there was a hookah, already lit, and a furnished opium cabinet — with a coconut oil lamp, steel needles, porcelain mushroom pipes, bowls, ashtrays, and cups. Paired with this was a liquor cabinet crammed with bottles of champagne and diverse spirits.

Manuscripts, some fashioned only of palm fronds or panels of sandalwood, filled a large, opal-encrusted, ebony bookcase.

"I must be in the home of some English industrialist who has come back from India," Robert told himself as he sat down unceremoniously on a divan.

No sooner had he sat down than he heard a growl under his seat. He stood up and took several steps back.

Beads of sweat moistened his brow as a tiger came out from under the divan. It stretched its legs and then moved to the center of the room with the undulating motions of a large cat. The feline leaned back on its hind legs, tested its claws on the rug, and moved slowly toward the visitor, its backbone sinuous, as if it was preparing to leap.

Robert had drawn his revolver and held it low against his thigh, ready to fire if the beast leapt. He was terribly pale, his heart was pounding, but he maintained his composure. With his finger on the gun's trigger, he waited. Three seconds passed; they seemed to him like three years. Man and tiger studied one another watchfully. Had Robert dropped his eyes, he would have been a dead man.

All at once, one of the golden, carved doors opened and a hollow, somber voice that seemed to come from somewhere far away cried, "Mowdi! Mowdi!"

The tiger recognized its master. It growled, then promptly lay back down under the divan.

Robert turned to the newcomer.

"Sir," he began angrily, "I find your joke in very poor taste, to say the least. Your Oriental and, frankly, ridiculous theatrics do not impress me in the least. I do not know your purpose in luring me to this deserted neighborhood, but I warn you that if your plan is to rob me, you'll be sorely disappointed. I have but a dozen shillings on my person and — I warn you — an excellent revolver . . ."

Robert stopped, reduced to silence by a will superior to his own and deeply disturbed by the appearance of the stranger facing him.

He was a man of small stature, and so emaciated that under the thin robe of black silk that covered him one could clearly make out the minutest details of his skeleton. His atrophied muscles, reduced to nothing, were no longer anything more than puppet strings, and he had the dry and discolored hands of a mummy. The figures from the *danse macabre* would appear plump by comparison.

His face alone was astounding. Imagine a skull with a gigantic forehead and two lively clear blue eyes, eyes sparkling with youth like those of a child: a skull and two cornflowers. His tiny ears were diaphanous, like two sheets of wax. Yet there was nothing macabre about this semi-skeleton. He had a noble profile and emanated considerable power and energy, a radiance of superabundant vitality. He moved with an easy grace and stood erect, and his smile was full of kindness.

"Sit down," he said, in the gentlest of tones.

Robert sat down. He was seized by vertigo; a thousand incoherent suppositions were whirling in his mind and he knew, with indescribable terror, that he was entirely in this stranger's power.

The latter tried to reassure him, and succeeded, despite his still hollow and faraway voice.

"First of all," he said in excellent French, "banish all fear from your mind. I understand your displeasure, and I regret, I assure you, having forgotten that my poor Mowdi was taking his nap in this room. He's a harmless beast that I caught in the jungle at a very young age. He has never harmed any of my friends."

"And your enemies?"

"I have no enemies. But he meets my needs."

"Well," murmured Robert with difficulty, "what do you want with me? And, to begin with, who are you?"

"Perhaps you have heard of the Brahmin Ardavena?"

"A thousand pardons!" stammered Robert. "That was the signature on your letter, but I don't recall ever having heard the name before."

"It's of no importance. I am the superior of the monastery of Chelambrum, a veritable city of temples and palaces, which houses within its walls a population of ten thousand Brahmins."

"I don't see how I can be of any use to you."

"Don't be so hasty. You are not unaware that we Hindu monks are sometimes capable of miracles that all of European science has never been able to reproduce or explain. You, on the other hand, possess knowledge of a different sort, a material power more practical than our own."

"I would very much like to see one of these miracles you claim to perform."

"Nothing could be easier," said the Brahmin with a condescending smile. "Try to stand up."

He stretched his hand toward Robert, piercing him with his blue eyes that, like precious stones, seemed to dance with fire.

The young man tried in vain to move. It seemed as if his whole body had become as heavy as a lead ingot, and his useless efforts caused him unbearable anguish. He was unable even to raise his arms.

"You see," said Ardavena, "if I had evil intentions, your weapons would hardly protect you. Now, I release you."

Robert stood up stiffly and took several steps, prey to a growing sense of dread. All his ideas of the real and the possible had been turned upside down. He was profoundly chastened.

"You are the stronger," he said with a rebellious cry. "But what do you want with me?"

"I don't want to influence your decision one way or another. If you find my projects distasteful, you shall leave here just as you arrived. I even insist, in the event that you refuse my proposal, on compensating you."

"I'm not asking for anything."

"Let us come to an understanding. I don't propose to compensate you for some material expense, but I imagine that the inconvenience that you have experienced, your dashed hopes, have caused you a harm that would be difficult to remedy. Here is what I expect from you: in addition to your creative imagination, you understand science, at least as the term is understood here. I propose to combine our two powers. You will initiate me into the sciences of chemistry, medicine, and mechanics. I will share with you the secrets of psychology and philosophy. Our mutual labor will give birth to marvels. We shall be the mysterious link in the chain that will unite the lost science of the ancient world with the powerful, though crude and foolish, science of the new one."

Robert, deep in a world of thought, said nothing. Ardavena continued, with some melancholy:

"I have knocked on the doors of many men of genius, and everywhere I have been dismissed as a charlatan or a madman; luckily, my own science has allowed me to discover you in the crowd of men as one finds a diamond in the alluvial sands of Golkonda. If you love Science and Truth for their own sakes, come with me."

"But . . ." Robert objected, already charmed by the beauty and solemnity of this discourse.

"Do not worry, I can anticipate your concerns. I know the miserable struggles that constrain a poor man in the West. You will live in luxury like a raja, and I will make you so rich that you will disdain wealth."

Ardavena had led Robert into the neighboring room. Here, there were only bare walls discolored by the damp, a straw mat, and a pitcher of water.

"These are my chambers," he said, "and I am a 'billionaire,' to use your terms. Anything is possible for one who can forgo everything."

"Well then," said Robert suddenly, "it's agreed. I place my feeble knowledge in the service of your wisdom."

"Are you certain? Once you have given your consent, you must obey me."

"My decision is made; we will meet again tomorrow, if you like."

"Why tomorrow? Nothing keeps you in London."

"Well then, so be it! I'll leave when you wish," said Robert, seduced and captivated by Ardavena's affable and at the same time imperious manner. "But don't you need some time to make arrangements?"

"They are already made; I knew in advance that you would accept."

Ardavena opened a door and preceded his guest down a long corridor paved with checkered black and white marble tiles. They descended a staircase and, suddenly, after exiting an obscure alley, found themselves on the sidewalk of another street. A cab was waiting in front of them. They got in. Five minutes later they were at Victoria Station, and eleven o'clock had not yet sounded when Robert Darvel and his bizarre associate, ensconced in a sleeper cabin on the Dover Express, were devouring the rails at a speed of 120 kilometers an hour.

At noon the following day, Robert was smoking a cigar on the bridge of the *Petchili*, a huge oil-fired steel steamer already two hours out of port en route toward the Far East.

Soon the white column of Longships Lighthouse at Land's End, then the pale gray coasts of Ireland, dissolved in distant violet mists.

Robert Darvel was on his way to India, a mysterious land where, unlike in our practical civilization, enchantments and the supernatural still reign.

V

....

The Castle of Energy

They enjoyed a pleasant and uneventful crossing on the *Petchili*. After the usual calls at Malta, Port Said, and Djibouti, the Brahmin Ardavena and his new collaborator disembarked at Colombo, capital of the island of Ceylon. From Colombo they made their way to Karnataka, home of the magnificent temple of Chelambrum.

During the voyage, Robert had become better acquainted with Ardavena. He had quickly discovered that the Brahmin was endowed with formidable erudition, and his embrace of seemingly incompatible specialties was rather disconcerting. In addition to Sanskrit, Tamil, and Hindustani, the three great dialects of India, he spoke English, French, and Italian with a remarkable purity of accent. He knew Arabic, Persian, and Chinese and had read the most celebrated authors in each of these languages.

Robert discovered that his new master even had a quite advanced understanding of recent scientific discoveries. But what disconcerted the young engineer most was the Brahmin's intellectual suppleness, his powers of deduction, the ease with which he moved from a minute detail to a rigorously established general finding. Ardavena analyzed with incomparable lucidity the most difficult problems and simplified everything through the clarity of his intellectual vision.

Robert, despite his diplomas and discoveries, felt rather inept and insignificant in the presence of this singular old man who seemed a living encyclopedia of human knowledge.

With respect to his material needs, however, he was quite satisfied. The day of their departure from London, Ardavena had remitted to him, in the form of a deposit, a bundle of bank notes amounting to roughly two thousand pounds sterling. Only one thing upset him. He reproached himself for not having informed his friend Pitcher of his departure and for not having shared his good news with him.

Several times he had wanted to write to him; the Brahmin Ardavena, who had guessed his intentions, had always dissuaded him.

"For what we must do," he said to him, "it is of the utmost importance that no one know what has become of you and that no one take an interest in you. Once word of a plan gets out, it is already half-ruined. I will provide you with a way to correspond with this Mr. Pitcher at a later date. Know, in any case, that he is hardly to be pitied at this time."

Robert had not dared to disobey his strange collaborator, but he was quite vexed to think that Pitcher might accuse him of ingratitude and indifference or, worse, believe him dead and mourn his passing.

Nonetheless, over time the novelty of a voyage to the Far East and his captivating conversations with Ardavena eventually helped the engineer forget about his old friend.

When they disembarked in Karikal, one of the few French possessions in India, Ardavena convinced Robert of the need to discard his European attire, and he procured for him a *chomin*, a white turban, and some slippers. A chomin is nothing more than a length of light muslin twenty-five to thirty meters in length that one wraps about the body.

To complete his transformation, Robert shaved his blond mustache and his long hair. With his long oval face, prominent cheekbones, and tanned complexion, he looked a great deal like a Hindu. Only his clear gray eyes and energetic gestures betrayed him. But it was understood that he would be making few public appearances.

After two days of rest in Karikal, the travelers set out by elephant for the monastery of Chelambrum.

It was a charming journey, along roads lined with verdant forests and prosperous villages. Robert marveled at every step. In his previous excursions around the world, he had never seen nature so generous nor so powerful, nor had he ever encountered such extravagant and beautiful scenery. There were forests of flowering trees that gave off an intoxicating scent, ponds surrounded by temples of pink marble and bordered by giant bamboo, cycads, and tree ferns. Then there were miles of red clay without trees or water, as if scorched by the all-consuming heat of the sun—all the varied enchantments of Oriental landscapes.

Robert eagerly drank in the wild, poetic perfumes of unsullied nature. He felt like he was being reborn into another existence. Like a child, he picked bouquets of enormous flowers, knocked down coconuts with stones, and launched projectiles at monkeys hanging nonchalantly from the branches of trees, upside down, by the tail.

But what astonished him most was the speed and luxury of the journey, as if all had been organized well in advance.

In Karikal, Hindu porters and a car awaited the arrival of the boat. The travelers had hardly touched the ground when they were welcomed into the palace of a wealthy babu, where their rooms had already been prepared. Servants waited on them, and they took their meals in a private room where no one ventured to speak to them.

All along the route, it was the same. At even the briefest halt, they were attended by obedient and devoted servants. Everything progressed with perfect regularity, something Robert had hardly ever seen in the countries he had had the good fortune to visit.

They arrived at the monastery of Chelambrum in the middle of the afternoon. The round cupolas, pyramids of gods and animals, and graceful columns of the monastery's minarets rose above a thick forest of palms, magnolias, and bamboo into the implacable azure sky. The ramparts, as vast as those of a city, were adorned with sculptures and surrounded by moats where young crocodiles, as alert and lively as lizards, were at play.

As he passed through the postern, Robert stopped, amazed. A succession of palaces and temples of white marble and pink and black granite, several of which rivaled the celebrated monuments of Egypt, surrounded a vast pool covered with aquatic flowers. There were rows of stone elephants, each twenty meters high, carrying on their backs divinities like the Virgin of Vanagui and the infant Krishna. There were elegant arches, forests of columns sculpted with an artistry more pure and more delicate than those of Greece or the Middle Ages, and a myriad of stairways with heavy banisters and light landings that made the inventions of Piranesi seem mundane.

Ardavena was leading him through a majestic courtyard girded with pillars and adorned with a gushing fountain, and Robert was delighting at the sight of so many masterpieces, when he let out a cry of horror.

On the bank of the sacred pool where the Brahmins make their ablutions and wash the statues of their gods, a hundred men were packed together in painfully contorted poses. The engineer was seized by anguish. He thought for a moment he had been transported to one of the circles of Chinese hell.

"Where am I?" he asked Ardavena, who remained impassive.

"It is here that fakirs voluntarily submit to tortures and ordeals in the hope of pleasing the gods.

"See, here's one who, to be faithful to his oath of silence, has sewn his lips together, leaving only a small hole. He can eat nothing but a little plain rice broth, which he sucks through a tiny straw. That one nailed his ears to the trunk of a tree years ago. The trunk has expanded and stretched the cartilage in his ears, which now resemble the wings of a bat. This one has kept his hands closed and roped together for so long that the nails have grown through his flesh. He must creep on the ground like an animal toward his bowl of rice."

Robert said nothing. He felt trapped in a nightmare.

A frighteningly emaciated fakir perched immobile on top of a column. He seemed devoid of life. His beard reached to his belly and birds had nested in his wild, bushy hair. Small golden lizards ran over his thighbones and skipped along his mummified toes.

Farther along, some fakirs agonized under piles of stone. Others were buried alive up to their necks in mire where insects devoured them. Some writhed on a bed of burning coals that they had to extinguish with their own blood, or rolled over sharp spikes that penetrated deeply into their flesh. A large, rapidly spinning bamboo wheel carried the bloody bodies of three fanatics whose loins and shoulders were pierced by iron hooks.

"Take me away from here," said Robert, who was feeling faint.

In his rush, he tripped over a body stretched on the ground. It looked more like a cadaver than like a living person: his eyes were ripped out and he had cut off his nose, his ears, and even his lips and part of his cheeks. His teeth were exposed. It was more than Robert could bear. He fled without looking back or listening to the explanations of Ardavena, who wanted to show him a *karavate*, a sort of primitive guillotine that allows the subject to cut off his own head. It consists of a very sharp crescent of steel that slides between two crosspieces; chains lead to the mechanism that sets the machine in action. The fanatic stretches out his neck, places his feet in stirrups attached to the chains, gives a violent kick, and his head rolls onto the ground.

"Enough of these horrors!" cried Robert. "How can you condone such monstrous outrages?"

"I do not condone them, but I cannot prevent them. I would lose all authority over those who obey me if I opposed the self-torture of these unfortunate fanatics. And, as you will see, I have done much to restrain and moderate the behavior of these hopeless martyrs."

"I still find it shocking."

"We shall discuss this later, in good time. Now, happily, I have more agreeable things to show you."

Robert said nothing. Now that he was fully in the Brahmin's hands, he had begun to regret having accepted Ardavena's offer so hastily. He recalled the old legends of those who sold their soul to the devil, and he wondered with a shiver whether the rapid and peculiar way the Brahmin had captivated him might not have had something supernatural about it. Then he began to feel the strange torment of not being able to think without his thoughts being known in an instant, of having this pale-eyed man who could read his soul like a wide-open book always beside him.

This initial, distressing impression dissipated little by little.

"Obviously," he said to himself, "Ardavena has told the truth, since I feel the effects of his power. Now it's up to me to study, to wrestle, to find logical, scientific explanations for these apparently inexplicable phenomena."

They had arrived in the part of the temple that served as living quarters for the superior of the Brahmins himself. These quarters included a palace and gardens fit for a raja. Everywhere there was flowing water, deep shade, and carpets of flowers; everywhere terraces, small stalls, and innumerable statues of the divinities of the Brahminic pantheon.

Robert noticed with pleasure that the quarters reserved for his use were located in a kind of tower completely isolated from the other buildings and surrounded by his own private garden. The whole was enclosed on all sides by thick hedges of cactus, nopal, acacia, and other thorny bushes.

"Here," he thought, "I shall feel at home."

His joy knew no bounds when, by means of a stairway of a good hundred steps carved out of the granite, Ardavena led him into a high, vaulted crypt into which fresh air and light were admitted through very high windows hidden within the exterior sculptures. The room was a veritable laboratory furnished with every modern convenience. There were cabinets of chemicals, a specialized library, electric kilns, and even a small dissecting room paved in white marble; nothing was lacking.

"As you see," said Ardavena, "you will be able to work; you are well equipped. And, if you need anything else, you have only to ask and I shall procure it for you within a few days."

The engineer noticed that everything in this vast laboratory was new. The flasks, carrying labels of English or French druggists, had never been opened, the equipment had never been used, and the books were uncut.

What pleased Robert most, as he rummaged gleefully through cabinet after cabinet, was the discovery of a whole collection of volumes and photographs related to the planet Mars.

"You can see that I thought of you," said Ardavena, "and, as you know, you can use anything here in any way you wish. You are the sole judge of the best way to carry out your studies. In addition, as I have told you, your work is constrained neither by time nor money. There are not many scientists in your position."

Robert's initial enthusiasm had returned. He surveyed his laboratory as if to take possession of it, dreaming already of incredible experiments, of discoveries that would change the face of worlds.

In the course of this rapid inventory, he was especially pleased to find a collection of recent works on psychology and on the physiology of the brain, including Flammarion's research on telepathy; Baraduc's articles on the photography of emotions; Roentgen and Curie's papers on the obscure rays emitted by certain substances; Metchnikoff's studies on longevity; the latest reports on the vapors that diamonds emit under certain conditions, vapors that seem to have a toning and purifying effect on bodily organs; and a host of other documents known only to specialists.

In the days that followed, Robert did not even see Ardavena. Apparently, he wanted to show his trust by leaving him completely at liberty. He had informed him as well that he was free to leave the grounds of the monastery. An elephant and its *cornac*, or mahout, were always at his disposal for the walks he liked to take in the forest.

Robert led a very pleasant life. Two servants were continually at his disposal, and a Malay, who had previously been a pharmacist's servant in Singapore, served as his laboratory assistant.

In the morning the young man would walk in the gardens filled with brightly colored birds, where he would wait for the rays of the sun to evaporate the dew. Then he would go to his laboratory, fresh and cool in its subterranean location despite the searing heat of the day. He would not come out again until evening, for dinner, and would finish his day with a meditative moonlit stroll through the ancient avenues of giant bamboo, baobab, and tamarind.

Only on rare occasions did he pay a visit to the Brahmin, whom he always found writing or reading in his cold cell, which was furnished, like his room on Yarmouth Street, with nothing more than a straw mat and a pitcher of water. There he became reacquainted with Mowdi, the tiger, with whom he was now on excellent terms.

Purring, Mowdi would come to the young engineer as soon as he saw him enter, and Robert never failed to stroke his beautiful orange and black fur.

The engineer enjoyed this calm, cloistered existence so much that he did not at all regret having left Paris to shut himself away in a Hindu monastery at the foot of the Ghats. Of course Ardavena did not make his guest share the privations he imposed on himself.

The food was exquisite and combined the refinements of European and native cuisine.

If he had had news of his friend Pitcher, Robert (who no longer had any family and had lost track of all his friends from earlier days) would have been perfectly content.

He complained about this to Ardavena one evening as they walked by torchlight down an interminable subterranean gallery whose walls were adorned with gigantic bas-reliefs carved out of the living granite.

The Brahmin reflected a moment.

"Do you absolutely feel you must reassure your friend?"

"I feel I must."

"Well then! I shall fulfill your wish: not only will you be able to reassure him, you will also see him, though you will be unable to speak to him."

Robert, truly touched yet a little skeptical, followed the old man to an elongated crypt with a Gothic vaulted ceiling supported by heavy pillars.

He felt he was in the nave of a cathedral; but in place of the altar there was only a large mirror illuminated by twin torches of vegetable wax that the fakirs had lit as they left.

Ardavena insisted that Robert remain utterly silent, under pain of death, no matter what he might see.

"I am calling forth formidable powers," he declared, "powers more difficult to control than electricity and steam."

Robert solemnly promised to remain silent, and Ardavena, after having placed golden tripods filled with glowing coals in a triangle, threw on some incense that he took from a small box hanging from his belt. Thick smoke soon obscured the air of the crypt. The flames of the torches faded, and the mirror was covered by a mist from which confusing figures slowly began to emerge. Then the vision became more luminous and distinct, while the other end of the crypt was plunged in darkness. Robert stifled a cry. A few feet in front of him he saw Pitcher in his little London boutique, busily dissecting a bird by the light of a lamp reflected in a large glass ball filled with water.

He observed the naturalist's work and heard him talk to himself as he often did. Mrs. Pitcher came in, scolding her son and reminding him it was time to go to bed. Pitcher obeyed, frowning, and the furnishings reflected in the mirror changed as he moved away. Pitcher went directly to bed and fell asleep.

Then Ardavena placed his hand on Robert's forehead and, obeying a will he was powerless to resist, Robert found himself in the house of his friend, a house he knew down to the smallest detail. Unconsciously submitting to a superior force, he walked to the workshop, took up pen and ink, wrote several lines, and placed this letter on the nightstand. Again he felt the hand of the Brahmin touch his forehead, and he found himself once more in front of the mirror, which no longer reflected anything but the pale light of the torches and the columns of the crypt.

He wanted to speak, but Ardavena gestured to him to keep still and threw incense once again on the tripods.

The mirror grew troubled as before, then cleared, and Robert discerned the delicate and noble profile of Alberte Teramond. She appeared full of sadness as she wistfully gazed at a photograph of Robert hanging on her wall.

VI

....

Marvels

Robert Darvel had completely adapted to his new lifestyle. He never dreamed of leaving the delightful gardens of Chelambrum and the splendid underground laboratory he had equipped to perfection. His sole interest now was to penetrate the mysteries of the human will, that marvelous and creative force that Balzac believed to be a material substance.

He had started down the path of truth but had not yet advanced very far. He was, however, already familiar with the fakirs' marvels and miracles that had at first so surprised him. He now performed some of the least difficult ones himself. He had participated in many absolutely stupefying séances. He had seen fakirs light and extinguish torches, make plants grow and flower, and ripen grapes solely by the strength of their will. He had seen them charm snakes, rendering them as rigid as sticks. Others gave themselves terrible wounds that they healed in an instant with no trace of a scar.

All of these feats are well known and confirmed by the accounts of thousands of travelers, and English officers and magistrates have gone so far as to testify to them in signed depositions.

One of the phenomena that most attracted Robert's attention — one mentioned in every popular work on the subject — is the phenomenon of levitation.

In the presence of Ardavena and the engineer, a fakir named Phara-Chibh asked for a cane, leaned heavily upon it with his left hand and, crossing his legs as he lifted into the air, rose slowly until he was two feet above the ground. There he remained, with no support but his cane. Then he cast this down, rose another foot or so, and held this position for a good ten minutes. After this, he started to descend gradually until he was sitting on the mat from which he had risen.

The same fakir, entirely naked, performed marvels that would have made European prestidigitators, with their theatrical cabinets, die of shame. He pulled from his mouth a cartload of stones that had to be carried off in a tumbril and then a tough, thorny vine no less than a hundred meters long that three men rolled up around the trunk of a tree, where its immense volume was evident to all. He recited entire passages by ancient and modern authors that he obviously could not have known. At his word, furniture rose up and began to walk in whichever direction he indicated. Doors opened and closed. At his command, spectators were unable to stretch out their hands or remove their hats. But the demonstration that most piqued Robert's curiosity was when Phara-Chibh was buried alive.

On the chosen day, and in the presence of English officers from the neighboring garrison who wished to witness the feat, Phara-Chibh appeared dressed only in a loincloth and pointed turban. He had spent the previous three days in meditation in the company of another fakir.

Under the eyes of the spectators, the fakir stopped his nose and ears with wax; his disciple pushed his tongue back so that it completely obstructed his esophagus. Almost immediately, the fakir fell into a sort of stupor and was then wrapped in a shroud-shaped sack, which was sewn shut and sealed. The sack was placed in a coffin that was also shut tight and sealed; the coffin in turn was placed in a pit thoroughly lined with stones and then covered with dirt that was packed down and trampled. Then the dirt was planted with seeds that quickly sprouted. A solid palisade was built around this tomb, and sentries, who were to be relieved every hour, were appointed to guard it.[3]

Robert Darvel, tanned from the sun and carefully disguised in his muslin chomin and turban, was amused to see the minute precautions the English officers took to avoid being victims of some deceit. They would certainly

---

3   Those of our readers who desire further information about these feats may consult Mr. Osborne's book, which contains the testimonies of Captain Ventura and Captain Mad, Monsieur Boileau's account, and Mr. McGregor's medical topography.

have been surprised had they known that a famous French engineer was sitting among the Brahmins, an impassive spectator of these preparations.

Phara-Chibh had set the moment for his resurrection at three months' time. Until that day, the English officers' surveillance did not lapse for a minute. A blanket of greenery now covered the gravesite of the living corpse.

"You must admit," laughed Ardavena one day, "that, even if you were to suppose (which is impossible) that my fakir managed, somehow, to receive help from the outside, you would still have to explain how he was able to live so long without either eating or breathing."

"You know how impatient I am for the day of his resurrection to arrive."

The day finally came. In the presence of the same witnesses, the tomb was opened. The plants, which had developed deep roots, were torn out, and the dirt was removed by the shovelful from the stone-lined pit. The coffin had sustained some slight water damage, but the stamps were intact, as were the seals, the knots, and the stitches of the sack that had served as his shroud.

Phara-Chibh, folded in two and terrifyingly thin, was as cold as a cadaver. His heart no longer beat. His head alone retained some meager vestiges of warmth.

The fakir was gently placed on a mat and his assistant began by replacing his tongue in its natural position. Then he removed the wax that obstructed his nose and ears and gently poured some warm water over the whole body of the exhumed man. This procedure produced some signs of life. The beating of his heart became perceptible, some color returned to his cheeks, and the slightest of shivers agitated his emaciated torso.

After two hours of meticulous nursing, including artificial respiration, the wholly resuscitated fakir stood up and, smiling, slowly began to walk around.

To Ardavena's great surprise, Robert Darvel, whom he had been carefully observing, did not show the amazement at this stupefying experiment that the Brahmin had expected. He returned to the shelter of the monastery without a word and shut himself in his laboratory, where he remained for two full weeks. When he came out again, he seemed transfigured. He leapt four steps at a time up the stairway leading to Ardavena's cell and burst through the door.

"Well," he shouted, "I've got it!"

"What?"

"Good God! The way to communicate with the planet Mars and go there even, not to mention a host of other marvels, next to which your miracles are child's play."

"Go on," said Ardavena coldly.

"It was quite simple once I stumbled onto it. Observing your fakirs' séances, I noticed this: the will of a single man concentrating over several minutes is sufficient to liberate him momentarily from the laws of planetary attraction. Imagine what one could achieve through the combined will of thousands of powerful men concentrating for a long period. They would be capable, I am sure of it, of completely liberating a body, for a given time, from the laws of the cosmos."

"Excellent," murmured Ardavena, who had turned pale as if from a sudden chill. "But you would need a device that could unite the rays of these scattered wills and then direct them toward some spiritual or material goal."

"I have developed a way, at least in theory. During my two weeks of deliberation, I have sketched out plans for an *Energy Condenser*. With my device, it will be possible to prolong the life of the dying, resuscitate the dead, kill kings on their thrones, stop overflowing rivers and armies on the march, and transport oneself from one end of the universe to the other at the speed of thought."

"How?"

"Isn't human thought infinitely quicker and more active than electrical fluid? People at the brink of death have been held back by the fierce will of a friend or family member who begged them, who commanded them not to die. What won't be possible for such a power amplified a hundred thousand times by the conjunction of a multitude of wills cooperating toward the same goal?"

"Certainly, but what about the machine?"

"I believe I can build it. It will be an immense darkroom. Only, unlike an ordinary darkroom, it will be circular, and the interior will be lined with a phosphorescent gelatin, whose formula I have devised, that manifests certain properties of cerebral matter. This delicate jelly, which will be very expensive to produce, works like an electric accumulator for the will. A huge glass carboy, filled with this same substance made even more powerful by an electrified liquid bath, will be, so to speak, a reservoir for all the energy beamed toward the oculus of the machine."

"Why the darkroom?"

"Because, just as I have tried with the phosphorescent gelatin to come close to the substance of the brain, with the darkroom I wanted to imitate the structure of the eye, the only organ in man that serves the will, that receives and transmits it to other organisms."

"I see. But, once you have accumulated the will in the cells of this sort of artificial brain, how will you be able to make use of it and project it over long distances?"

"Let me explain. At the back of the machine is a chair whose arms terminate in two metallic spheres, pierced, like sprinkler heads, with an infinite number of small holes. From these holes emerge electro-nervous wires of my invention, which descend into the middle of the gelatinous mass. To use the condenser once it is charged, one simply sits in the chair and places one's hands on the spheres. After a few seconds, the subject is able to profit from all the energy accumulated in the machine. His will, and consequently his creative force, is momentarily augmented by the combined wills of those who have contributed to the charging of the condenser. The power of his brain is thus multiplied almost to infinity."

"Give me an example so I may better comprehend."

"You showed me a fakir preventing one of his assistants from standing up, or even moving at all, just by looking at him. The same fakir, holding in his hands the orbs of my energy condenser, could render immobile a whole multitude. Only . . ."

"Ah, I see there is a limitation."

"Yes. The experimenter seated in the machine and projecting the unified rays of a multitude of wills will experience a terrible exhaustion that will last many days. It is even possible he will lose his mind after such a cerebral effort."

"I hardly think so," said Ardavena, laughing.

"In the meantime, I will search for a way to mitigate this drawback."

"Get to work, then. And spare no expense so that the end result will measure up to your dreams."

Ardavena had already taken several steps toward the door when he turned back abruptly.

"One more thing, please. You said a moment ago that you had found the secret of traveling to the planet Mars."

"Absolutely, yes. It is no more difficult than the other things I have just mentioned. Beginning with the principle of levitation, if a man can rise several feet above the earth by the force of his will alone, he can go wherever he wants if the conjunction of wills that carries him is sufficiently powerful."

Robert Darvel set to work with feverish energy. In a few days the exterior structure of the energy condenser was complete: it looked like a vast sphere with an enormous eye in the middle. It was mounted on a metallic pedestal surrounded by a balustrade that allowed one to walk around it, and upon which was located the seat reserved for the experimenter. The sides of the central carboy were made of very thick glass and furnished with tiny windows with nozzles for cleaning and filling it.

The fabrication of the phosphorescent gelatin, animated with a unique sort of life from a bath in an electric current, was more difficult, and Robert had to start over several times. But finally, with a little patience and a good deal of hard work, everything came together at last. The condenser had been set up in one of the large interior courtyards of the pagoda and hidden under a cotton tent, as much to protect it from the heat of the sun as to conceal it from curious eyes.

The evening it was all finished, Ardavena and Robert walked around the machine whose phosphorescent gelatin surrounded it, in the darkness, with a halo of white light.

"I worry that something will go wrong at the last moment, that we will forget some simple precaution and be forced to abort our first attempt."

"I have complete confidence," responded the Brahmin. "But how will you proceed?"

"It seems to me there are no two ways about it. We will begin with very simple experiments, which we will increase little by little in complexity and length to see how much tension our condenser can support."

"What if we were to begin right away?" suggested the Brahmin quietly.

"By God, I don't see any reason not to. Place yourself in front of the lens and concentrate all your willpower."

Ardavena obeyed with enthusiasm and for an hour he remained silent, absolutely immobile, his eyes fixed on the triple lens of crystal that seemed to absorb the emanations of his brain. Robert, his heart pounding with excitement, had the indescribable satisfaction of seeing the pale phosphorescence of the crystal sphere grow brighter, lighting up with small, passing flames and blue bolts of electricity as the phosphorescent gelatin absorbed the Brahmin's imperious will.

"That's enough," said Robert suddenly. "You mustn't tire yourself nor push the machine too far the first time."

Ardavena stepped away from the oculus and admired the beautiful glow that issued from the sphere and lit the surroundings with a light almost as bright as day.

"Now," Robert declared solemnly, "I know my invention works."

"Not entirely. We must now see whether I can transmit my will as well as condense it—whether I can, in one second, emit all the energy that I have accumulated over the course of one hour. Shall we try it?"

"As you wish."

Ardavena, grasping the two spheres that were crackling with blue flames, looked straight at Robert. Two long dark blue bolts shot instantly from his pupils, and the engineer, struck by this terrible gaze as if by a thunderclap, dropped to the ground, senseless.

Ardavena stood up, seized by a strange, giddy enthusiasm.

"You will never again see this world!" he cried, contemplating the inert body stretched at his feet. "Foolish man, suffer the consequences of your carelessness and your naïve confidence. I will be the sole master of your secrets, while you will go, at my behest and forever subject to my commands, to explore new worlds filled with inconceivable marvels."

The perfidious Ardavena lifted the body of the engineer onto his shoulders and carried him to the crypt where Phara-Chibh lived with another fakir. When they saw the superior of the monastery, both arose respectfully from the mat where they sat cross-legged.

"Master, how may we serve you?" asked Phara-Chibh.

"See this man," said Ardavena, "I leave him in your care. Know that his life is precious. No harm must come to him. But it is imperative that you place him in the same state you enter when you are buried alive for several months. For as long as possible, he must need neither to eat nor breathe, and he must feel no pain if he should be wounded."

"This is hardly possible. I have trained through long years of fasting and meditation. I'm afraid the crude faculties of this *belatti* (foreigner) cannot withstand the ordeal."

"I wish it," said the Brahmin with authority.

"I will try, master."

"How much time will you require?"

"A month, at the very least."

"That is acceptable. But above all remember my injunctions."

And without another word, Ardavena returned to his cell, his eyes shining, his face lit by a triumphant smile.

VII

....

The Catastrophe

And then you appeared standing on a thunderbolt.
D. Erasmus

A month had passed. No one had seen Robert Darvel, but a great transformation had taken place in the behavior of the ten thousand fakirs supported by the monastery and living within its walls. The bloody self-mutilations had ceased, as had the deafening processions of divinities conducted in boats around the sacred lake to the sound of trumpets and tambours and illuminated by Bengal fireworks. A mortal silence hung over the majestic domes of the temples. All the fakirs and other ascetics had withdrawn into their cells where they were fervidly focusing their will according to Ardavena's mysterious instructions.

Only the Brahmin was feverishly active. Each night he visited the energy condenser, now radiating light like a globe of fire, and, through repeated experiments, he perfected his handling of the terrible power he had acquired. Even he was terrified of the destructive force he now wielded. But, as with all superhuman power, this tyranny over the forces of nature had a cruel countereffect on the person to whom it was granted.

One night, Ardavena took his place on the metal seat, seized the spheres and, piercing the sky with his gaze, wished for a tempest to unleash its force on the forest. In a few minutes, he saw his wish fulfilled. As if painted by the fluid brushes that shone from his pupils, black clouds began to build. Thunder rumbled. A diluvial rain made the rivers overflow, and the fury of the wind smashed pines fifty meters tall as if they were reeds.

But after this experiment, the Brahmin had to keep to his bed for forty-eight hours, and it was only after attentive nursing that he prevailed over the deathly exhaustion that had overcome him. He recognized in this the truth of the old credo contained in the sacred books of every land, including the Vedas: the magician who succeeds in making spirits — that is to say, supernatural forces — obey him, always in the end becomes their victim.

Yet this warning did not deter the arrogant old man from carrying out his plans. Messengers left Chelambrum every day, stopping at the doors of monasteries and temples throughout the subcontinent to transmit Ardavena's orders.

Wherever these messengers went, the Brahmins, trained by long years of fasting, would begin to pray, projecting their energy toward the cupolas of Chelambrum. Flowing from every corner of India, a special atmosphere gathered above the monastery, and the condenser slowly absorbed it.

Obsessed with his plan, Ardavena passed days at a time engaged in astronomical calculations. A series of experiments had led him to conclude that thought travels at approximately half the speed of light. Given the speed of his passage from Earth to Mars, the engineer would have nothing to fear except being flattened or burned from the heat engendered by friction as he traversed the atmospheric layers. He made several trips to Calcutta and wrote to astronomers and metallurgists, who, never suspecting who their real correspondent was — imagining they were dealing with one of those amateur scientists found everywhere — graciously furnished him with all the information he requested.

Following their instructions, Ardavena arranged to build a sort of upholstered coffin, just large enough for a man. It had the shape of an olive and was formed of solid vanadium steel. This first envelope fit snugly inside a second, made of thick asbestos-board; this in turn was encased inside a third, made of wood infused with fire-resistant substances.

Ardavena had calculated that, given the incredible speed of his passage through the terrestrial atmosphere, Robert ran the risk of being crushed or burned only for a few minutes, and he believed he had resolved these two difficulties in the ways we have just seen.

The distance from Earth to Mars, at its greatest point, is ninety-nine million leagues, but when Mars is closest to Earth, when Mars, the Sun, and Earth are aligned, this distance shrinks to fourteen million leagues.

But as Robert himself had often explained to the Brahmin, the steel olive needed only to cross a little more than half of that colossal distance.

At that point, it would be in Mars's gravitational field.

Ardavena also knew that the strength of Earth's gravitational field diminished rapidly, that is to say, proportionally to the square of the distance that one moved away from it. This prodigious journey of eight million leagues was more terrifying in appearance than in reality, especially considering the speed at which psychic energy would propel the metallic coffin.

One evening, Phara-Chibh and his companion brought out the body of Robert Darvel, with the utmost care, on a palanquin. How he had changed! Even his face was unrecognizable: emaciated, skeletal, crosshatched with deep lines. The fakirs had, so to speak, petrified his defenseless body and refashioned it in their manner to make it capable of supporting a long artificial catalepsy. They had used the *pousti* plant, which causes emaciation and anemia, and many other poisonous preparations that make the organs appear dead while conserving a tiny spark of life deep in the brain, like a coal buried under a thick blanket of ashes. They had made him one of them.

At Ardavena's command, the body was placed next to the condenser that, now engorged with human energy, illuminated the farthest corners of the courtyard with a beautiful pale greenish-white light.

Phara-Chibh was prepared to believe that the moon, trapped by Ardavena's enchantments, was being held captive among these granite gods, leaving only its pale ghost to wander the sky.

The Brahmin didn't bother to correct him. He had Robert placed in front of him and, sitting down in the metal armchair, enveloped him, so to speak, in a protective armor of energy and health that his hands drank through the spheres from the vast reservoir behind him, as luminous jets of energy flashed from his eyes.

Then, under his gaze, Robert underwent the usual preparations. He was sewn inside a shroud and placed inside the steel, then the asbestos, and finally the wooden olive, with each lid screwed shut one after the other.

It should be pointed out that the two conical ends of the olive were armed with powerful spring-loaded releases made to automatically blow the cover off at the first shock.

At this moment, Ardavena had a moment of hesitation; something like remorse almost penetrated his despotic, frozen soul. There was still time to awaken Robert, to bring him back to life, to start the experiment over on different terms. In addition, self-interest mixed with these feelings of remorse.

"In sending him for good to this faraway planet, I will lose all the benefit of the discoveries he would certainly have made."

But the voice of pride spoke loudest.

"I will not share this power with anyone. I will make these discoveries myself. And, in any case, am I not powerful enough to bring him back from wherever I send him, whenever I wish, with a wealth of superhuman knowledge?"

The metal olive had been placed on a wooden tripod. Ardavena looked at the sky from time to time and consulted his chronometer frequently. At his signal, gongs and drums boomed. Their rhythmic and almost sinister call drew long files of fakirs from every corner of the monastery. As they entered the immense courtyard, the fakirs all knelt in a semicircle around the condenser, gazing at it with eyes hollowed by fasting and fever. Some were naked; others wore only a loincloth. They came from everywhere, from between the giant feet of stone elephants, from the depths of crypts, from temple gates; some descended stairways three by three, others surfaced like the spirits of reeds from the sacred lake.

Soon this silent multitude was complete, arranged in long, regular lines in the light of the flaming globe. All that could be heard was the sound of their ragged breathing. The huge shadows cast by the stone elephants added something solemn and terrible to the scene. Ardavena saw that his orders had been carried out, for a bluish mist was amassed above the half-glowing monastery. An arrogant smile played on his lips as he considered the millions of Indians bringing to his work, at that very moment, the magnificent contribution of their will. He experienced the delight of an unprecedented triumph.

The sphere had grown unbearably bright. Ardavena determined that the hour had come.

He sat on the metal armchair and stretched his emaciated hands toward the spheres. He experienced an extraordinary sensation; he felt as though his brain was growing, was becoming the brain of all humanity. His desiccated veins pulsed with new blood, full of youthful vigor and brilliance. It seemed to him he was drinking in, with one breath, the soul of an entire people. His intelligence seemed to him quasi-divine. He saw the present, the past, and the future, like three golden vases laid by destiny at his feet. His awareness of the power that now animated him even inspired him for a moment to give up his plan to communicate with Mars. He conceived of an even more audacious project. But he had made a promise to himself. He gripped the fluid-filled spheres more firmly and, with a supreme effort, two luminous jets of flame shot from his enlarged pupils to the projectile in front of him.

A moment passed. Then the steel olive disappeared as if in a magic trick, as if it had simply evaporated.

Ardavena smiled, but his smile was cut short by a terrifying cry of agony. The condenser, overcharged with energy, burst with a thunderous noise, pulverizing the crystal sphere. Debris rained down on the kneeling fakirs.

Ardavena, covered with blood, lay sprawled in the dust, his eyes burned out, still holding the two metal spheres in his charred hands.

The fakirs howled as they fled in every direction, imagining some celestial calamity. The following day some two or three hundred wounded and dead were removed from the rubble, all of them horribly disfigured on the battlefield of science.

Despite the Brahmins' professional discretion and their many precautions, the English government caught wind of this singular catastrophe. But the officers charged with the inquiry learned nothing precise about what had happened. They concluded that some ignorant fakirs had been maimed in an attempted chemistry experiment.

As for the Brahmin Ardavena, he was still breathing when he was found and he slowly recovered from his wounds, but he was blind and had lost his mind.

VIII

....

The Awakening

Despite the destruction at Chelambrum, the mad experiment Robert Darvel had devised was a complete success.

The vanadium steel olive indeed traversed the layers of the terrestrial atmosphere at the speed of thought, the friction turning its asbestos layer red. Fortunately it cooled almost immediately as it crossed the dark and lugubrious spaces of the Ether. A thick layer of ice formed around it, but this melted as soon as it entered the planet's sweltering atmosphere.

Mars is one of the planets with which we are most familiar. It is approximately six and a half times smaller than Earth. Its volume is barely sixteen hundredths that of our globe. From new telescopes with improved lenses and mirrors, and especially from the work of Giovanni Schiaparelli and Camille Flammarion, we know that Mars has a great many similarities to Earth. The seasons come and go there more or less as they do here, except that each, since the Martian year lasts 687 days, lasts twice as long, and even a bit more than that.

There, as on Earth, there are two temperate zones, a torrid zone, and two glacial zones. The last, thanks to the icecaps that envelop them during the winter that extend at their furthest approximately five degrees from each pole, are visible by telescope and even photographable, due to their whiteness, which stands out on the green and red crust of the planet.

The extent of these massive ice flows that assuredly form paleocrystic seas depends on the season in each hemisphere of Mars. Our terrestrial astronomers see them grow and shrink in a regular pattern over the course of one revolution (687 days).

Contemporary scientists are convinced that the planet is surrounded by an atmosphere almost identical to our own, though less dense, that holds great quantities of water vapor, just like our own sky here on Earth. For long periods of the year, thick clouds, perfectly visible from Earth, cross the sky and appear to form vast rings in the north and south of the planet, in the regions furthest from the equator, which are otherwise cloudless for months at a time. It has always been assumed that these clouds hover above bogs and marshes. They come and go according to the wind, pile up or dissipate, and it is certain that they are quite similar to our terrestrial clouds in composition, and that they should be classifiable as cirrus, nimbus, or cumulus.

For many years the Paris observatory has had an extensive collection of maps and photographs of the Martian oceans and continents. Through a telescope, the oceans present a more or less pronounced green coloration. From this it has been deduced that their seas are rich with alkaline chlorides and appear dark to us because they are deeper.

As for the islands and the continents, which are larger than the oceans and form an uninterrupted band around the planet's equator, these present those bright red and yellow-orange tones that are the planet's distinctive coloring. They have given the planet its name, which is, in pagan mythology, that of the god of war, to whom it had been consecrated. The oceans, especially in the northern hemisphere, are barely the size of the Mediterranean or the Caspian; interior lakes, or straits, like the English Channel, connect the regions covered with water. On Mars we do not find any ocean comparable to the Pacific or Atlantic. Only the boreal and austral seas have much in common with our own.

There are mountains on Mars, but only in small numbers and certainly none as high as our own. The appearance of white patches at regular intervals proves their existence; the high summits probably remain covered with snow even after winter has ended.

But the most striking aspect of Martian geography is that we have never discerned any rivers and that the whole of the solid surface of the planet is lined with immense canals whose lengths vary from a thousand to five thousand kilometers. These canals have regular, geometric designs. They appear to have been laid out intentionally by intelligent beings.

The raison d'être of these of these canals, discovered by Mr. Schiaparelli of Milan in 1877, has never been satisfactorily explained. They continue to perplex astronomers today. What is most extraordinary is that next to the lines formed by some of these canals, a second, parallel, and completely similar line forms and then disappears some time later.

Another striking feature of Mars is that, unlike Earth, which boasts only one satellite—the moon—Mars, more highly favored, possesses two of them, tiny, to be sure, named by astronomers Phobos and Deimos. Of these two miniature celestial bodies, one, Deimos, has a diameter of only twelve kilometers, and it completes its orbit in thirty hours and eighteen minutes; the other, Phobos, has a diameter of only ten kilometers and finishes its journey in seven hours and thirty-nine minutes. Phobos and Deimos, presaged by Voltaire in *Micromégas* and even by Swift, the celebrated author of *Gulliver's Travels*, were discovered by the American astronomer Asaph Hall.

As a result of its greater distance from the Sun, Mars receives about half as much heat and light from the Sun as does Earth. But this disadvantage, if it is one, is compensated by the length of the years, approximately twice our own.

By observing distinct features of the Martian surface, astronomers have demonstrated that Mars rotates completely in twenty-four hours, thirty-seven minutes, and thirty-three seconds, which means that days there are roughly one half of an hour longer than they are here.

It was into this strange world that the coffin-missile entered, in the midst of the Martian night, tracing a luminous trail like a meteor through the darkness.

Surging, rain-battered waves shrouded in mist closed around the metal shell and, contrary to the Brahmin Ardavena's expectations, as well as to Robert Darvel's, no shock triggered the springs at either end of the olive that would have permitted the prisoner to return to life and freedom.

Because the steel spheroid was hollow and had a wooden shell, and above all because of the diminished planetary attraction, it did not sink in the water. Nor did it rise to the surface. It hung in the water, a lamentable piece of flotsam, a plaything of the raging winds.

It floated like this for three days until a powerful wave, crashing on a cliff of red porphyry, thrust it through the mouth of a grotto, above the surface of the water, where it caught fast, miraculously suspended in the jagged teeth carved in the rocks by the waves. But the shock had been sufficiently strong. The springs worked and the olive's cover opened.

When Robert regained consciousness, he had the terrible sensation of having been buried alive. The energetic fluid with which Ardavena had, so to speak, impregnated his shroud before placing him inside the padded coffin gave him a superhuman vigor for a few minutes; it was enough to save him. With one swipe of his fingernails, which the fakirs had permitted to grow and had sharpened into claws, he ripped open the cotton sack that enveloped him and, since he couldn't breathe, he instinctively tore out the wax that plugged his nostrils. Next, still involuntarily, with a decisiveness born of desperation, he returned his tongue to its normal position and breathed in a huge gulp of air.

But the effort was too much for him. Robert lost consciousness and fell into a deep sleep, almost a coma, without having had the chance to pull his thoughts together, nor to begin to consider where he might be.

He was awakened by a pleasant feeling of warmth. He felt as though he were seated, with his back turned to the pale beams of a winter sun. He opened his eyes and saw before him nothing but a series of fantastically jagged red rocks and the mouth of a cavern that seemed to plunge deep into the bowels of the earth.

Wedged up to his neck in his steel coffin, he was just able to turn his head. He shuddered as he realized the peril he was in. The olive in which he was imprisoned was delicately, precariously balanced on several sharp points of rock. The slightest false movement might send it tumbling into the waters of a green and gray sea whose waves broke in the light of a reddish sun, veiled by fog, that seemed smaller to him than usual.

He had to extricate himself from this dangerous situation at all costs.

Robert made himself as small as possible and very cautiously attempted to slip out of the coffin without falling into the booming abyss beneath him. His endeavors met with success. To his great surprise, he felt endowed with extraordinary flexibility and vitality. He stretched out on the reddish sand of the grotto's floor, truly content. A confused humming filled his ears. He found the source when he felt the plugs of wax that stopped them, which he immediately removed.

He then heard the whistling wind and the melancholy surge of the surf against the cliff. He was cold and hungry. A strange dizziness overwhelmed him, like the vertigo that strikes explorers and travelers when they reach high altitudes. This abnormal faintness was in turn offset by increased muscular strength.

Dazed, Robert closed his eyes and tried to collect his thoughts. It seemed to him first of all that he must have been asleep for several days, and he surmised that he must be on the shore of the Indian Ocean, where he had no doubt come with Ardavena on some excursion.

His unease dissipated bit by bit. He tried to gather his memories, which required an enormously difficult effort. He went to the edge of a pool of water that shone in the darkness of the grotto and looked at himself. But he didn't recognize his gaunt, emaciated face nor his skeletal torso.

And why did he have such impossibly long nails?

He believed he had lost his mind or was dreaming. He pressed his hands to his temples in despair, then he stood up and began to walk, contemplating the ocean and the overcast sky. He was shivering. He was certain he was still dreaming when he noticed the length of his strides.

All at once his gaze lit on the olive, whose black wooden shell, battered and charred, stood out against the red sand.

"Yes," he stammered, "this must be some trick of Ardavena's. How I long to return to Chelambrum and the contentment of my lab and garden! But I must demand an explanation from the Brahmin. There is something incredible about all of this . . ."

His weakened brain couldn't piece any clearer ideas together. Hunger, thirst, and cold dominated his thoughts. He wrapped himself as best he could in what remained of his cotton shroud. He drew a little water from the pool in which he had glimpsed his reflection. The water, tossed there no doubt by the sea, was horribly bitter and salty.

Was he going to die of hunger and thirst in this cavern suspended between sea and sky on a cliff of porphyry?

His shining eyes cast about and eventually discovered in a corner of the crag little tufts of bluish plants, but their color didn't surprise him. They were, he figured, some variety of samphire or sea asparagus with which he was unacquainted. He tore up a handful and savored the refreshing juice with delight. He chewed them, spitting out the woody fibers, continuing to graze on all fours like this until a gnawing pain in his stomach warned him that he had eaten enough for the time being.

Robert had been deprived of food for such a long time that he became literally drunk on the few mouthfuls of juice from these herbs that he had imbibed; his head grew heavy, his legs unstable, and he couldn't keep his eyes open. Yet he had the strength and presence of mind to pull the metal olive from which he had emerged, like a chick breaking through the shell of an egg, to safety on the dry sand. After wedging it between two rocks, he climbed in head first, like an ostrich, twisted his shroud around his legs and fell at once into a deep, restorative slumber.

When he awoke — what a nightmare! His thoughts were hardly more coherent than before, and he was tortured by a terrible hunger.

"Nothing has changed," he cried, discouraged. "Since I awoke, I can think of nothing but food. If only there were some edible plants in the vicinity."

Fortunately, Robert had been fortified by his long sleep. The dizziness that had oppressed him had disappeared. He felt only a great appetite and an extraordinary agility in all his limbs. In one bound, he covered six or seven meters. He imagined for a moment that he had wings, and he had to be careful not to tumble, by accident, from high up the cliff into the sea.

At the mouth of the cave, he found a series of steps and crevices carved into the rock by the waves, and he decided to descend by this path to the surface of the water. He hoped to sound its depth and see whether it might not be possible, by wading through the water along the edge of the cliff, to reach a more hospitable location and find a way back to his cherished laboratory in Chelambrum. Despite all evidence, he believed it to be nearby.

All at once he shouted triumphantly. His voice, echoing from the rocks, sounded as resonant to him as the horn of a hunter. He stopped, frightened by his own booming voice.

He had just noticed, floating at water level among the seaweed, strands of bivalves that looked almost like mussels, only more plump, attached to the rock by their byssi.

"I'm saved," he said.

And he harvested an ample supply of mollusks and climbed back to his cavern to enjoy them. He felt his strength returning, so to speak, moment by moment.

Two days went by in this way, broken by long periods of sleep, with these nourishing but unvarying meals.

"I cannot," he thought, near the end of the second day, "spend much more time perched on this cliff like a seagull in its nest, grazing and eating bivalves. This would be too ridiculous."

Robert spent a good part of the night in thought. Strange conjectures slipped into his mind. The look of the sky, the presence of the machine that served as his bed, the absence of any other human beings and any boats on that ocean blanketed in fog, everything pointed to the fact that he must be far from Hindustan and that someone had taken advantage of his sleep and his catalepsy to strand him on this deserted shore.

"Perhaps Ardavena, coveting my discoveries, has transported me to northern Siberia, to get rid of me," he thought fearfully.

What strengthened this supposition was that he had noticed, although deprived of his chronometer, which Ardavena had unceremoniously borrowed from him, the unusual length of the days and nights.

And yet, he wasn't satisfied with this hypothesis.

"When the days are long," he told himself, "very logically, the nights are correspondingly short. Something doesn't make sense here."

Furthermore, the engineer could not judge these things very clearly. Since he had recovered from the effects of the narcotics the fakirs gave him, he felt a constant need to sleep and he hardly ever woke up, except to eat, and then he went right back to sleep.

That evening, he had evidently recovered enough strength, for sleep didn't come. The night seemed interminable. He had planned to climb to the top of the cliff as soon as it was light. But he slept, awoke, and slept again, but darkness still enveloped him. He feared for an instant that he might be lost in the eternal night of the arctic pole.

Finally the reddish glow of the shrunken sun slowly pierced the veil of mist. Robert rose, ate, and without further deliberation began to climb the rocks of red porphyry that rose above the cavern. It took more than an hour. He stopped to rest on every propitious ledge and made use of the tiniest bushes, the tiniest tufts of russet-colored plants to pull himself up a little more. At the top of the cliff, he stopped in amazement. A tall forest with red and yellow foliage, in which he recognized beech and hazel trees, rose all around him.

But he saw no traces of roads or paths into the interior. Russet-colored brambles, raspberry bushes with vermillion leaves, and brown mosses grew in a jumble of intertwining vegetation. On the misty horizon, the ocean stretched between two porphyry capes that framed the perspective in this direction.

Although surprised by the reddish color that dominated the landscape, Robert was full of childlike joy to find himself in the middle of the forest. He thought he might be in Canada, for he had read that there were, in that country, a great number of plant varieties with red foliage.

He made his plan at once.

"I'm going to strike out across this forest," he said, "always heading toward the south. I will use the stars and sun to guide me. In this manner I will eventually arrive in the southern part of the country, where the great cities and railroads can be found. Even if I have been left near the Arctic Circle, I won't be able to travel a full week without running into an Eskimo camp or a party of fur trappers or gold miners."

Before setting out, Robert decided to rest for a time in the forest. He ate plump golden raspberries and black currants. He picked red hazelnuts and violet blueberries. Then he set off.

A variety of birds resembling sparrows or thrushes fled at his approach, and he was overjoyed to discover a clearing covered with white mushrooms that resembled fairy-ring mushrooms, which furnished him a magnificent lunch.

To Robert's great surprise, the sun seemed to stand still in the midst of this layer of fog. The forest, clothed in red foliage, appeared to him like a beautiful and never-ending autumn morning in Eden. Yellow insects leapt in the vegetation; every now and then the cry of a bird could be heard. Robert felt increasingly listless. He imagined living in the profound peace of this sleepy, silent landscape forever. The changeless rhythm of the surf pounded the porphyry cliffs.

Once again overcome by sleep, Robert huddled between the roots of a great red beech tree and, exhausted, fell asleep on the moss. When he awoke, the sun rode low on the horizon. Huge lilac and green clouds floated above him, and his view of the red forest harmonized so perfectly with the color of the clouds and the dying rays of the sun that he feared for an instant that all the beauty that surrounded him might abruptly dissolve, along with all its glory, as if in a fairy tale.

But the sun, after hovering for a long time — such a long time that Robert couldn't recall ever seeing anything like it — sank beneath the inky, leaden clouds and disappeared. A bright lunar radiance almost immediately replaced the light of the vanished star.

Robert was delighting in the sight of fireflies flitting about in the bushes when, as he turned around to look at the sea, an extraordinary vision froze him in his tracks.

Two bright, white moons of enormous size were reflected in the waves.

"I am not mad," he said, "nor seeing things."

He closed his eyes, let himself fall to the ground, and thought. In an instant, the marvelous and terrible truth hit him. The metal coffin, the red foliage, the sad and diminished sun, and the two moons (Phobos and Deimos, no doubt) all added up.

"I am the first man ever to set foot on the planet Mars!" he shouted, filled with pride, and dread.

PART TWO

I

....

The Wilderness

Robert Darvel stood up, reeling from a strange feeling of vertigo: THE PLANET MARS! These magic words resonated in his ears, in the blowing wind, in the melancholy rustling of the leaves, in the monotonous murmur of the sea.

"The planet Mars!"

He had spoken these words aloud and they frightened him. A cacophony of voices seemed to respond from the bushes. He wheeled around instinctively, searching, his eyes wide with fear of the Unknown. It seemed to him that misshapen beings in the undergrowth were sneering and snickering as they softly echoed:

"Ah! Ah! The planet Mars . . ."

He took a few steps toward a clearing where the light of the two moons flowed pure and calm, luminously outlining the russet and pink shadows of the yellow willows and red beeches.

He felt a terrible urge to run, but he didn't dare, for he thought he heard someone treading close behind him, following in his footsteps, breathing softly on his neck. Animals were nibbling fruits in the trees; weary trunks were groaning in the wind; in the distance a spring was weeping: all of these noises added to his terror. Accounts he had read long ago of the strange inhabitants of other planets flooded into his memory. Was Mars peopled by monstrous cannibalistic brutes or by beings of a superior civilization, with the marvelous resources of a new science at their disposal? All these thoughts collided in his brain and he felt the same fears as the first men must have experienced in the forests of the Tertiary Period.

Large bats gliding on silent, velvet wings passed in front of him, and he dreamed of winged imps and evil dwarves and night prowlers who, hiding in caves and old hollow trees in the day, emerge only at night, like vampire bats, to suck the blood of their sleeping victims.

Robert felt his mind slipping away, tormented by a fear of solitude and of his own weakness. The calm night and quiet forest, redolent with decomposing foliage and damp earth, seemed to him full of peril. The horror of being alone made his blood freeze. The old home planet, Earth, which to him was now no more than a speck of light lost in the distance of the immense expanse of the heavens, appeared to his desolate soul as a place of delights, a privileged corner of the immense universe.

At the very least, there were men there!

Robert would have been very happy to be alone and without a home, protector, or money in the poorest neighborhood of Paris or London, even on the miserable Siberian steppes, even a prisoner of ferocious savages deep in Java or New Guinea.

He looked around frantically and an urge came over him, an irresistible urge, to cower in a hole in the rock or a hollow of a bush like a timid animal and wait for daylight.

Suddenly he happened on a brook that ran between two large red rocks, and whose clear surface gleamed in the light of the two moons, Phobos and Deimos. Reeds, rushes, and a mixture of succulents with spreading leaves adorned the waterway's banks, and quick golden fish as agile as trout darted among the plants. Huge trees admired their dark foliage in the water.

Robert had never beheld such a charming landscape illuminated by such soft glimmers of light. His courage returned; he was embarrassed by the fear that assailed him.

Kneeling on the damp grass, he drank water from his cupped hands and found it exquisite and soothing.

"No!" he proudly exclaimed. "I will not succumb to these senseless fears. I will be faithful to the role that I myself have chosen; I wanted to get to know new worlds, whatever the risks. Whatever enemies or dangers may await, I have come with all the venerable riches of human science. Whether

I succeed or fail I will have accomplished the goal I set for myself. I will have filled the page I wished to write and my mission will not have been in vain. I have no right to complain nor to be afraid."

Stimulated by this burst of enthusiasm, Robert found himself in complete control of his faculties. The strangeness of the situation revived him and he walked on at a brisk pace, leaving the spring and the clearing behind to plunge into a long avenue with a carpet of brown moss as soft as velvet under his feet.

If his friends on Earth had seen the young engineer at this moment, walking briskly with no idea where he was headed down the paths of an untamed forest, none of them, certainly, would have recognized him. Robert was as thin as a skeleton, his features were haggard, his shoulders were stooped, and his wild hair and beard were turning gray. His only clothing was the cotton sack that had served as his shroud, under which he was shivering, although it wasn't terribly cold.

He had made rudimentary sandals from thin strips of tree bark that he wrapped around his aching feet. And finally his incredibly long and sharp nails made him look more like a Stone Age man than a respectable mathematician who had graduated third in his class from the Ecole Polytechnique.

Robert Darvel, now certain that he had left the planet of his birth and that what he had taken to be a Canadian forest was instead a part of Mars, walked with great strides, as much to revive his sluggish limbs as to reach, as quickly as possible, some Martian settlement, the existence of which he was impatient to discover.

"If they are friendly and intelligent," he had told himself, "I will find a way to make myself understood and they will help me. If they are hostile and stupid, I will frighten them and they will be obliged to come to my assistance anyway."

Greatly fortified by these rather fanciful hopes, he pressed on, but after a quarter of an hour he was overcome by fatigue and, despite his sandals of vines, his feet were raw and terribly sore. He broke off a thick, mostly straight branch to serve as a cane and also as a weapon of self-defense.

To his great surprise, he had no trouble tearing off a branch that was bigger around than his wrist from the trunk of a red-needled pine, and he brandished this heavy bludgeon as easily as if it were a flimsy reed.

"Merciful heavens!" he cried suddenly. "I forgot that Mars is around six times smaller than Earth. By virtue of the law of gravity, my bodily strength must be proportionally greater. Let the inhabitants of Mars take note: if they pick a quarrel with me, I will surely be the stronger.

This childish notion of his own superiority made him smile. Thinking about it, he remembered a host of facts that confirmed his opinion that the lesser gravity of the planet had increased his physical strength.

"On Earth," he thought, "as exhausted as I was, I never would have been able to break free of the capsule, get out of my winding sheet, and climb the rock to reach the forest. As weary as I am, I never could have traveled such a distance."

Indeed, with almost no effort, Robert was taking enormous strides; he felt as if he were walking on air. To clear a log that blocked his path, he rose two or three meters into the air with one leap.

This observation encouraged him greatly, and his tireless imagination suggested he employ his newfound strength and agility to hunt the animals of the forest.

While making these reflections, he continued at great speed through a landscape brightly lit by the twin moons. Its calm lines, as if drawn in pink on a silver background, were like nothing he had seen before.

The avenue he had taken led to the top of a hill where a magnificent view opened before him: an immense ring of peaks, crowned with forests, surrounded the tranquil basin of a lake dotted with islands and fed by five or six waterfalls descending from the mountains.

But everything—the trees, the earth, the mosses and foliage—was a vivid vermillion or orange, or a deep violet, or a pale yellow; the color green, although found in certain species of plants, was not dominant. On the other hand, Robert saw some species of poplars with totally white leaves and some shrubs, of the pine family, whose fine needles shone as if gilded by some mysterious, charming shade of pale blue.

The splendor of this vegetation, colored blood, gold, and rust and illuminated by the magical, phosphorescent glow of the two moons, inspired an overwhelming feeling of yearning. In this golden forest, the blue and white trees were like ghosts sadly waving their arms, or perhaps young princesses who had lost their way, their white gowns blowing gently in the evening breeze.

Above all of this rose a pure sky and a mortal silence barely pierced by the vague rumors that rise from woods and earth that had, a few minutes earlier, so frightened Robert — the creaking of the breeze through the branches, the sound of wings, nocturnal feeding, all the secret, profound life of wild places.

Robert contemplated this magical scene for some time. He was filled with awe; the silence and majesty of the landscape got the better of him and he felt as if he were being invaded by a sort of sacred terror. He would have liked to scream out loud what he was feeling, but anguish seized him by the throat. Overwhelmed by his sense of isolation, he looked feverishly about, and he would have given the world to find a friend at his side — or anybody, even an enemy, with whom he could share the overwhelming, solemn impressions he was feeling.

He sat down on the moss — the beautiful russet and gold moss he found everywhere — and tried once again to master the sudden chill that had come over him.

What troubled him was that, although he keenly scanned the horizon, he couldn't see any sign of habitation anywhere: no smoke, no lights, no savage's or woodcutter's hut, nothing that revealed the presence of intelligent beings. Nothing but a magnificent and wild solitude, an untouched wilderness whose ancient trees had known neither fire nor axe.

In the midst of this mortal silence, he couldn't help cocking an ear, and his heart pounded at the thought of hearing the calls of hunters lost in the woods, a snatch of a shepherd's or some smugglers' song — in a word, the sound of a human voice. He turned his thoughts to his hunting trips in the jungle with his friend Pitcher, the naturalist. He would have gladly given up ten years of his life to have this loyal and brave traveling companion by his side.

What must he be thinking, ensconced in his little shop by the Thames? Surely he accused his friend of ingratitude and absentmindedness, and maybe he had even forgotten him in the countless preoccupations of the struggles of life.

This thought increased his unhappiness.

Oh! If Ralph Pitcher were here, how pleasant and stirring it would be to lay claim to a new planet, to venture together into marvelous uncharted territory.

But Robert was alone. As he thought of Earth, which was now no more than a tiny light on the horizon, he felt his courage falter. He was powerless to stop the memories that flooded over him and weighed heavily on his distressed soul.

He sighed as he thought of the charming Alberte, who had loved him and whom he would surely never see again. She too must have forgotten him, counting him among the lost or the dead.

The past rose up within him. He saw again, like the rapid flight of a procession of phantoms, everything that had happened to him: his childhood in a chateau outside Paris; the death of his parents, who had left him neither fortune nor protectors; his relentless academic pursuits; his inventions; his adventures in Siberia and at the Cape; and finally his stay with Ardavena and his journey through space.

"Come now!" he cried abruptly. "It's time to forget the past, time to bravely face the perils of the present."

He tightened the cotton robe around his waist, picked up his stick, and continued on his way, with that speed and lightness of foot to which he was still unaccustomed. After a moment's reflection, he decided to follow the shore of the lake, to pass through the curtain of forests that obstructed the horizon and reach the valley on the other side of the hills. There, perhaps, he would find some inhabitants.

After an hour's march he was hungry again. He felt an intolerable gnawing in his belly. He began by chewing on the shoots of young trees. Then, following a natural path along the edge of the lake, he saw, in a pool of water, a tuft of plants that, in everything except the brown color of their slightly plumper fruit, reminded him very much of the water chestnuts that grow in the ponds of western France.

He contented himself with this rather bland delight, but he vowed to discover a way to start a fire and prepare more substantial meals.

More or less fortified, he skirted the swampy shore of the lake, still happily served by the stunning physical strength he owed to the diminished centripetal force.

This night of forced marches felt as though it would never end. He felt bitterly disappointed that he had not encountered any of the marvels he had imagined long ago.

But underneath the large red beech trees, he was fortunate to find some mushrooms and then some beechnuts, which satisfied his hunger.

Dawn broke — a sad and shivering dawn in which the sun seemed veiled by a haze of smoke from a dying fire — as Robert reached the summit of the chain of hills on the far side of the lake.

From there an immense panorama opened before his eyes: a marsh the size of an ocean, uniformly dotted with ponds and clumps of reeds that stretched endlessly to the horizon. Above, flocks of birds wheeled in the sky.

But in all this desolate landscape, drenched with a fine rain and lit by an uncertain sun, Robert could find no trace of human habitation.

"How dreadful!" he cried. "How discouraging! Here I am, alone in a world without inhabitants, where there aren't even any dangers to distract me, that offers nothing but the prospect of brutish solitude . . ."

He felt a need to scream aloud, to talk to himself. He went on, in a sort of rage:

"Cursed be the dreamers and madmen who have supposed that other worlds were inhabited by beings and things veritably unknown and new. I understand now that the Universe is essentially the same everywhere! There is nothing new under the sun! Alas, even beyond the sun . . . I am punished by my own foolish pride. I will die here like a leper, without solace or friends, in solitude and despair . . ."

II

....

Dead from Joy

We must now return to Earth, though perhaps not as rapidly as Robert Darvel traveled to Mars, since we do not have, as he did, the power of millions of Hindu monks, nor the marvelous device that had permitted the Brahmin Ardavena to concentrate all of these scattered wills into a single beam.

As we mentioned earlier, the naturalist Ralph Pitcher had little by little forgotten his friend Robert.

But the latter's disappearance and the mysterious letter he had received from him remained with him, like one of those strange, inexplicable occurrences that one prefers not to think about but thinks about anyway.

The concern that he wished to brush aside kept returning, no matter what he did, inescapable and insistent; there were nights when Ralph would wake up suddenly, thinking his friend Robert was standing next to him, his expression filled with reproach.

Unable to resist this obsession, Ralph Pitcher returned to the old house on Yarmouth Street. The edifice was crumbling month by month in the wind and rain.

The rotted front gate was falling to pieces; it had come unhinged and the locks had disappeared, no doubt sold for scrap by some audacious thief in the night.

Ralph was thus able to enter easily into the courtyard now invaded by houseleeks, the hardy thistle, and that friend of ruins, the dandelion.

He searched each floor of the ancient residence but found no hint of what he was looking for, though he risked breaking his neck in the dislocated and damaged stairwells or falling into holes like secret dungeons that the rain had dug through rotten, disjointed floors.

Clearly, in no time at all the hotel would be a complete ruin and nothing but the thick walls would remain, their granite chimneys hung with heavy coats of arms dating from the time of Queen Elizabeth or Queen Anne.

Then a speculator would come with his steam-powered cranes, his trucks, and a regiment of Welsh masons and would erect, in place of these ruins, a twelve- or fifteen-story apartment building equipped with an elevator, electric wiring, and central heating.

Or so Ralph thought as he pensively descended the grand stairway with its forged steel banisters.

But, suddenly, he stopped, noticing something shining in the rotting wood of the steps.

He crouched quickly; he held, between his thumb and index finger a large opal, about the size of a fava bean.

He felt a sudden surge of emotion.

"It's not worth much," he murmured, "a crown and a half, if you had to sell it, three sovereigns at the most if you wished to purchase it . . ."

He stopped, pale as a ghost, and studied the little gem with green and pink accents; it was the stone that Robert Darvel usually wore as a tiepin.

"Someone lured him here," he cried, filled with rage and sorrow, "and then killed him."

"And yet, no, it can't be, for what then can explain the enigmatic letter I received?"

Ralph left Yarmouth Street greatly perplexed. This mystery dominated his thoughts all evening. After much reflection, he hit upon an expedient that he regretted not having thought of right at the beginning, since it was quite obvious.

The following day he went to the deeds office. There, after a long stay in the waiting room, he eventually discovered that, as the result of a legal dispute that had lasted more than a century between English and Hindu inheritors, for several months the house had been the property of a Hindu monk named Ardavena whose high esteem in the eyes of his countrymen was due as much to his fortune as to his erudition.

It was a place to start.

Ralph Pitcher resolved to pursue his investigation and, with a reference from an eminent professor at the Zoological Gardens who was a friend of his, he wrote a long letter to the resident minister of the Hindu province of Chelambrum asking for information about the character of Brahmin Ardavena and the possible presence in his monastery of a young French engineer.

It's important to note that Ralph's situation had recently changed from top to bottom; thanks to the treasure he had found in the crypt of the Buddhist pagoda, he had been able to give up his day-to-day work of ordinary taxidermy — the stuffing of bulldogs, foxes, and parakeets — to devote himself wholly to the study of natural history, a field about which he had some novel ideas.

He now signed with his own name the learned dissertations filled with discoveries that, in earlier days, he had happily ceded for a few pounds to established scientists, who derived both honor and profit from them.

Little by little he had made a name for himself among those true scientists, filled with a disinterested passion for the truth, who know one another throughout the world and form a sort of sacred brotherhood into which no one is admitted who has not proven his worth.

His book on the disappearance of animal species had made a splash, and his picture had been reproduced in notable publications in both England and France.

But despite these signs of nascent glory, Ralph had stubbornly refused to leave his little taxidermist shop — a touch of superstition perhaps.

And being obsessive, like many great scientists, he couldn't abide change; he loathed altering his routines.

He lived just as simply as before, setting aside for some ingenious enterprise the capital that he allowed to accumulate in the Royal Bank, which now exceeded the sum of a hundred and fifty thousand pounds sterling.

In any country other than England, this strange behavior would have seriously damaged Ralph's reputation; but there, it only added to his growing popularity. Ralph was taken for an eccentric; people wanted to see his shop and take his picture.

Noble ladies, listed in *Burke's Peerage*, considered it an honor to bring him commissions, and automobiles adorned with heraldic emblems stopped in front of the workshop, to the great bewilderment of Mrs. Pitcher.

Ralph was thus a well-known figure, and he imagined that his request for information about the Brahmin Ardavena and his friend Robert Darvel would not be ignored.

Once the letter was on its way, he felt happier and more relaxed than he had in quite some time. He worked that evening with incredible energy on a microscopic examination of an Aepyornis egg that he had received a few days earlier from Madagascar, the study of which formed the basis for a new, sensational theory.

Toward evening, his brain a little tired, he went down to a tavern with a cosmopolitan clientele on the banks of the river where he had become accustomed to go to read the foreign press.

He had barely opened the massive pages of the *Times* and absentmindedly glanced at the editorial when a headline with enormous letters caught his attention:

DEAD FROM JOY!

A Self-Made Man. — The Tragedies of Speculation. Useless Billions. — Miss Alberte Unlikely to Die: Doctors Hope to Save Her.

He read:

"As we go to press, we have learned of the death of the honorable John Teramond, the prominent banker, whose loss will be unanimously mourned by the financiers of the London stock exchange.

"Mr. John Teramond has expired in the most extraordinary of circumstances.

"It is well known that he had made a name for himself as one of the most fearless players in the Transvaal War.

"With the reestablishment of peace, against the advice of all his friends, he devoted the whole of his capital to the acquisition of a vast claim that had previously been prospected by a young French engineer, a Mr. Darvel, in whom he had complete confidence, though they later had a falling out.

"What is stranger still is that, since that time, neither Mr. Teramond nor anyone else has had any news of the Frenchman. He has most likely been killed in the course of one of the rash explorations of some deserted wilderness that he was wont to undertake without notice.

"At first, everything went well. The yield from the gold deposits was considerable, fulfilling the French engineer's expectations. The Teramond Bank was able to disburse fabulous dividends to its investors.

"But the seams soon dried up, the profits ceased to match the operation's expenses, with the Teramond Bank's costly publicity campaign, and the value of the shares plummeted. Soon they ceased to be listed among the serious stocks and the market was flooded with them; it was a case of getting rid of them at any cost, selling at a villainously low price.

"Others would have cut their losses before it was too late and looked for a more solid venture.

"But deaf to every objurgation, to every remonstrance, Mr. Teramond displayed incredible tenacity; he repurchased shares by the bucketful in a market without competitors since news from the gold fields grew worse and worse. They had reached a bed of marl that seemed to mark the end of the gold field, as numerous experienced old miners affirmed.

"Mr. Teramond had faith in his claim. He didn't stop work for a single day, devoting the last remnants of his capital to the task.

"In recent weeks, Mr. Teramond's situation appeared to be hopeless. His magnificent gallery of paintings had been sold along with his princely hunting grounds in the north of Scotland, when, yesterday, a radiogram from the Cape abruptly changed the face of things.

"After having cut through the bed of marl where the seams of gold ended, the workers had reached a deposit whose abundance recalls the heroic epoch of the first California mines; nuggets of pure gold weighing several kilograms had been brought to the surface.

"At the moment when this news burst like a thunderbolt in the Exchange, Mr. Teramond was in desperate straits. He had just arranged for the sale of his home. Receiving one cable after another that confirmed this unprecedented success, he had been unable to withstand the violence of his emotions; he was struck down by an embolism.

"Mr. John Teramond has died from joy!

"That very evening, shares of the Teramond Bank made a prodigious leap, jumping from three pounds to one hundred and sixty pounds sterling;

everything signals that this rise will only continue on an upward path tomorrow and in the days to come.

"The honorable banker succumbed just as the enormous sum of more than a billion was about to spill into his account.

"The sole heir to this colossal fortune, Miss Alberte Teramond, fainted when she learned of her father's tragic death and spent the night teetering between life and death. We have just learned that, despite the seriousness of her condition, there is hope she will be saved.

"Let us recall, finally, that Mr. Darvel, the engineer who discovered the marvelous claim, had previously proposed to Miss Alberte; but after some disagreements between the young engineer and Mr. Teramond, the latter had not permitted this proposal to go forward . . ."

* * *

Ralph Pitcher reread the article twice, unable to put it out of his mind. He spent the following day locked in his laboratory, which only happened, as Mrs. Pitcher pointed out, when he was in the grip of some serious concern.

Three days later, properly gloved and freshly shaved, Ralph presented himself at the Teramond estate and asked to be received by Miss Alberte.

At first he was refused admittance; the young woman was indisposed, overcome with grief. She asked that her visitor return another time; for the moment she wasn't receiving anyone. The servants had been given formal instructions.

Ralph had expected this difficulty. He calmly insisted that the valet return to his mistress and inform her that he had some important news for her about Robert Darvel.

These words worked like magic: a few minutes later, Ralph was ushered into a small green and white salon full of fine furniture in light silks and red sandstone, done in the style incorrectly called "art nouveau."

Ralph Pitcher had expected to find himself in front of some pretentious doll entirely occupied with fashions and sport, jewelry and receptions.

He was caught off guard by the solemn look in her thoughtful blue eyes, under a head of copper-colored hair. Her prominent forehead, determined chin, and softly arched nose suggested that she had inherited all the will-power of the speculator now dead from joy.

Alberte showed her visitor to a seat and then addressed him in a voice that, despite its sweet musicality, was penetrating and imperious.

"Mr. Pitcher," she said, "you are the only man that I would receive in these somber circumstances, and for two reasons.

"Robert Darvel spoke your name once"—her voice was laced with sadness—"and I have read your books. I know that you are a brilliant, yet modest, inventor. I knew immediately that you had not come to me on some frivolous pretext."

These straightforward words put Ralph immediately at ease.

"No, Miss," he murmured, "you are not mistaken. It was absolutely necessary that I speak to you. What I am about to tell you will undoubtedly surprise you, but I can promise you that it is true in every detail."

And, all in one breath, the young man told her of Robert Darvel's mysterious disappearance, of the inexplicable letter, and the recent steps he had taken to try to find him.

Miss Alberte listened to him without interrupting, but as he spoke her face had been transfigured. The lines of weariness and disenchantment that pulled at the corners of her lips had disappeared. She had gathered herself.

"Mr. Pitcher," she said, "I put absolute faith in what you have just told me and admire your fidelity to your missing friend.

"Believe me when I say that these are not just empty words.

"The agonies that my father suffered before the triumph that cost him his life have given me experience at a very great cost.

"I have seen everyone turn their backs to us. I saw ruin at our doorstep. I have suffered the insolence of creditors and even the contempt of servants."

And she added, with a movement of her head that showed her energy,

"Now they are all coming back, seeing who can be the most despicably flattering; the most insolent have become the most servile. They imagine that they can easily take advantage of a young woman with no business experience.

"They are mistaken.

"My father did not leave me just his millions. I have also inherited his insight and his determination. I have already taken all the necessary measures to protect my interests. None of these beasts of prey that prowl about me and imagine that the game is already over will have any part in the scramble for the spoils of the gold fields.

"I am a billionaire, but I will do just what I please with my gold.

"If my father were still alive, he would approve. I only ever had one argument with him, when I reproached him for his ingratitude toward Mr. Darvel, whom I loved, whom I still love.

"But I have already decided what I will do. I wasn't waiting for your visit, Mr. Pitcher, to make my decision."

"What do you mean to say?"

"I want to find Mr. Darvel and marry him.

"I promised myself that I would have no one but him for my husband."

Hearing these words, Ralph's heart swelled with joy; even with the most optimistic perspective, he would not have dared envision such a reception. And her Anglo-Saxon personality — fiercely loyal, brutally frank — pleased him beyond words.

"Miss," he said, "I can see that we will get along perfectly. I didn't come to ask you for financial assistance. Obviously, compared to you, I am very poor, but I nonetheless have something like a hundred thousand pounds in the bank. Let's not speak of that . . ."

"What do you want from me then? I am ready to place at your disposal a check for any amount you would like."

"It's not a question of money," said Ralph Pitcher, slightly agitated. "Now that I know you, I won't hesitate to ask you for it. But what I've been trying to say is this: with the prestige that you enjoy at the moment, you can accomplish anything; your smallest wish is an order. Write as I have done, that is all I ask. I am sure you will receive a much quicker response than I will.

"What is a poor taxidermist, what is even a scientist next to a gold queen like you?"

"There is some truth to what you say. I'll write immediately and you will deliver the letter to the post office. Only, I shall allow myself to add one small improvement to your plan. It won't hurt to offer a reward of five hundred pounds to whoever can bring us news of Mr. Darvel."

"I hadn't thought of that," said the naturalist naïvely.

"I really am my father's daughter, am I not? I have learned, to my cost, to recognize the power of money."

And she displayed a melancholy smile.

But she had already sat down in front of a small olive-wood desk encrusted with silver and mother-of-pearl (one of Maple's latest creations), and her graceful handwriting already raced across the mourning-paper.

Ralph Pitcher arrived at his shop filled with hope.

The following day, the naturalist was still in bed when Mrs. Pitcher, as was her custom, brought him his mail along with a large bowl of excellent coffee.

This was, for Ralph, one of the best parts of his day: while taking little sips of the fragrant brew, he would slide open, with the tip of his finger, the numerous scientific reviews that filled his mail. He would skim them absentmindedly, deep in thought. He would plan his work for the day. And it was only after having hit on a good idea that he would make the effort to get out of bed. Waking up, recommencing his intellectual endeavors, was a keen pleasure for him.

He had begun to leaf through a series of spectroscopic photographs of the planets that he found especially interesting when his eyes came to rest on a letter that had a stamp of the British Raj: he opened it feverishly.

It was an official communiqué that bore the insignia of the resident minister of Chelambrum.

The news, drafted by some clerk in a very musty style and almost buried under tiresome administrative turns of phrase, left the young man deeply stunned.

The resident minister's clerk recounted in his own words the catastrophe that had occurred at the pagoda and the Brahmin Ardavena's madness. He confirmed conclusively the presence of a French engineer, whose name was unknown to him, among the Brahmin's entourage; but he was certain that he must have been a victim of the audacious experiment, whose objective remained a mystery, that had cost the lives of several hundred yogis.

Ralph Pitcher had hardly finished reading when, leaving the rest of his mail untouched, he leapt from his bed, dressed, and charged down the stairs.

Five minutes later he jumped into a cab and was on his way to Miss Alberte's residence.

He came home again deep in thought but mostly satisfied.

Within a week all the English press was aflutter with a sensational bit of news.

Miss Alberte Teramond, the newly minted billionaire, had just paid a king's ransom for a yacht with the latest improvements and modern comforts, built for one of the Vanderbilts. She had left on a cruise and no one had been able to discover where she was going.

Some journals categorically affirmed that, being a woman of action like her father, she had gone to assess *de visu* the yields of her famous claims. Others insisted she was simply making a tour of the Mediterranean.

But what had really driven the curious to distraction in this mysterious departure was that Miss Alberte was taking with her the placid naturalist Ralph Pitcher.

Even the most audacious reporters hesitated to advance the idea of a marriage of love between the taxidermist and the billionaire.

They lost themselves in speculation.

III

....

The Conquest of Fire

Robert Darvel did not remain discouraged for long. Since he felt very tired, he lay down beneath a spiny genista bush, taking care to put down some freshly cut grass for a mattress.

He slept peacefully for five or six hours. His survey of the surrounding country had reassured him that at least for the moment he was in no immediate danger. He was certain that, in the region he had reached in such miraculous fashion, there were neither dangerous beasts nor inhabitants. And thus nothing to fear.

When he awoke, he gathered several handfuls of red hazelnuts, to which he added some water chestnuts and mushrooms. Such a menu would have enchanted a vegetarian. But Robert wasn't exactly a confirmed follower of that faith, and he told himself that as soon as had chosen a place of residence he would devote himself to hunting and fishing, find a way to light a fire, and build as comfortable a home as he could manage.

Above all, Robert was a man with a creative imagination; he had brought with him from Earth neither a container loaded with rations and tools nor a case filled with instruments of the latest design. But he had a deep understanding of chemistry, mechanics — all the capacities of the inventor — and he looked, with good reason, on this intellectual arsenal as something more precious than an entire flotilla of provisions and machines.

First, he would choose a place to live, then he would make tools for hunting and fishing, clothe himself, and make shoes. Once he was armed and his subsistence was assured, he would find a way to extract from the bowels of the earth, from the alluvial mud of the lakes or from the atmosphere itself, the substances needed for a grand project that he had conceived just after he awoke.

With his excellent memory, he would retrace the outlines of the Martian continents that, long ago, he had studied so intently that he could remember even the smallest of them. To be more clear, he would add the names that terrestrial astronomers had given to the canals and seas: Erebus, Titanum, Arcus, Gigantum, Cyclopum, Nilus, and so on.

He had several reasons to believe he was in the neighborhood of Avernus. His extensive knowledge of astronomy would allow him to choose the spot on the planet most visible to terrestrial observers and, alone, with no one's assistance, he would find a way to build luminous signals like those he had installed the previous year on the Siberian steppes. The sole difference was that he would not use the same signals. He would quite simply reproduce either the twenty-four letters of the French alphabet or the dots and dashes of Morse's telegraphic code.

"Then," he exclaimed joyously, "it will only be a matter of time before my signals are seen by the astronomers of Earth. They will answer me and we will establish regular communications. I will recount my incredible adventures in great detail. Old Ardavena will be arrested and will have no choice but to avail himself, in order to bring me home, of the same methods he used to send me here. I will return to Earth, enriched with a completely new understanding, after having successfully carried out the most audacious expedition ever undertaken by man . . . and, perhaps when I return," he thought to himself, "Alberte's father . . ."

* * *

Ever since the audacious hope of returning to Earth had first shone in his eyes, Robert had undergone a complete transformation. The discouragements, uncertainties and terrors of his first moments were gone. He had a newfound courage. A mysterious force animated him, and he now felt able to face any difficulty and resolve any problem.

He stepped out of the thorny bush that had sheltered him as he slept and stretched luxuriously. It was the middle of the day. The landscape presented a series of marshes and ponds, broken here and there by small pockets of trees and covered with a crop of half-dried reeds whose stalks chimed eerily in the blowing wind. For Robert, shivering under his light covering of cloth, the brittle stems evoked the image of a blazing fire. He decided that the first thing he would do after seeing to food would be to try to light a fire. In this damp and swampy country, illumined by a pale sun, on this planet whose equatorial regions weren't likely to be much warmer than the south of England, life without fire was impossible.

Robert's first thought was to search for a flint then retrace his steps to the place where he had left the debris of the metal shell and strike sparks from the steel into a pile of very dry moss or what was left of his cotton shroud. Unfortunately, he had covered a lot of ground in twenty-four hours, and when he tried to get his bearings he discovered to his great distress that it would be impossible to retrace his path; he was feeling a little disheartened as he made his way back when a flock of fat birds rose honking from the undergrowth.

Instinctively, Robert seized a large stone and threw it with all his strength. Whether by luck or by skill, the stone struck one of the fowls and it fell with a broken wing, while the rest of the band flew off, their discordant squawking redoubled.

Robert rushed to seize hold of the bird that, wounded though it was, was attempting to take refuge in a patch of gladiolus. He seized it by the foot and, ignoring the fury of its beak, managed with some difficulty to wring its neck. It was a superb animal; a type of bustard, larger than a goose, with beautiful brown plumage and a belly covered with a dense layer of white down.

"At least I will be able to make myself a feather bed!" Robert laughed. "This down is every bit as good as eiderdown."

As he spoke he had begun to pluck his bird. Once he had finished — it took no more than three quarters of an hour — he had the good fortune to find a bluish stone, from the shale family, a sort of slate, that broke easily into shards. With considerable time and patience, he fashioned it into a long triangle-shaped blade, sharpened its edges, and embedded it in a piece of soft wood.

With the help of this primitive knife, he carefully cleaned and cut up his game, which he was obliged to eat raw; but it had been so long since he had tasted meat that he thoroughly enjoyed this savage meal and it gave him a true feeling of well-being.

For the time being he had eaten only the two thighs. He had hung the rest of the animal with a strand of bark from the highest part of the bush that served as his bedchamber. He promised himself that before the sun went down he would find a way to light a fire so that he could cook the rest of his game. He would obtain salt by evaporating seawater. He would build himself a house. He would make weapons. Before setting off on his grand exploration of the planet, he intended to build a comfortable place to live. He would not leave on his expedition until he was well rested and well equipped.

He worked tirelessly all that afternoon. With his stone knife, he cut down a young tree with a perfectly straight trunk; from its foliage and resinous aroma he had recognized it as a close cousin of the pine or cypress. His intention was to make a bow, and he recalled that in the Middle Ages branches of yew and other resinous trees were commonly used for this purpose.

After an hour's labor he held in his hands a perfectly round and straight piece of wood just over two meters in length. He had also broken the slate blade of his knife, but it wasn't difficult to remedy this loss.

There remained the bowstring. To make one, Robert pulled threads out of his cotton shroud, wove them together, then twisted them to make a sturdy cord that he coated with resin from the same tree that had furnished the wood for his weapon. Perfectly straight reeds, which he armed with sharp flint tips, fletched, and weighted with a heavy pebble, furnished him with excellent arrows.

The results pleased him. None of the complicated inventions he had previously devised had given him such pleasure. As happy as a child with a new toy, he wondered whether he should shoot his arrows standing with his hand at shoulder height, like the Greeks; on one knee, like some medieval archers; or reclining on his back, one foot braced against the bow, like the first crusaders and the *caboclos* of Brazil.

He was soon rescued from his uncertainty; a flock of birds like the first he had killed rose again from the marsh. Taking cover behind the trunk of a tree, he had the pleasure of testing his new weapons, with great success: seven bustards lay slain, and Robert was astonished by his own strength, seeing that several of them had been pierced clean through.

His astonishment diminished the more he thought about it. Had he not read in Garcilaso de la Vega's *History of the Conquest of Florida* that an arrow, although shot from a very great distance by the Indians, had gone clean through a Spanish knight's thigh, literally nailing him to his horse?

He finished off his victims with a club and hung them triumphantly in his larder. Now he was certain not to die of hunger. Next, with the down from his birds (he now felt sure he could kill as many as he wished) he could make himself a mattress and some pillows. New birch bark would provide the necessary fabric and rushes from the marsh the rest. Shivering under the foggy sky he could already picture himself in the near future covered with a cap and warm clothes of woven rushes stuffed with bustard down. Dressed in this way, he would be able to hazard every kind of bad weather. And this was not the only benefit he hoped to obtain from his hunting: from the bones he would carve needles, fishhooks, and awls; with the finest parts of the fat, mixed with red clay, he would make ink.

And finally, he counted on recovering the wreckage of the steel shell, out of which he would be able to form tools and weapons of every description: axes, sabers, knives, saws, files, hammers, and so on, a complete armorer's and ironmonger's arsenal.

"But to do this, I need to find a way to build a fire. It's of the utmost importance, and it shouldn't be too difficult. But I will need to discover a way!"

Buoyed by these many triumphs, Robert was confident he would succeed. He left the peninsula where he had set up his temporary encampment and made for the rocky hills. As he walked, he carefully gathered dried leaves and mosses that he found along the way. These he ground into a fine powder that he collected in a large water-lily leaf that he had taken care to bring.

When he judged that he had enough, he chose two sharp flints and struck sparks from them above his improvised tinder. But try as he might, the sparks flew and fell without starting any fire; the tiny sparks struck from the flint cooled before they could set the moss on fire.

Robert deeply regretted his lack of a striking steel. He kept at it, however, with the patience of a saint, trying a thousand different methods without success. He mixed powdered resin with his ground, dried leaves. In place of a striking steel, he tried a small rock that appeared to contain traces of iron. Nothing worked.

Evening descended slowly over the immense marsh. Consumed by these efforts, the afternoon had passed like a dream.

Stretched out on his bed of leaves, sated on the fowl's raw flesh, Robert couldn't fall asleep. He was cold, and muffled cries and the rumbling of beasts in the forest made him shudder despite himself.

Restless and also frustrated by his lack of success, he decided to go for a short stroll in the dazzling light of Phobos and Deimos, as much to keep himself warm as to calm his frayed nerves.

He had walked for only a few minutes, skirting the pools of water, when he stopped, dumbfounded.

He was walking in a heavy fog up to his shoulders that rose from the marshes but did not diminish the clarity of the sky, since it remained low to the ground.

Through these light shadows, on the surface of the water, danced thousands of blue flames that burst into view, went out, fluttered, stopped, disappeared, and reappeared at unpredictable intervals and in capricious patterns.

"Will-o'-the-wisps!" shouted Robert.

And the old legends of the French countryside, told to him long ago by his nurse and read in beautiful gilt-edged books of fairy tales, came to his mind. He sighed bitterly. How far he was from Earth, from his childhood, from all whom he loved! He would grow old miserably, in a solitary world, forgetting even the sound of the human voice.

Fortunately, Robert never remained discouraged for long. The chemist soon overtook the dreamer and the romantic.

"Will-o'-the-wisps!" he repeated in a voice as level as if he were responding to an examination question at the Sorbonne. "Will-o'-the-wisps are nothing more than swamp gas or ethylene. It is generally accepted that their combustion is due to the presence of organic phosphorus released by decomposing matter in the stagnant waters . . ."

He suddenly dropped his doctoral tone:

"Heavens! What was I thinking? Aren't I trying to start a fire? And it's right here and excellent too! All you have to do, as they say, is reach out and grab it . . ."

But Robert knew, if only from the tales of his childhood, that will-o'-the-wisps are by nature capricious. If you approach them, they flee. If you flee, they follow. If you stop, they dance or go out, yielding to the smallest breath of air. He therefore resolved to take the necessary precautions.

He broke off the long, straight trunks of two young pines and stripped the branches. He had chosen two of essentially equal length and, thus prepared, he advanced to the tip of a peninsula bordered on either side by lagoons in which the blue flames appeared more numerous than in any other spot. Then he began to stir up the mud. Seething bubbles of gas emerged, almost immediately ignited by neighboring flames; for a moment, a true flame burned.

Encouraged by this initial experiment, Robert dug into the bark and wood of one of the poles with the help of a sharp piece of flint in such a way as to make a sort of spoon at one end, which he filled with a kind of artificial tinder made of moss, crushed leaves, and a little cotton.

His heart was pounding. With a trembling hand, he stirred deep in the mud, a large blue flame shone, and he quickly stretched forth his tinder. But as fast as he was, the flame went out and he had to start again.

Finally, after three fruitless attempts, the powder caught fire. With what care he drew in the precious pole, and how delicately he revived the grow-ing spark that he had quickly placed on some fuel he had prepared on a large piece of slate!

Oh, how he blew with care, holding in his breath for fear of sending his fragile fire flying!

Finally, like a new Prometheus, he felt the inexpressible joy of seeing a small flame crackle. He fed it with bits of reeds, then tiny branches until it became a real bonfire, in front of which he joyously warmed himself.

As he stretched his hands in front of the flames, he thought that he must certainly be the first man who had ever made fire on the planet Mars.

Once there was a large pile of glowing coals, he filled his stone, as a sort of shovel, and carried his fire like a treasure back to his hut.

That evening, he didn't go to bed before savoring a morsel of grilled bustard, which he found delicious. He covered his fire with an enormous blanket of branches to be sure he would still have some coals in the morn-ing, and his sleep was filled with rosy dreams.

IV

....

The White Beast

Waking after several hours, Robert undertook an exploration of his surroundings, although it was still dark. After about a hundred steps he unexpectedly found himself at the edge of the sea. A deep bay cut into the land like the mouth of a river. The reddish sand, turning violet in places, was strewn with shells of different colors: purple, pink, orange, and yellow; some of them, though few in number, were a beautiful azure blue.

He came across the remains of an enormous crustacean whose strange shape caught his attention.

Nearly the size of a man, the body was wider than it was long and protected by a scaly carapace. The animal must have moved very slowly, for its very short legs, out of proportion with the body, were no more than a few centimeters long. In compensation, two feelers armed with formidable pincers reached out like oversized arms.

It was an animal built exclusively for defense, made to live in some crevice in the rocks, but undoubtedly formidable if one were to attack it.

Robert broke off one of the pincers, for a curious keepsake as much as a weapon in case of need.

He continued on his way, under the magical light of the twin moons that literally turned the landscape red and pink.

He amused himself, as he had often done on terrestrial beaches, by hunting for shellfish, whose presence was signaled by small, regular holes in the sand.

In this way he caught some triangular bivalves as large as oysters that looked like two small three-cornered hats made out of stone.

He found them delicious.

Arriving at a shallow pool of clear water, he saw swimming in it what appeared to be a sort of tiny octopus with innumerable tentacles, each hardly bigger around than an ordinary earthworm.

He stretched out his hand.

The animal disappeared into the ground without a trace. The sand where it had been was barely wet.

Robert noticed a kind of rosette formed by an infinite number of small holes, comparable to the imprint that the bottom of a large colander might leave in the sand.

He presumed therefore the existence of some fantastic shellfish.

Armed with the pincer of the giant crab, he began to dig into the sand.

Soon he had uncovered a long white worm with a red head, then a second and a third. Each hole corresponded to a worm. But all his efforts to pull them from their hiding place were futile.

The engineer was lost in speculation. He wondered whether he wasn't dealing with marine creatures that live in a colony, as certain insects do.

He stopped digging. At the moment when he least expected it, all the worms he had exhumed disappeared at the same time.

The sand had instantly closed over them and was once more flat and riddled with tiny holes that diminished in size from moment to moment.

"Now that's strange!" the young man exclaimed.

And, seizing a large shell for a shovel, he again began to dig.

At first it was a complete waste of time.

The deeper he dug, the smaller the holes became, until they disappeared completely. To his great surprise, he found no more of the white worms.

The hole was growing deeper and beginning to fill, little by little, as water seeped in.

Then, all at once, something began to seethe beneath the surface of the sand.

Thousands of worms surged from the sand, bunched together like a head of white and pink coral.

This teeming mass glittered with iridescent reflections, like opal or mother-of-pearl, changing colors under his gaze.

Robert retreated instinctively.

Suddenly, with disconcerting speed, a form leapt up and bounded on the sand.

Robert was transfixed with horror.

The monster he saw was more terrifying than the most extravagant nightmare.

Try to imagine the crude appearance of a human face made out of transparent and viscous gelatin.

Its lidless eyes had the dull, glacial expression of an octopus. But its nose, with its quivering nares, and its enormous mouth, fitted with black teeth, gave it an expression of melancholy ferocity and scorn.

This fantastical face was surrounded on all sides by thousands of white tentacles that the engineer had at first taken to be sea worms.

The young man felt more afraid than if he had found himself face to face with a lion or tiger.

This unthinkable being suggested a creation that had been aborted at the mollusk stage, resulting in a hideous half-baked design midway between man and octopus.

Forgetting for a moment the real danger to which he was exposed, he was lost in this extraordinary revelation.

"The intelligence we possess," he conjectured, "has not necessarily only evolved within the order of mammals of which man is the crowning masterpiece!"

And he had a frightening vision of planets peopled by plant-men, insect-men, and reptile-men, equaling—even surpassing—the intellectual prowess we have attained.

Why couldn't it be so?

Even on the terrestrial globe, some animals, such as the elephant, approach human intelligence.

Perhaps they lacked nothing but a more useful tool, a hand, a more conducive environment or more felicitous evolutionary circumstances to reach a standing equal to ours.

In any case, Robert had always believed that, for the simple reason that our brain can imagine them, all the conceptions of our minds, even the most absurd, must exist somewhere.

Every creation of our imagination, every affirmation of our reason corresponds to a reality.

Only negation corresponds to nothing, and there must exist a psychological space where all that is affirmative and creative is complete and finally reconciled, despite apparent contradictions.

Robert was still lost in thought when his attention was abruptly called back to his strange adversary.

The human cephalopod now pressed itself to the ground like a flat disk; it looked like those primitive representations of the sun in which we see a man's face surrounded by rays.

Then, just as it had changed form, it changed color. It became the same reddish color as the sand, from which it was now hard to distinguish it.

Like the octopus and other mimics, it had the ability to adopt the color of its surroundings. Like the chameleon, it moved successively through every shade.

Then, its appearance changing again, it became a shapeless, gelatinous mass, as if a tub of spoilt flour paste had been spilled on the ground. Any resemblance to a human face had disappeared.

Robert Darvel had recovered from his initial fear. He was preparing to back away when the monster suddenly rose up, surprising him yet again with a third transformation.

It was a now wheel rolling over the sand with dizzying speed. Its long white tentacles were moving with such speed that they appeared rectilinear.

In the center, the hideously swollen face snickered, its pendulous lip contorted in diabolical fury.

It had changed color again: it was now blood red, and the protruding white globes of its eyes were terrifying.

Seeing its rapid flight over the sand, Robert had at first assumed that the cephalopod, frightened by his presence, was attempting to flee, was going to find another hole to hide in farther away. This was not the case.

He soon realized that the monster, after making an enormous circuit, had begun to retrace its path, still in the fantastical form of a living wheel, and was now tracing around him a series of ever tightening circles.

"Apparently," he reasoned, "this must be the tactic that this Martian octopus commonly uses to catch its prey. It must fascinate it, dazzle it, hypnotize it after a manner with its spinning and perpetual changes of color and shape. But I won't wait for it to rush toward me."

And Robert started to walk toward the shore, above which rose the red forest we have attempted to describe.

But first, to his great surprise, and then to his great terror, the cephalopod, still spinning with dizzying speed, was able to maintain a position between him and the shore. He began to see that no matter what he did his gaze was inexorably drawn to this undulating mass that, without ceasing to gyrate, continually changed its color and aspect, picking up flashes of precious stones from the moon's reflection, then changing, suddenly, into a rag seemingly carried away in a furious whirlwind.

In spite of his best efforts, he was yielding to its fascination.

He couldn't stop himself from following the rapid movements of this abject yet strikingly human visage and its large, glaucous eyes that flashed, from time to time, with phosphorescent gleams.

His eyes were growing tired and he began to feel lightheaded. His steps were becoming increasingly unsteady and, each time the monster moved closer, he involuntarily took a few steps to the right or the left.

Not only was he not moving forward, but he did not realize that he was being led, little by little, in the opposite direction from where he had come, to where the waters formed a kind of marine marsh covered with algae and all kinds of organic debris.

In the end, however, he rebelled.

"If I don't break this spell," he murmured, "I'm finished! No doubt this creature must be eager for new prey. It must think it has already caught me in its gluey embrace and will soon drink my blood from the thousands of suckers at the ends of its tentacles. But this is not the case!

"This human octopus must not be different from its earthly cousins.

"Let's see!"

Robert Darvel firmly grasped the claw of the giant crab with which he had armed himself and marched straight at the cephalopod.

It took flight, continuing its movements, perhaps in the hope that Robert would pursue it and that it could, in this manner, lead him closer to the ocean; but the young man did nothing of the sort.

This time he continued walking straight toward firm ground, appearing to show no more interest in his enemy.

It moved closer then, as if to engage in combat, but remaining well out of reach of his club.

Robert was focused entirely on carrying out his new tactic when he felt a sharp pain in his leg. He instinctively bent down and reached out his hand to see what had happened.

He realized with horror that another octopus, hidden in the sand and undoubtedly associated with the other in its hunt, had already encircled his leg with several of its tentacles and was beginning to suck his blood.

He glimpsed his own end, ingloriously devoured by hideous beasts in this sandy marsh. A sudden fury seized him.

With his improvised club, he began pounding on the half-buried octopus like a madman, severing by the dozen the tentacles whose suckers were trying to fasten onto his flesh.

Completely caught up in this battle, he had forgotten his first assailant.

He had just managed with great difficulty to free his leg.

And stand up.

When all at once a cry of inexpressible anguish burst from his chest. An unbearable weight had suddenly fallen on his shoulders and he felt enveloped in a coat of soft and slimy flesh.

Then it was as if a swarm of insects were crawling over his face and neck, their icy viscidity filling him with loathsome horror.

As one might guess, the first octopus that had whirled around him for such a long time had finally pounced on its prey.

It had taken advantage of the diversion afforded by the attack of the second, undoubtedly planned in advance.

Robert's blood rushed to his head. He had to steel himself with an incredible strength of will so as not to faint. He felt the monster's flaccid lips press against his skull while thousands of suckers wandered over his flesh, searching, undoubtedly, for veins and arteries before attaching themselves.

The tremendous weight of the vile creature was crushing him.

His legs were giving way.

An appalling smell both insipid and briny rose to his nostrils and turned his stomach to the point of nausea. Yet he fought with a fury born of despair.

He shook himself. He tore with his nails at the gelatinous mass whose liquid he could feel running through his fingers.

Nothing worked.

Suckers were steadily latching onto his neck and his cheeks and he felt his strength failing.

Frenzied, he began to run frenetically toward dry ground, but the monster didn't let go. It held him and held him fast.

To crown it all, Robert's foot caught the edge of a large rock. He lost his balance and fell headlong to the ground.

It was all over.

Life was draining out of him drop by drop, drawn out by thousands of thirsty mouths . . .

Robert lost consciousness . . .

* * *

When he came to, he felt extremely weak.

He was dazed and sore, as if emerging from a narcotics-induced sleep. Then he felt a painful stinging on his face and neck as if, while he was unconscious, he had been bitten by thousands of mosquitoes. At the same time, he had the sensation that he was smeared with something thick and sticky like bird-lime.

He struggled to sit up and looked around.

But what he saw immediately brought back the horror of his situation.

A few paces away, the hideous cephalopod, to which he had almost fallen victim, was flailing desperately in spasms of agony in the grip of a creature that Robert took at first to be a gigantic bird but on second glance appeared more like a giant bat.

The young man quickly guessed what had happened.

While the octopus was intent on devouring him, it had been surprised, in its turn, by an enemy undoubtedly fond of its flesh, as albatross and seagulls are on our planet, more than happy to feed on cuttlefish and squid left behind by the waves.

A moment's reflection convinced Robert that he could expect nothing good from such a savior.

Marshaling his strength and his courage and without a single curious glance behind him, he made it back to solid ground and stretched himself out, overwhelmed, on a bed of moss under the gigantic trunk of an old red beech, not far from the bonfire that he had lit.

He fell instantly into a sleep as deep and irresistible as death.

V

....

The Vampire

Fate had decreed that after the monsters of the sea, Robert would also face, that very night, those of the sky.

After only a few minutes' rest, he was awakened by a sensation so singular and painful that he thought it must be a nightmare. It felt like someone was on top of him, placing all their weight on his chest in order to suffocate him. At the same time, he felt a sharp sting on his neck, close to his ear.

He instinctively reached out his hand and was profoundly horrified when his fingers brushed against something velvety and warm, like the eiderdown of a bird or the soft, plush skin of a bat.

Quietly, a dark mass rose above him. In the dark of the night his gaze met two large, phosphorescent eyes just as a violent blow struck the side of his head, half-stunning him.

He tried to yell, to call for help; but he was paralyzed by fear and could only moan plaintively.

His brief struggle with the mysterious vampire that had chosen him as its prey had lasted all of ten seconds. With the sky completely veiled by clouds, the night was pitch-black. All Robert could see, a few feet away, were the incandescent eyes of the monster, poised above him with beating wings, no doubt preparing to pounce again.

The young man thought he was finished. He understood now that this planet he had believed to be uninhabited was peopled with horrific beings, the misshapen remains of primitive creations, and that he would be devoured with no hope of rescue from anyone.

Yet, despite the freezing terror that seeped into the marrow of his bones, the sudden thought of a possible means of defense hit him like a bolt from the blue.

"Fire!" he exclaimed hoarsely. "Fire! These nocturnal monsters must be afraid of flames."

He rushed like a madman from his resting place to where, the previous evening, he had built the bonfire that he had so carefully covered with branches.

"What if it's gone out?"

His teeth chattered with fear at the thought.

Luckily it had not, and Robert was overjoyed to find a large mass of red coals smoldering beneath the ashes and branches.

In a flash, he tore a blazing brand from the fire and hurled it with all his strength toward his enemy. For a few seconds, the light from the fiery coals illuminated a truly diabolical apparition: a creature worthy of a place among the most hideous demons of medieval imagination.

Imagine a bat, about the size of a man. Nothing could hope to give an idea of its appearance, except perhaps the giant Chiropterae of Brazil or the vampire bats of Java. But its wings were much smaller and its finger-joints, grouped at the extremity of the forearm, formed a true hand armed with sharp claws. In addition, its lower extremities terminated in similar hands, and it was by these claws that the vampire, when Robert caught sight of it in the brief light of his flaming projectile, held itself fast to the sturdy branch of a beech tree.

To the unfortunate exile from Earth, everything about this apparition augmented its horror: the dull yellow of its membranous wings; its face, human down to the last detail and filled with guile and cruelty; but above all its flabby, blood-red lips and its blinking, scarlet-rimmed eyes, like those of an albino. It had a turned up nose, like a bulldog, set in a bloodless face; long, rounded ears, out of all proportion with the head, completed the hideous picture.

Robert observed all of these details with indelible clarity, and he was so startled by them that he let the second brand he had seized fall from his hands.

Luckily for him, his missile had hit its mark.

Its stomach scorched, and dazed by the flame, which must have been unbearable to this nocturnal creature, the vampire let out a cry of agony, followed by a series of lugubrious groans, and then tumbled, reeling, from its perch.

After this surprising success, Robert rushed forward, armed with a huge firebrand, prepared to finish off his victim. But the vampire, who appeared to be deathly afraid of the flame, began to hop right and left, as awkwardly as a kangaroo, groaning all the while in an almost-human voice.

Robert pressed it but, just when he thought he had it in his grasp, it leapt onto a large branch and disappeared from view.

Somewhat reassured, the young man returned to his fire and added some small branches of dry wood. A clear blaze soon arose, one of those joyous, crackling blazes that fill one with warmth and chase away all the phantasmagoria of the night.

Robert sat down and, with a little less apprehension, reflected on the unusual attack from which he had miraculously escaped.

Like all people who are alone, he had acquired the habit of thinking aloud:

"I don't believe I have anything to fear from this horrifying creature during the day," he said. "It is while I slept that it began to suck my blood." And he instinctively touched a small, round wound that still bled a little, just behind his ear.

"These vampires are unquestionably nocturnal. Now I have been warned, and as they say, forewarned is forearmed. For the moment, it's a question of keeping a good fire and a good guard. As soon as it is light, I am going to search for a cave where, when night arrives, I can barricade the entrance with stones and branches . . . I will make myself a lantern, with marrow from the rushes and the fat of birds . . . then I will always have fire to defend myself."

Despite these and other reflections by which he attempted to reassure himself, Robert couldn't stop thinking of the horrible creature whose image appeared to him as soon as he closed his eyes.

At the slightest rustling of leaves, the slightest creaking of reeds, he would leap up and strain his ears in terror. He was certain he heard in the darkness the gentle beating of the monster's velvety wings.

"What if he brings reinforcements?" he wondered, trembling. "How can I hold out against a troop of vampires once my store of firebrands is exhausted?"

And he pictured himself on the ground, dismembered alive by a swarm of beings with blinking eyes and thick, bloody lips in livid albino faces.

His head was spinning from fear of the unknown. Would he not have to battle other strange perils, other unheard-of beasts, in this melancholy world that he now suspected was peopled exclusively by terrifying creatures?

Haunted by these thoughts, Robert felt a sense of deep joy and deliverance at the sight of the sun rising like a pale globe through the fog, above the water and brown rushes.

He laughed, he sang, he scoffed at the notorious vampires. His splendid self-confidence, which is the making of great men and great enterprises, had returned with the sun.

"Bah!" he laughed. "I must be the meanest of cowards; with my muscular strength multiplied by the planet's weaker gravity, I will put all the vampires to flight. But first, I'm going to eat."

Having measured his strength against certain danger, Robert felt braver and more cheerful, and then the sun lit up the clouds beautifully, the puddles of water were filled with light, and countless flocks of birds rose honking from the grass. Robert felt filled with strength to face the trials of this new day, which seemed to smile at him through misty veils.

In front of a pond as clear as a mirror, he calmly examined the wound on his neck. It wasn't much after all: a red mark a little swollen around the edges.

At the same time, this brief examination started him thinking.

"Good God!" he exclaimed. "It appears that these vampires understand anatomy. This sore is located right along the jugular vein and the carotid artery. It surely was, as they say, five minutes to midnight when I awoke."

Robert applied to his wound a compress made from fragrant herbs that seemed to him close cousins of sage, mint, lemon balm, and rosemary, all plants from old Mother Earth.

They differed from their congeners only in details hardly worth mentioning: leaves that were more deeply indented or more brown, flowers that were smaller or different colors.

"I shall donate," he exclaimed, "these curious specimens to the gardens of the Museum de Paris, if ever I manage to return home."

He then returned to his larder, which fortunately had not been destroyed by the vampire. He prepared a succulent meal of grilled meat accompanied by several dozen water chestnuts, which took the place of the bread and vegetables of terrestrial meals. He shouldered his bow and arrows, threw several logs onto his fire, and set off, after having tied what remained of his game on his back with straps made of woven rushes.

But, along the path he followed through the marsh, he took care, every dozen steps or so, to break the reeds so that — like another Tom Thumb — he might easily find his way back to his hut and, more importantly, his bonfire.

He walked in high spirits for a quarter of an hour, like a sightseer almost, pleased with the appearance of the sky, which didn't portend any rain capable of putting out his fire.

Suddenly his way was blocked by a hill covered with a novel variety of large yellow and red water-willows, glowing in the morning sun.

He took a few steps down an alley that seemed to have been regularly laid out between the trunks, as if by a human hand, and then he stopped short, stunned and also amazed.

He had stumbled upon a Martian hamlet of sorts, whose rustic simplicity encouraged him to explore further.

VI

....

Captain Wad's Experiment

Reports in the press of the *Conqueror*'s arrival in the Canary Islands reassured the nervous world of investors.

"There you have it," they said, "just as we had suspected. This silly girl is going to spend the winter in these Iles of the Blessed, the Nice of the truly wealthy; obviously, she does not take after her father."

But public opinion changed completely when it was learned that the *Conqueror* had stopped in Las Palmas just long enough to replenish its stores of coal.

The same question posed at the beginning of the voyage was posed anew; the account books of financial circles recorded sizable wagers.

The practically inclined celebrated noisily when a cablegram from Cape Town reported that the *Conqueror* had dropped anchor in Table Bay.

"Good Lord!" exclaimed in unison the clan of serious men. "We knew it, we were certain of it: she's a true businesswoman. She has gone to visit her claims . . . This is a bold first step!"

But the businessmen experienced a cruel slap in the face on learning that the *Conqueror*, after no more than the time needed to refuel, had again set sail for an unknown destination.

The eccentrics and those with a fertile imagination, who had wagered that Miss Alberte was on a world tour, saw their shares rise considerably. Their stock had taken a tremendous fall; now they were quoted at fifteen to one.

This time it was a near certainty: Miss Alberte would stop in Australia and then return, undoubtedly, through the flowery suite of oceanic islands springing up like fresh bouquets from their ring of white coral. The public's opinion of the banker's daughter plummeted. She was surrendering to the puerile fantasy of a tour around the world in her very own yacht; she was no longer someone to be taken seriously.

Opinion swung a third time when it was learned that the yacht had left its passengers in Karikal, in French territory. From there, Miss Alberte and her royally outfitted escort had set off toward the Ghats.

This time, the speculators celebrated yet again. The goal of this mysterious voyage was no longer in doubt to anyone: each now understood the presence of the naturalist, Pitcher, in the expedition.

Everything was clear: everyone knew that Ralph was as knowledgeable in geology as he was in zoology; his travels in previous years through the jungle were well known. From this point on, no one doubted that Miss Alberte, guided by Pitcher, was on the trail of a diamond mine, a lode of uranium or some other equally valuable mineral.

"What determination!" repeated the men of the stock exchange. "What flair! Her father had discovered Darvel, the engineer; she has straightaway latched onto Pitcher, the naturalist!

"She is going to double the tremendous wealth of the Teramond Bank. She is indeed extraordinary."

As is often the case, the enthusiasts as well as the detractors were both completely wrong. As the reader has no doubt surmised, Miss Alberte and Pitcher were quite simply pursuing their investigation into Robert Darvel's unexplained disappearance.

All throughout the voyage they had discussed it; they had told each other what they knew and had concluded that Robert must still be alive. It is easy to believe what one hopes to be true.

But if he had died — something they refused to believe — they wanted to know how and to punish, if need be, the guilty.

For if Robert had not been ambushed, it did not enter their heads that he could have died a natural death.

"Come, Miss," cried Pitcher exultantly, "I put it to you, is it at all possible that Robert has simply perished of dysentery, an attack of fever, or sunstroke like a common worker in the Rand? Like an ordinary, badly acclimated Chinaman?"

"I have never believed it for a second," replied the young woman, her brow furrowed by a crease of stiff obstinacy that, in moments of anger or excitement, made her look exactly like her father.

"You understand, Miss," Ralph continued, "that a scientist of Robert's caliber doesn't just die in that way.

"A physicist, chemist, hygienist, physiologist . . ."

"Enough already," Miss Alberte impatiently interrupted. "You could exhaust all the words that end in *-ist* in the encyclopedia without achieving your goal."

"I simply meant that if Robert had been ill, he was too learned to not know how to heal himself and too bold, too robust, and too intelligent not to defend himself against his enemies.

"There is something else beneath this, something hidden."

"We will uncover it, Mr. Pitcher!"

This conversation took place in the sitting room of the opulent field motorcar that the banker's daughter had had built especially for the expedition.

It was, in effect, a large caravan mounted on wheel trucks and equipped with a five hundred–horsepower motor. Built by a major London manufacturer, its cost of construction amounted to fifty thousand pounds; the luxury trains of certain comfort-loving rulers might give the reader some idea.

At this moment, the car was slowly climbing a path lined on either side with palms, latanias, and other equatorial species.

Bands of small red monkeys played among the branches, and some, to the great astonishment of Miss Alberte, ventured onto the motorcar's foot-plates from where they would bounce back into the lower branches with the elasticity of a rubber ball.

But soon the forest gave way to rich fields of cotton, tobacco, and white poppies bordered by sturdy hedgerows of spiny prickly pears.

Ralph smiled with satisfaction.

"I recognize the signs," he said, "of the practical spirit of colonization. We must not be far from the home of the resident minister, Captain Wad.

"Why, look, here we are."

And with that patriotic joy that is an integral part, so to speak, of the English soul, he pointed out a bamboo pole at whose summit flew the Union Jack.

Several minutes later, Miss Alberte's car, and those that accompanied it, stopped before a delightful residence, at once palace and cottage, with a highlander nonchalantly standing guard before the door.

India is perhaps the only country in the world where rigorous and persistent experimentation has devised ways to protect man from the heat.

Ralph Pitcher and Miss Alberte were led into a high-ceilinged room refreshingly cooled by a liquid air ventilator.

Only in fusty old Europe do we still use bladed contraptions that merely stir up stale air without renewing it, producing deathly drafts with no cooling effect.

The liquid air ventilator, which gently diffuses sanitized, glacial air through sixty openings, is especially valued in the equatorial zone.

This innovation has rendered obsolete the punkahs that, operated by slaves in the households of wealthy Hindus to this day, agitate the air with their double wings, like a gigantic butterfly.

Ralph and Miss Alberte were not kept waiting in the anteroom; Captain Wad himself soon appeared.

They had expected to find a bureaucrat stupefied by the climate, suffering that disease of the liver that attacks Europeans, and especially the English, stubbornly attached to their habitual regimen of alcohol and rare red meat.

They were surprised to see a lively, affable personage appear, dressed in loose-fitting green-and-pink striped pajamas and boisterously expressing his joy at the chance to entertain his compatriots.

"Nothing," he said, "could please me more than your arrival.

"I could almost say that I have been waiting for you, so much so that I have here at hand a detailed account of the Ardavena case that has been written just for you.

"As for the ridiculous letter that you received, it came from the hand of one of these Hindus who, proud to know a little English and to be in the service of His Majesty, manifest in every occasion a notorious incompetence . . ."

"Captain," Miss Alberte interrupted brusquely, "before you say anything else, tell me, I beg you, whether Monsieur Darvel is alive."

The officer, suddenly serious, frowned.

"Miss," he said, "about that, I know no more than you. I cannot affirm anything.

"The Chelambrum affair is a mystery that has intrigued me greatly, and that I haven't managed to solve; I run into incredible obstacles at every turn.

"However, in my heart, I don't believe that Darvel is dead. My inquiry has established that it was he who agreed to collaborate with the Brahmin Ardavena in psychodynamic experiments that I do not yet entirely understand."

"What leads you to this conclusion?"

"One thing in particular. After the catastrophe, I took in the yogi Phara-Chibh. He knows the secret of being buried alive and passing many weeks in the ground like a cadaver, without apparently suffering any ill effects from the experience . . ."

"So where is this man?" Ralph Pitcher impetuously demanded.

"He is here, you will soon see him.

"Phara-Chibh claims to know that the engineer is quite alive."

The officer put a finger to his lips.

"But there is nothing I can say. You must visit him and see for yourselves what miracles this ragged ascetic is able to perform."

"But," murmured Miss Alberte, insisting, "what does he maintain?"

"He will tell you himself," replied the officer.

And he added, in a tone that cut short any insistence:

"We will see him after dinner. First, I wish to enjoy the pleasure of receiving guests who have come all the way from England."

There was a tone of honest cordiality in Captain Wad's rather stiff manner, and it appeared certain that Robert Darvel was alive. It was more than Ralph and Miss Alberte had dared to hope, and they resolved to be patient.

In any case, they had no time for further reflection. A gong rumbled and domestics dressed in light muslin appeared to lead the resident minister's guests into a delightful dining room.

It was Captain Wad's creation, and he was obviously proud of it.

Tumbling from fifty different points in the stucco vault, delicate ribbons of water refreshed the room and created the illusion of the entrance to a grotto of naiads, with an enchanting bed of lilies with diaphanous foliage.

A few steps away the sun's terrible heat cracked the earth and caused the seeds of wild balsams and cacti to explode in bloom, but here it had been disarmed.

The table was laden with all the refinements of European luxury, spiced with Indian splendor.

The centerpieces displayed huge blooms of magnolias, double water lilies, cacti, and unclassified orchids. Stationed behind the guests, smartly dressed domestics respectfully presented vintage wines: the celebrated port-wine from the citadel of Goa, more than a century old; calabashes of palm wine; ginger brandy; and those spirits of myrtle, jasmine, and wild lemon so skillfully refined by Anglo-Indian distillers.

The inescapable curry dressed venison and fish that would have cost a fortune in London. Fruit was piled in crystal dishes as if fallen from the Promised Land. The narrow columns of the jets of water murmured in song, and at the end of the room the bay window opened wide to the distant rumbling of the forest and a breeze laden with wild scents.

Miss Alberte and Ralph were enraptured.

They now understood what had seemed inconceivable a few days earlier: the profound aversion of many Englishmen to return to Europe once they have lived a few years in India.

The art of living has been studied there for thousands of generations.

In addition, Captain Wad was a charming conversationalist. He understood the art, so little practiced today, of not only letting others speak but of enticing each listener to speak, of drawing from each person, for the pleasure of the group, the interesting things he had to tell.

"I intend to prove to you," he said laughing, "that we are not as savage as people like to say. I have tried, as best I could, to avoid the physical and mental sluggishness that overcomes those bureaucrats fond of gin and opium."

"One can see," murmured Pitcher, "that you are a friend to the yogis."

"Certainly; but, if this is an attempt to remind me of my promise, I am ready. Phara-Chibh awaits us. We can go see him whenever Miss Alberte wishes."

"Right away, Captain," exclaimed the young woman. "I must confess that, despite the delights of your table, which would make Lucullus, Brillat-Savarin, and several billionaires of our acquaintance blush with shame, I have a burning desire to see this thaumaturge."

Captain Wad rose from the table and led his guests through a gallery of bamboo columns with a magnificent view over the forest and the moonlit gardens.

But it should be noted that Captain Wad, until then a most considerate host to his compatriots, had undergone an abrupt transformation.

There was something hard in his gaze and his tone was imperious and gruff.

"You are the only people to whom I would show the extraordinary spectacle you are about to witness," he said.

"But I warn you that you must remain absolutely silent during the experiment. One gesture, one word, might trigger your immediate destruction."

"I understand," said Miss Alberte resolutely. "After the anguish I have endured in this world, the wonders of the unseen world do not frighten me."

Captain Wad said nothing in reply. One of the boys had handed him a torch that smelled of resin and burned in the calm night air with a beautiful, clear flame.

"Now," he said, "we are going to climb the tower.

"The fortifications of this residence are built on the site of the former palace of a raja.

"Nothing remains of it but a solitary tower, richly adorned with sculptures. But what is special about it is that it has no windows of any kind.

"It is the paradox of a subterranean crypt raised into the air. Each of the vaulted rooms, formed of massive blocks of stone, is completely dark, and, despite careful study, I have never been able to discover, hidden among the carvings, the conduits through which flows the air needed for respiration."

Captain Wad had opened a door.

Ralph Pitcher and Miss Alberte could see, in front of them, the first steps of a black granite stairway cut out of the large blocks that formed the outer wall of the tower.

The leering faces of the bas-reliefs carved in the wall seemed to climb with them; slitted eyes winked as they passed, muzzles of tigers or elephants seemed to flare at them, and this procession of monstrous divinities grew more numerous and more contorted as they mounted the steps.

"These people had imagination," murmured Ralph Pitcher.

Then he closed his mouth.

Captain Wad, raising his torch, led them into the room that made up the first floor of the tower.

They saw idols with vacant and fierce faces, whose intertwined arms and legs rose in bizarre movements toward the vault, crowned with a delicately sculpted lotus flower.

On the floor lay a pile of bones.

They hurriedly fled this place, filled with the oppressive weight of cruel centuries.

The next floor was perhaps even more terrible in its nakedness.

The circular walls were carved with a hundred niches, now empty, but undoubtedly occupied not long ago by statues.

Captain Wad explained that the gold, silver, and copper idols had been looted during the Indian Mutiny; only the niches remained, like so many holes filled with shadows.

"I didn't want to change any of this," murmured the captain. "It seemed to me that I would have been committing a sacrilege! . . . But be patient, we have only one more floor to climb, the last one. The room is very large — I don't know whether you have noticed, but the tower is shaped like a pine-cone, much narrower at the base than the summit."

Ralph and Miss Alberte were rather surprised to find this room completely bare; there were no sculptures, no paintings, and only a few columns that formed Gothic arcades as they met near the ceiling.

In the center of the room, Phara-Chibh was crouched at a sort of low altar with his legs spread out, so immobile that he appeared to be carved from the black rock of the tower.

He was completely naked and so frighteningly thin that Miss Alberte inadvertently drew back.

Phara-Chibh was now no more than a skeleton covered with brownish skin, his muscles gone, his ribs protruding, the skin of his stomach almost pressing against his spine.

Only his enormous head, with clear, blazing eyes, seemed to have preserved, for itself alone, the vitality of the rest of the body.

At the sight of the newcomers, he neither rose nor greeted them. He remained fixed in place, as if he were an interesting idol displayed to curious visitors.

But under the stream of fire coming from his devouring pupils, Ralph and Miss Alberte recoiled instinctively, their heads spinning.

The naturalist later admitted that he had been less uncomfortable when the Thugs had tied him to the mouth of an old cannon and left after positioning a lens above the powder-filled touch hole.

He knew that once the sun had risen high enough above the horizon the cannon would fire, and yet he had not experienced the same anguish he felt under the yogi's oppressive gaze.

There was a moment of solemn silence.

"You understand," murmured Captain Wad, as if to dispel this impression, "that Phara-Chibh is no ordinary magician; he has a knowledge of cosmic theories whose depth and audacity have astounded me.

"He claims, for example, that in the first age of man, wheat was brought by a yogi from a neighboring planet.

"He knows the secrets of Atlantis, where the men were almost gods and a magus, having imprudently confided his secret to a woman, caused the submersion of an entire continent and the regrettable loss, forever, of great secrets of the will.

"He also knows why the pyramids were built. The pharaohs made them into tombs, but they had a purpose that historians have never discovered.

"Their very shape itself proves it: they were a refuge from the incessant rain of meteors that, in other epochs, had depopulated Earth!

"Didn't the Gauls fire arrows at the sky?

"The poor, brutish people of those times sweat blood and tears, dying in harness, to build refuges from death."

At this very instant, from a corner of the room, a tiger rose to its feet and came to Miss Alberte, lightly brushing against her dress. It stretched its claws on the black granite of the floor and, with a knowing look, lay down at the young woman's feet.

Ralph Pitcher, at the sight of the beast, had taken three steps back. Miss

Alberte had grown a little pale, but she had not recoiled. Everything she saw was a revelation; she understood that the tiger was necessary, portentous, that it was an integral part of this ensemble of surprising impressions unfolding in front of her.

But Captain Wad had promptly stepped between the animal and Miss Alberte.

"Have no fear," he said, "he is completely harmless. Down, Mowdi!

"He was trained by Ardavena, whose every command he obeyed."

"I know," said Ralph, who had come closer, somewhat reassured by these words, "that the secret of mastering and taming all sorts of animals, of endowing them with quasi-human intelligence, has almost been lost, that only a few Indian temples have maintained it."

Mowdi had withdrawn at the officer's words and was curled up in a ball.

There was a moment of silence; despite their best efforts, they all felt forlorn, troubled by the yogi's burdensome gaze that glided over them replete with mysterious emanations.

"Now," said the captain, "you will witness one of Phara-Chibh's most extraordinary experiments.

"I repeat my earlier advice: whatever you see, whatever you hear, do not respond with any noise or movement.

"If Miss Alberte were not to feel up to it, it would be better—and I say this in all seriousness—to put off this performance until later."

"No!" Miss Alberte sharply exclaimed. "I am not one of those weak women ruled by their nerves. I promise I will not be afraid."

"Good," said the captain gravely, and he pointed out, to his guests, some chairs carved out of the rock whose arms terminated in crocodile heads.

Ralph and Miss Alberte, without being aware of it, had been set on edge by the strangeness of the decor and by Captain Wad's mysterious conduct.

He spoke in a low voice with the yogi. Then, with his torch, he lit seven thick candles arranged in the form of a star, each of which, to Ralph's great surprise, burned with a flame of a different color.

They were the seven fundamental colors, produced, the naturalist supposed, by metallic oxides mixed with the vegetable wax of which the candles were formed.

There was something fantastic about the whole thing.

Next, the captain took various colored powders from a box and, inside the stone chandeliers that held the candles, he traced a circle around the altar where the yogi squatted.

Then he threw other powders onto large bronze incense burners, where smoldering olive pits lay covered with white ashes.

Plumes of thick smoke rose toward the vault; a haze began to build in the vast, windowless rotunda.

An acrid, stomach-churning smell emanated from the smoke.

Ralph recognized the harsh smell of venomous and hallucinogenic plants, most from the families Solanaceae, Umbelliferae, and Papaveraceae.

In the candlelight, the smoke, which ranged in color from pink to blue and green, exhaled the nauseating bitterness of rue, Datura stramonium, hemlock, belladonna, Cannabis indica, and white poppy.

The air in the room had become nearly unbreathable. Ralph and Miss Alberte were covered with sweat, their hearts pounded with inexpressible anguish, and their eyes started from their sockets, as if a band of hard iron were squeezing their temples. Their suffering was intolerable.

Then, little by little, it grew calm. A sensation of algidity, a glacial chill, invaded their extremities. Finally, all of these painful sensations were replaced by a strange feeling of comfort. They found themselves in a serene and beatific state. They enjoyed a marvelous intellectual lucidity; they felt able to solve the most difficult problems, to follow the most complicated logic, with ease.

The air, at once luminous and heavy, now seemed to them perfectly clear, and Phara-Chibh seemed to move in a vaguely phosphorescent atmosphere, enveloped in a sort of halo, like those that primitive painters placed around the heads of saints and magi.

On the ground in front of him, right in the center of the circle formed by the seven candles, Phara-Chibh had placed a sort of dark-colored rag, with five points, which appeared to be an old bit of very worn leather still covered, here and there, with gray hairs. He picked up a flute that lay next to him, one of those primitive and rudimentary musical instruments that poor Hindus carve out of bamboo, and he began to play very softly, his long skeletal fingers stretched over the holes.

Miss Alberte couldn't help shivering, thinking of those musicians of the *danse macabre* who joyously drive the wedding party toward the open grave.

The air that the yogi played was one of those haunting, tuneless Oriental melodies, where the same notes interminably return in a mechanical rhythm.

This strange scene held its spectators' rapt attention.

They knew that there was something more here than a simple magic trick like those of which they had read that at first glance seem almost miraculous but soon reveal a logical explanation.

Phara-Chibh gradually picked up the rhythm of his song, and something strange happened as the slow cadence was replaced by a faster and faster tempo.

The shapeless strip of leather at first seemed to shiver, as if agitated by an intangible breath, then it jumped, twisted, stretched, and finally shriveled up like a parchment thrown onto white-hot coals.

There was something distressing in the convulsive movements of this inanimate thing struggling to live, seeming to grudgingly obey the all-powerful will that animated it.

The rhythm grew feverish, imperious; between the desiccated lips of the yogi these few notes became a tyrannical order that even nature dared not disobey.

"You must! It is my wish! . . ." the reed flute seemed to be tirelessly repeating.

And, under the impulse of this all-powerful will, the indefinable thing stretched, grew longer, began to swell and take shape.

A moment later it fluttered above the floor. Ralph made out the still-vague silhouette of a sort of bat.

"Faster! Faster! It is my wish!" repeated the imperious flute, whose staccato notes now spun in a whirlwind, in a mad crescendo.

The resurrection—perhaps the creation—of the winged beast, at first so faltering, now progressed at a dizzying speed.

The apparition was now the size of a man and, standing on its feet, it opened its membranous, dull-yellow wings, which grew with the speed of certain phantasmagorical tableaux.

Miss Alberte had grown pale. She braced herself against the anguished terror that was beginning to overwhelm her.

Ralph Pitcher showed only slightly less alarm.

There was something both human and animal in this monster magnificently created by Phara-Chibh; similar demons can be found in the miniatures of medieval books of sorcery.

It was a sort of large, human bat, but, unlike the species found in Guyana or Java, its hands, armed with sharp claws, were at the tips of its wings.

Its face had a high brow and outsized jaws and displayed a powerful, more than human intelligence—but made above all for craft and cruelty. Its pendulous lips, the hideous color of blood, showed sharp, white teeth. Its short, turned-up nose, hardly more than two holes, could have been compared to that of a bulldog. Its deep-set eyes, bordered by enflamed red eyelids, blinked as if unaccustomed to the light and seemed drawn to the green and blue candles.

As for its ears, they had the same design as the human ear but were impossibly distended; vibratile as two rounded wings, they gave an abject expression to the monster's physiognomy.

The illustrators of the Middle Ages had certainly never invented a more hideous demon.

It was floating at some height above the yogi, with no apparent effort, flapping its membranous wings just enough to maintain its balance.

It appeared to be entirely unaware of the presence of those around it and even of the person it was obeying.

It was beset by extraordinary distress and suffering.

Suddenly, with a great beat of its wings, it attempted to fly toward the ceiling.

Its red-rimmed eyes flamed as it became intensely real and alive. Now it was the yogi Phara-Chibh who had grown indistinct and hazy, who seemed an apparition; Ralph supposed that the volitional fluid of the ascetic must have diminished to produce this extraordinary vision.

But one of the scaly wings broke the circle of candles, and, amazingly, the part that passed through it disappeared completely, dissolved, cleanly cut by a line, just like an engraving at the edge of the paper.

The monster, as if it understood that it could not exist outside the magic circle, quickly returned to the place it had occupied.

Abruptly Phara-Chibh stopped playing; a few seconds of silence followed.

The mysterious apparition grew faint and the yogi became once again a real and palpable being.

At the same time it seemed to the spectators that the candlelight dimmed, that a rain of shadows fell, so to speak, from the vault, and that other human bats — innumerable — were slowly emerging from the mist.

Phara-Chibh had begun to play again and, without changing a note, simply by the particular rhythm he gave to the melody, the song had become funereal, oppressively melancholic.

The other apparitions slowly dissipated.

All at once, the pale profile of Darvel the engineer began to emerge from the darkness, spectral and transparent.

The monster flung itself at him, claws first.

But it was more than Miss Alberte could bear. She screamed in fear and fainted.

Several minutes of indescribable terror ensued.

At the young woman's scream, the seven candles had gone out, the apparition had vanished, and Ralph had felt a sudden shock, not unlike that from a battery of several thousand volts.

Like Miss Alberte, he fainted . . . When he reopened his eyes again, Captain Wad stood before him, pale as death, his lips drained of blood, holding, in his trembling hands, the torch he had managed to relight.

"Miss Alberte!" cried Ralph in distress.

"I don't know whether we can save her," murmured the officer in a hollow voice.

And he pointed to the young woman, still lifeless, in the stone chair.

"And Phara-Chibh?"

The officer gestured in desolation.

"This is all that remains of him!" he said.

On the altar Ralph saw with horror a large pile of white ashes in the middle of which some blackened bones still smoldered.

The naturalist, deeply upset, said nothing.

"It is my fault too," said the officer. "I have been irresponsible.

"I should have been able to see that Miss Alberte, as courageous as she is, did not have the strength to endure such a spectacle."

He added with bitterness:

"The sacred texts are correct when they say that women must be kept far away from magic operations and commerce with invisible spirits . . ."

The two men looked at each other, terrified.

They felt profoundly exhausted and increasingly dizzy; they found it impossible to keep their eyes open. Their legs were wobbly.

"We must not succumb to this torpor," said Captain Wad with difficulty. "We have to leave this accursed tower and its air still saturated with fluid poisons; staying here another quarter of an hour will be the death of us, and of Miss Alberte.

"You must help me carry her out of here."

Both of them set to work; but even though the officer and the naturalist were each blessed with more than average strength, increased further by sporting pursuits, it was only with the greatest effort that they managed to lift the young woman's inert body, which seemed to them as heavy as if it had been a leaden statue.

They were succumbing to an invincible fatigue; their nerves slackened, their joints hurt, and their muscles ached.

It took them more than an hour to descend the tower's stairway.

When they finally reached the lawns of the garden, suffused with the fragrance of Bengal roses, Persian jasmine, lemon and citron trees, and magnolias, they were at the end of their strength.

They lay Miss Alberte on a marble bench with an inclined backrest and Captain Wad ran to look for smelling salts, ether, and cordials—anything that his travelers' pharmacy could provide to revive the young woman from her swoon.

On his return, he had the satisfaction of seeing she had regained her senses. But she was extremely weak; the shock she had received had left her limp and exhausted, unable to speak.

The domestics carefully carried her to her room, where she was lavished with every care her condition demanded.

A sepoy rushed at full gallop to find the doctor from the neighboring station, who came immediately when he learned that his patient was nothing less than a billionaire.

After a careful and thorough examination, during which he had listened with an air of skepticism to the explanations that Captain Wad felt obliged to give him, he declared that she would live, but he could not promise that her mind had not been irreparably damaged.

"The most urgent thing," he said, after having written a prescription, "is to save the life of the patient, to prevent nervous excitement that could cause even more serious problems since she is predisposed toward cardiac ailments."

"Her father died of an embolism," said Ralph.

"That does not surprise me," he said. "Another reason to be extremely careful with our invalid, to spare her any excitement, even the slightest."

Ralph and Captain Wad fortunately had little to fear: Miss Alberte slowly recovered and soon they were able to hope that the fantastic drama she had experienced would have no lasting effect on her mind.

In the meantime, on the very day after Phara-Chibh's death, Ralph and the captain came up with an explanation.

"I am certain," the officer had said, "that the scene we witnessed happened in reality somewhere.

"The engineer Darvel is not dead. He may be facing great danger, but he is alive."

"Yet, the monster that appeared to us certainly does not exist in terrestrial zoology."

"I never claimed it did; and in any case, there are still many unexplored caverns holding many mysterious and surprising creatures.

"Wasn't a strange winged lizard captured a few years ago in an unexplored cave in China that had precisely the complicated, contorted shape that previously was believed to exist only in the imagination of the painters of the Empire of Heaven?"

But Ralph Pitcher remained quiet.

His mind was at work. The words spoken the night before about wheat brought from a neighboring planet by the power of a yogi came into his mind; he recalled Robert's former projects.

He stood up swiftly, in the grip of unspeakable excitement.

"Captain!" he murmured. "Do you want me to tell you the truth? I have just had an intuition and I am certain I am right.

"Robert Darvel has fulfilled his longstanding dream. He has succeeded in reaching the planet Mars!

"It cannot be otherwise! . . . And the monster that appeared to us is nothing other than one of the denizens of Mars with whom Robert, armed with all the knowledge of the old planet, undoubtedly wages some awful battle."

"I thought as much," said Captain Wad, after a moment of silence.

VII

·······················

The Martian Village

The whole of the village looked something like a cartoon conceived and drawn by a child. It was a collection of low, round cottages thatched with woven reeds and with no visible chimneys.

The huts were spread along the edge of a pond teeming with ducks and a very plump sort of bird, which to Robert looked like a type of penguin. On one side the marsh was divided by hedgerows of reeds and formed into fields bursting with cress, water chestnuts, and those large-leafed water lilies with edible roots that Robert had already seen. In short, the marsh showed signs of purposeful cultivation.

The inhabitants of this lakeside hamlet, grouped in front of their doors or engaged in various tasks, were a comical and surprising sight. They were scarcely taller than ten-year-old children and exceptionally plump: their bellies, in particular, were especially well developed. Their round faces were fresh and pink; their long hair and beards were an unpleasant reddish hue; and, above all, a rather childish smile beamed perpetually on their innocent countenances. Their cheeks were so fat as to almost hide their noses, and their small, slightly dull blue eyes angled toward their temples, like those of the Chinese.

The little children looked like veritable balls of fat, fowls fattened for some solemn feast.

They were playing, in their plodding and clumsy way, with fat, tame ducks and two kinds of animals with whiskers. One, Robert easily recognized, was a type of seal, and the other a type of otter. He even noticed some large water rats, gravely sitting on their haunches on top of the roofs or moving through the crowd; no one seemed at all bothered by their presence.

There were also some white birds with red beaks and feet, close cousins to the cormorant, lined up on large horizontal perches.

The Martians' outfits were no less strange. They were all dressed in long, very heavy robes woven with feathers of every color. They also wore sharply pointed hats that Robert later learned were made from the longest feathers of the wild goose, bound at the top and the bottom with small strips of leather.

Some of them (most likely the laborers or sailors of the band), wore hooded overcoats embellished with colorful designs including, Robert was surprised to find, a primitive image of the vampire he had defeated the night before.

All of these beings in feather robes moved in an awkward and graceless way, and they walked only at a very slow pace. Robert could not help thinking they resembled, in every particular, the marsh birds that lived among them.

"They are veritable penguins with human faces," he murmured.

Yet as unrefined, as childish, as grotesque as these creatures were, they were nevertheless human, the crude draft of a race of intelligent beings like those on his home planet, and he was overcome with joy: his chest swelled, his heart beat faster, and his eyes filled with tears. He wanted to embrace all of these smiling monkeys, like so many enormous, chubby infants, as if they were long lost friends.

A thousand thoughts plagued him. He sensed that he stood face to face with people who were—undoubtedly—simple and good, perhaps also a bit stupid; he even pitied them.

"The poor devils!" he exclaimed, after a glance around the village. "They do not know how to use fire nor, consequently, metal . . ."

He was deeply moved. He conceived a thousand humanitarian projects. In a few days, in a few months, he would shepherd these mild, unsophisticated brutes through several thousand years of progress. He saw himself as a king, almost a God, and he no longer felt the slightest fear.

Smiling, he advanced with open arms and slow, measured steps toward the leaders of the village.

In their dull, slow-moving brains, shock did not have time to give way to fear; he was among them before even the smartest of them had begun to consider what to do about him.

Still smiling, he patted the children, amiably offered up morsels of his remaining meat, and finally sat down on a grassy bank by the door of one of the huts like a man happy to be alive, pleased to have finally reached the end of his travels, and who was making himself at home among friends.

A portly old man, whose feathered robe — green in front and brown in back — made him look rather like an obese wild duck, advanced toward him making conciliatory gestures and patting his cotton shroud.

"He must feel sorry for me," Robert thought, "and think me very poorly dressed."

The elderly Martian, with a crowd of astonished and smiling people pressing together behind him, seemed above all shocked by Robert's emaciated appearance, and, by means of gestures — slapping his chubby cheeks and his round paunch — he demonstrated his sincere concern. Then he pronounced several phrases whose words seemed to Robert exclusively composed of vowels, and two young girls, in white feathers and with their red hair gathered in a leather bag under their pointed caps, unhurriedly brought wicker baskets filled with fresh, pink-and-green-speckled eggs, joints of raw meat, water chestnuts, and mushrooms.

They also brought a wooden vessel carved from the trunk of a tree and filled with some sort of sweetened water; water-lily roots, carefully peeled and scrubbed; and finally, on its own, a handful of salt on a red wicker tray, which all the assembled seemed to eye with envy, most likely the dessert for this unique meal.

"How unfortunate these people are," thought Robert, "never to have tasted cooked food and still regarding salt as a delicacy. We will soon change that: in less than six months they will be acquainted with Brillat-Savarin, Carême, and Baron Brisse."

The idea of selling the illustrated works of celebrated gourmets to the Martians caused him to laugh madly for a few moments, but he soon recovered himself. He understood he must show respect for the meal offered to him and, although not the least bit hungry, he ate what they brought him with gusto.

The spectators showed their satisfaction with a great clamor. Their joy knew no limits when, stuffed with this indigestible fare and desiring a little exercise, he took by the hand the old man with green feathers on his belly and one of the girls in white plumage who had served him, to tour the village.

Along the way he caressed the friendly otters that lounged along the edge of the water and the tame seals that barked as he passed with almost human voices. A fat rat climbed onto his shoulder and nibbled his ear, cormorants came up to peck at his cotton robe, and the crowd of women and chubby young children escorted him with a kind and deferential curiosity.

The president of France and the king of Spain are neither more pleased with themselves nor more proud in the course of a state visit to a friendly nation, and Robert Darvel, unlike these potentates, had little cause to fear anarchist bombs; he had even blithely left his bow, his arrows, and his cudgel on the grass where he had been seated.

Meanwhile, the sun climbed above the horizon, and the Martians, despite their downy robes, huddled together on their doorsteps and soaked in the heat with beatific smiles.

Robert was surprised at the sight of thirty or so Martians busily building a hut. After raising four beech-wood posts, they wove a roof out of reeds at a slow and steady pace, progressing more quickly than the most frenetic workmen.

The old man with the feathered belly made Robert understand, with his hands, that this house was intended for him.

Robert was touched by such consideration.

"Our civilized men," he thought, "have much to learn from the benevolence and sensitivity of these savages."

He felt a flush of shame as he thought of the battles for money, the cutthroat attitudes in the stock exchange, and all the cruelties he had witnessed on Earth.

Yet he also felt proud as he thought of the knowledge he would bestow on these unfortunate souls who did not even know how to use fire and were satisfied with raw meat and roots.

He had already noticed that the language of his hosts was made up entirely of vowels. He took his young guide by the hand, solemnly embraced her—this appeared to give her much pleasure—and, after some expressive mimicry, he managed to learn her name. She was called Eeeoys. With the help of similar courtesies, he also succeeded in learning the name of the old man, who was called Aouya.

His repetition of their names seemed to make them happy.

The village was humming with extraordinary activity. Men were boarding reed boats covered with seal skin and unloading sacks of roots and mounds of game that, with no sign of dispute, women and children distributed to each house with unequaled joy and zeal.

"What happy folk," Robert exclaimed. "Their idea of property has not been pushed to the point we have reached in our old civilizations."

He sat down on the grass a few steps from his future home. But, all at once, Aouya took Robert by the shoulder and led him deep into the village, toward a sort of portal constructed of branches and unbaked clay, under which stood a sinister-looking image.

It was a crude idol that depicted, with striking realism, a vampire similar to the one that had attacked Robert. The body was carved of wood, and the wings, supported by small branches, were made of leather colored with a paint that Robert supposed was made of finely ground gray clay mixed with oil. The idol's face was horrifying: its deep-set eyes, bulldog nose, and gaping maw had been rendered with scrupulous fidelity.

What surprised him more was to find, at the foot of the crude altar that housed this grotesque divinity, a crowd of animals attached to small stakes by leather cords.

There were seals, cormorants, even rats: in short, a sampling of the country's fauna. Robert even found an animal he had not encountered since having arrived on the planet.

It was a species of cow with very short legs, the tail of a horse, and immense horns that brought to his mind the Himalayan yak, the Cape gnu, and the Canadian musk ox.

The bellowing, whimpering, and barking of these animals, furious at being tied up, made a deafening din.

The sight of this spectacle was like a flash of light for Robert.

In an instant he understood that, to the honest inhabitants of the region, the vampires were a sort of parasitic divinity to whom the best of the beasts and game were sacrificed. And it was plain to see that whenever the

Martians forgot to pay their tribute of living prey, they themselves became the victims of these bloodthirsty monsters.

He could see, too, from the reverential terror in the Martians' usually placid eyes and from how they were shivering in their feather robes, that the vampires inspired overwhelming fear in them.

He turned from Aouya to Eeeoys and, with the help of expressive mimicry, asked them the god's name.

"*Erloor*," they answered in unison, with a shiver of horror.

Robert was struck by the fact that all the words he had heard in the Martian village had been composed of nothing but vowels. This sinister word, *Erloor*, was the only one containing consonants. This gave him something to ponder.

Lost in thought, he allowed himself to be led toward another temple, more or less like the first, when an anguished thought clutched at his heart.

"My fire!" he cried. "They have probably extinguished my fire! . . ."

VIII

....

Public Festivities

Robert Darvel's blood froze in his veins at the thought that they might have extinguished his fire in his absence.

He was desperately worried.

With supplicating yet imperious looks, he made his guides understand that they had to go with him as quickly as possible.

Their presence, of course, was not absolutely necessary, but he wanted from the start to acquire great influence over them and win their admiration.

From the bottom of his heart he blessed these brave folk, and he vowed to defend them from their enemies and to wage a merciless war with the Erloor.

Although Aouya and Eeeoys were rather surprised, Robert was able to convince them and, forcing a smile despite his concern, he set off with his friends along the tracks of the small wood of red willows, where he easily found the path he had taken.

It wasn't a long journey. But the closer he drew to his shelter and his fire, the faster his heart was beating. It took all his courage to continue to smile at the two Martians who had each taken one of his hands and were following him blindly, watching his every move like two small children.

At a bend near a stand of large reeds, Robert let out a cry. He was mere steps away from his fire. Thick smoke rose from the huge pile of branches, as if someone, out of nowhere, had doused it with several buckets of water. The flames were dying down, sputtering and crackling, yet no one was there. Robert leapt forward. A large incandescent mass was still burning in the middle of the pile. Oblivious to burns, he snatched up all the coals that the water had not reached and placed them in a dry, rocky spot.

Then, in a kind of frenzy, he piled dried plants, branches that were still green, dead wood, and anything that came to hand on these few coals he had rescued.

On all fours, his brow beaded with sweat, he blew with all his might, with desperate force.

A clear flame, crowned with beautiful, blue smoke, soon rose from this bonfire that quickly grew as large as the other.

He finally stood, out of breath, and mopped his brow with a corner of his shroud.

"That was a narrow escape," he murmured, "but it won't happen again! . . ."

He looked around. Aouya and Eeeoys were at his sides, filled with fear. Robert's frenzied activity had terrified them, and they were astonished beyond belief by the sight of the fire.

Robert comforted them with smiles and affably patted the young woman, and then he began to investigate how the Erloor had succeeded in putting out his fire.

To his immense surprise, he found that a sort of canal or ditch, as straight as if laid out by a master surveyor, had been dug in the space of a few hours from the marsh to the fire.

It even appeared that the invisible builders of this ditch had been interrupted in their work by his sudden arrival. As it reached the fire, the canal divided into two branches and was taking on the form of a circle that, once finished, would have completely engulfed his fire and extinguished it for good.

Robert was perplexed. These signs of advanced knowledge frightened him. He thought of the famous Martian canals discovered by Schiaparelli in 1877, and he was puzzled that he had not yet happened upon one of them. These canals, noted by every astronomer, vary in length from a thousand to five thousand kilometers and are almost always more than one hundred and twenty kilometers in breadth.

He recognized, from the skill with which the work had been carried out and the expert manner in which the clumps of reeds and grass had been thrown to the side, that he was dealing with very accomplished ditch diggers.

But the work was too perfect, in Robert's opinion, to have been carried out by intelligent beings. Self-awareness always implies a certain inexactness in handiwork: bees or beavers don't make mistakes; men do.

Here the clumps of turf and loamy earth were arranged left and right with a perfect, inimitable skill. None was larger or smaller than another, they were all cone-shaped and bore noticeable claw marks.

"But," Robert quickly told himself, "it cannot have been the vampires, the Erloor, who accomplished all of this in such a short time. I could tell, from the structure of their eyes, that they can only see to make mischief during the night."

He conjectured that the Erloor must have some formidable allies, but this only increased his desire to oppose them.

"We will do battle!" he shouted. "I much prefer a planet peopled with monsters to a deserted world. I come bearing earthly science. One day perhaps I will be the emperor or the god of this universe and then the woman I was prevented from marrying must surely come join me and share my power."

Lost in these ambitious — and perhaps slightly childish — dreams, Robert had forgotten his two small companions, who were chilled to the bone at the sight of the rectilinear canal dug from the marsh all the way to the fire. He understood that all his power depended on the confidence of these embryonic humans.

With a thousand engaging smiles, he led them to his fire that now burned like a conflagration and demonstrated how to stretch out one's hands and warm them by the fire.

The two Martians imitated him with incredible pleasure. He even had to stop them before they burned their fingers.

Robert Darvel gave them an astonished look filled with pity.

"I wasn't mistaken," he murmured. "These poor people do not understand the benefits of fire! I must be their Prometheus."

He smiled as he considered all the looks of surprise and astonishment he would undoubtedly witness.

First, he took from his pantry a quarter of raw meat and, making a skewer from a beech-wood branch, he began to prepare, then and there, a succulent roast. The most agreeable scent soon tickled the nostrils of the

Martians, who both approached with great interest, smiling, their eyes filled with longing.

"Exactly," said Robert, forgetting for a moment that his listeners did not understand his language. "It's a roast, an excellent roast, which you have probably never had an opportunity to eat. But there's a first time for everything."

Putting theory into practice, he seized a sharp piece of slate, delicately removed two perfectly grilled legs and, with an engaging smile and meaningful gestures, he offered one to Aouya and the other to Eeeoys, who did not hesitate to sink their teeth into the delicate morsels that were offered to them.

To inspire their full confidence, he followed their example and ate heartily.

From the joyful and admiring expressions of his companions, Robert could see that they were close to considering him a veritable divinity; Aouya was bowing before him with veneration; Eeeoys was respectfully kissing his hands.

While they greedily finished off the rest of the game, Robert gathered some rushes and red-willow sticks that he wove together into a rough semblance of a large basket. He lined the bottom and sides with a blanket of moist clay and, once this was done, he used a flat stone as a shovel to fill it with burning coals, which he covered with several handfuls of ashes.

To finish the job, he tied his fire basket firmly to the center of a long pole; Aouya took one end of it while he took the other. Eeeoys preceded them, carrying the game and the bow and arrows. In this manner, Robert Darvel made his triumphal return to the village. Before leaving his former encampment, he had taken care to throw new fuel on the fire so that it would continue to burn for several more hours in case some accident befell the treasure he was carrying.

As they entered the village, Robert and his companions were greeted with cries of joy. The population gathered in the square eagerly awaited them. Their enthusiasm turned into delirium and frenzy when Robert, assisted by Aouya and Eeeoys, solemnly placed his coals on a spot of dry, elevated ground and lit a great bonfire whose spirals of blue smoke rose majestically into the sky.

An hour later, the entire Martian village was enveloped by the smells of the kitchen. Ducks and bustards were browning over the flames; a whole beef, solidly placed on stakes in the form of a cross, was slowly roasting, its stomach stuffed with aromatic herbs; piles of water chestnuts, cooking in the hot coals, spread the wonderful odor of fresh bread.

The Martians had never seen such a feast. Most of them, watching attentively in their feather robes, were armed with wooden spoons, ready to collect their portion of this gargantuan feast.

Their admiration for the fire was such that they had already begun to build a solid fence all the way around it.

IX

....

War with the Idols

Upon reflection, Robert decided this precaution was not unwarranted.

But in the midst of the general gaiety, one thing surprised him. Aouya and Eeeoys kept pulling him by the hand, as if they had something important to tell him.

When he finally consented to see what they wanted, they led him to the temple that housed the hideous idol of the Erloor. Aouya's mien was sad and anxious. Eeeoys's eyes were brimming with tears.

Robert smiled and reassured them; then, determined to strike a decisive blow, he tore the idol from its pedestal, seized it by its leather wings, and threw it into the middle of the fire. Then he cut the ropes that tethered the victims destined to be sacrificed to the hunger of the nocturnal god.

No missionary destroying the fetishes of some small tribe in the interior of Africa ever felt such satisfaction.

Yet despite the gallant impulse that propelled him to act, as it were, without thinking, he had some apprehensions about the consequences of his actions.

Seeing the image of the vampire topple over, seeing it consumed in the flames, the Martians had let out a long, anguished lament and the pressing crowd had grown still and silent. They were pale and trembling with fear. Aouya and even Eeeoys had recoiled involuntary in terror.

"This time," Robert mused, "I have maybe gone too far."

It was now a matter of reassuring and comforting the terrified Martians.

It wasn't easy at first. They backed away from Robert in dismay and hardly dared to look at him. Some had tears in their eyes, doubtless imagining the Erloor's bloody reprisals! They surely expected to be sacrificed en masse, as soon as the sun went down, to the voraciousness of the vampires.

Robert was deeply moved. A single glance had shown him the emotional state of these humble savages.

"No!" he cried, in a voice full of authority, the imperious tone of which appeared to have a striking effect on his listeners. "This will not come to pass! I will protect you from the Erloor, you have my word. The battle will begin today, and I will triumph, I am sure of it!"

Taking advantage of the good impression his confident acts had produced, he stretched his hands before the fire, then looked at what was left of the idol and shrugged his shoulders. He picked up a large brand and gestured as if he would throw it at the temple, and he encouraged the Martians to do the same. In short, with a thousand ingenious gestures he tried to make his new friends understand that with his protection and the help of fire they would have nothing more to fear from the vampires.

The crowd looked at him with fond attention but did not understand what he was trying to say. Eventually, Aouya and another old man managed to grasp what he was trying to make them understand and explained it to the others with great exclamations of joy, in that language composed almost exclusively of vowels to which Robert was not yet accustomed.

This news had a beneficial effect. Although still a little frightened, the multitude slowly calmed down and soon began to express again, boister-ously, the joy that the culinary preparations had given them.

Aouya and Eeeoys had returned and, to Robert's great surprise, they pulled him once again by the hand. He followed and they led him first of all to the hut they had built for him. It was almost completed already and as comfortable in its simplicity as any of the most beautiful in the village.

The walls, made of little bricks of clay intermingled with branches, were very thick and offered sufficient protection from the cold. In place of a door there was a curtain of plastered cane; it had a slate floor, a little rough but just about level, covered with a red mat.

What pleased Robert most was the sight of a sort of bed draped with a bustard-feather blanket, which promised to be very comfortable, especially in winter. There was also a host of furniture and utensils: a wood and rattan bench, beech-wood dishes and spoons, carved stone vessels, long flint knives, and other primitive weapons. Slabs of meat, vegetables, and water chestnuts had been placed in a corner of the room. There was also a small provision of salt, by which Robert was truly charmed.

But he didn't stay long in his new abode. After doing his best to thank his new guides, he placed the longest and most solid of the stone knives in his belt and picked up a short, very heavy club, which must have been used to kill the Martian seals and oxen, and followed his hosts, who were leading him away once again.

They led him to a temple that was similar to that of the Erloor, where their kind faces betrayed some apprehension. They wanted to see whether their guest would show the same courage and composure in front of this second deity.

Robert choked back a cry of astonishment.

He stood in front of a hideous monster, long and heavyset, mounted on six very short legs that terminated in curved red claws that were quite long and seemed to Robert specially designed to dig the earth. The animal, carved carefully though crudely, had something in its appearance of an insect, a reptile, and a mole all at once. Its face, a reddish brown like the rest of its body, had no sign of eyes, but it had numerous teeth sticking out of its mouth like a boar's tusks. Its nose stretched into a trunk tipped with a very tough nail, which surely made any attack by this animal most dreadful.

Robert stood there for some time, silent and perplexed. He wasn't frightened, but he was trying to understand the nature of this mysterious creature, while the two Martians watched him, filled with distress. He understood that he could not show the slightest sign of fear: to do so would completely undermine his prestige.

"Here we have," he said, forcing a smile, "a beautiful specimen of a burrowing herbivore, similar to the terrestrial mole but grown to a gigantic size. Now I recognize the skilled worker who dug the ditch that almost put out my fire, and I understand why the floors of Martian huts are paved with thick slate. I am no longer surprised that Mars is crisscrossed with canals."

While he was speaking, Robert had wrapped his arms around the idol and unceremoniously toppled it from its pedestal and was now shoving it out of the temple with his feet.

He eventually got Eeeoys to divulge the name of this monster in the Martian language. It was *Roomboo*.

"Very well," he cheerfully exclaimed, "the Roomboo will suffer the same fate as its friend."

And he dragged the hideous statue to the bonfire where it quickly burned up like the other.

He was very pleased to see that the Martians, visibly shocked the first time, seemed much less perturbed by this second performance. It appeared that, despite their slow wits, they had managed to understand.

Yet Robert did not want to let their minds dwell any longer on the consequences of his coup.

It was almost time to eat, and the feast, which had everyone licking their chops in anticipation, made for a welcome diversion.

Nothing could be more comical than the expressions of the Martians as they removed the meat from the spits. They seemed torn between the joy of warming themselves and the fear of being burned, not to mention the problem of staining their feather robes nor the greediness that made them lick their lips and breathe in the delicious smell of the roast meats.

When the victuals, finally taken off the fire, had been arranged on wooden platters, men with large flint knives arrived to skillfully carve the meat.

Robert, concerned above all else with maintaining the influence he had acquired, did not wait for the distribution of the food to begin. He autocratically chose for himself the filet of beef, some duck and bustard wings, and the largest and best roasted water chestnuts, placed them all on a large platter, and carried them into his house.

He shrewdly ate alone, to maintain his standing, to preserve in the eyes of his hosts his nature as an exceptional, quasi-divine being, and he congratulated himself on the energy and presence of mind he had displayed.

At first he ate like an ogre: the fasts and privations he had lately endured had given him a ferocious appetite. He could not satisfy his hunger. Everything tasted delicious.

Outside, he could hear the sounds of the Martians feasting around the fire and devouring their food with such gluttony that he could hear them chewing.

Eating all alone, he felt as proud as the king of Spain; his brain was filled with dreams of glory.

"These humble Martians!" he exclaimed. "Imagine everything that I shall teach them! This week, I shall show them how to make pottery. Their dishes have too many flaws. After that, woodworking: they have no tables . . . Later, after I have found iron and copper ore among the rocks—and why not gold, platinum, or radium?—I shall introduce them to metallurgy. It will be an exquisite thing to reconstruct civilization piece by piece, to recreate, one after another, every stage through which human-kind has passed."

His beatific reverie was interrupted by the appearance of little Eeeoys, who was standing in the doorway and smiling somewhat sadly at him, with a mixture of timidity and unease. She took him by the hand and led him outside. She gestured first toward the horizon, where the sun was sinking behind a curtain of purple clouds, and then pointed to the fire, which was nowhere near as bright as it had been an hour earlier and was now sending up only thin wreaths of smoke.

Robert crossed the village with a heavy heart. He found Martians seated two by two on the ground, their wooden dishes on their knees, and so stuffed with food that they appeared incapable of moving. He shuddered at the thought that in two hours at the most it would be completely dark, and the Erloor vampires, thirsting for vengeance, would most certainly fall upon these poor, defenseless souls.

He bitterly reproached himself for his laziness and idle dreaming. Fortu-nately, there was still, so he thought, enough time to take serious defensive measures.

Eeeoys watched him, trembling with fear and instinctively drawing closer to him, as if imploring his protection and support. Her mute supplication deeply moved him, and the innocent smile that greeted his assurances—to which she listened in silence, trusting him even though she couldn't under-stand—inspired him with new energy.

His first concern was to furnish an abundance of new fuel for the fire. Then, with Eeeoys's help, he revived the least sleepy of the revelers, among others the venerable Aouya, who, after a long yawn and a good sneeze, finally realized the gravity of the situation.

Robert had great difficulty, however, in making them understand what he wanted. In their naïveté, the Martians imagined, as far as Robert could ascertain, that all danger had disappeared with the destruction of the idols. Only Eeeoys had more foresight, and he was very grateful for her perspicacity.

Finally, after half an hour of pantomimes and negotiations, they arranged their defenses. A circle of logs was placed all the way around the village, and loads of dry wood were piled nearby so that the brilliant light of the flames would not diminish for an instant. In addition, each home was surrounded by large pieces of slate, in order to thwart as much as possible the subterranean maneuvers of the Roomboo.

Robert stationed sentries at each fire and showed them all they had to do: keep awake and not allow the flames to die down.

As for himself, aware of his responsibilities, he had vowed to not close his eyes for an instant and to make his rounds continually, every hour, to scold inattentive sentinels and thwart the enemy's stratagems.

Thinking, with good reason, that he needed to have an observation post in a central location, Robert established his headquarters close to the first fire, in the middle of the small village square. From there, he could see and watch over everything.

Eeeoys, lying not far away from him on a mat, quickly fell into a deep sleep.

Night arrived. Phobos and Deimos rose over the horizon, surrounded by a radiant cortege of clouds. One by one, awakening from the heavy somnolence of their digestion, the Martians had returned to their huts. The flames of the bonfires, infinitely reflected in the calm, mirrorlike waters of the marshes, rose high into a night sky perfumed with the pleasant fragrance of fresh herbs.

Everything presaged a night free of alarms; the illuminated village shone in the darkness, encircled by a dazzling aureole that would surely keep the demons of the night in check until dawn.

Robert made his first round and noted with satisfaction that all was well; the sentinels appeared fresh and alert and were calling out to one another every quarter of an hour with a guttural cry.

A second and third round gave the young man full confidence in the

Martians' vigilance, and he paid no heed to the condition of the sky, which had become entirely veiled by clouds.

It could have been midnight — according to terrestrial measurements of time — when, a little tired after his long day and relaxing in the warmth of the fire, Robert stretched out on a mat and surrendered to sleep, promising himself not to rest for more than an hour or two.

Incoherent nightmares infiltrated his sleep.

He dreamed — as for some time he had frequently done — that his terrestrial fiancée had come to join him, accompanied by his naturalist friend, and with them he shared his reign. Miss Alberte, now a queen, had taken little Eeeoys as her maid of honor, his friend Pitcher was prime minister, and the venerable Aouya, assigned to his post in view of his great appetite, was the overseer of provisions; as for the terrible Erloor and their probable allies the Roomboo, they had been so well tamed that they had become extremely handy servants.

Robert — still dreaming — went for delightful nighttime rides around the planet in a gondola pulled through the air by a dozen vampires, whom he guided with a sharp-edged goad and whose velvety wings gently rustled as they glided above forests and lakes.

Borne by these miraculous chargers, he went so far as to visit the satellites of Mars, Phobos and Deimos, the first no more than twelve and the second no more than ten kilometers in diameter. These two tiny moons were first seen from Earth in 1877 by the astronomer Asaph Hall.

Then, his dream following its own internal logic, he saw himself back on Earth, loaded with spoils: maps, minerals, precious stones, and animals that amazed all the men of science. He received letters of congratulation from all the rulers of Europe and had the singular honor of being inducted into the Royal Academy in London and the Académie des Sciences in Paris.

But when he entered the lecture hall of the celebrated Académie, he was astonished to find himself in a large, gloomy cavern filled with the deafening sound of beating wings. Hundreds of Erloor fluttered through the air, darting black looks at him with their phosphorescent pupils as they circled him in the darkness . . .

He opened his eyes, his brow beaded with sweat. He was slipping into sleep once again, exhausted, when a heartrending cry roused him completely.

X

....

Nocturnal Battle

Robert leapt to his feet, filled with dread. The harrowing tone of the cry for help, quickly tailing into a sort of death rattle, left no doubt. One of the fire's guardians had been attacked, was maybe already dead. The young man raced in the direction from which the desperate plea had come, stopping only to grab his large stone knife and club.

It came from the very edge of the village, deep in the swamp. Along the way, he collided with Martians who appeared, terrified, on the doorsteps of their huts. These poor souls must have understood the significance of this agonized howl, for their whole bodies were trembling and their innocent, pink faces were pale and colorless. They must have bitterly regretted putting their trust in the stranger who had brought fire and destroyed their idols.

The thought cut him to the quick; he reproached himself, as for an act of cowardice far beneath him, at the weakness he had displayed in giving in to sleep.

His dismay knew no bounds when, arriving at the edge of the water, he found the fire almost extinct and the sentries in flight. He looked around: a couple of steps away an unfortunate Martian was holding on to the willows on the bank with all his might, struggling in the powerful claws of a beast hiding in the grasses—undoubtedly the aquatic Roomboo, the giant burrowing mole. It had been he, attacked by the animal as he was peacefully sleeping, who had let out the terrible shriek that had awakened Robert.

Robert saw in the shadows, shining like fireflies at a respectful distance from the fire, scores of phosphorescent eyes of a troop of Erloor watching from the reeds.

There was no time to waste. He struck the Roomboo behind the head with his club and the monster immediately let go of the Martian, stunned by the blow. Before it had time to recover, Robert drove his stone knife deep between its shoulders.

The beast howled in pain, thrashed the muck with its six feet, vomited great spurts of black blood, and finally grew still.

As for the Martian, he had prudently retreated to the fire onto which he was hastily and fearfully tossing armloads of wood.

Determined to make the most of his victory, Robert pulled the corpse of the Roomboo onto dry ground and dragged it next to the fire.

It was a superb animal. Its feet had webs for swimming and claws for digging, and it had perfectly white ivory tusks and dense, thick fur like that of a sea otter.

Before the grateful Martian, he placed his foot on the monster and signaled to him to gather other Martians to witness his triumph.

Soon there were twenty or more, grouped in a circle, their faces expressing astonishment and fear.

To teach them that they no longer had any reason to fear the Roomboo and should consider them ordinary game, Robert sliced into the animal and partially skinned it, detaching one of the legs, which he set to roast over the coals.

This had a great effect on the spectators. Led by his compelling example, each of them set to work. In the blink of an eye, the Roomboo's carcass was skinned and cut up.

The Martians joyfully danced around the fire, drinking in the smell of grilled meat.

Turning around, Robert found little Eeeoys at his side, smiling up at him. She had gotten up when he awoke and had quietly followed him. He was touched by her graciousness and almost animal-like fidelity and rewarded the young girl with the gift of one of the Roomboo's legs, which she immediately set about devouring.

He enjoyed some too. It was very juicy meat, quite red, a bit tough, but with none of the gaminess he had expected.

The entire village was bustling with activity. In every direction, people were throwing fuel onto the fires. The women and children, dressed only in the slips of bark that they wore in place of nightshirts, were passing slowly before the remains of the Roomboo. Many knelt before Robert and some respectfully kissed his feet.

To completely capture their imagination, Robert sent Eeeoys to find his bow and arrows and, in front of the attentive crowd, he attached a flaming brand to the tip of an arrow and bent his bow toward where the eyes of the vampires glowed in the darkness like a swarm of fireflies. He let fly and the arrow whistled in the rapt silence of the spectators. Robert must have aimed true; anguished cries arose from the Erloor camp, a heartrending whimpering followed by a dull and plaintive clamor, and the constellation of shining eyes disappeared into the night with discordant cries, among which Robert thought he heard supplications and threats proffered in an unknown tongue.

At that moment, the fire sputtered and sent up a column of steam and smoke. The Roomboo's subterranean mine had reached its target.

But this time, Robert was ready. He shoveled the coals to higher and drier ground and, with shining torches, he lit up the vast expanse of water. When the aquatic miner emerged from its tunnel, he attacked it first with his club and then with his stone knife, and the townspeople had a second victim to flay and cut up.

It was only then that Robert was struck by the Roomboo's strange anatomy. The animal was flat in the middle, like certain reptiles. Its six feet were especially remarkable.

The front feet, very long and sharp, had such strong ivory claws that they must have been able to dig through the stoniest ground in a matter of minutes. The second pair, short and shrunken, were formed of large membranes whose claws were no longer anything but a reminder of the general design and must have helped the blind animal find its footing in the thick waters and mud of the bogs.

These feet, almost flippers, emerged at the edge of its ribs. From there, its spine curved in, its waist contracted, like a wasp's, and its body terminated in a formidable rump with disproportionately large legs armed with outward curving claws that must have helped the animal to dig its way out of cave-ins or to finish the work of the front legs.

The monster's face was terrifying, horrible, eyeless, with a horn over its nose, rudimentary ears, and an expressionless maw filled with ivory tusks more massive and harder than those of an elephant.

On the whole, Robert noted, at approximately two meters long, this was a formidable monster. Its flexible waist gave it the ability to draw itself into a ball and lunge like a tiger. With its webbed feet and claws it could live in the water as well as underground. Blind and as well armed as a rhinoceros, it was guided only by its sense of smell and would not retreat from anything, precisely because it could not see anything. And finally, its teeth demonstrated that it could nourish itself equally well with the flesh of animals and reptiles that it might catch in the water as with the roots of plants it encountered as it dug its tunnels.

Robert, who had been comfortably self-assured for some time, promised himself he would make a lot of money someday by selling to the director of the Jardin d'Acclimatation a specimen of this phenomenal mole, which the most notable Martians were at that moment cutting up before his eyes with grunts of joy.

The village took on a festive atmosphere in the light of the bonfires. It was a sort of nocturnal Bastille Day. The Martians were returning to their homes, each carrying a morsel of the Roomboo, chanting guttural songs that must have been triumphal hymns. After showing themselves to be quite fearful during the catastrophe, they appeared arrogant after success.

Little by little they retired to their huts and Robert was left alone near his central fire, next to little Eeeoys who, overcome with fatigue, was again lying on her mat.

Robert himself did not sleep. Far from being intoxicated by his recent triumph, he now had a clear picture of the perils that surrounded him. The weight of his responsibility frightened him, and he considered with dread that it would take nothing more than a heavy rain to put out his fires and deliver the entire village to the rapaciousness of the vampires.

He was uneasy, nervous, agitated; and the serenity of Eeeoys, who slept with a smile on her lips, was not enough to calm his nerves.

With great impatience he watched for the first signs of a liberating dawn.

Several times, his club in hand, the stone knife in his belt, he walked around the village, waking the sentries who were asleep, adding wood to the fires, inspecting the surrounding area, without a doubt more preoccupied than Napoleon on the eve of the Battle of Austerlitz.

The clouds had grown thicker. The flames from the bonfires were now blood-red and the only sounds that broke the silence were the lugubrious cries of night birds that seemed to be crying "Woe! Woe!" in their cawing voices.

He returned to sit by his fire and there he noticed some disquieting phenomena. A very fine sort of rain, as if someone were silently tossing small handfuls of gravel, was falling on the fire, and it was already covered with a thin whitish layer.

He raised his eyes. High up, a darker shape emerged from the night sky and, from a spot nearly lost in the clouds, a rain of red, moist sand was falling. It had begun imperceptibly, with tiny handfuls. Then it had grown stronger, and now it was a veritable downpour of sand that fell on the fire and threatened to put it out.

What could he do? The Erloor were out of reach. He watched them descending in bands, wheeling around the village, and then flying up again, no doubt laden with new projectiles.

What frightened him was the wisdom of the vampires in choosing to attack him instead of the sentries at the other fires, who would have been much easier to overcome. He could see that soon his fire would be literally buried under a pulverulent heap.

He had already awakened little Eeeoys, who otherwise ran the risk of being buried alive and suffocated by the diabolical rain.

Robert was starting to despair. He knew that after putting out this fire, the vampires would attack another, and once the entire village was plunged in darkness they would come after the unfortunate and demoralized Martians, who had no way to defend themselves.

"Yet let it never be said," he shouted in rage, "that I was bested in this fight!"

He couldn't think of anything. It served no use to shake off the brands and blow on them to revive them; the whirlwind of sand continued to fall, slowly, inexorably.

He took his bow and arrows and, with all the strength of his muscles increased tenfold by the lesser gravity, he shot flaming brands at the sinister cloud.

This tactic had some success at first, sowing some confusion in the assailants' ranks. The sand fell with less regularity, and some of the Erloor, frightened by the proximity of the winged torches that Robert continued to shoot at them without interruption, fled with piercing screams. But they soon returned to the fray with a new enthusiasm.

All that Robert gained from this tactic was to see the phalanx of vampires mount to an inaccessible height, from which the rain of sand continued to fall. He was trying to figure out what to do when Eeeoys, who was pressing tightly to him in fear, had a fortunate inspiration.

At dusk, the Martians had begun to surround the fire with a palisade.

Eeeoys made Robert understand through her gestures that he needed to place a horizontal roof on the stakes. He rushed to put this idea into action, and soon the fire was covered by solid branches and pieces of sod; it would be a long time before the flames began to pierce this shell, and, in this way, there was a good chance of making it to dawn and keeping the Erloor at bay until the liberating rays of the solar star appeared.

This expedient, which was a complete success, gave Robert another idea, which, if it succeeded as well, would undoubtedly lead to a decisive victory.

Taking care to arrange some air vents, he busied himself in concealing the light of his fire with mats and sod, then he lay down nearby, as if overcome by sleep, next to Eeeoys, but took care to keep his knife and club close to hand.

As he had hoped, the Erloor, exhausted from staring much of the night at the brightness of the bonfires, could not fully keep track of his movements.

His ruse was a complete success.

He saw the troupe of vampires slowly descend and the bravest land abruptly on the ground, and he heard the soft noise of their wings.

Next to him, Eeeoys was trembling like a leaf and, with her face pressed against the ground, was too terrified to make the slightest movement.

Robert felt his heart pounding precipitously, but he had the courage to wait until he felt the cold hands of the Erloor brush against his face.

Then he suddenly leapt up, tore off the mats that concealed the flames, and fell upon the blinded vampires with his club. They were so surprised and afraid that their pale faces grew gray with terror. The miserable monsters, whose pupils only dilated in complete darkness, stumbled into the fire, screamed, and struggled, and Robert, inexorable, bludgeoned them.

With an intelligence that surprised him, Eeeoys threw armfuls of wood onto the fire, and the flames soon rose in a livid column that illuminated a veritable field of death, a hideous slaughter of gray beasts writhing in the blood and the dust.

Some even begged Robert for mercy with tears and almost human gestures. He turned away, filled with disgust at this butchery.

The Martians, awakened by the blinding light, had come out of their houses. After a moment's hesitation, a clamor of vengeance had broken out and they had rushed, knives in hand, to cut the throats of the victims that the club had stunned.

Blood ran in rivers, and the vampires, hypnotized by the flames that now reached the palisades, were tumbling on their own, like moths entranced by a lamp at night, into the middle of the burning coals, where they perished.

The rainy dawn illuminated a battlefield littered with the dead and injured. The vampires had suffered a terrible defeat; their bodies were piled by the hundreds around the fire, which their blood threatened to extinguish.

Robert was astonished to see the peaceable Martians display a ferocity he did not think they had in them. He excused their behavior, surmising that they must have had centuries of tyranny to avenge.

They calmly divided up the bodies and carried them to be roasted for provisions. Any Erloor who still showed signs of life were mercilessly finished off.

Robert had great difficulty saving the life of one of these strange creatures who had only sustained a slight wound to his wing and was struggling piteously on the ground like a huge human bat. Eeeoys had already raised her club to smash his skull when Robert stepped in and, with an imperious gesture, made her understand that this was his property, his portion of the spoils.

He bound his captive tightly with strips of willow bark and led him to his hut where, in the darkness, the Erloor seemed to feel a little reassured. Robert placed him on a mat and left him some roots and some meat. The Erloor refused to touch the food and remained motionless, crouched on the ground and full of fear, for quite some time. Then he tried to climb up the walls and uttered some inarticulate groans; his eyes were blinking and his whole body shivered as he stretched his limbs against his bonds like a wolf in a trap.

The light, especially, appeared to make him extremely uneasy. When Robert opened the door, he would nervously beat his gray wings, scratch at the walls with his claws, and begin to wail with small, sharp cries.

Robert suspected that this being would be difficult to tame, but he promised himself he would make every effort. It was only through the Erloor, he thought, that he would be able to discover all the planet's secrets.

XI

....

Explorations

The following week felt truly enchanted to Robert; time flowed with the swiftness of a dream.

Robert now held a more than royal sway over his Martian subjects. He dressed in a magnificent robe of red and green feathers and wore a cap of his own design that, in his vanity, he had given the shape of a diadem, and he was accompanied by a dozen robust and well-armed bodyguards wherever he went. In addition, Aouya and Eeeoys followed him everywhere, tasked with the special mission of teaching him the finer points of the Martian language that he had begun to speak reasonably well. It wasn't difficult, since this idiom was composed of hardly more than two hundred words, formed of vowel combinations, with a few, rare consonants for expressing terrible or noxious things.

Robert was also venerated by his subjects, and their affection for him reached heights of fanaticism and adoration.

He was surprised one day to find his image, roughly sculpted out of wood, clay, and colored leather, placed in one of the temples where the idol of the Erloor had formerly reigned. He made his interpreters understand that it disgusted him to take the place of these beasts of prey. He had come with his hands full of gifts; he wanted only abundance, justice, and good-ness for everyone.

His ideas harmonized so well with those of his naturally peaceful subjects that it was inevitable that they would win him great popularity.

And, too, he had been of great service to them.

The day after the vampires' attack, he had had raised around the village a ring of tall chimneys, built of uncured bricks, with pointed roofs and lateral openings equipped with wind blocks to counter the rain and the vampires' sand. The floors of these furnaces were built of massive stones against which the tunneling prowess of the Roomboo stood no chance.

Furthermore, weighted traps had been placed here and there for the latter, and the Martians had the pleasure of catching four that very day, their heads crushed by the mass of the counterweight.

Now the village slept peacefully, encircled with a ring of bright fires.

The following day, Robert boarded one of his subjects' reed-and-leather boats and had the pleasure of passing several hours boating on one of the famous canals known to terrestrial astronomers.

He surmised, from his own calculations, that it must be the Avernus.

Picture if you will an enormous river, like an arm of the sea, whose two banks, from a vantage point in the center, are lost in the mist, and whose salty water flows slowly southward.

Robert paid no heed to the skill of the paddlers, who steered the vessel with spoon-shaped paddles made from a large reed fitted at each end with a leather pouch. Armed with a slate and a sharp stone, he traced the contours of the planet's continents from memory, according to Schiaparelli and Flammarion.

He was struck by a peculiarity in the rough sketch he had just completed. All the oceans were in the North and all the continents in the South.

In one stroke, he believed he had discovered what astronomers and men of science had been searching for so long.

"It's plain as day," he cried enthusiastically. "I can't believe no one thought of it sooner: the whole of the planet Mars, with its landlocked pole and its aquatic pole, is nothing more than a vast swamp, and all would be submerged by the melting ice after a winter of six months, just as all would be withered up after a spring and summer both of which also last for six months, if the Martians had not dug these vast canals that drain from the North the living water that is lacking in the South.

One fact, however, bothered him: the presence, noted by astronomers, of mountains near the equator whose summits turn white in the winter.

"It doesn't disprove my theory," said Robert, as if responding to an invisible interlocutor, "if there are some mountainous regions in this vast swamp. It's not impossible . . . But, if there are mountains, there must be valleys, delightful spots, warmed by six months of summer, where all the plants and fruits of the tropics must flourish, where winter must be reduced to inconsequential showers. The astronomers who have repeated without thinking that Mars is farther removed from the Sun than Earth have forgotten one thing: the Martian year has six hundred and eighty-seven days.

He had fallen into a deep reverie. He understood now the strength and vigor of these trees and plants, which must live twice as long as their terrestrial counterparts. He imagined, like a feast for the senses, the marvelous six-month autumn, where the passing away of things must be filled with infinite and subtly nuanced colors unknown in earthly seasons.

He foresaw nature's slow awakening after a long sleep, and the thousands of different flowers that would surely, after such a long repose, hail the arrival of the sun. He could already savor the charm of these successive flowerings, the leisurely pace of their unforgettably voluptuous development . . . And the torrid and endless summer, in gold-colored forests . . . And the scarlet reeds of autumn, and the clouds of birds with their melancholy cries.

His imagination was catching fire. He began to think like a botanist. Plants that were able to withstand such long periods of cold and heat stood out clearly in the herbarium in his memory.

He pictured cool ravines lined with orange trees, coconuts, and other palms, where the Erloor must retire after sucking the blood from their victims.

He bristled with anger:

"I haven't seen anything!" he cried. "I know nothing of this mysterious planet. I probably know no more than I would if, arriving on Earth, I had landed with the Eskimo or in Tierra del Fuego . . . . Perhaps, besides the Erloor, there are other beings: wise, powerful, intelligent, who live among fertile fields in regions caressed by the sun, where happiness reigns."

He noticed, at this point, that Aouya and Eeeoys were listening and looking at him anxiously. He reassured them with a smile, and the unexpectedness of the landscape soon gave his obsession a respite.

The boat had just run aground on a bed of admirably carved granite.

From studying the breaks in the stone, Robert observed that, just like the ancient Egyptians, the builders of these canals had made use of the expansive strength of water transformed into ice to split the blocks of stone without tools.

Robert saw swimming through the reeds a large number of those animals, at once aquatic and fossorial, that the people of the village worshipped under the name of Roomboo. He was going to fell one with his club when Eeeoys restrained his arm and made him understand, although not without great effort, that on the canals the Roomboo were useful and sacred beings, almost public servants.

"They eat many fish," she said, "but they clean the riverbeds, and they are absolutely necessary. We should only kill them if they attack the villages, which will no longer happen now that their masters, the Erloor, are defeated."

Robert disembarked. After about fifty paces through a terrain filled with red plants, his path was blocked by a wall of huge, irregular blocks, built without mortar, in the manner of cyclopean stonework.

He then understood why astronomers on Earth saw a double line on the banks of the canals, and he also recalled having seen, during his voyage, stone shelves, veritable dams, that permitted the conservation of polar waters in the summer, while in the winter the water must flow furiously between the two ramparts of the canal.

Robert was lost in these reflections when his hosts — *my subjects, rather*, he thought — showed him a steep sort of stairway by which one reached the top of the dike.

He moved from astonishment to astonishment. Not much farther, he found a veritable Martian city made up of more than two thousand huts. He was received with enthusiastic huzzahs.

True to the line of conduct he had been following, he pushed forward the prominent Martian whom he had chosen to carry a slate basket filled with hot coals. The repetition of earlier scenes followed: flames came to life, roasting meat perfumed the air, the idols of the Erloor and the Roomboo were dragged to the stake and the village was soon encircled by a protective ring of bonfires.

Robert Darvel, now indifferent to the people's expressions of respect, took his leave after a light meal and, like a minister on tour, visited another village where he received the same solemn reception.

Wherever he went, fear of the Erloor vanished. They could even be found nailed alive to the doors of huts.

Robert savored the delights of his well-deserved celebrity. He was showered with caresses and gifts, and he enjoyed the compendious pleasure of being admired all at once as a general, an admiral, a politician, a doctor, a druggist, an engineer, and so on.

Fire towers were built everywhere according to his instructions, and security reigned where only recently terror had prevailed.

The vampires were no longer a threat. The Erloor, chastened by the hard lesson they had learned, no longer attacked anyone. They had undoubtedly retreated to regions where their influence had not yet waned.

Nevertheless, Robert captured two of them who had foolishly fallen face first into the flames. With the usual prudence of a head of state, he ordered that they be provisionally imprisoned, pending the outcome of their trials for disturbing the peace, breaking and entering, murder, and vampirism; the simpleminded Martians did not yet have an inkling of the gravity of these charges.

The fifth day of this triumphal tour, after interminable journeys through red forests and along canals as wide as the sea, Robert stopped in his tracks. He stood before the crumbling ruins of a palace of pink sandstone overrun by ivy that brought to mind as much by its general shape as its details the Gothic architecture of Earth.

It was a maze of towers, turrets, balconies, and minarets that appeared at first glance to be impossibly intertwined. There were crumbling stone stairways of two hundred steps that abruptly stopped in mid-air, leading to no terrace or landing. The disintegrating flying buttresses remained standing only through some disconcertingly audacious miracle of balance, like half-arches of a bridge. Balconies clung precariously to single blocks of stone, turrets swayed on a single remaining pillar, and majestic pediments crowned with foliage rested on animal-headed caryatids with missing arms.

This grandiose rubble was overgrown with hardy vegetation: crimson ivy, beech, and birch that covered them in a leafy blanket and also supported them with root and branch as if to prevent their final collapse.

The Martians shrank from these ruins in a kind of horror, and Robert noticed that the figures, though roughly hewn, were a perfect likeness of the Erloor, opening their wings on the temple's pediments or doubled over in laughter around the columns.

Robert, in his attempts to explain what he saw, ran into countless contradictions. How can one reconcile the presence of these grandiose ruins — undeniably the work of artists and thinkers — with the state of ignorance and brutishness, if not savagery, of the planet's inhabitants? And these canals, built with such skill? Even assuming that the tunneling beasts, the Roomboo, had excavated and built them, what engineer had drawn the plans, determined the width and depth and, above all, had conceived of the idea of the dual rampart and the dams that helped to prevent both drought and the floods caused by melting polar ice?

"I must be walking," Robert mused, "through the ruins of an ancient and refined civilization in the process of slowly returning to barbarism!"

His reverie was interrupted by his entourage's arrival at the gates of a village, where he had to submit to the customary chore of acclamations, ovations, and banquets.

He began to understand the dark concern visible, even in their most joyous effigies, in the faces of potentates and emperors . . .

Robert went to sleep mulling over philosophical concerns, rolled up in his superb feather cloak, a cloak of honor, almost as beautiful, in its own way, as the robe once offered to the Duchess of Berry by the city of Rouen, which, according to Vaulabelle, author of *The History of the Two Restorations*, was composed entirely of green and gold down from the heads of ducks skillfully sewn onto muslin.

XII

....

Progress

Months had passed and Robert Darvel now enjoyed the prerogatives of a true monarch. The Martians, following his plans, had built a spacious and comfortable abode for him that, in comparison to the surrounding huts, he could call without impertinence a presidential, maybe even a royal, palace.

The Martians had learned to no longer fear the Erloor. The smallest hamlet surrounded by workshops and cultivated fields was now protected at night by a circle of bonfires, and each one, built on a solid stone foundation and covered by a stoutly built canopy, protected from both rain and ash, defied the endeavors of the Erloor and the underground sorties of their allies.

Unheard-of prosperity and perfect security now reigned over an immense expanse of land.

The signs of tremendous activity were everywhere: larger and more comfortable ships were built from new designs Robert had provided; fishing and hunting techniques had been improved; and bows, blowguns, and fish traps and hooks, not to mention a host of other devices, had been added, for the time being, to the primitive tools of the Martians.

Granaries and reserves had been established with winter in mind, and the fabrication of preserves, unknown until then, had spread remarkably quickly. You could now see in every cabin salted legs of beef, smoked bustards, and provisions of vegetables preserved in an oil that Robert had found a way to extract from water chestnuts and beechnuts gathered from the forest floor.

While exploring in the mountains, he had found vines of a type of wild grape and had planted the stocks with great care on the slope of a hill well exposed to the sun. He counted on soon being able to give the Martians a taste of his own vintage and to become the Bacchus or Noah of these simple folk, just as he had already been their Prometheus, their Solon, and their Hannibal.

To his great joy, he had discovered excellent iron ore in the rocks and, processing it with the primitive methods still used today in Catalan forges, he managed to form several blocks of pure metal from which he forged knives and steel hammers, hardened with the help of powdered carbon, in an oven made of clay.

Many, in Robert's place, would have been happy, but, now that some of his projects had been realized — and he even hoped to be able to one day enter into communication with Earth — a gnawing melancholy engulfed him. He would have much preferred to be back in London, in Mrs. Hobson's tavern, in the company of his friend Ralph Pitcher.

And another thing concerned him.

Little Eeeoys had fallen in love with him and wished to marry him in the Martian tradition, which was little more than an opulent banquet followed by tuneless songs.

Robert had resisted this offer for many reasons. Miss Alberte Teramond was always present in his thoughts, and each time he searched the cloudless sky and saw his home planet twinkling among the stars, his heart flew to this young woman, and he looked on all the Martian women with their rosy cheeks and bright smiles with the most complete indifference.

Eeeoys, however, was wasting away. She no longer left Robert's side for a moment and she now spoke French sufficiently well to make a jealous scene upon the slightest pretext. Her love for Robert had led her into an exaggerated coquettishness. She never left her room in the presidential residence except dressed in precious furs, adorned with necklaces of seeds and sparkling stones.

Robert grew increasingly tired of her advances, and he often undertook long excursions on the canals to distract himself from his troubles. In this way he had reconnoitered the major part of the northern regions and sketched out their topography.

It should be noted that the appearance of the land changed but little in all the areas he had visited. Everywhere there was the never-ending red foliage of the forest and the never-ending marshes, vast empty spaces where here and there he would find small populations, more or less similar to those that he already knew.

He knew that in the South, near the equator, there were lands with lush vegetation, but it is important to note that the pilots absolutely refused to turn the prows of their skiffs in that direction, and they let it be known that those beautiful lands were the domain of the Erloor and other beings as formidable as they. This only increased his curiosity.

"It is certain that I am only acquainted," he told himself, "with the most savage regions. I must visit the entire planet."

This desire grew within him from day to day, and the thought of the dangers that lay ahead only whetted his appetite.

He came to think that the Erloor he had captured the night of the combat might serve to initiate him into the mysteries of this forbidden territory.

He consequently employed all his care in supplying food for the animal that he had chained up in a cave and nourished on raw meat.[4]

---

4 Translator's note: There exists a substantial gap here in the account that has reached us of Robert Darvel's adventures.

XIII

....

The Crystal Mountain

Robert was happy, to the point where he could almost say he was as happy as it was possible to be.

Yet he had not lost his old love of adventure. And before he attempted a comprehensive exploration and invented a means to communicate with Earth and perhaps return to the planet of his birth—a grand but temporarily deferred project—Robert had no greater pleasure than venturing out on his own without any of his brave Martians, whose naïve affection was growing tiresome.

For quite some time he had listened to little Eeeoys's stories of a terrible valley in the South where even the Erloor feared to venture.

The existence of this valley was a very ancient tradition, but even the old men could not tell him anything precise about the location of this terrible place. All that was known was that it lay between two extraordinarily high mountains and was inhabited by horrific monsters that could be found nowhere else.

The Martians named this valley Lirraarr and pronounced the word with the guttural intonation of the Spanish *jota*, which in their language signified death.

This alone was enough to make Robert want to visit this mysterious place that everyone advised him to avoid.

Besides, the accursed mountains were not very far from the principal

Martian village. According to the old men, he would see their peaks after a three days' march.

He was all the more excited by the prospect of this excursion because he had hardly had a chance to see mountains of any height.

One morning, therefore, after obtaining the most precise information he could, he set off, warning the people of his entourage that he would not return before a week or two had passed.

They were accustomed to his absences, and the Martians had such a high opinion of his courage and intelligence that it didn't occur to them for an instant that he might run a genuine risk.

Eeeoys alone shed a few tears; Robert comforted her with a promise to bring back, as he often did, new varieties of fruit or sparkling gems.

Robert had divulged the goal of his voyage to no one.

Once outside the hut that served as his palace, under the arching canopy of the great red forest, he felt an indescribable sensual pleasure: the weather was very mild and before him opened grandiose landscapes, lent a sumptuous melancholia by tones of copper and tarnished gold unknown in terrestrial climes. At each step, he discovered a stone, a plant, or some new insect.

And the forest now seemed familiar. From the moss that grew on the leeward side of tree trunks and with the help of the stars, he could now find his bearings; he was certain he wouldn't get lost.

He recalled similar impressions from his childhood during hunting parties in the woods of Sologne. He knew that apart from the Erloor there was no real danger to fear.

The first three days of his journey passed without incident: he ate, hunted, and slept in the shelter of a hollow tree or beneath thick shrubbery.

Just as the Martians had told him, at the end of the third day he spied jagged peaks that were nearly equal in height and shape.

He walked all the following day before reaching the foot of the mountains. The landscape's appearance had abruptly changed. The lush vermillion forest had given way to a clayey plain, strewn with cracks and crevasses into which darted fat red lizards with the small, ferocious eyes of crocodiles.

After this he came to a rocky cliff of reddish sandstone that formed the base of the mountain, a cliff that appeared to have been hewn by human hands.

It was a sheer rock face without a single ledge or fissure.

Robert walked for a few hours along the foot of this impassable wall. The heat was growing intolerable, something he had not yet experienced since his arrival on the planet. He was exhausted, and his exhaustion was accompanied by a sort of vertigo; he thought he saw a red haze rising from the inaccessible summits, but nothing in the terrain appeared volcanic.

The entire region appeared hostile and inhospitable. He was surprised to realize that he almost regretted having ventured so far from his good Martians.

He put off the next step of his journey until the following day and passed the night in a crevice in the ground, from which he carefully chased the red lizards before fortifying it with large stones.

He slept badly.

He awoke several times in the grip of an inexplicable anguish, a cold sweat on his brow, his chest tight, gasping for breath.

Overcome by fatigue he would fall asleep again only to reawaken, tormented by the same anxiety. The coming of the morning felt like a deliverance; he got up and continued his journey.

He was surprised by the sudden rise in the temperature that he had noticed the day before. Plants he had never seen before grew from crevices in the rock, with succulent, bright yellow leaves topped with a spiny efflorescence like those of the cacti of Central America. Insects with huge wings and fat, goitered reptiles: an entirely different fauna evidenced the abrupt change of climate.

The heat was growing increasingly intolerable. Robert was sweating profusely and making very slow progress. He was still walking along the sheer base of the rock wall that continued, bare and unchanging, along an almost imperceptible curve.

But, after a sudden bend, the landscape transformed with the speed of a scene-change in a play . . . The rock face stopped, ending in a sort of gigantic pylon whose summit rose into the clouds.

The cliff gave way to an immense forest composed of species that grow in the most torrid zones. Robert was not surprised to discover trees similar to those on Earth, relatives of the banana, bamboo, and palm.

"Nature," he murmured, "is consistent in her designs. The infinite varieties of her creations always follow an almost identical theme.

"Just as atomic chemistry shows us the systems of yet-undiscovered bodies, sufficiently rigorous logic should be able to divine every 'possible' species of plant."

Despite this readymade theory, Robert was continually forced to acknowledge that he had never seen, even in the marshes of India and central Africa or the layered forests of central Brazil, such vigorous, exuberant, even riotous vegetation.

Trees with violet or scarlet leaves shot like rockets into the sky, reaching heights of two or three hundred meters, their thick, fleshy foliage as vast as the sails of a ship. Other trees had sprouted from the lower boughs, where they branched off from the trunk, their roots clinging to the smallest fissures, sending lively shoots creeping toward the soil in search of more substantial nourishment. It was a forest that was twenty or thirty stories tall.

Everywhere the abundance of vines and branches trapped forest debris from which other seeds sprouted immediately, intertwining roots and flowers, stems and fruits in a superabundance of vitality that resembled — on a grander scale — the frenzy of a tempestuous sea.

There were corollas the size of a garden, palms that could shelter an entire village in their shade, towering cycads.

Robert was rooted to the ground, stunned by this vegetal splendor rendered even more inexplicable by its apparently restricted space of existence and because it had shot up in front of him, as it were, so unexpectedly.

This fact overturned everything he knew about climatology.

"Yet there must be a cause," he murmured, "likely a very simple cause.

"It is up to me to discover it."

But no matter how much he searched, he did not find the explanation for this magical forest, for this abrupt change of temperature that occurred in the space of a few hundred meters.

He noticed at the same time that this sudden, unexpected forest was home to a host of animals that he had not yet observed on Mars.

As in the primeval forests whose trunks, slowly carbonized in the absence of air, formed our coal mines, reptiles dominated.

There were the entire contemplative society of lizards and chameleons, tree snakes gliding from branch to branch, and, hopping on the ground, strange, almost man-sized green toads with blood-red splotches.

There were many insects, too: splendid butterflies whose wings seemed to be made from a strip of rainbow; moths of blue and green gold the size of pigeons, delightful and ornate, like monsters in an old Japanese print.

On the other hand, there were very few birds—a few deep-billed wading birds that were nonchalantly gulping down the smallest reptiles, some vultures, whose blood-red plumage made them stand out clearly in the bright sky. As for mammals, Robert Darvel saw none.

These observations occupied him for over an hour.

Robert did not dare to venture into this tangled bush, surely teeming with ravenous or venomous beasts. It was clear to him that a man lost between the earth and sky in these forests suspended one above another might wander for weeks from branch to branch, never touching the ground, never able to get his bearings.

He was disconcerted; his entire body was soaked with sweat, and it seemed to him that the forest blew suffocating gusts of heat toward him; and yet he still perceived, at a relatively negligible distance, the shadows of the northern tree species that he had left the day before; it was completely baffling.

For a time he followed the edge of the giant timber forest. As in all virgin forests, the ground between the trunks, deprived of air and light, was shadowy, barren, and fetid, cluttered with fungi and reptiles; it would have been ill advised to enter into those damp passages.

But it was hardly in Robert Darvel's nature to admit to being beaten, to stop in the face of an obstacle, whatever it might be.

By dint of searching and poking around, he ended up discovering a giant cedar, isolated in a sort of clearing and separated somewhat from the virgin forest, that climbed majestically more than a hundred meters.

Scaling this colossus didn't present any difficulty; on the broad lower branches, two riders would have been able to run their horses at a gallop without fear of getting in each other's way.

Robert thought that by reaching the crown of this coniferous patriarch he would perhaps obtain a panoramic view of this bewitching region.

Reassuring himself that the cutlass of steel-coated iron hanging from his belt was well within reach, he started his ascent.

The branches, which almost touched one another, formed a series of paths covered by fine blond needles; this cedar was, itself, a whole forest.

Robert's passage disturbed only inoffensive red squirrels, which leapt by the thousands into the branches. He had no trouble climbing to the top.

When he had reached it and was able to scan the horizon, he remained literally dazzled.

From his lookout post he was able to make out almost the whole of the forest. It formed a vast oval around three or four leagues wide; he was unable to gauge its much greater length.

Half of this oval lay enclosed in the mountainous chain by a half-ellipse of sheer walls as precisely defined as if they had been traced out by a land surveyor.

But that wasn't the chief wonder; the perfectly equal peaks of the mountain chain — which he hadn't been able to see as long as he had remained at the foot of the exterior wall — cast dazzling beams of light, as if the entire mountain were formed of the purest crystal.

A forest from the age of the mammoth crowned with a rainbow — such was the magic spectacle opening to Robert's eyes.

Looking more attentively, he recognized that the planes of the crystal were arranged following certain curves.

"Parabolic mirrors!" he exclaimed.

He was stunned with admiration before this masterpiece that must have taken centuries of work. Its very conception presupposed the most grandiose ideas.

But the reality was there in front of him, indisputable.

Robert Darvel understood everything now.

It was the walls of the mountain that, by collecting and concentrating the rays of the sun into this stunning valley, created this exceptional climate, to which without a doubt other scientists had contributed devices that he couldn't yet guess.

He was lost in thought.

It was certain that neither his subjects nor their enemies, the Erloor, had been able to design and execute such a marvel, and he mused with sadness that perhaps the intellectual race of Mars had disappeared ages earlier.

But suddenly, an objection arose in his logically ordered brain.

How was it that the continuous action of those mirrors, which Archimedes — by means of a system that has remained a mystery to this day — used to burn the Roman fleet, had not set fire to the forest itself?

It didn't take him long to find the explanation.

Exactly in the center of the ellipse, in the middle of a thick cloud of steam, he made out a glistening cone that seemed to him the peak of an elongated pyramid. He realized that the rays were focused on this monument, from there splitting off into all the enchanting valley to create the eternal tropical summer there.

He supposed that the effect of this mechanism, whose details still escaped him, was accomplished with metals of a special conductivity. This valley was all in all a perfected and gargantuan greenhouse.

The steam showed that a lake, perhaps divided into irrigation canals of nearly boiling water, must have completed the effect of this ingenious arrangement, producing that warm humidity indispensable to tropical plants.

Robert quickly climbed back down.

He had decided to explore the forbidden glen, no matter the cost; he no longer regretted having ventured far from his timid subjects.

In any case, he was soon able to confirm his previous hypotheses.

At a hundred steps from the giant cedar, he found himself on the edge of a canal filled with black, smoking water; it gave off an acrid, sickly smell that reminded him of formic acid, whose power for stimulating vegetation is so great.

Robert dipped his finger into the water and tasted it: it had a bitter and metallic flavor.

In his capacity as a chemist, he was proficient in the assessment of all known substances; the nerve fibers of his oral papillae, trained at length, detected at first blush the oxides and the bases, the acids and the salts.

After a moment's reflection, he recognized beyond any doubt that the water of the canal was saturated with those salts that have the property of holding a given temperature for several hours and even several days.

These salts are moreover widely used in industry for the fabrication of boilers, cooking pots, and so on.

Thus, no means had been neglected. Everything contributed, by virtue of the intentions of a specific will, to create this lush vegetation.

The engineer moved from astonishment to astonishment. And yet the tangled forest still presented him with an impassible barrier.

Using his cutlass in place of a machete, he moved forward for a time along the banks of the canal, which split at regular intervals and was divided into a mass of branches as complicated in their meanderings as the bends of a labyrinth.

But suddenly, a strange spectacle caught his eye.

A few steps away from him rose a tree of average height that appeared to be composed of a tangled lacework of lianas bristling with spines and arranged in the center of a large corolla that was itself encircled by high thorns.

The bizarre flower might have been a half-meter wide. Its center was blue and black, with yellow circles that gave it vaguely the appearance of a human eye; but, for eyelashes, this vegetal pupil was flanked with large yellow stamens, from which there escaped a nauseating scent of musk.

Robert was about to step back when a red squirrel approached softly, sniffing and shaking its tail, evidently attracted by the flower's smell.

Hesitantly, it passed between the barbed lianas and approached still closer.

The yellow and blue pupil twinkled, the circular spines trembled.

Then suddenly the lianas released with the dry crack of a whip.

The squirrel was surrounded, garroted as if it had been seized by a hundred snakes; in the blink of an eye it was carried toward the flower whose "gaze" had taken on, so to speak, a ferocious appearance.

The animal had let out only one cry of agony: already the yellow stamens were planted in its flesh.

All this had occurred with dreadful speed, in an instant.

Robert, terrified, took a step backward, but so clumsily that he slipped and tumbled to the ground.

He almost didn't get back up again.

He was half asphyxiated the moment he hit the ground.

He recognized with distress that a deleterious atmosphere, composed no doubt of carbonic acid, floated at ground level, carbonic gas being, as one knows, heavier than ordinary air.

Robert climbed back to his feet with a desperate effort, inhaling with delight a gulp of pure air and, with unsteady steps, made his way out of the poisonous forest.

Despite all his curiosity, all his desire to learn, he understood that he was not sufficiently armed for such an exploration, that he would never reach the center of the valley alive.

While he slowly retraced his path, he thought about this series of phenomena and tried in vain to determine why this dreadful environment had been artificially created.

Was it an experimental park, a torture garden, the monstrous caprice of some tyrant?

None of these hypotheses were satisfactory.

He slowly made his way back to the Martian villages, determined to return en masse and armed to this crystal mountain whose secret he had been unable to discover.[5]

---

5   There is another sizable gap here.

XIV

....

The Photographs

A week had passed since the death of Phara-Chibh.

Captain Wad and Ralph Pitcher (who had become in a few days the captain's inseparable friend) were sipping iced drinks in a gazebo in the residence's gardens, next to the convalescing Miss Teramond, who no longer bore any mark of the torments she had passed through save a captivating paleness. These three individuals understood one another perfectly.

The more they had reflected and debated, the more convinced they had become of one truth: that Robert Darvel had reached the planet Mars, that he had fulfilled that tremendous dream of scientists, poets, and madmen.

A thousand little circumstances, insignificant in themselves, developed into convincing proofs when combined.

Captain Wad had reopened the previously undertaken investigation into the catastrophe at the Chelambrum monastery. Through a patient interrogation of the Hindu monks, he had managed to discern a large part of the truth.

In the subterranean laboratory Robert had occupied, he had found the notes, the preliminary plans, and the working drawings from which the engineer's project clearly emerged.

Now Ralph no longer found anything extraordinary in the mysterious letter he had found, which he had before considered inexplicable.

But what truly caught his attention was the discovery, in a notebook filled with notes and formulae of all sorts, of these few lines in Robert's handwriting:

Today, Ardavena found the means to show me my dear Alberte, in one of his magic mirrors whose workings no longer seem so extraordinary to me . . . I don't think she has forgotten me. But it was a terrible jolt. I have been unable to work for two or three days . . .

Pitcher took it upon himself to present the notebook to Miss Alberte, who was profoundly touched.

"I knew," she murmured, "that Robert could not have forgotten me.

"He has been thinking of me, just as I have been thinking of him; but we shall find him! If he has truly succeeded in crossing the gulfs of the ether to reach Mars, why can't we join him? Why can't we achieve what he has managed to achieve?"

Captain Wad shook his head in silent discouragement.

"No," said Ralph, "it isn't possible. Robert must have benefited from a conjunction of circumstances that doubtless will never occur again."

"We shall see," murmured Miss Alberte, now pensive.

At that moment, the gong in the vestibule rang out and some domestics arrived in distress at the gazebo where this conversation was taking place.

"Captain," said one of them, "they have just arrested a prisoner and the sepoys are bringing him to you."

"A prisoner," exclaimed the officer moodily. "Was it worth the trouble to disturb me over that? No doubt he's some thief who hoped to steal our rice or spuds.

"Lock him up and let me have some peace!"

"But," the man insisted, "he isn't a native. We wouldn't have bothered you over so little. He is a European and, we believe, a spy.

"He speaks English with a strange accent, he is miserably dressed, and we found on his person a series of very unusual photographs."

"You did well to warn me," said the officer to the servant, recovering his professional demeanor. "Bring him in, I will interrogate him at once.

"I suspect," added the captain, after the domestic had withdrawn, "that what we have here is simply one of those international stalkers, roustabouts, or vagabonds, to which no country is inaccessible."

"Here he is now," said Ralph.

The sepoys brought into the garden an individual with a long blond beard and very light blue eyes. Just as the domestic had said, he was miserably dressed and covered with dust, and he seemed overcome by fatigue.

But despite these sorry trappings, there was a sincerity and nobility of appearance about him that impressed one at first sight.

To the great surprise of everyone there, he let out a cry of joy as he caught sight of Alberte and made the handcuffs with which he was chained ring out noisily. Then, giving a hint of a bow:

"Is that really you, Miss Teramond? I am truly delighted to have finally found you!

"Luckily your photograph is displayed on the front page of every newspaper."

Captain Wad thought he was in the presence of some desperate go-between who, discovering by chance that the young lady was in India, had devised the ingenious trick of having himself arrested to get to her.

"Quiet," he said harshly. "I'm the one you have business with.

"I warn you that if you intended to engage in some ill-mannered stunt, you will be most disappointed. And for starters, where are your references, your papers?"

"As for papers," said the man good-humoredly, "I possess a convict's record printed on yellow paper and perfectly in order."

"What sort of joke is this?" asked the officer, frowning menacingly.

"It is no joke," replied the prisoner in a slightly cheeky tone, "but, unless things have changed, I don't think that liberal England is in the habit of handing over the political convicts of other nations who come searching for refuge on its territory."

"That's enough," grumbled the irritated Captain Wad. "I am going to clear up your case and I guarantee that it won't take long.

"To begin with, who are you? Where do you come from? What is your name?"

The prisoner seemed to pay no heed to the menacing tone with which the officer pronounced these words.

"I have come from Siberia," he answered calmly. "I am a Polish scientist and my name is Bolensky."

Ralph nearly fell out of the rocking chair in which he was seated.

"Bolensky!" he interrupted suddenly. "I know . . . I know: didn't you collaborate with a Frenchman named Darvel on some luminous signals that were to be directed at the inhabitants of the planet Mars?"

Suddenly, Captain Wad had set aside, like a mask, his official and stiff physiognomy; he was now deeply attentive.

"Precisely," said the Pole cordially. "Now we're getting somewhere! It wasn't easy."

Captain Wad gestured discreetly to two impassive sepoys whose white uniforms set off the light bronze tone of their fierce faces; Bolensky's handcuffs were removed and the officer himself brought a chair for him.

To Miss Alberte's great astonishment, Bolensky seemed not at all surprised by this change in attitude.

"It was absolutely necessary that I see you," he said, turning toward the young woman. "I have very important news for you.

"This is not the first time, Miss, that I have heard your name spoken. How often my friend Darvel spoke of you when we were camping together in Siberia! You heard, perhaps, that I was arrested, that I was sent to join my Polish compatriots in the penal colony, in despair at having to abandon our marvelous attempt at interplanetary communication.

"At the last moment I managed to escape.

"I made it to Japan, where, in order to make a living, I joined a large scientific photography firm in the capacity of director.

"I had had no news of Robert, but I had not forgotten our dream.

"With the powerful apparatuses that I had further perfected at my disposal, I obtained negatives of the planet Mars of a perfect clarity."

"Well?" asked Miss Alberte, breathless with emotion.

"You shall see these photographs as soon as the sepoys who confiscated them from me have returned them."

"Egad!" interrupted the captain. "It must be those Martian photographs that made my overzealous sepoys mistake you for a spy."

"Precisely; I had more than a hundred and I would have had many more if, one fine morning without the slightest excuse, the Japanese, no doubt sufficiently initiated into cosmographic photography, hadn't suddenly dismissed me.

"That very day, I was awaiting the departure of a steamship for San Francisco when I happened to catch sight of a newspaper that contained Miss Teramond's portrait and the details of Darvel's life.

"My mind was instantly made up. Instead of going to San Francisco, I boarded a ship for Karikal. By the time I arrived, I had essentially no money left.

"I had to pass through a thousand dangers, a thousand hardships, to find you."

"Your collaboration will be invaluable to us," said Ralph, as he stood up. "Robert Darvel certainly told you of his friend Pitcher."

"Upon many occasions!"

While the two men exchanged a cordial handshake, a domestic, at Captain Wad's command, brought a small, grimy case.

"My photographs," exclaimed the Pole, his eyes shining with joy.

He opened the suitcase with a frantic hand; he scattered piles of unmounted prints on the pedestal table of the gazebo; on all of them the planet appeared with its dark mass crisscrossed by the lighter lineaments of Schiaparelli's canals.

At first glance, there appeared to be nothing out of the ordinary in these photographs.

"But don't you see?" exclaimed Bolensky passionately.

"Look here, this white mark followed by a line, then on this other one, a dot, a line, and a dash!

"Again on this one, two dashes and a dot."

"What is it?" asked Miss Alberte.

"Don't you understand . . . Morse code?

"There is a man up there who is signaling Earth, and this man can only be Robert Darvel!"

XV

....

"RO-BERT DAR-VEL"

Once Bolensky had, thanks to the attentions of Captain Wad, resumed the outward appearance of a gentleman, he promptly won everyone over; the escaped convict showed himself to be man of intelligence and heart, and a true scientist; indeed, the first care of his friends was to not leave him in the precarious situation in which he found himself.

One morning, the domestic who was assigned to his service handed him three letters, which surprised him no end; he wondered what well-informed correspondent had already been able to discover his new retreat.

He opened the first letter, from which fell a check for one hundred pounds. It was from Captain Wad, who explained to him with all sorts of oratorical precautions that, a post for a geological engineer just having become vacant, he had thought it might please him to be chosen to fill it.

The salary was two hundred pounds, and he had enclosed in the envelope six months' pay in advance to get him started.

Enchanted by the captain's behavior, as refined as it was generous, Bolensky opened the second letter. His surprise grew when he discovered that it contained a check for one thousand pounds payable on demand at the Royal Bank of India.

This second missive bore Ralph Pitcher's signature. The naturalist recounted, in rather vague and tangled sentences, that he found himself owing a considerable sum to Darvel the engineer and that, the latter not having been able to compensate the Pole for the material and moral injuries resulting from the breakdown of their partnership, he, Pitcher, was taking the place of his friend and placing at Bolensky's disposal such a sum as might be useful to him.

"I didn't need this," murmured the Pole with emotion, "to know that Mr. Pitcher was a good soul; one would say that these good people have passed the word around to sign these checks directed at me."

While saying this, with a flick of a fingernail he broke the black wax seal of the last envelope.

He was left speechless upon finding in it a third check, this one for ten thousand pounds.

The letter was from Miss Alberte; in a few sentences, none of which would have wounded even the touchiest sensibility, the young woman entreated the engineer to come work for the Teramond Bank, which needed highly competent men for the mining of the gold fields.

Bolensky rubbed his eyes to make quite sure that he wasn't having a waking dream, then he quickly went down the staircase that led to the residence's dining room.

His friends had already taken their places.

"Hurry up then," said the captain, "we were going to start without you."

"I apologize from the bottom of my heart," said the Pole mischievously, "but I confess that I was detained by the gravity of my morning mail.

"Imagine this: I have received, along with a bundle of checks, several highly advantageous proposals."

The three guests lifted their heads as one.

"My dear friends," he continued, placing the three letters and the three checks on the table, "all three of you have had the same generous thought . . . I will be always grateful to you: but it is truly impossible for me to accept . . ."

A discussion began; but despite his opposition, Bolensky did not gain the upper hand.

They forced him to keep the checks and, after they had begged repeatedly, he ended up consenting, with this condition:

"This is veritable moral coercion; but I demand at least that this money be used for the installation of sophisticated equipment for astral photography. It is absolutely essential that we have here the same equipment that I had at my disposal for a few weeks during my stay in Japan."

Miss Alberte smiled.

"It's a bit late for that, Mr. Engineer," she murmured mockingly.

"Why do you say that?"

"Because the equipment you want has already been ordered and is en route!"

At this news, Bolensky could not contain his joy; he forgot for several minutes the battle of selflessness that he was carrying out against his friends.

"All right," he cried enthusiastically, "all is well; we are going to be able to set to work immediately." Then he added with a touch of sadness:

"As long as Robert Darvel hasn't grown discouraged, hasn't stopped sending his signals!"

"As for that, you may be sure," responded Pitcher, "that our friend Darvel has given countless proofs of his tenacity. He knows better than anyone that it is not from one day to the next that his signals may be noticed by the stargazers of Earth.

"The man I know will continue his attempts at inter-astral communication for years if need be.

"He must persevere all the more as he has resolved the two most difficult parts of the problem: he has reached the planet, and he has found the means to make his signals visible."

"How has he been able to do it?" interrupted Miss Alberte.

"I don't know what to tell you; however, from the appearance of the signals—the very clean, luminous lines that he draws on the dark face of the planet—I assume that he has found powerful sources of energy and of light that could hardly be anything but electric."

During this conversation, Captain Wad had remained silent and thoughtful.

"It's a pity," said Ralph, "that we can't make Robert aware that his signals have been noticed."

"Perhaps there is someone," said the officer, "who could do what you suggest."

"Who?"

"The Brahmin Ardavena.

"Unfortunately, since the unexplained catastrophe at the Chelambrum monastery, he has remained buried in a sort of coma. He has become more or less an idiot."

"Who knows?" murmured Miss Alberte.

"We shall see," continued the captain, "but before dealing with him, I believe that there is something more important to do.

"Mr. Bolensky has not yet tried to arrange the famous photographs so as to make a translation."

"How was I supposed to do it?" responded the Pole. "It was impossible!

"The whole time that I wasn't in front of my cameras—I had no time to sleep or eat—I was spied on by the Japanese. I didn't want them to steal my secret.

"All that I could do was number and file the proofs with the greatest care."

"But on the ship?" questioned Miss Alberte.

"That wasn't any easier. I wouldn't have ventured to start such a delicate task in the lack of privacy of a third class cabin, in the midst of crude and brutal émigrés, under the unceasing rhythm of pitch and yaw."

"I understand. But what about since you arrived here?"

"Miss, to be absolutely frank, I didn't dare undertake the reading of the Martian signals, though no doubt it is very easy.

"I feel like I am about to enter like a thief into a mysterious sanctuary, that I am going to learn things forbidden to man, to pick the fruit of the tree of knowledge.

"I tremble at the idea of what those signals—which have crossed thousands of leagues at the astounding speed of a ray of light—will teach me.

"I want you all to be there for the reading of the first message sent from one heavenly body to another, by the genius of man."

Bolensky had pronounced these words in a solemn tone; his emotion, his religious terror, at the threshold of the mystery, took hold of his friends.

"Then so be it!" said Miss Alberte.

"Together, united by the same thought, we will begin the translation of the document.

"But it would be a crime to delay any longer. Why not start today?"

"As you please," answered Bolensky. "For my part, it would not upset me to be delivered from this uncertainty, from these anxieties . . ."

Captain Wad struck a gong and a domestic appeared; then, after a brief command given in Sanskrit by the officer, he came back laden with the case of photographs.

Everyone came closer, driven by a powerful curiosity.

Bolensky trembled a little as he took one of the bundles of proofs and cut the strings that bound it.

But suddenly he let out an exclamation of rage, surprise, and despair.

The proofs, though carefully fixed, now had a uniformly black surface, with not a single detail, line, or mark.

A terrible silence hung in the room for a few moments.

Throats tightened in anguish; all looked on in alarm, incapable of uttering a word, as if lightning, suddenly, had fallen in the midst of them.

Bolensky was livid; perhaps only one of the bundles of proofs had deteriorated thus.

He took up a second, then another, then yet another: all were blackened beyond remedy.

"Only electricity, in certain circumstances, can produce similar effects," Ralph Pitcher murmured.

"But," cried Bolensky, whose despondency was giving way to anger, "my proofs were still intact yesterday evening.

"I can't explain this . . ."

"There's something else," said Captain Wad. "This destruction of the proofs occurring precisely on the day when we need them, in these conditions, can be explained only by malice."

"But," asked the Pole, "who would be interested?"

"Only one man in the world: Ardavena."

"But you said he was mad."

"He must have recovered. He alone possesses the power to produce these fantastic catastrophes.

"But we shall soon find out: the monastery in which he is committed is only a few miles from here, and my automobile will take us there in a quarter of an hour."

Everyone stood; they were eager to finally have the key to the alarming mystery that seemed to be growing increasingly inscrutable the more they strove to penetrate it.

Soon, the captain's car, into which they were crammed willy-nilly, was careering at full speed down a dusty road bordered to the right and the left by forests of tall palm trees.

They were no more than a mile or two from the monastery when Captain Wad, who had taken up his binoculars and was absentmindedly scanning the horizon, threw them down with a shout of surprise.

"What is it?" asked Bolensky.

"I don't know," said the officer with agitation, "but a large cloud of smoke hangs above the buildings and people are running away; a fire has just broken out in the monastery and I have every reason to believe that this phenomenon coincides with the deterioration of your proofs and is related to Darvel's fate."

At a sign from his master, the native chauffeur shifted into third gear; a few minutes later, they stopped in the middle of a horrified crowd, facing the buildings of the monastery from which a high column of flames now shot up, crackling evilly.

At the sight of the resident minister, the Hindus moved respectfully aside and he was able to approach and obtain information about the disaster.

An old Hindu declared that lightning had started the blaze.

"You've got some nerve," replied the captain. "The sky is perfectly clear and blue and there certainly wasn't any thunder. It must have been something else."

"And yet I swear it's the truth, sir," said the old man, "and everyone will tell you the same thing, that we saw a long white flash of lightning and that we heard a dreadful detonation."

The officer, at first incredulous, ended up bowing to the evidence: all the Hindus that he questioned—threatening to flog them if they didn't tell the truth—were unanimous in their testimonies.

Meanwhile, thanks to the presence of the resident minister, help was organized; a battalion of sepoys, rushed in from the neighboring fort, put two pumps into operation.

It didn't take long to gain control of the fire, which, after having consumed the roofs and the warehouses where rice straw was stored, was stopped by the heavy stone walls.

As soon as possible, even before the fire was completely extinguished, the captain and his guests made their way to the cell that Ardavena had occupied in this monastery.

But it was written that on this day they would lurch from one surprise to another.

A sort of circular pit, its edges blackened by flame, was all that marked the location of the old Brahmin's cell, the roof of which had collapsed and burned.

Bits of brain, hideous debris still sticking to the stone, left no doubt as to the fate that he had suffered.

"My friends," cried Captain Wad with a voice quavering with emotion, "some things are now clear to me.

"Lightning did not start this fire.

"It was a fireball!

"And this fireball came without a doubt from the planet Mars."

The officer wasn't wrong.

The meteoric mass, which because of its rapidity and its glow the Hindus had taken for a bolt of lightning, had successively collapsed three solid vaults of stone, passing through them with a frightful penetrating power, and it had struck in its passage the Brahmin squatting on his mat.

Miss Alberte and her companions remained silent. They felt that they had been pulled into a series of marvelous events beyond their control. It was Ralph Pitcher who spoke first.

"We must absolutely find this meteor," he declared, "especially if, as you suppose, it comes from the planet Mars."

"But what makes you believe this?"

"I have all sorts of reasons that I will explain to you.

"You will see that I am not wrong."

Guided by a domestic, they reached the lower levels. The vaults had been pierced by the projectile, which had left a hole as clean as if it had been made by a die-cutter, but they had to descend all the way to the crypt to find the meteor.

At first they saw only a white-hot mass sunk vertically into the ground, which gave off a suffocating heat. But, to the three scientists' great surprise, this bizarre aerolite had a perfectly regular shape—one might have said an elongated olive or an enormous and very short cigar; it wasn't composed of rock or of inert ore, as meteorites generally are.

In spite of their impatience, the captain and his friends had to wait for the object, heated up by the formidable atmospheric friction, to cool down before they could approach it.

Finally, with great effort, thanks to a squadron of sepoys armed with winches, the planetary projectile was lifted from the cavity that it had dug and transported into an interior courtyard. They could then see that it was hollow inside, and that one of its orifices, hollowed like the neck of a bottle, carried the traces of a screw thread and a spring that must have served to secure a hatch.

"My friends," said the captain solemnly and with emotion, "we have before us a fact of capital importance.

"This fireball can only be the projectile that Darvel described so precisely in his notes.

"But," interrupted Ralph, "how then are we to explain that it is empty, and above all that it fell directly on Ardavena?

"Believe me, it is no coincidence."

"Assuredly not," added the Pole, "but will you permit me to give my explanation?"

"As for me," said Ralph, "I don't see one."

"We will probably never have an exact explanation; but let us attempt to assemble the facts.

"For me, one thing that is beyond a shadow of a doubt is that Ardavena had come to be completely cured of his madness; it is he, without any doubt, who destroyed our photographic proofs out of maliciousness or jealousy.

"It is also he who must have made this steel olive come back to Earth.

"It was surely the power of his will that launched it to Mars, and he remained in communication with this piece of metal through the volitive fluid attached to the metal's molecules; just as he had made it leave, he was able to make it come back."

"I don't see it quite that way," objected Ralph Pitcher. "If that was it, he wouldn't have gotten himself killed so foolishly."

"No doubt he didn't consider that the olive, attracted by his volitive energy, would arrive straightaway, with a speed increased by the laws of gravity, to the very source of that energy—that is to say to his own mind.

"As for his intentions, I don't know what to tell you: we mustn't flatter ourselves that we will ever be able to see very clearly in this darkness.

"Perhaps he wanted to deprive Darvel of the vehicle that could facilitate his return to Earth? Perhaps he had established contact with him? . . ."

"I myself believe that we will never know," murmured Captain Wad in a muffled voice. "But I am certain of one thing.

"From now on, I am sure of it, our proofs will no longer be damaged by invisible hands. Ardavena's death frees us from a formidable enemy."

"Provided," murmured Pitcher, "that our friend has persisted with his signals."

"We will know in a few days . . ."

They had to stick to this verdict and return to the residence, to which the metal olive was transported with care. The captain took it upon himself to question some of the servants of Chelambrum who had perhaps had the opportunity of seeing the projectile in Robert Darvel's laboratory.

In the meantime, not two days had gone by before the fragile and costly cameras for interplanetary photography arrived from Karikal in an automotive van.

Bolensky, aided by Ralph Pitcher, spent the entire day arranging them properly on one of the terraces of the residence.

It was not without emotion that Ralph submitted the first plates to the effects of the developing agents.

"There are signals!" exclaimed Captain Wad. "I would have wagered as much, since that rascal Ardavena is dead."

"I hope," said Miss Alberte, very nervous, "that we will not be as guilty of negligence as Mr. Bolensky; I wish to take responsibility for the task of taking down as they appear the dashes and dots that constitute Morse code."

She soberly took her place facing Captain Wad's desk and started to write down the information that Ralph Pitcher slowly dictated to her.

Everyone was filled with anxiety.

Suddenly, Captain Wad who, standing behind the young girl, spelled out the characters as they came, moved forward, prey to an extraordinary agitation.

"My friends," he declared in a solemn voice, "we weren't mistaken in our expectations. The engineer is quite alive and he lives on Mars; we have the honor of recording the first telegram between the two planets . . ."

And he began slowly declaiming the syllables:

RO-BERT DAR-VEL . . .

Communication between Mars and Earth had been established!

XVI

....

Darkness

At nightfall, despite the tears and supplications of Eeeoys and his entire retinue, Robert started into the great tropical forest. Only the vampire, whom he believed he had tamed and who fluttered ponderously before him, went with him.

Well provided with weapons and provisions, he followed the banks of a canal for several hours until, having reached a clearing and now separated from his people, he was abandoned by his guide and attacked by a swarm of Erloor, who swooped in from all parts of the wood.

With the help of a lighter with which he was equipped, he tried to start a fire, his habitual means of defense; but before he was able to, a heavy circular net, a sort of conical cast-net with weighted edges, dropped over him, and in a moment he was bound, muzzled, and carried away.

As he struggled, he was hit in the forehead by one of the stone balls of the net, and he fainted.

When he regained consciousness, he was chained in darkness, and a muffled murmur whispered in his ears; the shadows rustled with the fluttering of wings and warm breath passed over his face. In the distance, he heard the roar of a torrent.

The darkness to which his eyes adjusted little by little was pricked by thousands of glistening eyes, enough to create a phosphorescent haze.

The place where he found himself seemed to him imposing and sinister: it was a spacious cavern, as high as a cathedral, and its craggy walls were covered, like funerary curtains, by the wings of vampires pressing against the rock and so close together that they covered the walls from floor to ceiling.[6]

6 This incomplete fragment is the last known. Robert Darvel, following in his signals the order of events, was not able to explain to us his means of communication. This passage is placed, in the English edition as here, after the account of Miss Alberte and her friends.

Translator's Note

This narrative, having appeared for the first time in the Bulletin of the Anglo-Indian Society, under the title *The Prisoner of the Planet Mars*, was entirely drafted by the efforts of Major Carl Bell, friend and collaborator of Ralph Pitcher, following the notes of this latter, who only organized the interplanetary messages, often too concise, truncated, or abruptly interrupted, which is the only reason that prevented their publication in full.

We will not review the profound sensation produced in Europe and America by *The Prisoner of the Planet Mars*, to such a degree that many people saw this volume as only a work of pure imagination.

French readers will note that, with the drama playing out at once on the planet Mars and on Earth, the setting is sometimes abruptly displaced, at the same time that the reader is forced into certain flashbacks.

Whatever it is about these imperfections that might have shocked English and American readers, we are certain that *The Prisoner of the Planet Mars* will pique the interest and curiosity of the French public all the more since, in spite of the efforts of scientists from Europe and America, the fate of the valiant engineer Robert Darvel still remains a mystery.

The signals were suddenly interrupted, and it was only after three months of helpless waiting—when it became sadly obvious that the engineer Darvel had lost the means of communicating with Earth, as a result of his death or for some other reason—that Miss Alberte Teramond finally consented to the publication of the interplanetary messages, compiled, and sometimes explained by, the learned naturalist Ralph Pitcher.

This catastrophe is all the more unfortunate in that it leaves the scientific world uncertain of the explorer's fate.

Did he tire of sending messages to which no one responded?

Was he deprived of the electrical energy necessary to produce the luminous rays over the expanse of several dozen leagues, which would be nearly impracticable—although not impossible—even for terrestrial industry? Is he dead? Or a prisoner? So many questions, probably forever insoluble.

The most interesting part of his voyage of exploration in the Martian tropics, the narrative of his struggles and of his likely triumph over the Erloor, has not reached us.

Finally, there would have been considerable advantages for science to know the method he used for the luminous signals.

It can be conjectured that, after having been the vampires' prisoner, he ended up learning their language, imposing his ideas on them, and perhaps ruling them.

Perhaps they communicated to him the secrets of some ancient Martian civilization, provided with a knowledge that, if not superior, is at least different from ours.

The creation of shining bands of such sustained intensity and such considerable luminous power presupposes an in-depth knowledge of natural forces.

As for Miss Alberte, on the subject of whom the reader must understand that we are held to the utmost discretion, we cannot communicate any new information.

The young billionairess has withdrawn into complete seclusion.

If the more or less unreliable reports of certain major English or French journals are to be believed, Miss Alberte is preparing, in the greatest secrecy, a grandiose undertaking, with the devoted collaboration of the honorable Ralph Pitcher, Captain Wad, who just recently tendered his resignation, and Bolensky the engineer.

The hostility that official scientists have expressed for interplanetary communications and the tragic or mysterious catastrophes that have followed all attempts of this sort do not permit us to share this news without grave reservations.

THE WAR OF

THE VAMPIRES

PART ONE

....

The Invisibles

I

....

Zarouk

"You wouldn't believe, Mr. Georges Darvel," said the naturalist Ralph Pitcher, "how pleased my friends Captain Wad and Bolensky the engineer will be to see you! They are most impatient to meet you. If you only knew how much trouble we had finding you."

"I still wonder how you did."

"An old letter of yours set us on the right track. We found it in your brother's private papers after the catastrophe at Chelambrum."

"It is the last I wrote to him," murmured the young man sadly. "Since then, I have had no news . . ."

"Don't get discouraged; there is still hope. If it's not already too late, I swear to you, all that human science and wealth can do will be set in motion to save him!

"But let's return to your letter," continued Ralph Pitcher, trying to conceal his excitement. "It had a postmark from Paris but no return address. You spoke of your studies — rather vague information, you must admit; but Miss Alberte insisted on making your acquaintance, and you know that our young billionaire has an altogether Anglo-Saxon resolve.

"Her agents searched every school, placed ever more notices in the papers . . . But without a truly timely stroke of luck, all of that would have been for naught."

"I had finished my exams and was looking for an engineering position abroad and, with a diploma from the Ecole Centrale . . ."

"You have found a position now! But I must bring you up to speed. You know only what the newspapers have written about your brother's extraordinary adventure."

"I have read the translation of the interstellar messages. And I know that Miss Alberte has withdrawn from the world."

"When it became clear that the luminous signals had definitively stopped, Miss Alberte called upon us: myself, Captain Wad, and Bolensky. 'My friends,' she said, 'I am disheartened, but I have not given up hope. Since Robert Darvel found a way to reach the planet Mars, we must find it too. And we shall find it, even if I have to sacrifice my entire fortune.

"'I know I can count on you.'

"And then she added," the naturalist modestly continued, "that nowhere in the world would she find three scientists with such original minds, with a creative faculty more . . .'"

Ralph Pitcher reddened like a schoolboy and became tangled in these laudatory phrases, which he was obliged to address to himself.

"Well," he finished, "you understand that we accepted enthusiastically. It was a unique opportunity."

"Miss Alberte provided us with unlimited credit; she advised us to spare no expense whenever we found something of interest. Few scientists are so fortunate and, from now on, you are one of us! It is a given."

Georges Darvel, red with pleasure, stammered a thanks, which Pitcher cut short with a vigorous handshake.

"That's enough," he murmured. "By partnering with you in our work, we settle a sacred debt to the memory of our friend, the glorious scientist whom we will find again someday, I am certain."

Both of them were deep in thought as they walked in silence under the spreading shade of the cork-oaks, carob trees, and Aleppo pines, which make up in large part the great forest of Kroumiria.

They followed at this moment one of the forest roads that crisscross the wild region between Ain Draham and Chehahia.

So that his new friend could enjoy the beauty of the country, Pitcher had proposed they travel on foot. A pack-saddle mule, laden with baggage and led by a Negro, followed some twenty paces behind.

This verdant corner of arid Tunisia contains some of the most beautiful landscapes in the world.

The forest road, its large blocks of red sandstone covered with a velvety moss, wound through a land of valleys and hills that, around each bend, offered the surprise of a new prospect.

Sometimes a wadi bordered with cactus and tall oleanders would force them to ford its bed strewn with large glistening stones. Sometimes the moors — genuine labyrinths of wild myrtle, arbutus trees, and heather as tall as a man — gave off, under the voracious heat of the sun, a steam of heady scents.

Elsewhere, a Roman ruin hooked its crumbling vault to the side of a hill, and old olive trees, contemporaries of Apuleius and Saint Augustine, thrust their roots between the blocks and shook their spindly foliage, like hair, above the pediment of a temple. Farther along, an enormous fig tree, its trunk bowed by the wind, was itself an entire grove swarming with birds, chameleons, and lizards; and occasionally they would spy, at the very top of the old tree whose gently sloping branches forr'ed easy paths, the horns and beard of a kid eagerly eating figs.

Then the forest would reappear, with pathways that receded into an azure fog and deliciously craggy ravines, which were veritable abysses of foliage.

Every now and again the bright colors of a red beech or Lombardy poplar, with ever-rustling leaves of white silk, would burst through the light-gray foliage and the slight, vaporous silhouettes of the pines and Algerian oaks.

But most enchanting of all were the remains of vineyards reverted centuries ago to their savage state and exploding, from the humid depths of the ravines to the summits of the tallest trees, in a prodigious firework of leafy vines and abundant fruit.

It was a riot of luxuriant foliage, enough to make one believe that the entire earth would one day be overrun by this impetuous upsurge of sap.

The shoots lifted in elegant bridges and scalloped hammocks to an often prodigious height, from which thousands of blue woodpigeons and white-and-pink turtledoves would suddenly be startled into flight in a flurry of beating wings and chirps by the brown shadow of a vulture inscribing great circles in the blue sky.

In swampy areas, herds of small boars fled between the tall lances of the reeds, and the cry of the hyena, which resembles an ironic laugh that continually moves away as one gets nearer, rang out occasionally.

But it must be said that the crowning grace of this virgin forest, of the proud, supple vigor of these never-pruned trees, was the glades of flowers and tall grass and that haunting fragrance of myrtle and oleander, which is like the embalmed breath of the magical forest.

"Look at those vines!" cried Ralph Pitcher with admiration. "Those rootstocks are perhaps fifteen or eighteen hundred years old; in the autumn they are still loaded with excellent clusters; if you pressed them you would rediscover, no doubt, the lost vintages of the decadent Romans, the wines mixed with snow and served to Trimalchio in golden bowls . . ."

Georges Darvel didn't respond at first; his thoughts were far from these classical reminiscences relished by the erudite Ralph Pitcher.

"How then," suddenly asked the young man, "did you come to be in Tunisia? I would have expected to find you in India or England."

"It is precisely to throw the curious off the scent, and also because of the beauty of the locale and the climate, that Miss Alberte chose this little-known country, rarely visited by tourists.

"Here, we are certain that no one will disturb our work with flimsy pretexts: we are sheltered from reporters, photographers, socialites, from all those whom I emphatically call 'time bandits.'

"It has the deep seclusion of an alchemist's laboratory in some abbey of the Middle Ages, but an abbey provided with the most complete and powerful equipment that a scientist ever had at his disposal.

"Once, during a cruise in her yacht, the *Conqueror*, Miss Alberte had the opportunity to visit Kroumiria, and she retained fond memories of the region.

"Some months ago, through the intermediary of her Malta correspondent, she bought the Villa des Lentisques, a marvelous Arabian palace deep in the forest, an extravagance that a Sicilian banker, since incarcerated for being a fence for the Mafia, had the idea of building in this wilderness.

"In any case, you will be able to judge for yourself.

"We have almost arrived. Look a little to your left; that large white structure is the Villa des Lentisques . . ."

"At last I shall see Miss Alberte!" exclaimed Georges Darvel. "And be able to express all my gratitude for her heroic efforts on behalf of my brother!"

"You will see her no doubt, but not today, nor tomorrow. I haven't had the chance yet to tell you that she will come back some time later in the week.

"She left us a fortnight ago; the interests of her mining concerns urgently demanded her presence in London."

"That's a shame," murmured the young man, a little disconcerted.

"While we're on the subject, did you know that the prodigious flow of gold from the mine your brother discovered has never dried up?

"It's as if the Pactolus itself flows into Miss Alberte's coffers! Our laboratory expenses are only a drop of water drawn from this overflowing torrent of wealth."

A strangled cry abruptly interrupted Ralph Pitcher. At the same time, a flock of birds, startled, tumultuously took flight from the nearby trees.

"That's Zarouk, my Negro," murmured the naturalist. "I'll go see. I should say that he is often frightened over nothing."

Zarouk was right in the middle of the path, motionless, as if petrified by fear; his face had gone from deep black to ghastly gray and his contorted features and rigid torso signaled his intense horror.

Georges then noticed that the Negro was blind—his bulging eyes were covered with a white film—but this infirmity didn't make his face at all hideous or repulsive; his forehead was high and domed, his face handsome, his nose slender and straight, and his lips were not so thick as to stamp a bestial expression on his physiognomy.

In the meantime, Ralph approached him.

"What is it then, my poor Zarouk?" he asked affectionately. "I didn't take you to be such a coward! Is there a panther nearby?"

Zarouk shook his head, still too distressed to answer; his limbs were trembling under his burnouse of white wool. With a convulsive hand, he squeezed the bridle of the mule, which, strangely, seemed to share the Negro's fear; it balked and was wracked by a powerful shudder.

"Now that's strange," said Georges into his friend's ear. "And what about the birds that suddenly took flight a moment ago?"

"I don't know what to think," responded the naturalist, glancing around in concern. "Zarouk has obviously sensed some danger, but what? Apart from a few scorpions nestled underground and a few wild cats, the forest of Ain-Draham harbors no harmful animals."

"Aren't there hyenas? . . ."

"They are the most cowardly and fearful of beasts; they never attack people. Zarouk couldn't be frightened over so little."

"Just now you mentioned panthers?"

"They are extremely rare in Tunisia, even in the south; sometimes five or six years go by without a single one being captured.

"Besides, Zarouk, who was born in the Sudan and brought to Gabès by Shambaa caravans as a small child, wouldn't be any more frightened of panthers than of hyenas. It must be something else."

"We'll soon know; Zarouk is starting to recover."

"Well," resumed Pitcher, turning toward the Negro, "will you speak now? You know very well that with us here with you there is nothing to fear.

"Really, I thought you were more brave."

"Master," retorted the Negro in a strangled voice, "Zarouk is brave, but you have no idea. . . . It's horrifying! Zarouk is not afraid of the beasts of the earth or the birds of the sky; but he is afraid of evil spirits!"

"What are you trying to suggest?"

"Master, I swear to you, in the name of the living and merciful God, by the venerable beard of Mohammad, Prophet of Prophets, just now, I was brushed by the wing of one of the djinns, or perhaps Iblis himself! . . .

"The blood froze in my veins . . . I had just the time to pronounce three times the sacred name of Allah, which puts djinns, ghouls, and afreets to flight . . . For one moment, a horrifying face, drawn in lines of fire, emerged from the depths of the everlasting darkness that envelops me. Then it rushed off rapidly, borne by its wings . . . Yes, Master, I swear to you, for one second, I saw!"

"How could you have seen?" interrupted Ralph in a tone full of incredulity. "When we who can see perceived nothing? You have had some hallucination, like those who are intoxicated with *dawamesk* or opium.

"Here, take a swallow of *boukha*[7] to buck you up and forget this silly fright."

The Negro happily seized the flask Ralph Pitcher held out to him and drank in long draughts; then, after a moment of silence:

"I am sure that I did not dream," he said slowly. "You and your friend the Frenchman, you saw the birds take flight and the mule start to sweat and shiver as if a lion were approaching, for they too were afraid.

"Isn't it possible that by the all-powerful will of Allah, the evil spirit became for several moments visible to my dead pupils, so as to warn me of some danger?"

"I still believe that you had a hallucination. In your fear, without perceiving it, you shook the bridle abruptly, which frightened the mule, and at the same moment a vulture might have passed . . ."

Zarouk shook his head without answering, making it clear that Ralph Pitcher's rational explanation had left him unconvinced and that he persisted in his belief in the djinn.

They continued walking, but the Negro drew closer to his two companions, as if he feared the terrible apparition might return and attack.

For his part, Ralph Pitcher was completely at ease.

"Zarouk," he explained to Georges, whose curiosity had been singularly piqued, "is the best and most faithful of servants. His blindness doesn't prevent him from being of great service. Like many of his fellows, he is gifted with an exquisite sense of hearing, smell, and touch.

"In our laboratory, he knows the exact place of every object and can quickly find anything without ever making a mistake or blunder. He even manages to apprehend certain states of the exterior world of which other men ordinarily have a notion only through their eyes. I have not yet been able to explain to myself what elusive notation of sensations aids him, or by what subtle association of ideas he achieves it.

"For example, he will say with certainty that a cloud has just passed over the sun and, if there are many clouds, he can even count them. On hunting parties, we have put a gun into his hand and he has filled us with wonder

---

7   Boukha: a brandy made from figs

at his aim. Wherever he goes, he recognizes without the least hesitation people whom he has met only once."

"All of this is marvelous," said Georges, "but it is not absolutely inexplicable; a great number of similar examples have been cited."

"You will have the leisure to study him yourself. Zarouk is certainly much more amazing than you suspect.

"There are moments when I am tempted to believe that, behind the corneal opacity that covers them, his pupils are sensitive to the obscure rays of the spectrum, invisible to us, to x-rays and perhaps to other, weaker and more tenuous radiances.

"Why, after all, wouldn't such a thing be possible?"

Georges reflected a moment, powerfully intrigued by this audacious hypothesis.

"Why, then," he asked in turn, "haven't you operated on his cataracts?"

"Captain Wad was the first to think of this. Zarouk has always tenaciously refused."

The two friends continued for some time in silence; behind them, the Negro had commenced one of those mournful and interminable chants sung by the camel drivers of the great desert. In spite of himself, Georges was moved by this monotonous tune, in which the same notes repeated indefinitely. It seemed to him to imitate the heartrending moan of the wind in the dismal plains of the Sahara.

"You know," he said to Pitcher, laughing, "what you just told me is hardly reassuring; if Zarouk — like a blind bat that can fly in a straight line and avoid any obstacles — really possesses such finely tuned senses, there must be something real in the apparition that frightened him, even if it is invisible to us."

"Who knows?" murmured the naturalist, lost in thought. "Didn't Shakespeare say that there are more things in heaven and earth than our weak imaginations can conceive of?

"Perhaps Zarouk is one of the precursors of an evolution of the human eye that, in hundreds of centuries, and perhaps much sooner, will perceive radiances that didn't exist in the first ages of the world.

"Already, certain subjects, in a hypnotic state, see what is happening far away or on the other side of a high wall and yet, at the moment when they display this hyperacuity of vision, their eyes are closed.

"The day when science manages to construct a solid theory about it . . ."

Ralph Pitcher didn't finish his thought; there was a new silence.

"What are djinns exactly?" asked Georges abruptly. "I must confess that I don't know the least thing about them. Study of the sciences has caused me to substantially neglect Mohammedan philosophy."

"I could explain it well enough, but Zarouk will tell us about it.

"When it comes to these questions he has an inexhaustible loquacity. Like all the people of the desert, he has an imagination crammed with the marvelous tales repeated around the campfires in every caravan.

"Zarouk!"

"Master," said the Negro, coming forward with an eagerness that had nothing servile about it. "I heard your friend's question. But is it prudent to speak of these terrible beings while they yet may prowl around us?"

"Have no fear. Didn't you yourself tell me that the strength of their wings can carry them hundreds of leagues away in a few hours?"

This thought seemed to bring the Negro much comfort.

"Without doubt," he answered, letting out a sigh of relief, "that is true and I did not lie. And, am I not under the protection of the invincible and merciful God?"

And he continued in a nasal, singsong voice:

"Djinns are invisible spirits who inhabit the space that stretches between the earth and the sky. Their number is a thousand times greater than that of men and animals.

"Some of them are good and some evil, but the latter are much more numerous. They serve Iblis, to whom God has accorded complete independence until the Day of Judgment.

"The wise sultan Suleyman (Solomon), who even Jews and infidels revere, received from God a green stone of dazzling brilliance, which gave him power to command all evil spirits; until his death, they were perfectly submissive to him and he employed them in the building of the temple of Jerusalem; but since his death they have dispersed throughout the world, where they commit all sorts of crimes . . ."

This was a subject upon which Zarouk, like all the Arabs of the desert, was inexhaustible.

Georges Darvel and his friend Pitcher were very careful not to interrupt him and obligingly let him enumerate the various kinds of djinns, afreets, toghuls or ogres, ghouls, and other fantastic beings, all gifted with a power as dreadful as it was marvelous.

In listening, they felt the same pleasure that they had experienced as children hearing the *Thousand and One Nights*.

They were far indeed from the grand scientific hypotheses that they had debated a moment before, and they couldn't stop themselves from smiling at Zarouk's gravity as he reeled off these astonishing fables that he no doubt believed with all his heart.

The Negro, moreover, with the fluency that all Orientals possess for languages, expressed himself despite his barbarisms in very clear French; like nearly all Arabs he was a born storyteller.

Ralph and Georges Darvel were still enthralled by his tales when, coming around a clump of almond and carob trees, they suddenly found themselves before the Villa des Lentisques.

II

························

The Villa des Lentisques

Built in the middle of a deep valley, the Villa des Lentisques rose like an island of white marble from a sea of flowers and greenery. It was a grandiose dream brought to life through the magical power of wealth.

The finest features of the Venetian style—its noble, magnificent lines and brilliant colors—had been harmoniously fused with the Oriental marvels of Arab architecture. Galleries carved *à jour* at great expense by sculptors from Morocco and Baghdad were balanced on slender white columns that stood out cleanly against mosaics that looked like sumptuous brocades and colored bricks that imitated the azulejos of the Alhambra.

The gilded roofs and azure cupolas sparkling in the sun seemed to encircle it with an otherworldly nimbus, with a dreamlike quality.

It was too beautiful to be real; one couldn't help thinking that a gust of wind might dispel the glorious apparition like a mirage of an oasis that haunts the sterile sands of the great desert.

Following Alberte's instructions, the old trees of the valley had been preserved; a single opening—to the north—permitted a glimpse of the yellow sands of the faraway coast and the Mediterranean, a narrow blue band against the deep azure of the sky.

Georges Darvel had stopped in his tracks, caught up by an admiration so deep that it bordered on stupefaction.

The ideal perfection of the Villa des Lentisques was beyond anything he had seen, or even read about, except perhaps Poe's miraculous domain of Arnheim.

"What do you think of our little place?" asked Ralph Pitcher good-naturedly.

"I think," said Georges, "that Aladdin's palace would seem a squalid dump, an abject hovel, next to this villa."

"Let's not exaggerate, my young friend," answered Ralph with an air of false modesty, "but it is true that the Villa des Lentisques unites in one structure the effort and genius of three civilizations.

"In it, the noble elegance of Italy combines with the languid opulence of the Arabs and, to complete the picture, the meticulous British knack for comfort."

"It looks like part of the roof is made of glass."

"Yes, that's our laboratory built on the largest of the terraces; we also installed our telescope in one of the cupolas, all accomplished, I can say, without spoiling the architectural profile of this magnificent residence.

"No one would suspect that this fairytale palace is one of the most formidably armed arsenals of modern science.

"In any case, you will be able to judge for yourself . . ."

During this conversation, the blind Zarouk opened both sides of a tall cedar door with arabesque metalwork, revealing a spacious vestibule paved in mosaic and supported by stucco columns; from the vault hung an ancient Turkish lantern in finely worked copper, whose design was as complicated as a Gothic monstrance.

The vestibule opened by way of a triple oriel onto the patio, a vast interior courtyard planted with orange, lemon, and jasmine and cooled by the spray of a monumental fountain adorned with a bronze nymph.

A cloister with spindly colonnades enclosed the patio and, with its armchairs of Venetian leather and deep couches, provided a convenient shelter from the heat. In the silence broken only by the murmur of running water, it was an ideal spot for meditation and reverie.

A young woman appeared, dressed in raw linen, her ears adorned with heavy rings.

"Chérifa," said the naturalist, "show this gentleman his room and then conduct him to the laboratory, where I will await him. Arrange for our guest to be provided with everything he needs."

Georges looked at the young woman. Her light bronze skin, large black almond-shaped eyes, aquiline nose, and prominent lips and the bluish tattoos that marked her forehead and arms clearly revealed her origin.

She might have been fifteen or sixteen years old; she was among her kind an ideal beauty.

"Chérifa," explained Ralph Pitcher in a low voice, "is the daughter of a nomadic sheik of the Chehahia.

"Miss Alberte cared for her when she had smallpox, one of the illnesses that ravage the Arabs; ever since, she has devoted herself entirely to her benefactress and has never left her side. She is a sort of voluntary slave, a humble friend who has Miss Alberte's complete confidence.

"Chérifa is cheerful, sweet-tempered, charming, and intelligent, and she renders us great service through her constant vigilance and precocious good sense.

"She's an example of what the Arabs could become, if one appealed to their reason and their heart, instead of robbing and mistreating them, which happens unfortunately still much too often."

Georges followed his guide to a tall and spacious chamber on the third floor with delightful Gothic windows of stained glass that opened onto a balcony overlooking the countryside.

He was surprised by the brilliant melding of comfort and simplicity in the room's design. The rounded angles of the walls, tiled with brilliant arabesques, and the gently vaulted ceiling gave asylum neither to dust nor to germs. The drapes of Murano beads filtered the brightness of the light without intercepting it completely. Last of all, the furniture, designed by a student of Walter Crane's, was made of forged copper or porcelain, in the fashion beginning to take hold in the salons of some billionaires.

Many-hued sprays of glass flowers concealed the bulbs of the electric lamps, and a large bookcase housed handsomely bound editions of the latest scientific publications and the eternal masterpieces of poets.

A vast washroom adjoining the bedroom contained all the equipment necessary for hot and cold baths, electric baths, and light baths.

It was the epitome of taste and princely simplicity.

"You'll be comfortable here," said Chérifa with a radiant laugh that revealed her white teeth. "Here is the telephone, and this is the electric button for calling the servants at any hour of the day or night.

"Now, you must be hungry. Wouldn't you like some refreshment?"

"Thank you, but I had rather a large lunch at Tabarka."

"All right. I'll leave you then . . ."

As quick and light as a desert gazelle, whose tender, large, and pensive eyes she shared, Chérifa had already disappeared.

Left alone, Georges Darvel took a bath. The heat and the dust of the road made him particularly appreciate its beneficial effect. He then exchanged his traveling clothes for a pajama jacket and pants and went down to the patio.

There he found Chérifa, who showed him to the laboratory that was the sole thing occupying the largest of the villa's terraces. It was an immense crystal cube formed of five gigantic panes supported by four steel columns and an equal number of girders, entered through a sort of trapdoor inside.

Thick felt curtains made it possible—merely by depressing an electric button—to produce day or night, the brightest light or total darkness, at will.

Although Georges Darvel was familiar with the best-equipped laboratories of Paris and London, he found a profusion of equipment he hadn't the slightest idea how to use or at least that he had never seen before.

There were photographic plates with a surface area of several square meters, mirrors coated with a special silvering that held in focus for several minutes the most fleeting images of clouds and birds.

Gigantic tubes were trained toward the sky with powerful microphones set up to convey the most imperceptible noises of heaven and earth to the ears of the experimenters.

The young man saw even more unfamiliar apparatuses, consisting of lenticular mirrors linked to powerful batteries and to flasks fitted with tubing and filled with liquids of every color.

From the laboratory a spiral staircase led to an annex where cabinets of chemical products, powerful electric ovens, and refrigerators could be found, as well as the richly stocked library of the most rare books of alchemists and Talmudists.

The whole constituted a unique and marvelously complete facility.

Georges Darvel was awestruck as he entered this sanctuary of science, and he remained speechless for some time.

Ralph Pitcher hastened to meet him.

"My dear friend," he said to him, "from this day forward you are one of us. Allow me to present our collaborators, and devoted friends of your illustrious brother, Captain Wad and the engineer Bolensky."

At these words, two individuals in long laboratory coats, who with Zarouk's assistance were decanting the contents of a demijohn into a large glass vat, abandoned their task and rushed forward.

There was a striking contrast between the Englishman and the Pole. The engineer, who was tall in stature and had very light blue eyes and a long, pale blond beard, was affectionate and spirited. All the impulsive aspects of the Slavic character — frankness, loquacity, a quick and bold, even reckless imagination — shone as it were in every word, every gesture.

Captain Wad, of average height with a long, already graying mustache and black, almost stony eyes was stiff, dour. His rare gestures had the precision of an automaton.

He had the look of a very serious man, one who is precise in even his most insignificant words; but under this somewhat dry exterior, the captain was the most loyal and generous of men.

He took Georges's hand with genuine warmth and shook it with eminently British vigor, assuring him of his wholehearted sympathy and devotion.

"You should know, Mr. Darvel," said Ralph Pitcher, "that these are not just empty words. The captain says nothing lightly. He weighs the meaning of his words and he rarely makes such declarations."

The engineer, for his part, was overjoyed and kept staring at the young man who, somewhat intimidated, was effusive in his courtesies.

"It's astonishing" exclaimed the Pole with emotion, "how much Mr. Darvel looks like his brother! It seems to me that I'm seeing him just as he was when we lived together in the Siberian wastes.

"A moment ago, when I first saw him, my heart skipped a beat. Although I had been apprised of his arrival, I couldn't help thinking, for a second, that our dear hero had returned. I thought the explorer of the sky, the conqueror of the stars, had suddenly appeared before me, triumphant!"

There was a moment of silence as the four scientists looked at one other; they had just had the same thought.

"Do you sincerely believe, gentlemen, that my brother is still alive? That he may succeed in returning to Earth?"

"I firmly believe," responded Captain Wad with all seriousness, "that your brother is still alive."

"But, those abruptly interrupted signals," objected the young man ruefully. "I confess, I can't bring myself to share your hope, your confidence . . . I would very much like to be wrong, I swear to you, and yet . . ."

"But the fact that the signals have stopped proves nothing, young man!" interrupted the Pole in a booming voice.

"Our friend could be very much alive, simply without the means to continue his communications with Earth, something that is very difficult, even for us!

"Consider this: Robert Darvel reached the planet Mars safe and sound, and he acquired enough power over the inhabitants to make those luminous lines that we have been able to photograph. Why should he have perished?

"We have no reason to suppose such a thing."

"And yet," the young man objected again, "what about this strange story of captivity among the Erloor, after which the signals no longer appeared?"

"This proves nothing. Robert must have escaped from peril, since he was able to tell us about it.

"He was speaking of a much earlier event."

"Let me add something too," said Captain Wad in turn. "Robert Darvel cannot be dead; there are deep and mysterious causes for the success of such an unheard-of endeavor: it can *not* have been for naught. The conscious force that governs worlds and regulates phenomena with the most rigorous logic cannot have permitted such a voyage needlessly.

"Accuse me if you will of being a mystic, but I believe that it was an *absolute* necessity — I was going to say for all eternity — that Mars and Earth, the two sister planets, enter into communication! Robert Darvel *had* to succeed just as he *has* to return to *Earth*, to enrich it with all the knowledge, all the science, of a new world!

"It's a truth as limpid and as clear to me as one of Euclid's theorems . . ."

Captain Wad, so cold a moment earlier, had spoken these words with such unreserved enthusiasm and warmth that Georges was half persuaded of the providential role attributed to his brother in the destiny of the two planets.

"In any case," added Pitcher, with his habitual aplomb, "we won't wait for Robert Darvel to return; we will join him, and very soon."

"Have you already found a way?" stammered Georges who, little by little, felt the ardent faith of the two scientists winning him over.

"We are nearly there," answered the captain, suddenly pensive. "We are held back now only by some practical details in the construction of our device, quite minor technical difficulties that we are sure to resolve.

"It's a matter of a few weeks.

"I must admit moreover that what I was able to salvage of your brother's notes from Chelambrum has been of enormous assistance."

"I will help you!" cried Georges, his eyes sparkling with joy.

"You are aware," resumed the captain who, absorbed in his thoughts, hadn't heard him, "that all physical, mechanical, or chemical phenomena can be reduced to just one: movement.

"It is now a commonplace truth.

"Heat is a certain mode of movement, just as light is another.

"We see every day movement transformed into heat, heat into electricity, electricity into light.

"It is therefore logical to presume that under certain conditions electricity can be transformed into volitive fluid, into *will*.

"Man will accomplish anything he desires on the day he is able to add to his feeble brain the nearly infinite power of electrical currents, when he is able to charge his nervous system with volitive fluid as one charges a storage battery with electricity.

"Then, he will no longer know fatigue, nor sickness, nor perhaps — who knows? — death.

"He will face no more obstacles; he will be able to do all that he would like!

"Your brother found a way to collect volitive fluid; we have been looking for a way to transform electricity into volitive energy."

"Have you found it?" asked Georges, breathless, filled with wonder, alarmed almost by the grandiose horizons opening to his imagination.

"As I just told you, we are hindered only by some technical details."

"Plus," interrupted the impetuous Bolensky, "we are in a position right now to show you practical results. Our discoveries are not mere theories!

"You may judge for yourself."

The Pole retrieved, from under a bell jar, a strange helmet of glass and copper ending in a bundle of platinum wires connected to a battery.

A slight smile played on Captain Wad's lips as the engineer placed the helmet on his head. Thus attired, the captain rather resembled a deep-sea diver.

"You see," continued the engineer, proceeding with his demonstration, "that at this moment, the current furnished by the battery is being transformed into volitive fluid that is then stored in our friend's brain.

"See how his eyes flash, what a strange expression of calm and might his physiognomy has acquired; it now appears surrounded with a sort of unreal light!

"His will has now been doubled, tripled, multiplied tenfold . . .

"He could order us to do whatever he wished; in spite of ourselves, we would be forced to obey him."

Georges Darvel remained silent; Bolensky took this silence for incredulity.

"You want proof," he said. "The captain will mentally order you to kneel; try to resist him!"

"I would be curious, actually . . ." murmured the young man, steeling himself with all his might.

The captain shot, through his mask, a searing glance.

Georges Darvel felt a sharp burning sensation in the pit of his stomach.

It was no use bracing himself; his face was flushed and his forehead was beaded with sweat as, despite himself, his muscles slackened, and he kneeled.

"It's dreadful," he stammered. "Who could resist such power?"

"Science is supreme," said Ralph Pitcher proudly.

"You understand perfectly well," added the Pole, "that if our friend ordered you for example to take that scalpel from the counter and cut off the head of good Zarouk, who is listening to us from his corner with astonishment, you wouldn't be able to prevent yourself from doing so."

"In fact, as you can see, you have already started to obey the captain's silent injunction."

As pale as death, his teeth clenched, his face tense, Georges Darvel was indeed headed for the knife with stiff, angular movements, the constrained movements of a human marionette.

Letting out a deep sigh, he took the weapon, gripped it convulsively and walked straight to the Negro, who recoiled, somewhat alarmed.

The blade had already been lifted, when a look from the captain stopped the reluctant murderer in his tracks, freezing him in the pose of an ancient sacrificial priest.

Georges's face expressed unspeakable suffering and fatigue.

"I beg you," he murmured, "stop this terrible experiment for a moment . . . What I feel is atrocious . . . It seems to me that another being has settled within me, that I am no longer me.

"I now believe all that I have read about possession and bewitchment . . ."

"With the difference," explained Bolensky, "that these phenomena of domination of one being by another, which used to occur only in rare circumstances and with exceptionally sensitive temperaments, we can now produce whenever we wish, with the greatest ease."

"However," said Ralph Pitcher sharply, "it is not necessary that these experiments, prodigious as they may be, cause you such pain.

"We only wished to persuade you that the possibility of reaching the planet Mars is not some mad dream."

"I am now absolutely persuaded," answered Georges, who was recovering little by little from the effort he had made to resist the all-powerful will of Captain Wad, "nothing should be impossible for you."

"Now," said the engineer, "here's something else. Watch carefully."

He spoke a few words into Zarouk's ear. The Negro tripped an electric switch and a trapdoor installed in the glass roof folded in on itself. Next, the Pole cautiously removed from a case a spiral spindle of glass tapered at both ends.

He gripped it between thumb and index finger and held it before the captain's eyes.

A few minutes passed in the most profound silence; suddenly Bolensky opened his fingers. As rapid as an arrow, the spindle of glass shot up, whistling as it disappeared through the half-open trapdoor.

Georges Darvel was speechless, lost in a world of thought.

Captain Wad, who had just removed the glass helmet, approached him, smiling.

"I see," he said kindly, "that these little experiments — simple laboratory experiments — have made a certain impression on you; but they are nothing, absolutely nothing, next to what we can achieve by the same means."

Georges Darvel bowed respectfully:

"Permit me," he murmured, quite moved, "to thank you once more for the great honor that you do me in making me a partner in your marvelous work."

"I am convinced that you will soon become an invaluable collaborator."

"I will try," the young man said modestly, "although I can't imagine, truly, how an ignoramus of my sort can be useful to scientists such as you."

The captain did not respond to this forced complement. He had liked Georges Darvel from the start. He was secretly persuaded that the young engineer would show himself worthy of his relation to the explorer of the skies, that he was of that race of true researchers who form something like a band of outsiders, whose elect recognize one other by mysterious signs among the unthinking and addled human crowd.

Georges was now carefully examining a statue of black bronze set on an onyx plinth in the center of the laboratory.

It represented an adolescent holding a bell in one hand and presenting tablets with the other. The delicate yet powerful torso had been sculpted in the style of the Italian Renaissance. The pupils, after the manner of the ancients, were represented by sapphires, and the lips, a proud and graceful curve, were slightly open as if the statue was about to speak.

"You are admiring our everyday messenger," explained Ralph Pitcher.

"This masterpiece of French sculpture serves, quite simply, to conceal the apparatuses of a powerful telephonic loudspeaker.

"It is a marvel, a princely gift from Miss Alberte, who paid four thousand pounds sterling for it."

"I have rarely seen anything more beautiful!"

"That's not surprising in the least. This statue is one of the last works of Falguière, the master of elegance. See how the physiognomy expresses so well the anxiety of a messenger bearing news whose nature is yet unknown to him . . ."

At this moment the bell rang.

A clear voice issued from the bronze mouth.

"It is I, Miss Alberte . . .

"I hope at the very least that I'm not interrupting you in the middle of some delicate experiment?"

"Not at all, Miss," answered Pitcher, speaking close to the tablet in the statue's hand. "I trust that you are well, that no misfortune has befallen you . . ."

"Everything is fine. I have finished my business, which, in the end, detained me at Malta not nearly as long as expected.

"The *Conqueror* will be able to set sail as early as tomorrow.

"I hope therefore to be back at the villa in the evening."

"Should we inform Chérifa? I don't think she was expecting such a prompt return."

"She has already been advised, thank you. We have agreed that she will wait for me at Tabarka with the automobile . . .

"But I almost forgot: has Mr. Darvel arrived?"

"Yes, Miss, not two hours ago."

"Tell him how happy I shall be to see him, what pleasure his presence in our refuge gives me.

"Now, farewell, or rather, until tomorrow. I have a crowd of importunate visitors to face and a meeting with my lawyer in a quarter of an hour to discuss the suit that the Transvaal State has suddenly decided to bring against me."

The statue grew silent once again, but Georges remained under the spell of that fresh, musical voice that seemed to still be ringing in his ears many minutes later.

"I wish you could have spoken with her," said the naturalist. "You could have introduced yourself. But she was too busy, as you must have realized.

"In her business travels, she never has a moment's rest.

"One must have an exceptional intellect to get the better of, as she does, all the bandits of international finance joining forces against her billions."

"You will come to appreciate," added Captain Wad, "her intuitive and penetrating intelligence."

"Even in science?" asked Georges.

"Even in science. There are days when she astounds us with the accuracy and the audacity of her insights.

"Without a doubt Miss Alberte is the ideal mate for your illustrious brother, the beloved companion chosen from among all others."

Georges Darvel remained silent. Now that the enthusiasm that the three friends' stupefying demonstrations had excited in him was beginning to wear off, he kept dwelling on the dreadful distance that separated Robert from his old native planet, and doubt began again to infiltrate his thoughts.

III

....

A Meal Worthy of Lucullus

Dinner at the villa was served at precisely six o'clock.

The day was coordinated with an almost bureaucratic or monastic regularity, without which any difficult undertaking is impossible.

At the sound of a gong that, after an Indian custom, announced the beginning of the meal, the four scientists made their way to the large, brightly colored dining room, with walls paneled in Cordovan leather and joists of carved and gilded cedar.

Georges admired the Italian credenzas laden with Benvenuto ewers; vases by Ballin and other masters of the goldsmith's art; precious Wedgwood, Rouen, and Meissen porcelains; gleaming Hispano-Moorish urns; and modern fired stoneware.

There was a prodigious heap of artistic riches, and he was more than a little intimidated by these splendors as he took his place on a luxurious chair encrusted with ebony, mother-of-pearl, and coral, a piece of rare and exquisite bad taste.

The chairs, in the rococo style nearly impossible to find today, had been rescued from the looting of the imperial palace in Brazil.

"You will see," said Bolensky, who had taken the seat next to Georges, "that this rather archaic splendor is in no way incompatible with the refinements of modern comfort.

"Observe that gilded wheel that turns above the Venetian chandelier with the multicolored blossoms."

"A fan, no doubt," murmured the young man.

"It is indeed a fan, yes, but not one of those ineffectual devices that do nothing but stir up polluted air and promote the spread of germs with no real benefit to hygiene or health.

"Each of the spokes of that wheel dispenses frigid air from a flask of liquid oxygen inside it.

"On even the hottest of days, here the air is pure and fresh.

"Moreover, dinner is served automatically, and the wines, in buckets of ice, rise directly from the cellar to the table by means of a special small elevator. That silver oval that appears to be a hotplate is nothing but its platform. Dishes arrive hot from the kitchens in the same way, at the precise moment when they are at the height of their flavor."

While the Pole was giving these explanations, Georges absentmindedly skimmed the menu in front of him.

The classics of French haute cuisine mingled with refined exotic delicacies, such as pâté of moray eel with *terfas*, or white Tunisian truffles, curried pheasant, blackbirds with myrtle, and other gastronomical rarities.

"This is, certainly, a meal worthy of Lucullus," said Georges mechanically.

Pitcher was just then offering the young man some slices of *bottarga* that were to be followed by an Italian *frittura* of calamari and giant prawns.

"You won't believe how right you are," he said, laughing. "We have this very day one of the favorite dishes of the famous gourmand: tongues of *phoenicopteri*, or, to be more modern, the tongues of pink flamingos, for which, as you know, the Romans paid a king's ransom."

"This delicacy must indeed cost an incredible amount. The flamingo is both very rare and very difficult to kill. I read that even the Arabs themselves, skillful marksmen as they are, only rarely bring one down."

"You're quite right, but a few days ago, an entire flock of flamingos exhausted by a gale descended on one of the ponds in the forest. Hunters killed some thirty of them, which Mr. Frymcock, our chef, hastened to buy.

"He has, in these matters, an impossible erudition.

"He knows Carême's books on the cuisine of antiquity by heart and I would not be surprised if he himself one day translated *De re coquinaria*, the gourmand Apicius's famous treatise."

Pitcher had spoken these words in an enthusiastic tone, proving that, though a scientist, he was not at all indifferent to the pleasures of the table.

"Let's hope," replied Georges, laughing, "that he doesn't get it into his head to serve us, like Lucullus, nightingale tongues sprinkled with pearls and diamonds."

"He is quite capable of such a thing. He is someone you must not challenge to any eccentricity.

"Do you know that one day he organized a shark fishing party with the sole goal of procuring one of their fins, which are one of the indispensable ingredients in the preparation of the Chinese delicacy bird's nest soup!"

"This Mr. Frymcock must be no ordinary man.

"What you've told me makes me very much want to make his acquaintance."

"This is easily done: like many artists, Frymcock is most vain; a well-turned word of praise flies straight to his heart.

"His story, moreover, is far from ordinary, and I don't believe I'm being indiscreet by sharing it with you.

"Frymcock is the only son of a genuine lord from Sussex. He was an excellent student at Oxford and no one doubted that he would one day become a celebrated chemist.

"By the age of twenty, he had made a name for himself with original articles published in special compilations.

"Then, old lord Frymcock died unexpectedly and his son found himself heir to a colossal fortune.

"The first use that he made of his wealth was to give a colossal banquet for thirty of his friends; there were murmurs in the British press for quite some time about this extravagance without precedent in the annals of gastronomy.

"The meal was served in a vast hall transformed for the occasion into a garden filled with the rarest flowers and shrubs.

"Magnolias, roses, jasmines, and lilacs provided shade for the table. Birds from the islands and butterflies from the tropics had been released by the hundreds in these enchanted groves.

"The young lord wanted the Sardanapalian meal that he offered his friends to be an exquisite delight for all the senses.

"No expense was spared in the pursuit of this goal.

"A large orchestra concealed in the foliage played a suite of compositions specially written by the most illustrious musicians to accompany each of the dishes on the dazzling menu."

"I don't entirely understand," said Georges Darvel.

"I will explain: for example, the green rye soup was accompanied by a delicious pastoral for flute, guitar, and oboe.

"The composer had delightfully evoked the awakening of spring on the Russian steppes, the rye billowing like the sea beneath the April breeze, and the unchanging songs of the muzhiks celebrating this renewal with the strumming of balalaikas.

"The lobster à l'américaine began with Breton bagpipes and ended with "Yankee Doodle" accompanied by trumpet and banjo, all of it interwoven with and sustained by the powerful voice of the organ, imitating the whistling of the wind and the roar of the storm."

"And the plum pudding?" asked Georges, laughing.

"You shouldn't laugh," rejoined the naturalist gravely. "I can assure you — I was one of the fortunate guests at this feast — that the effect of these musical pieces was more magnificent and moving than you can imagine . . .

"The plum pudding was accompanied by a mellifluous Christmas carol, in which could be found the themes of "God Save the King" and the touching romance "Home, Sweet Home."

"Each dish was in addition presented by an ingeniously symbolic procession.

"Some Romans of the decadent period, preceded by lictors and eagles, carried the monstrous turbot dear to Domitian, and Gothic ladies the venison tournedos, announced by a sounding of horns.

"Even the sweets and cakes gave an excuse for a parade of young Parisian girls with mischievous, fresh faces dolled up with rice powder.

"An elephant's trunk, in a headily spiced sauce, was served by a black monarch with a cortege of savage splendor.

"The most lavish sets in the theater pale in comparison to the Oriental splendors that accompanied the coffee and liqueurs.

"In addition, on a stage placed at the back of the hall, a succession of ballets emphasized for the eyes the nonetheless quite clear meaning of the music.

"I won't even mention the wines; to touch on this one subject would require an entire volume."

"This incomparable feast lasted a day and half of a night; this period of time, by all appearances considerable, seemed to us all hardly sufficient, so rapidly did it pass."

"Only one thing puzzles me," objected Georges, "and that is that the guests were able to eat and drink for such a long time without feeling the unhappy effects of gluttony."

"This had been provided for. Next to each guest, the Amphitryon had placed a small flask filled with an elixir of his own invention.

"A few drops of this liqueur, no doubt made up largely of pepsins, sufficed to greatly accelerate one's digestion and entirely restore the appetite in a very short time."

"Even if we accept that, this miraculous elixir must not have stopped the fumes of the excellent wines from going to your head?"

"You couldn't be more wrong; during the entire meal, everyone remained wonderfully cheerful and entirely composed.

"No brutish drunkenness disturbed that beautiful gastronomic solemnity, and this also thanks to another of Mr. Frymcock's discoveries."

"Could he have found a way to suppress the effects of alcohol?"

"Almost. Here's how: it's a well-known fact in tropical countries that the ingestion of a large quantity of pure alcohol is enough to heal the bite of serpents.

"Beginning with this fact, Frymcock reasoned that the reverse must be true. From the venom of certain cobras, he concocted a serum that had the property of making the body momentarily resistant to the consequences of alcoholic intoxication.

"Tell me again that he's not a genius!"

"I wouldn't think of it; but I am curious to know the rest of his adventures."

"I was absent for a time, traveling in India as I have no doubt told you. When I returned, young Lord Frymcock was completely ruined. After the banquet that I attended, which had cost no less than a million, he had organized others. In no time at all, his inheritance had evaporated in the smoke of his kitchens.

"There is more: spineless slanderers spread a rumor that, at one of these feasts, he had served to his guests the thighs of a young negress in a Yambuya sauce for which a well-known explorer had given him the recipe.

"I am certain that our friend was innocent, but people were outraged and there was a general outcry against him. He was jailed under an accusation of cannibalism and had great difficulty obtaining an acquittal.

"When he left prison, the friends he had so thoroughly regaled turned their backs on him, and the populace hounded him, calling him a cannibal.

"When I ran into him again he was seriously contemplating suicide.

"I comforted him with kind words and, convinced that this eminent gastronome would be a precious acquisition for Miss Alberte, I told her the whole story.

"She laughed until she cried, and a few days afterward, as I had hoped, she hired young Lord Frymcock at princely wages.

"He has free rein, spends as much money as he pleases, and we eat divinely as a result . . ."

"Hold on," interrupted Bolensky, leaning toward one of the windows, "there he is now, crossing the patio."

Georges Darvel rushed to the window, expecting to see some spirited and jovial character like Cruickshank's caricatures of certain potbellied commodores.

He saw instead a long, gaunt, and wan being, with thin lips and a melancholy face, walking with measured steps, as though troubled by some grave concern.

"He doesn't at all correspond to the idea you had of him, does he?" said the Pole. "He looks like a cross between a splenetic lord and the pierrot of macabre pantomimes.

"In fact, he has a merry disposition and is a good companion, in spite of his demeanor."

Georges returned to his seat, promising himself to get to know the extraordinary lord cook at the first opportunity.

He then noticed that Captain Wad had still not touched any of the delicacies that Pitcher and Bolensky had nearly polished off.

The captain sustained himself in a most bizarre fashion.

A large platter loaded with countless miniature flasks sat in front of him, next to a dish filled with a pink jelly and a carafe filled with a violet liquid.

The captain would take a bit of jelly, add to it a drop from one of the flasks, and swallow it all with gusto. From time to time, he refilled his glass with the violet liquid, returning to the mysterious flasks before quenching his thirst.

Georges Darvel observed this merry-go-round with bewilderment.

The captain, observing this, said, "I see that my way of eating intrigues you; there is, however, nothing strange about it. I am simply more logical.

"I eat as everyone will eat, without any doubt, in a century or two, perhaps well before that.

"This pink jelly is a complete food, chemically prepared, containing only the nitrogen and carbon that the body requires with none of the useless or harmful materials contained in animal or vegetable substances."

"A pitiful delicacy," the young man couldn't resist saying. "I must confess that I prefer Mr. Frymcock's sophisticated menus."

"You could be mistaken: with these flasks, I give my *vitalose* — that's the name of the complete nutrient — whatever flavor I desire."

Georges read the labels with astonishment: essence of trout, essence of *pré-salé*, essence of partridge, essence of salmon, essence of almonds, and so on . . . Every possible delicacy was encapsulated there, quintessenced in several drops of perfume.

"Here," continued Captain Wad with a tranquil smile, "would you like to taste pheasant wing?"

And he offered the young man a spoonful of jelly on which he had let fall a drop of essence.

With a grimace of hesitation, Georges Darvel swallowed the suspect jam and was obliged to admit that the illusion of flavor was complete.

"In the same way," resumed the captain, "I give at will to this violet liquid the taste of whatever vintage I please."

"You must be very proud of such an advance beyond ordinary mortals."

"I take no vain pride in it, believe me.

"It is, to tell the truth, an experiment that I am conducting on myself. I am persuaded that such a diet must have a beneficial influence on the body.

"With a system of nutrition so complete and yet so condensed, the role of the stomach is reduced to next to nothing, it becomes useless; intrepid surgeons have already proven many times over that one really has no need of it.

"I believe that in several thousand years, by means of a gradual transformation, man will be freed of his cumbersome digestive apparatus, no longer of any value, and since he will hardly make use of his arms and legs anymore . . ."

"Do you mean to suggest that in the future man shall become in some measure a purely spiritual being?"

"No, but his brain will attain a considerable size and will substitute for the other organs . . ."

The conversation had now returned to scientific terrain. All took part in it with animation; Georges Darvel was able to prove to his new friends that he possessed extensive and solid knowledge in all branches of learning.

Then they talked at length about Robert. With an emotion that he didn't try to hide, Georges recounted the kindness his older brother, whom he saw only at long intervals, had shown him.

As soon as he had earned a little money, he had placed in Georges's name a small sum sufficient to permit him to finish his studies, and he had never stopped watching over him from afar with the most lively solicitude.

"Robert," said the young man, "successfully completed a superhuman undertaking that will make our name eternally glorious. But I have to tell you that I would renounce all that glory to have my brother among us once again."

"Man of little faith," shouted Bolensky excitedly, "didn't I tell you that we shall find him again! You have seen what we can do! Can you still doubt us?"

"I know," replied Georges swiftly, "that if a plan as fancifully audacious as this one can be successfully completed, only you can do it. Forgive me that moment of discouragement."

"Don't apologize. I know better than anyone these alternations of hope and uncertainty. But you still know only a slim portion of our discoveries . . ."

"Let's go see the planet Mars!" interrupted Pitcher abruptly.

"Just what I was thinking," murmured Captain Wad.

A few moments later, all four stood on one of the upper terraces of the villa, under the velvet blue sky bejeweled with stars.

All around them, the huge forest rustled, pale silver and blue in the dusk, refreshed by the evening dew that it seemed to imbibe avidly. After the oppressive heat of the day, there was something like a shiver of well-being in the song of the nocturnal leaves, with a great stillness barely disturbed here and there by the laugh of a hyena or the baying of a dog in one of the *douars* lost in the bush.

No cloud obscured the still, dazzling sky, in which the red planet seemed to shine with particular brilliance, distinguishing itself clearly from the other heavenly bodies.

For a long time, they contemplated it in silence, while at that very moment Robert Darvel may also himself have been observing Earth, which, for him, was nothing more — as Mars for them — than a small twinkling light in the immensity of the heavens.

All at once, Georges stretched out his hand.

"A falling star!" he cried. "There's another and another."

"It's a veritable display of celestial fireworks!"

Soon they were falling by the dozen, tracing a brief line of flame before disappearing.

"In my country," said the Pole, "the peasants believe that they are souls delivered from purgatory making their way to paradise."

"The truth," said Georges, "is just as poetic. The falling stars that one observes at any given moment are fragments of old, shattered stars that have been wandering for years, for centuries perhaps; attracted by another force in the infinite dark of interstellar space, they end up falling into the sphere of terrestrial attraction. In the friction of our atmosphere, they become incandescent, which is why they are taken for stars; in reality they are simple bolides."

"Who knows," said Pitcher. "Perhaps one of them has been hurled from one of the volcanoes of Mars?"

"Why not?"

The discussion of bolides continued.

Why couldn't man travel from star to star, since these inert masses manage to do it? Hadn't some been found that weighed as much as four hundred kilograms, still intact, neither disintegrated nor melted by the terrible friction of the atmospheric strata?

Isn't this one more proof of the possibility of interstellar travel? The day man finds a way to animate some sort of projectile with sufficient initial speed, the problem will be solved.

Hearing these hypotheses deduced with such inescapable logic, Georges started to hope again.

The four scientists didn't part until very late. In spite of all his concerns, once Georges had returned to his room he quickly fell asleep. He dreamed that his brother was on his way back to Earth in a fantastic chariot, harnessed to falling stars, and laden with Martian curiosities.

Eventually fatigue overcame the latent work of his cerebral cells, and he slept without dreaming again until morning.

IV

·····················

The Invisible Being

Georges Darvel awoke in excellent spirits. It seemed as if his doubts, uncertainties, and discouragements had slipped away under cover of night.

His well-rested brain benefited from that lucidity, that clarity of thought that is characteristic of intellectual health.

He felt, also, capable of adding to the treasure trove of discoveries, of demonstrating that he was the brother of the inspired explorer of the sky, as much by intellect as by flesh and blood.

Reflecting on his ample material security and, thanks to the generosity of Miss Alberte, the ease with which he could henceforth work, he felt a deep debt of gratitude. He was firmly determined to show himself worthy of the good fortune that had come his way.

In this state of mind, at a very early hour, he made his way to the laboratory; there he found Captain Wad, already at work in the company of Zarouk.

The Negro seemed to have completely forgotten his terror of the previous day and he greeted the young man, from the doorway, with typical Oriental grandiloquence.

As he subjected Georges to a sort of open-ended examination of his practical knowledge of physics, chemistry, and above all radiography and cosmography, the captain shared some of his secrets.

In his attempts to solve the mystery of Robert Darvel's disappearance, he had made some interesting discoveries; this largely explained why their interplanetary expedition was not yet ready.

Georges worked with determination and enthusiasm throughout the day, astonishing the three scientists with the lucidity of his insights and the clarity with which he summed up the most perplexing questions.

At the same time, he demonstrated his skillful mastery of experimentation and of the latest laboratory practice, without which no scientist is truly complete.

That day, there was a dreadful hot spell. The heat was blazing, suffocating, and they had to make extensive use of the liquid air ventilators in order to produce a tolerable atmosphere.

In the middle of the afternoon, as Captain Wad was explaining one of his discoveries to Georges, they were witness to one of the strangest phenomena ever recorded by science.

"Observe this glass vat," he said. "The liquid it contains has the property of making certain imperceptible rays visible to our eyes as they pass through it; for example, it permits us to see x-rays very clearly . . ."

The captain's demonstration was abruptly interrupted.

Zarouk, who happened to be standing behind Georges Darvel at the time, had just let out a dreadful cry.

"The djinn! The djinn!" he babbled in a hoarse voice.

With a horror-stricken gesture, he pointed to the glass vat, whose limpid contents seemed agitated by a sort of eddy.

Georges saw that his face had once again turned that ashen gray he had observed the day before that is an indication of extreme terror in people of his race.

The four scientists looked at one another in astonishment.

The Negro retreated as far as he was able; his frizzy hair stood on end in twisted locks; his sightless eyes rolled upward, as if they wished to leap from their sockets, almost as if they were mounted on mobile stalks like those of certain crustaceans.

"Master! Master!" murmured his white lips.

"What is it, ninny?" cried Ralph Pitcher. "Out with it! Are you losing your mind?"

But the Negro appeared to be paralyzed. His tongue was stuck to the roof of his mouth in unholy terror and he was mumbling incoherently.

"Come now, explain yourself!" resumed the naturalist, more gently. "Tell me, what has frightened you so? I have already explained that you have nothing to fear . . ."

Zarouk shook his head desperately in disagreement.

With his legs wobbling beneath him, the Negro, as if impelled by some unseen force, continued to back away slowly from the crystal vat, which was blazing at that moment with the brightness of the sun.

"He's seeing things, I tell you!" muttered Bolensky, shrugging his shoulders in agitation.

It must be said that patience was not one of the Pole's strong points.

"That's enough!" said Pitcher, grabbing him with both arms.

The naturalist's face was flushed with emotion.

"How do we know," he added, lowering his voice, "that this blind man, so differently disposed than us, has not seen a being that our pupils, accustomed to the coarse light of day, are not delicate enough to perceive?

"I have often thought that since there are x-rays, why couldn't there also be x-beings, invisible beings?

"It's a daring but defensible hypothesis . . ."

Not waiting for another word, Captain Wad rushed to an optical device he had built specifically for the study of x-rays that happened to be trained at that very moment on the glass vat.

The silvering of the mirrors, formed of several superimposed layers, was capable of vibration as if it had been formed of nerve cells, and it was complemented by a system of plates coated with substances more sensitive to luminous rays than the most delicate photographic devices.

"If it were possible . . ." stammered Ralph Pitcher.

"We shall see," said the captain in a voice trembling with emotion.

And with a flourish, he pressed an electric button.

In an instant, every corner of the vast glass enclosure of the aerial laboratory was thrown into total darkness.

With his eye glued to the lens, the captain peered through his device.

But, despite his scientific zeal, despite his satisfaction in seeing one of his boldest scientific hypotheses proven, he recoiled in terror, trembling uncontrollably, his heart frozen with dread.

Ralph Pitcher, who followed immediately after him, showed no more sangfroid. He leapt backward with as much haste as if he had stepped on a snake.

At that moment a crystalline voice rang out from the telephone loudspeaker:

"It's Chérifa."

"What do you want, my child?" answered the captain in a strangled tone. "We're busy at the moment, very busy . . ."

The captain was caught up in one of those thrilling instants where a scientist sees and hears nothing.

"Mr. Frymcock wishes to speak to you," repeated the child.

"I don't give half a damn about Frymcock!" he replied with anger. "And I don't have time for kitchen talk . . .

"Tell him to come later, I can't deal with him right now! He will have to wait! Not now . . ." And, without awaiting Chérifa's response, the captain abruptly cut off the call.

During this brief exchange, Georges Darvel had taken his turn in front of the lens. What he saw explained the horror that had seized Captain Wad and the naturalist.

A monstrous creature floated motionless in the phosphorescent liquid of the vat, like an octopus concealed in its cavern or an enormous eye deep within its socket.

It was a grayish mass, barely distinguishable from the shadows by a slight phosphorescence. It had large pupilless eyes, no ears, no nose, and a small, bright red mouth.

"To hell with these interruptions!" shouted the captain. "We never get a moment's peace!"

Its large head, maybe three times the size of a human head, had a large, prominent forehead.

It lacked a body; in its place, at the base of this gelatinous mass swarmed bundles of feet, hands, or suckers—it was difficult to tell which.

Moreover, this nightmarish creature seemed indifferent to the presence of those around it; it must have been unaware of their existence.

After recoiling instinctively, Georges had the courage to take a second look at the monster; this time he made out, on either side of the head, what looked like two dirty white scraps of cloth, which must have been folded up wings, that recalled a hideous butterfly torn from its cocoon before its time.

Georges gave a shiver of disgust and horror as he thought that it was no doubt this terrifying larva blind Zarouk had taken for a djinn when it brushed past him in the forest of Ain-Draham.

Ralph Pitcher then took the young man's place before the lens.

Breathless and with beads of sweat on his forehead, the naturalist was caught between delirious elation and overwhelming repulsion, unable to take his eyes off the monster, the sight of which, so to speak, hypnotized him.

But at the same time he experienced a bitter disappointment.

Were these the invisible beings, the x-beings of which he had so often dreamed, that he had pictured as gracious as elves and undines, with a vaporous and mystical beauty?

He felt a rush of nausea.

So it was these revolting creatures, these abominable, demon-faced abortions, that haunted the depths of the sky and the sea, imperceptible to man.

The four scientists had had the same thought: they remained silent, in the shadows barely lit by the pale fluorescence from the glass vat. They almost regretted having lifted a corner of the veil that hides from us the mystery of things.

Bolensky alone searched, without success, for some way to capture the strange apparition.

Suddenly, there was a quiet knock at the door. And then another.

"Who is it?" asked Ralph Pitcher.

"It's Mr. Frymcock," answered Zarouk in a cracked voice.

"Well in that case, be quick and open the door for him so that we may know what he wants. I shall get rid of him quickly."

While giving this order, Pitcher had pressed the electric button and the felt curtains retreated into their recesses; light instantly flooded the room from every direction, replacing the gloom; it was blindingly bright.

All who had observed the scene turned as one toward the glass vat.

Now, it no longer appeared to hold anything but a perfectly limpid liquid, in which the rays of the sun seemed to make fistfuls of opals and diamonds sparkle . . .

In the meantime, Mr. Frymcock, smartly attired in a khaki-colored suit, had entered and made his way to the middle of the laboratory. A cavalier smile enlivened his long, melancholy clown's face.

"Gentlemen," he said courteously, "pardon me for disturbing your learned experiments, but I felt I must inform you that Miss Alberte will not return until quite late tonight instead of this evening as she had hoped.

"I have just received a telegram from Malta; Miss Alberte didn't have the time to telephone herself."

As he spoke, the lord cook had unconsciously made his way to the glass vat and absentmindedly raised his right hand above the limpid liquid to gaze at the reflection of the rings on his fingers . . .

"Keep back! . . ." bellowed the Pole. "Get back in the name of God! You have no idea! . . . You don't understand . . ."

The warning came too late; the horrible monster seized him, and Mr. Frymcock's hand and wrist plunged into the liquid.

Eyes wide with fright, the poor man struggled, calling for help in a hoarse voice; he was unable to free his hand and already a cloud of blood was staining the liquid.

His face was suddenly livid; his eyes expressed a terror approaching madness.

Recovering from their initial astonishment, Georges and Bolensky rushed forward; using all their strength, they managed to wrest the victim away from the hideous embrace.

Nearly immediately, the water of the vat began to boil; drops leapt, spattering and splashing. A barely visible form, like the shadow of a wisp of smoke, crossed the laboratory and disappeared through the open trapdoor at the apex of the glass ceiling.

With much-appreciated speed, Zarouk dashed forward and pressed the button that closed the trapdoor.

There was a general relief. Every chest breathed a little easier.

"At last it is gone!" cried Pitcher joyfully.

"We have done something foolish," replied Bolensky, still following his initial idea. "We should have captured it. It was a unique opportunity! We will regret not having taken advantage of it."

"You may be right," murmured Captain Wad. "We lacked the sangfroid, and you above all; but there is no use railing about what has passed.

"We should rather see to poor Frymcock, who seems to me in an extremely sorry state."

Both of them approached the lord cook. Georges Darvel and Pitcher were administering smelling salts, and he was recovering little by little from the terrible jolt he had experienced.

They then noticed with surprise that the victim's hand and wrist were covered with little red wounds all along the lines of his veins.

"If we had not come to his aid, Frymcock would have been bled alive, as if he had fallen into the tentacles of an octopus."

"So! How do you feel?" asked Georges.

"Well, sir," murmured the cook with a sigh, "I've never felt better . . ."

Then he added in a thoughtful tone:

"That, however, is an animal I have not yet had the opportunity to taste . . ."

"Ah," said Ralph Pitcher, laughing, "his love of the culinary art is returning; he will be all right. I was afraid for a moment that fear had driven him mad. I'm delighted to see that isn't the case.

"Have no fear, Mr. Frymcock. If you ever capture one of those monsters, we will permit you to prepare it in whatever sauce you please, although, for my own part, I have no desire to eat that repugnant beast."

During this exchange, the captain washed the wounds with a potent antiseptic and quickly bandaged the wounded man's hand and wrist.

As one might suppose, once the lord cook had withdrawn, none of them dreamed of continuing the work they'd begun. They had not yet recovered from the extraordinary event that they had just experienced.

As their initial terror subsided, scientific zeal took its place and they bitterly deplored—as Bolensky had foreseen—not having captured a creature that had not yet been classified among terrestrial fauna.

They questioned Zarouk, but the Negro, who had not yet recovered, could offer only obscure and vague responses; he remained persuaded that he had come face to face with the evil genies of Oriental legend.

Captain Wad came to think that there could be a basis of truth in all those tales: the fairies, kobolds, and will-o'-the-wisps of folklore, those fantastic beings found in the traditions of all peoples, were perhaps only an invisible race that had until now evaded the investigations of science.

It wasn't absurd to suppose that some organisms might have the same properties as certain luminous rays and be invisible to our eyes.

They were forced to admit that Zarouk's eyes, protected by his blindness from the brutality of light, possessed an exquisite sensitivity and received immediate impressions from radiances that the most complicated apparatuses barely manage to reveal to us.

But this time, these hypotheses were supported by an event, an undeniable event had taken place in the presence of serious witnesses and had left material traces.

V

....

The Catastrophe

In their customary place on the terrace overlooking the valley, Georges Darvel and his friends continued during the meal the discussion that had captivated them concerning the strange incident of that afternoon.

In the course of the conversation, Georges learned all about his companions' various discoveries that had not yet been made public.

Captain Wad had discovered z-rays, which, ever since, have permitted the exploration of mines through many kilometers of geological layers; thanks to this discovery one can now explode a powder magazine or incinerate a fleet from unthinkable distances.

Bolensky the engineer had perfected the *telephote*, which is for the eye what the telephone is for the ear, surpassing the wonder of magic mirrors that allow one to see those who are absent no matter how far away they may be.

He had also devised aerostatic medical sanatoriums located above the clouds, where in a chemically pure atmosphere saturated with vivifying ozone most illnesses can be cured in a matter of days.

Ralph Pitcher had grappled with the problem of wireless energy; he was on the cusp of finding the means to transport electric currents over great distances, without the intermediary of any conductor, as the telegraph and the telephone presently use. The glorious culmination of this research will revolutionize all the sciences; inaccessible waterfalls, even the power of tides and hurricanes will be at our disposal; the batteries of airplanes and submarines will be able to be charged at a distance effortlessly and instantaneously.

Despite his admiration for these brilliant discoveries, Georges Darvel couldn't help thinking that if they had focused their efforts they would have successfully completed the exploration of Mars long ago.

With the indiscretion of youth, he made this reflection aloud. Pitcher was the one who took it upon himself to reply.

"My dear Georges," he said to him, "you sound like a child. Human knowledge is a whole of which the parts are closely linked one to another. One cannot control the process of discovery. Like a miner in his tunnel, the scientist is obliged to follow the vein of new truth that is offered to him, and it is much more our discoveries that lead us than we who lead our discoveries."

"Trust, in addition," added Captain Wad calmly, "that the exploration of Mars is no worse off for this.

"On the planet where we will land, science is the most formidable weapon in our earthly arsenal . . ."

At this point, the conversation quite logically turned to the means of making oneself invisible.

The captain modestly confessed that he had wrestled with this strange problem in the past.

"The chimera of invisibility," he said, "has haunted the human mind forever; for me, this is proof that it is possible.

"All that man dreams—and even *all that he can clearly envision*—is realized sooner or later.

"It is contrary to reason to think that our mind can conceive of a thing that might never exist.

"From the dawn of history, in old Egyptian and Sanskrit myths, one already finds gods and magicians who appear or disappear at will.

"Ancient Greece has the fine fable of Gyges's ring that one can read in Herodotus; Arab and Persian tales are full of similar stories.

"Even today, this dream has preoccupied poets and novelists."

"Have you had any concrete success?" asked Georges with some skepticism.

"No. But I am convinced it is possible, and I have recorded a large number of facts concerning this hypothesis to which today's events give new solidity.

"In fact, if nature has created invisible beings, there is no reason why we should not manage to uncover this secret.

"Without mentioning the miracles of the Hindus I have witnessed, in certain nervous afflictions—I'm speaking not of madness but only an excited sensitivity—often the patients have been brushed or even jostled by beings that are quite palpable but *invisible*.

"How do we know that what we call hallucination isn't simply a more subtle reality?"

"What if we went back to the laboratory?" interrupted Bolensky suddenly. "It's oppressively hot here; the liquid oxygen will at least give us a little cool air.

"A terrible storm must be on the way; my nerves are as tense as fiddle strings."

"Let's go inside," murmured the Captain. "I've been feeling apprehensive ever since the sun went down."

At that moment a great silent flash of lightning rent the heavens, revealing a gathering chaos of tormented black clouds with livid edges, like madly tortured mortuary velvet.

The landscape, with its jagged, red peaks and the pale line of the sea, was visible for an instant before it was again plunged into darkness.

A steam heavy with the scent of foliage and flowers was rising from the forest; there wasn't a breath of wind; nature seemed exhausted; the silence was broken only by the barking of jackals and the hooting of nocturnal birds of prey, which acquired a plaintive and heartrending quality in the despondent gloom.

"Yes," repeated Ralph Pitcher after a moment of silence, "let's return to the laboratory; I don't know why, but I feel very uneasy . . . If I were superstitious, I would think that some misfortune was about to befall me."

"Though you might laugh at me," murmured Bolensky, "it feels to me like the hideous monster from this afternoon is on the prowl, circling around us."

Nobody considered making fun of the engineer: all felt more or less the same instinctive apprehension.

"We should perhaps have gone to meet Miss Alberte," said Georges, struggling to breathe the sultry air.

"The automobile has already left for Tabarka," answered Ralph, "and in any case, the road is neither long nor treacherous and, unless lightning strikes..."

He didn't finish his thought, though the young man's words had left him somewhat ill at ease.

A few minutes later, the four scientists entered the laboratory, where nothing had been moved since the invisible being's escape.

Bolensky turned on the electric lamps and started up the liquid oxygen ventilator.

"Do you want me to close the curtains?" he asked.

"No, no," said Captain Wad. "This way we will be able to watch the spectacular storm that is gathering; there are moments when the laboratory is surrounded by lightning on all sides—it feels like you are in the center of a raging furnace..."

Zarouk entered at this moment. He had a wild look in his eye and was holding something under his burnoose.

The first thing he did was hurriedly close the trapdoor in the glass ceiling that Bolensky had absentmindedly opened when he came in.

"What is it?" asked Pitcher.

The Negro was shivering with fear.

His only response was to throw the object that he was concealing under his burnoose onto the laboratory table; it was nothing but the body of a young jackal.

"What do you expect me to do with this, you coward?" said the naturalist.

But then Pitcher let out a cry of surprise. He had instinctively run his hand over the animal's coat. The jackal was no longer anything but a sort of long flaccid sack, entirely emptied of all living substance, a limp skin hanging off a skeleton.

Captain Wad came closer and spread apart the yellow hairs just behind the ear. He revealed to the others the epidermis riddled with red blotches.

"Just as I suspected," he murmured, lowering his voice. "The same bloody marks as on Mr. Frymcock's hand and wrist!

"This jackal was bled dry by the *invisible creature*!...

"Or invisible creatures... For all we know the human race may be about to face an invasion of these monsters, disturbed in their ancient refuges by the clearing of forests, and by railroads, submarines, and airplanes."

"If that is the case, we shall fight!" exclaimed Pitcher, with some enthusiasm.

"If these monsters exist outside of our understanding, we will have to quickly find the flaw in their armor.

"What is the use, truly, of being heirs to five thousand years of human discoveries if we let ourselves be defeated at the first attack!

"These invisible drinkers of blood would have stood a chance of success in the ignorant days of pagan Rome when they would have been taken for gods, in the dismal Middle Ages when one would have seen devils in them, but now, no!

"Science is armed against all enemies, against all catastrophes. In her eyes, nothing is impossible!

"Let us rejoice, instead, to have been the first to discover the presence of these strange beings!

"The honor of this immortal discovery will be ours!"

These words dispelled the painful impression made by Zarouk's discovery; the Negro was questioned in minute detail.

As usual, after dinner he had gone to rest in the villa's garden, at the foot of one of the porphyry stelae that bore large ceramic vases from Nabeul, painted a hodgepodge of bright colors, next to an ancient olive tree perhaps two thousand years old whose elongated fruits, of a variety that the Arabs call "camel's tooth," were known to the Carthaginians.

His masters knew that each day Zarouk spent many hours there, his face brightened by a distracted smile and his ears alert to all the murmurs, all the rustlings of the garden.

His incredibly sharp senses could discern the beating wings or elytra and the drone particular to each sort of insect, the creeping of chameleons and grass-snakes, the surreptitious movement of porcupines and wildcats through the branches. He could even make out the moaning of trees producing sap and the crackle of ripe grains bursting their hulls in the sunlight and tossing their seed to the wind.

Subtle fragrances told him the location, near or far, of each plant and animal.

In these ecstatic meditations, Zarouk experienced, a hundred times over, the delightful pleasure that sublime music performed by a flawless orchestra gives to a dilettante.

It was without doubt in the course of these raptures that his hearing and his sense of smell were so keenly sharpened and came to compensate for his lack of sight.

Zarouk's ecstasy had been suddenly disturbed by a confused beating of wings soon followed by a groan of agony.

Sweating with fear, he hadn't stirred from his hiding place, recognizing again the presence of the dreadful "djinn."

Once the noise had ceased, the Negro had grown bolder, and he had no difficulty finding the vampirized corpse of the jackal; it was then that, trembling at his own boldness, he had taken refuge in the laboratory.

After Zarouk's story, there was a moment of silence. All four were lost in thought.

"Without a doubt, these hideous beings," said Bolensky finally, "possess a formidable intelligence, for why else would they resemble, in such an explicit fashion, a brain?"

The discussion continued, fiercer and more impassioned.

"In the future, no doubt," murmured Captain Wad thoughtfully, "man will become similar to these gigantic brains; it is an evolution that is certain to occur in a few hundred centuries.

"It is a well-known truth that all unused organs are resorbed; already — this is a most simple example — in civilized peoples, the toe atrophies or even disappears completely.

"I explained to you yesterday, at dinner — and we owe this discovery to Berthelot — that a chemically simplified food will lead to the resorption of the intestine and the stomach and consequently make certain functions of the liver redundant.

"Man, sustained by products that he will digest almost immediately, will make do with a shorter and shorter digestive tube.

"After that — I am certain of it — the daily wear and tear of the organism will be neutralized by the direct injection of a special substance into the arteries.

"The entire digestive system won't have a reason to exist anymore."

"I'm quite willing to accept," interjected Georges Darvel, "that by the gradual suppression of the organs, these monsters — let's call them, if you will, Vampires, in memory of the human bats described by my brother — have come to be no more than brains, but this doesn't explain their invisibility.

"What of their noses, eyes, and ears, which appear to be simply vestigial?"

"I will answer you," retorted the captain, "and without even mentioning obscure rays that would quite suffice to justify the hypothesis.

"Quite recently, a Hungarian scientist succeeded in restoring vision to the blind by acting directly on the optical lobes, that is to say, on the parts of the brain that control vision.

"That is an invaluable proof; its incalculable consequences will be evident in the future.

"In my opinion, the crude mechanism of the senses is destined to disappear; the nerve cell will perceive, without their help, all exterior impressions.

"Taste, hearing, smell, and touch will no longer have, so to speak, a raison d'être.

"Have the Vampires perhaps then arrived," Georges Darvel said next, "at that ideal state that we only suspect exists? You will allow that many objections may be raised against this attractive hypothesis."

"For example?"

"To cite just one: would you admit that the muscles and muscular strength must disappear? It seems to me . . ."

"It seems you are in error," continued Captain Wad, animatedly. "I am now going to postulate a thesis whose utterance will send into a rage every champion pugilist, boxer, cyclist, one-legged man, and all the rest . . .

"Muscle is a heavy and crude mechanism, dependent on the digestive system of which the brain, having arrived at the height of its perfection, will have no need whatsoever.

"It is muscle that joins the human being and the animal, that debases his dignity as a thinking being!

"But for the rare exception, the men of genius who have dominated the world have never boasted great physical strength.

"Those who have subdued nations and subjugated nature have more often than not had a feeble constitution.

"Nobody imagines Newton, Louis XI, Sixtus V, Michelangelo, or Napoleon as capable of athletic exploits.

"Mind dominates matter—the brain rules the world!

"Through force of intellect and willpower, emperors and philosophers have held multitudes under the yoke from the sick beds to which they were confined.

"Voltaire, Renan, and Descartes were infirm valetudinarians.

"I could cite many more examples."

"That's quite all right. I understand . . . So, in your opinion, muscle is fated to disappear."

"But it's obvious! It's staring you in the face. The slightest reflection should suffice to convince you."

"It is simply a matter of several hundred centuries," interrupted Ralph Pitcher, not without irony.

"That is true," continued the captain, "but already, in our time, the inhabitant of a great city uses his muscles less and less.

"Thanks to automobiles, railroads, and airplanes, soon he will no longer bother to walk.

"Less and less often must he bear a burden.

"Soon, condensed foods will save him even the trouble of digestion.

"Physical exercise will be no more than a luxury or an occupation."

"But factory and field workers," said Georges, surprised by this strange paradox. "You will agree with me . . ."

"That they supply muscular labor. Agreed! I have never dreamed of denying it. But this labor tends to diminish day by day.

"Machines, more powerful and more compliant than the worker, are beginning to replace him everywhere.

"The laborer, the farmer has recourse to threshers and electric or steam-powered reapers for his harvest.

"Hundreds of horses would be needed to carry out the work of a lone locomotive, which a train driver runs with the simple pressure of a finger on the regulator.

"The day when the machine will have completely replaced man is near, very near! . . ."

The captain was interrupted in the middle of his eloquent harangue by a rumble of thunder.

The storm, which had threatened to burst for some time, was finally beginning. All talk ceased as the four scientists watched the spectacular display outside the glass walls.

The storm was preparing to unleash its force on the deep valley in which the villa had been built.

The sky, rent again and again by great silent flashes of lightning, was livid. The distant forests and rough terrain of the countryside emerged from the deep darkness, drawn with strokes of pale blue fire. At times, the lightning unfurled in huge pale sheets.

It was as if, suddenly, the floodgates of a vast lake of light had opened, victoriously drowning the shadows, forcing them to retreat before an impetuous flood of fantastic rays.

Luminous fountains, pyrotechnics, even the bombardment of a city by a fleet of armored ships would pale into insignificance next to this grandiose spectacle.

The rain started to fall in enormous drops: but it was a singular sort of downpour, a phosphorescent rain that called to mind some fiery, infernal shower.

Dante would have been able to cull a most frightful description, one of the cruelest scenes in his *Inferno*, from this chaotic vista.

Georges Darvel and his friends contemplated this spectacle with a mixture of admiration and terror. Although they were used to the region's frequent storms, never had they experienced a cataclysm such as this.

They were pensive, reminded of all that is unknown in the world that surrounds us and of the uncertainty of our science, so primitive, so weak, left with nothing more than hypotheses about everything of interest.

This was certainly no ordinary storm; as if in a gigantic condenser, a dreadful accumulation of energy had been produced within the mountainous circle that surrounded the villa.

This fantastic phenomenon had unleashed its cascades of flame unceasingly for more than an hour when its character abruptly altered.

The horizontal bursts of blue energy were joined by vertical bolts of lightning, of a blinding red, slicing across the sky in perfectly straight lines, with none of the cracks, gaps, or zigzags of ordinary lightning.

They crackled around the villa with muffled explosions. An old cork oak a hundred paces away was hit, and it collapsed with a resounding crash.

Ralph Pitcher and Captain Wad looked at each other anxiously.

"You will never convince me that those are ordinary bolts of lightning," murmured the naturalist, shaking his head.

"Perhaps it would be best not to stay here."

"Bah," said Bolensky, "you really believe we might be in danger here?"

"Yes! I do. We should leave."

"I disagree," exclaimed the Pole disdainfully, "and I can't imagine what sort of danger you are alluding to.

"Do you think that we will be better sheltered in the villa?

"Don't forget that this laboratory is equipped with four lightning rods . . ."

Before he could finish, a sudden dazzling light appeared above the glass ceiling, which blazed as if it had caught fire.

The next second an incandescent body, a ball of fire, crashed into the laboratory with an appalling whistle, followed by a dull concussion.

Georges Darvel screamed as he was thrown backward by it, half-blinded, his right hand burnt, his clothes smoldering.

The glass walls were shattered: in an instinct of self-preservation the young man lunged onto the terrace that was level with the laboratory.

He retraced his steps almost immediately when he heard heartrending cries rising from the smoking rubble.

At that moment, blinding white flames broke out; the tank of ether and other combustibles were catching fire.

This dismal white light rising into the lightning-streaked sky completed the sublime horror of the catastrophe.

All of this had occurred with lightning speed; all told, the drama had lasted less than a minute.

Darvel was stumbling around in the debris of broken glass, his hands and eyes in horrific pain. He had lost his head and felt drawn to the great white flame from which arose horrific screams.

Suddenly, a man lunged toward him, beard and clothing burnt, waving his arms like a madman in the flames.

"Georges, my boy, is that you?"

At the sound of his voice, Georges Darvel recognized Pitcher the naturalist.

"Is that you, Ralph?" he stammered, "I can't make you out! . . . My eyes are shot with blood, my pupils are on fire! . . .

"It's dreadful! . . . But what of Captain Wad and Mr. Bolensky?"

"They are both dead, I'm sure . . ."

"And Zarouk?"

Pitcher pointed to a motionless form a few steps away.

"I don't know," he said, "whether he was killed instantly or has only fainted.

"Help me pick him up . . . We mustn't stay here another moment . . . There is picrate here and other, more dangerous explosives down below! I'm surprised that it hasn't all blown up already!"

Panic-stricken, Pitcher and Georges picked up Zarouk's body and carried him to the far end of the terrace.

"Only the wing that holds the laboratory will blow," Pitcher had said.

Both of them were dazed with shock and fear after the violent jolt and the instinctive urge that had made them flee. They remained numb, mopping their blood-covered eyes with their handkerchiefs.

It didn't even occur to them to try to escape from the villa, to get out of harm's reach, like the servants whose cries of terror could be heard as they ran desperately into the forest.

At that moment, the thin silhouette of Mr. Frymcock appeared on the terrace.

"Well, sir," he said, as calm as could be, "what has happened? Did lightning strike the laboratory?"

"It wasn't lightning," stammered Pitcher. "I don't know what it was . . . Wad and Bolensky are under there."

And he pointed to the rubble, above which the great white flame of the ether undulated like a giant plume.

"But we must rescue them!"

"It's no use, besides it's all about to blow! . . ."

And Ralph Pitcher gave a mad laugh.

"Yes, it's going to blow," repeated Georges mechanically.

"By God!" muttered Frymcock, "They've lost their minds from fear! Hey," he cried, "shake off your stupor. We must combat the fire and rescue Captain Wad and the engineer from the blaze if we can.

Ralph Pitcher stood up straight and raised his hand to his forehead in an expression of weariness and bewilderment. His face, scarred by burns and gashes from splinters of glass, was tense with the effort that he made to regain his composure.

"Yes," he murmured, "we must! I will help you . . . I have just had a terrible attack of despondency and despair."

Stimulated by his example, Georges had gotten up as well.

"Let's show a little pluck, gentlemen," said Frymcock. "The three of us together can perhaps prevail over this misfortune.

"If only I knew where to find the fire extinguishers."

"They are not far at all. There are some on each terrace of the villa," said Ralph who was slowly recovering from his terrifying jolt. "But there's something better. I will open the canister of fire-retardant gases.

"Why didn't I think of this sooner?"

Like many dwellings, the villa was provided with those glass canisters that, when broken, release gases that inhibit combustion; but as an extra precaution, there was a gasometer near the laboratory filled with enough alkaline gas to extinguish the most violent blaze.

Ignoring the imminent risk of explosion, Ralph Pitcher opened the gasometer while Georges Darvel and Frymcock opened the taps of the terrace's water tanks.

After a few minutes, the flames disappeared, replaced by a mass of acrid and nauseating steam; the danger of explosion had been averted. The villa now seemed to be swallowed in a white cloud.

When it had begun to dissipate, Ralph and his two companions, joined by Zarouk, who had indeed only fainted, made their way through the smoking rubble armed with lanterns, which little Chérifa, who alone among the villa's staff had not taken flight, had found for them.

It was a pitiful spectacle.

Nothing remained of the marvelous glass-walled laboratory but the four iron girders of the frame; the precious instruments that had cost so much in effort and in money were smashed; blackened and grotesquely twisted by the violence of the fire, the statue that housed the telephonic equipment was lying in the rubble. There was now a smoking black hole in the center of the room, half-filled with debris.

At the edge of the hole, the rescuers found the hideously maimed body of Bolensky; his brains oozed from his skull, which looked as if it had been split by a blow from an axe.

The unfortunate engineer must have been killed in an instant; his eyes were wide open and his face still held a sort of smile that the clots of blood and the burns made a dreadful sight indeed.

"Poor Bolensky," murmured Pitcher, trying to hide the tears rolling down his cheeks. "He was so full of enthusiasm, so full of life, only a moment ago! . . .

"Try as I might, I can't explain such a catastrophe . . ."

"Perhaps Captain Wad has somehow survived," murmured Georges. "Let's look. You never know."

"I'm afraid it's hopeless," said Ralph. "There he is!"

And he pointed to the abyss yawning at their feet.

"But we must be certain," declared Frymcock. "If you'd like, I will be the first to go down."

"You should not risk your life," interrupted Zarouk. "I will go down if you wish."

"I'm the one who will go," said Georges Darvel in turn . . .

At this moment the sound of an automobile horn rang out in the night above the rumble of thunder.

"It's Miss Alberte!" cried Pitcher with despair.

"How are we to tell her that Bolensky and the Captain are dead?"

All four looked at each other, filled with consternation.

The sound of the horn drew nearer.

"We must make a decision," said Ralph Pitcher . . . "I will go, or rather, no, let's all go; it's the better course to take."

Sick at heart, they finally convinced themselves to go. They crossed the patio, whose beautiful mosaic had been blackened by the smoke, and arrived at the main entrance just as the car came to a halt.

VI

....

A Strange Meteorite

Miss Alberte Teramond leapt anxiously from the car. She appeared deathly pale to Georges in the glow of the automobile's headlamps; dark shadows underlined her blue eyes, her dark golden hair was disheveled, her traveling clothes were spattered with mud.

"I hope, Mr. Pitcher," she said breathless with anxiety, "that we have suffered only material losses! . . . I saw the glow of the blaze . . . I realized that lightning must have struck the villa."

Then catching sight of Georges, who bowed shyly:

"Mr. Darvel, no doubt? Welcome . . . But where are the captain and Mr. Bolensky?"

She had spoken with such volubility that Pitcher hadn't been able to get a word in.

"Miss," he stammered, trembling.

"But you are dreadfully burned, my dear Pitcher!" she continued, deeply distressed, "and you too, Mr. Darvel!"

"Ah! I see that Chérifa and Mr. Frymcock are here, safe and sound, fortunately."

Then, struck by the dismay etched on every face:

"So, will no one tell me what has happened to Captain Wad and Mr. Bolensky?

"Speak, I must know, I cannot bear this awful uncertainty."

"Miss," stammered Pitcher, steadying his voice, "our two friends perished in the disaster . . . Such is the painful truth!"

A long moment of poignant silence followed; the young woman was transfixed by the fatal news.

She emerged from her despondent state only to burst into tears.

"My God!" she murmured, sobbing. "But this is terrible! To think that with all my billions, I am not able even to safeguard the lives of my dearest friends!

"Who could ever replace their devotion, their knowledge, their boundless generosity?"

Yet there was too much natural energy in her soul; the daughter of the speculator who had died of joy could not remain sunken in despair for long.

Her recovery was extraordinarily quick.

In a few brief sentences, she had Ralph Pitcher explain what had happened in minute detail.

"Perhaps," she said, "Captain Wad is only wounded and has been miraculously preserved, as often happens in these sorts of catastrophes.

"It is our duty to do all we can to save him.

"I will not rest until I am certain of his fate . . ."

Chérifa advanced toward her mistress, whose hands she tenderly embraced.

"I was so worried," she murmured. "The storm must have been terrible at sea! . . ."

"Yes, I thought that the *Conqueror* would never reach the port of Tabarka; the sea was boiling, the waves and even the clouds seemed as if they were on fire.

"There were abrupt lulls, then suddenly a groundswell high as a mountain would toss the yacht to a vertiginous height . . .

"Two men were thrown overboard and were lost.

"The sailors insisted that they had never experienced such a strange storm; the captain, who has sailed for forty years, had never before seen the terrifying, unfathomable shooting stars of this horrific night."

"You must be exhausted," broke in Chérifa insistently. "Despite our disarray, your supper awaits . . ."

"There's no time for that," exclaimed Miss Alberte, impatiently. "I thank you for your attentions, but help us instead save the captain if there is still time."

Without a word, Chérifa followed Miss Alberte, who had already set off for the laboratory.

Zarouk had taken advantage of these few minutes to obtain torches, as well as pickaxes and shovels, which he had taken from the gardener's shed.

While climbing the stairs, the young woman asked Ralph Pitcher what he thought had caused the catastrophe.

"I know nothing for certain," answered the naturalist, still completely overwhelmed. "Though I suppose that lightning . . ."

"But the laboratory was fitted with lightning rods."

"There are, as you may be aware, cases when the most skillfully constructed lightning rods are of no use, and we don't know why . . .

"As I told you, whatever happened to us was a most abnormal and extraordinary phenomenon."

"But you mentioned a ball of fire?"

"Lightning very often takes this form . . . To be honest, I cannot confirm anything."

"We shall soon find out."

They arrived, by way of the interior stairway, at the door of the dispensary, which was located just beneath the glass laboratory.

Pitcher opened the door; there was a jumble of broken beams, smashed equipment, and half-consumed furniture, and the unpleasant smell of the gases used to extinguish the fire permeated the room.

"Miss," said the naturalist once again, "you know that there is a cylinder of picrate in here; it is truly a miracle that it didn't explode.

"The fire may still be smoldering. A blow from a pickaxe may cause it to explode . . . please leave, I implore you; it is most imprudent to risk your life in this smoking rubble."

"You are risking your own life, Mr. Pitcher," retorted the young woman curtly. "It is my duty to set an example."

"It is not at all the same thing," muttered the naturalist with dissatisfaction. "Is it not our job, as scientists, to wrestle with physical or chemical phenomena?"

"Do not insist, Mr. Pitcher," she said in an imperious tone that permitted no reply. "I consider it my duty to share the danger, if there be any . . ."

Pitcher fell silent, well aware that his remonstrations were useless. He handed tools to Georges, Zarouk, and Frymcock. Miss Alberte and Chérifa each grabbed a torch.

Lanterns set on the floor brought light at last to the desolate scene. In the center of the wreckage, sections of iron girders emerged, like the masts of a floundering ship, from the gaping maw of the round pit.

With utmost caution, they started clearing the rubble; the beams and blocks were removed and carried onto the terrace; the bottles of chemicals, many of which were still intact, were placed out of the way in a remote corner of the room

The men worked tirelessly for an entire hour without finding the least trace of the captain.

Miss Alberte was beside herself; she couldn't stop bombarding Ralph Pitcher with questions.

"How is it that we have found nothing?" she asked. "Could the captain have been reduced to ashes by the lighting?"

"It wasn't lightning," responded the naturalist, after a moment of reflection. "If it were, the copper and the steel would have melted. But no, the edges of the girders are clean and shiny as if they have been cut. It must be assumed that they yielded under the pressure of a considerable mass . . ."

Suddenly he stopped: his pickaxe had just struck the wicker corselet of an enormous cylinder.

"The picrate!" he cried. "It's truly fortunate that I didn't strike harder.

"I am still astounded that the entire villa wasn't blown to pieces. When you consider that a single blow could have detonated it.

"This big fragment of the roof that fell just above it formed a sort of protective niche for the cylinder. Its wicker corselet hasn't even been scratched."

The formidable explosive was gently eased from its cavity and placed safely on the terrace.

Pitcher was lost in thought.

"I can breathe again," he murmured. "A moment ago it was as if we had a volcano under our feet.

"We won't find the body of our poor friend here. The incandescent mass must have carried him with it as it fell through the floors below.

"We have planned our search poorly, and it is my fault."

Little by little they were coming to understand the terrible phenomenon.

The incandescent object whose nature was as yet unknown had plummeted like a cannonball straight through all the floors beneath the laboratory.

They descended to the room below, which housed Arab baths, a Tunisian hammam with walls of white marble.

There wasn't much debris here, but on the edge of the circular gulf bored through the mosaics on the floor, Georges Darvel silently pointed out, for Miss Alberte, a long streak of blood.

"Let's keep going," murmured the young woman sadly.

"You know what I've been thinking?" said Pitcher suddenly. "This catastrophe has strange features in common with the one that caused Ardavena's death."

"What conclusion do you draw from this?"

"That we have experienced a rather common atmospheric phenomenon . . . It's a simple meteor, a bolide, or, if you prefer, a large shooting star that has fallen on the villa."

"But this bolide?"

"That's what tore this circular hole, just as a cannonball smashes through the different bulkheads of a ship's hull.

"I can now say it with confidence: I have no doubt that the bolide is lying beneath our feet, at the bottom of the hole."

These words had a profound effect on the young woman; she and Georges Darvel exchanged glances without daring to say aloud what they were thinking.

Without a word, they all hastened to the floor below; it consisted of an immense vaulted cellar built in the days of the Roman occupation.

It is a well-known fact that all of this region of Tunisia is covered with huge ruins dating from this period. The villa had been built on the site of an ancient fortress, and the architect had needed only to utilize the abundant materials readily at hand.

He had had no trouble refitting the cellars, which had remained nearly intact, for their new purpose.

With their heavy, surbased vaults and squat pillars made from large blocks held together with indestructible Roman mortar, they were more like crypts than cellars. A steam engine, installed in one of the outer vaults, powered the indispensable dynamos that provided the lighting, heating, and other electrical needs of the villa.

But the boiler's fire was going out; the stoker and the mechanic had panicked and run off, imagining no doubt that the villa was collapsing around them. It was another stroke of luck that the bolide had not killed them and smashed the machine.

It had in fact landed only a few meters away.

"I knew it!" cried Pitcher, waving his torch wildly. "It's definitely a bolide! And a spherical one at that! Here it is, half-sunk in the ground!"

Everyone rushed forward. The torchlight revealed a globe maybe three meters in diameter that looked to be made of a sort of half-vitrified granite with a hard, rough surface sparkling with mica.

A thick steam hung all around it. Frymcock, who had been among the first to dash forward, suddenly threw himself backward with a cry of pain.

He had foolishly placed his hand on the still-incandescent meteor and had severely burned the tips of his fingers.

"*By Jove!*" he cried with a grimace, "It's like red-hot iron!"

"The captain is under there," said Pitcher sorrowfully.

"Who knows?" murmured Miss Alberte. "As long as we haven't found the cadaver, we have the right to hope."

"Unfortunately," said Georges Darvel, with a shiver of horror, "there is no longer any possible doubt . . ."

And he pointed with dread to a clenched and half-charred hand trapped under the stony sphere.

Miss Alberte closed her eyes, and her beautiful face darkened with the shadow of death. It required an incredible effort on her part not to fall unconscious.

Pitcher was crying like a child.

Everyone was filled with consternation.

"Please go, Miss," murmured Darvel softly, "spare yourself this lamentable spectacle . . . We beseech you."

"No," she cried with a stifled sob, "I will stay to the end. Despite the evidence, I still can't accept the awful truth . . . If you knew how much I cared for Captain Wad . . . If you had been able, like me, to value his devotion, his modesty, his profound erudition . . . I considered him almost like a father . . ."

Without a sound, they set to work freeing the body.

Attempting to dislodge the enormous, still burning rock was unthinkable. It was simpler to try to break it, minerals of a crystalline structure being often quite friable.

Georges Darvel was the first to take a pickaxe to it.

A large fragment broke off. The young man was surprised to find that the interior of the meteorite was a different color than the outer surface.

The latter was a reddish brown with green splotches like some stoneware fired at high temperatures; underneath this sort of bark lay a white substance, crisscrossed by red-colored tubes; some of these tubes, with tapered ends, had been broken by the pickaxe, and droplets of a thick liquid were leaking out.

The young man had stopped, paralyzed by indecision.

"What should I do, Mr. Pitcher?" he asked. "Never has any scientific account mentioned an aerolite made of materials such as this."

"It's simply crystallization," grumbled the naturalist, still apparently distracted by his grief.

"I have never seen crystallization that enclosed an interior fluid. What's more, this shape is as uniform as if it had been fashioned by human hands.

"I have a feeling that we are on the trail of something extraordinary! . . .

"Think! This strange stone comes perhaps from some faraway planet . . . If I reduce it to dust, it will be impossible to study it.

"I truly don't know whether I should continue . . ."

Everyone was breathless with impatience.

Miss Alberte and Ralph Pitcher exchanged a strange glance.

"Keep going," said the naturalist hurriedly, "but take care to make as few small fragments as possible."

Georges had just cautiously moved his hand close to the broken fragment.

"Here's another oddity," he murmured feverishly. "The surface of the sphere is red-hot, but the interior is perfectly cold, nearly frozen."

"How do you explain that?"

"I don't know," said Pitcher anxiously. "Let's keep going."

With a shaky hand, Georges Darvel struck it again; a larger piece of the shell broke loose.

The same shout of amazement rose from every mouth.

A human foot had appeared, liberated suddenly from the stony gangue where it had been interred.

Georges dropped his pickaxe in surprise.

"A man!" he stammered, losing his head, "A man! There's a man inside this rock!"

"A cadaver at least," murmured Pitcher sorrowfully.

"It doesn't matter, I have to see!" cried Georges excitedly.

"Don't you understand?" he added in a hoarse voice. "It's Robert Darvel — it's my brother who is in there, buried in a stone! . . ."

"Dead or alive: I have to know!"

"How could he possibly be alive?" said Pitcher sadly. "I have been thinking the same thing for the last ten minutes, but I didn't dare open my mouth! . . ."

And he gestured toward Miss Alberte, who was leaning, petrified and pale, on Chérifa's shoulder so as not to faint.

She suddenly stood up straight, eyes aflame, arms outstretched, trembling with a mad hope.

In the gleam of the torches beneath the vaulted ceiling, her delicate beauty acquired a tragic quality; she resembled some blood-covered heroine out of ancient Aeschylus, summoning the gods as witnesses.

"No, gentlemen," she said solemnly, "Robert Darvel is not dead — he cannot be dead. A man like him does not perish in this way. A secret voice cries out to me that he has triumphed!"

"Believe me, I beg you. Robert is alive."

Then she added in a tone of absolute belief:

"Would he be here if he had perished? Nothing is impossible to the conqueror of the heavens! If he has returned, it's because such was his wish."

Pitcher's conviction began to wane as he listened to her impassioned speech; he struggled in vain to recover his composure; his blood was coursing through his veins and his head was spinning.

"But," he stammered, "we still don't even know whether this is Robert Darvel."

Before he had finished his sentence, Georges had seized his pickaxe with a sort of sacred fury and started to strike wildly at the rock.

It was a kind of madness. Under his blows, large chunks broke off and the smashed tubes on the inside released a pungent fluid.

Pitcher was forced to moderate this fury.

"Be careful, man," he said to him. "You're hammering away like a madman. You might injure him . . ."

The young man, struck by this thought, continued his work more measuredly.

A human form began to emerge little by little from the rock, like a statue hewn by an inspired sculptor.

The still indistinct form lay in a crouched position, huddled up in a ball with its knees at its chin and its hands crossed under its knees, like the Guanches of the Azores—descendants of Atlantis—or the mummies of certain Incan peoples, some of which are enclosed in large clay urns.

Pitcher, struck by this similarity, shook his head in discouragement.

And yet he noticed that the tubes that Georges Darvel's pickaxe had broken were wider at their base and narrowed at their ends; this base was attached to the epidermis like the spines of a sea urchin to its shell: he conjectured that these tubes, which appeared to be made of some type of glass, contained antiseptic liquids intended to preserve the mummy.

But this explanation didn't satisfy him. He did not remember ever having read a description of such a device.

While he indulged in these reflections, the torso had been completely freed; only the face remained to be uncovered.

George hesitated, paralyzed by uncertainty.

He was afraid to take the final step. His heart constricted dreadfully at the thought of the despair perhaps awaiting him.

The body maintained its peculiar position with lifeless rigidity.

"Finish the job," murmured Miss Alberte, "so we may at least be free of this accursed uncertainty, so that we may know for sure!"

"I haven't the strength to do it," stammered the young man, his voice choked with anxiety.

"Then I must do it," said Pitcher, brandishing a wide-bladed penknife.

With an unsteady hand, he started to cautiously remove the stony crust mixed with what remained of the tubes.

He found his task less difficult than he had expected; as he carefully slid the blade along the cheek, with gentle pressure, the stone mask ceased to adhere and broke loose all in one piece.

A face was revealed. It was emaciated and discolored and its eyes were closed, but it carried proud and noble features, a high forehead, and a gracefully drawn mouth over which a slight smile still seemed to play.

"Robert!"

"My brother! . . ."

The two cries rang out in the same instant. But this time the shock was too much for Miss Alberte.

Ralph Pitcher and Chérifa had just enough time to dash forward to catch her in their arms as she fainted.

Georges had steeled himself for this moment in vain.

With a glint of madness shining in his feverish eyes he rushed toward the lifeless body, so miraculously exhumed from its stone coffin.

He put his hand on Robert's forehead; it was ice-cold.

He strained to hear the elusive beating of his heart; his chest was still and cold.

"He is dead," he babbled, and he sank aghast among the fragments of the sphere, seized by the most dreadful despair.

A few steps away, Zarouk smiled enigmatically.

VII

....

A Potent Cure

A dreary dawn, pale and damp, revealed the night's devastation; in the forest, countless trees had been shattered or uprooted, the furrowed earth rolled with torrents of water reddened by blood-colored clays, and all the majestic countryside was obscured, as if behind a veil, by the wan crosshatching of a slow shower that seemed as though it would never end.

The servants had recovered from their panic and returned one by one to the villa, although they were persuaded at heart that it was the "sorcerers" whom their mistress sheltered whose evil spells had called down the fire from the sky and made the giant abyss where the beautiful laboratory with crystal walls once stood.

Through Mr. Frymcock's care, the horribly mangled bodies of Captain Wad and Bolensky had been laid in a room transformed into a chapel of rest where they awaited their solemn funeral rites.

Everything was as it had been before, except that the servants had all been forbidden, under any circumstance whatsoever, to enter the room that had belonged to Captain Wad.

There, poignant new developments were unfolding in this mysterious drama.

It was there that they had carried the body of Robert Darvel.

Although the engineer displayed all the signs of certain death, Ralph Pitcher and Miss Alberte herself had not given up hope.

They had even managed to reassure Georges; they had explained to him that these signs of death did not constitute proof; they had told him of the prodigies they had witnessed in India, of the incredible resurrections of sleeping yogis in the monastery of Chelambrum.

Georges had regained hope; Alberte, once she had recovered from her fainting fit, had seen to all the necessary arrangements herself.

Robert had been laid on the bed and wrapped in burning hot blankets. To revive him they had made use of every conceivable revulsive agent: they had rubbed his body vigorously; they had applied caustic mustard plasters to the soles of his feet; they had even managed to get him to swallow, by means of a feeding tube, several drops of a powerful cordial.

Nothing had worked.

Day was breaking and Robert Darvel had not shown the slightest sign of life.

Discouragement was creeping into their hearts.

"Anyone can see," murmured Georges Darvel with inconsolable grief, "that my brother is dead!"

"Do not say that," retorted Miss Alberte. "You should have more confidence in our care and in your brother's genius.

"It must be that the hour he calculated for his return to life is yet to come.

"We must not despair. We must be patient . . ."

But there was a hint of weariness in the young woman's voice as she spoke these words. The others could sense that she no longer had the same faith that they would succeed, the same superb enthusiasm that, a few hours before, had galvanized Pitcher's skepticism and lifted Georges out of his overwhelming grief.

It was now Pitcher who showed the most enthusiasm; the very uselessness of his efforts seemed to spur him on.

"Goddam!" he cried. "Miss Alberte, you must send the automobile to Tunis or to Bizerta . . ."

"Whatever for?"

"To bring the best surgeon that can be found.

"There is an operation we can try, a desperate operation, which succeeds ten times out of a hundred."

"Tell me more, quickly . . ."

"It's called heart massage . . . , it's very risky, Miss. As I told you, it succeeds ten times out of a hundred, and many practitioners will not take the risk . . . The surgeon severs the muscles of the chest, then he saws through two ribs and opens a 'window' in the sternum.

"Once the heart is laid bare, he takes it in his hands, compresses it, tries to start it beating again, like setting in motion the pendulum of a stopped clock . . ."

"Yes, of course," interrupted Georges Darvel with a slight shrug of the shoulders, "I have read about that as well somewhere; but this operation, the most dangerous there is, has only ever been tried on subjects whose heart had stopped beating for a very short time. This case is different . . ."

"It doesn't matter," said Alberte. "It is our duty to try everything in our power."

She had already reached for the room's telephone receiver and was giving orders.

"That's taken care of," she said after a few moments. "The car is going to leave in ten minutes and will be back at noon with the surgeon from the hospital in Bizerta . . ."

"And yet," objected Georges Darvel again, "if my brother has set his awakening for a later date, as Mr. Pitcher mentioned a moment ago, wouldn't it be an atrocity to dissect him alive like this?

"Yes, of course," answered Miss Alberte, "but the doctor will perhaps have some good ideas . . ."

"A thousand pardons, Miss," interrupted Frymcock, who until then had been sitting quietly by himself, "but while we await the doctor's arrival, which may take some time, there are some methods that we may try to which we have not yet resorted.

"The application of an electric current, for instance, or injections of ether, from which surprising results have sometimes been obtained."

Pitcher leapt to his feet.

"Electricity!" he cried. "Why didn't I think of that?

"Luckily we have a current at our disposal . . ."

He rushed out of the chamber then returned at once, armed with the necessary instruments; after making a slight incision in Robert's shoulder and knee, he applied the end of a conductor to each and started the current.

The effect was instantaneous: his arms and legs relaxed, his eyes opened.

The body no longer had the posture of a mummy but lay stretched out on the bed.

"Just as I suspected!" cried Pitcher triumphantly.

"This doesn't prove much," retorted Miss Alberte. "You know as well as I that electric current has a similar effect on cadavers . . . His muscles have moved, it's true, but his body is still cold and lifeless. His eyes are blank and his heart . . ."

"Be patient, Miss," cried the naturalist enthusiastically. "I am now going to apply a very weak and slow current for a moment or two, then I will give an injection of ether!"

Everyone had drawn closer, without much hope but eager nonetheless.

The initial effect of the current was nearly imperceptible.

However Pitcher, ever the optimist, pointed out that Robert's muscles and joints had gradually lost their rigidity.

The application was repeated; there was an appreciable relaxation of the muscles of the face, and the entire body recovered a certain suppleness.

"This is the moment to give the injection," said the naturalist, trying to hide his deep apprehension.

The others were filled with anxiety as they watched him fill a Pravaz syringe.

They were all aware of the strong effects of ether, which, injected into a vein, can galvanize even the dying for a few moments.

If this treatment proved ineffective, they would be forced to abandon all hope.

Miss Alberte's eyes were bright with fever as she watched Pitcher slowly insert the hollow needle under the epidermis of the forearm.

Three seconds passed in dreadful silence.

The crystal barrel of the tiny syringe was empty and Robert Darvel remained lifeless.

Miss Alberte's heart was in her throat; she exchanged a look of distress with Georges.

At that instant both of them would have willingly given years of their life to see a few minutes into the future.

At long last a little color returned to Robert's cheeks, his eyelids fluttered, and his torso was agitated by a weak movement. Then he made an effort to sit up, cast around him with vacant, unseeing eyes, and fell back on the pillow.

"He lives!" cried the young woman, drunk with happiness.

Pitcher signaled her to be quiet.

"He lives, without a doubt," he murmured in a low voice, "but the thread that holds him to life is so tenuous that the slightest shock would suffice to break it. He didn't have even the strength to raise himself up. His gaze is vacant—he is just staring into space.

"I don't dare give him a second injection; I don't know whether he is strong enough to bear it . . ."

They started to massage him again, with increased vigor; but the engineer remained in a state of profound stupor, as if cataleptic. He did not recognize any of those around him, and the feeble throbbing of his arteries was the only sign that the vital spark wasn't completely extinguished in this body ground down by fatigue and danger.

Ralph Pitcher frowned, haunted by the specter of this man, so close to death, slipping once more into a lifelessness from which he would never emerge.

Suddenly he turned to Georges.

"What did you do with the fragments of the sphere?"

"As you requested, I took what remained to your room and placed it carefully on porcelain trays and in crystal vats . . .

"I even picked up all the fragments of the broken red glass tubes in order to collect some of the colorless and viscous liquid that they contain for future analysis."

"Good. Bring me all that you have of this liquid."

"What do you plan to do?"

"I don't know whether my hypothesis is correct, but I am persuaded that this liquid has tonic, nutritive, and restorative properties. Many medications and even some foods can be absorbed through the skin."

"We can always try," said the young man, after a moment of hesitation. "I believe, like you, that these strange tubes contain the traveling provisions and perhaps the breathable air that my brother carried with him from Mars . . ."

A few minutes later, Georges brought an alcarraza half-filled with the mysterious liquid.

With a small sponge, Pitcher started to rub some of it on the invalid's torso and soon had the satisfaction of seeing the medication work its magic.

Minute by minute, color returned to the engineer's face, his eyes lost their haggard expression, and he recovered the ability to move.

After a half hour of treatment, he seemed to have regained consciousness; a smile brightened his emaciated face and a singularly gentle expression entered his lifeless pupils.

"Georges! . . . Miss Alberte!" he spluttered in a voice so weak that it seemed to come from somewhere far away. His eyes never left the two young people leaning over his bedside.

But this mental shock must have been too violent, for after a few moments his eyes closed and he slumped back on the pillows, asleep.

"He is saved!" cried Pitcher. "Let me assure you, it is now only a question of rest and proper care."

The doctor from Bizerte arrived a little later and confirmed this diagnosis.

The patient, though emaciated, was in good health; in a fortnight, he would be completely recovered.

The doctor, for his part, listened with polite skepticism to Pitcher's story of Robert Darvel's incredible adventures.

To convince him of their truth, they were forced to show him the wreckage of the sphere.

His incredulity then changed to utter astonishment, and he asked immediately for permission to take one of the tubes of red glass in order to analyze its contents, which he declared at a glance to be highly oxygenated.

Ralph Pitcher felt no need to deny his request, but only on the express condition that the doctor maintain the strictest silence about the events that had transpired at the villa.

From then on, Robert Darvel's state rapidly improved. He still was able to speak only rarely, and with great effort, but his sleep was calm and deep and his stomach accepted without revulsion the consommés prepared by Mr. Frymcock's skilled hands.

The villa once again bustled with life and, if not for the death of Captain

Wad and Bolensky, no shadow would have darkened Miss Alberte's happiness.

Zarouk alone remained gloomy, besieged by continuous terrors, repeating endlessly that the Vampires—the djinns as he continued to call them—now thronged in great number around the villa.

He claimed to hear the noise of their wings both in the silence of the night and during the boisterous activities of the day.

Haunted by this obsession, the unhappy Negro was listless and hardly dared to venture out into the villa's grounds.

He was all the more upset that nobody, or almost nobody, paid attention to his statements.

Robert Darvel's return had driven all other concerns from the minds of his friends.

Besides—this was Pitcher's response to the Negro's never-ending laments—now that the explorer of the planets had returned, he would certainly know how to repel the Invisibles' attacks and find a way to capture them if need be.

The Negro, unconvinced, shook his head ruefully. He was so frightened that, if not for his attachment to Miss Alberte and the naturalist, he would have fled. He would have returned, without hesitation, to the distant oases of the far south where he was born.

PART TWO

The Martian Mystery

I

Robert Darvel's Tale

Pitcher was dying of curiosity. He struggled to refrain from torturing his patient with the hundreds of questions swirling in his head. Yet, despite his impatience, he had decided that Robert Darvel should not break the account of his experiences into bits and pieces.

They agreed to wait until he had completely recovered, until he was able to speak, an hour or two at a time if need be, to relate in one sitting the full account of his extraordinary odyssey.

Never had time moved so slowly for Miss Alberte and her friends.

Robert Darvel, whose state was rapidly improving, seemed to suffer himself from his inability to speak.

Before a week had passed he was able to get out of bed.

Supported by Pitcher and Georges, he ventured into the garden.

He was moved to tears by the exquisite pleasure of breathing air fragrant with the scent of myrtle, lemon blossoms, and jasmine — all the familiar flora that he rediscovered like a friend believed to be lost forever.

Only one scent bothered him, seemed even to inspire in him a sort of horror: the scent of oleanders; he fled their fresh and beautiful corollas with the most intense repulsion.

Georges and Miss Alberte were not at all surprised by this; the sap of the oleander, especially in spring, is a poison all the more potent as the climate is hotter. A drop of this venomous sap on a recent scratch can be deadly.

Pitcher alone, his imagination always at work, deduced from this simple fact all sorts of hypotheses, imagining the planet Mars covered with accursed forests, under whose foliage one was destined to die, as in the fabulous shade of the legendary manchineel tree.

More intensely than an ordinary convalescent, Robert enjoyed the many little pleasures accompanying the return of health after a long illness; was he not also recovering from a voyage through interstellar space, which still troubled his silences and dreams?

At first, his shrunken stomach could barely manage a few spoonsful of chicken broth; then soft-boiled eggs and partridge wings, the delight of convalescent patients, were permitted him; rare meats and aged wines, their warmth hidden beneath mellow, languorous bouquets, finished the work of mending his exhausted tissues.

Now Robert Darvel looked much as he did in London before his departure for India in the company of the Brahmin Ardavena; some stray white hairs, a few premature wrinkles around his still-clear blue eyes, were all that betrayed the fatigue of an otherworldly adventure; he appeared at first glance younger than Pitcher, and even than Georges, momentarily disfigured by his burns from the fire.

As the engineer himself said, laughing, he felt in fine fettle, ready to start over. It was he himself who cut short the delay fixed for the narration, awaited with such impatience, of his interstellar exploration.

It had been agreed that they would meet after dinner in the large sitting room of the villa, with a veranda overlooking the superb vista of the forest and the faraway sea.

From the outset, the gathering took on a solemn character, which was not at all forced. The silence, which reigned from the moment Robert Darvel had settled himself in the place of honor reserved for him, was due as much to admiration as to curiosity.

Ralph Pitcher and Georges took their places on either side of the explorer of the stars; Miss Alberte sat across from them, her face beaming with happiness. Behind her sat Mr. Frymcock, who had claimed the honor of serving as stenographer to the speaker; finally, Zarouk leaned on the back of Pitcher's armchair and Chérifa squatted on a cushion at her mistress's feet.

The electric lamps, whose corollas of precious stones were lost among the flowering arabesques of the ceiling, threw a soft and enchanting light on this group seemingly arranged by some artist of genius.

"My friends," started Robert, all eyes upon him, "would you rather I take up my account from the beginning or continue it from the point where my signals were interrupted?"

"Obviously," Pitcher replied, "you should continue from where your signals were interrupted!

"You said yourself that the story published in the newspapers is sufficiently exact, and we know it by heart! . . .

"You must take pity on our curiosity, which has been severely tested for many days."

"So be it . . ." acquiesced the engineer, smiling.

"You were at the point where the human bats had taken you prisoner and carried you to their cave."

Robert's face took on a sudden gravity. His gaze seemed lost for a moment in the vastness of space.

"Ah! Yes, the cave," he murmured. "I can still see its high shadowy vaults, supported by thousands of stalactites. It was like a vision of hell, where thousands of glowing eyes pricked the inky darkness, creating a sort of half-light, like a furtive, unnatural twilight. I could just make out the glimmering shafts of columns and the walls, papered, as it were, with a hideous, mortuary velvet of innumerable wings.

"An appalling stench, the acrid odor of guano mixed with the fetor of a charnel house, permeated the cave; I was afraid of course—I can't imagine anyone in my place not feeling afraid—yet I felt more disgust than fear.

"I was continually brushed by hideous wings, whose hairy and membranous caress provoked a sense of overpowering nausea. I would have fainted if the very excess of my terror hadn't stiffened my nerves.

"I was in the center of a covey of Erloor who stared at me with fiery eyes filled with a ferocious curiosity; some approached so close that the insipid loathsomeness of their breath washed over my face.

"Pressed into a cleft in the rock, unable to move thanks to the net of bark fibers that imprisoned me, I expected to be devoured at any moment. I had no illusions on that score. I knew that I had already been condemned.

"The Erloor grew in number from moment to moment. The infinite number of stars, the multitude of lights of a great city seen from the basket of a balloon, would hardly give an idea of these swarming eyes of flame glinting in the darkness around me, encircling me with a dreadful aureole.

"The monsters shoved and jostled to get a better look at me, from time to time grunting with rage and frantically beating their wings.

"New swarms constantly arrived to join those already there; they dropped from the ceiling, they rose from the floor of the cave.

"Sabbath dances, the 'temptations' of visionary painters, are nothing next to this demonic swarm, from which now issued a deafening drone, punctuated by sharp cries, like the murmur of a wrathful crowd.

"I trembled, suspecting that they were most likely fighting over who would devour me, that they were perhaps going to tear me limb from limb while I was still alive. I never knew the subject of their quarrel; but after an hour during which I suffered all the throes of death, the hideous crush died down.

"With a great clattering of wings, the cave emptied bit by bit, and the glistening eyes were decreasing in number, withdrawing little by little.

"Soon I was plunged into a darkness so profound it was almost palpable, like that spoken of in the Bible.

"If it wasn't salvation, it was at least a respite from my agonies.

"I speculated, plausibly enough, that the essentially nocturnal Erloor had gone in search of food.

"My newfound solitude brought me immense relief.

"I was exhausted and famished; for a second, I nearly fell asleep, but the fear of danger kept me awake.

"It occurred to me that I might stand a chance of wearing down the strands that bound me against the wall of basaltic rock, and I set to work immediately.

"It was a labor of patience, but I had the entire night, and the woven fibers of the cast-net in which I had been caught were not nearly so durable as the thin cords of our terrestrial hemp.

"I had already succeeded in freeing my left arm when I received a blow so harsh and painful on the back of my hand that I couldn't stifle a cry. My hand was bleeding, and see, I still bear the mark of the Erloor's claws!"

Robert Darvel extended his hand, where five reddish scars were still clearly visible.

"I hadn't noticed," he continued, "that one of these monsters, no doubt charged with keeping me under surveillance, was glued to the great rock wall behind me.

"Turning around, I found myself so to speak nose to nose with him. His burning eyes searched mine and his menacing growl made it plain that I was to stop my escape attempts.

"I took his warning to heart and didn't move a muscle the rest of the night. In the end, I succumbed to fatigue and fell asleep."

"I think I would have been too afraid to sleep," murmured Miss Alberte, with a slight shiver.

"No fear, no emotion holds out against a certain level of fatigue. I have experienced this many a time, and the oft-cited fact of artillerymen sleeping on their guns, in the middle of a battle, doesn't surprise me at all.

"In any case, when I awoke, the cave was just as quiet as before, but it seemed to me that the night had given way to a crepuscular shade. The silhouettes of the stalactites and stalagmites, which formed natural pillars, stretched on forever, vague shapes lost in a haze of shadows.

"I could make out none of the details. The scene resembled those water-colors with a black background against which, if you look carefully enough, you can make out even blacker silhouettes lit by an almost imperceptible diffusion of light.

"But a rhythmic, muffled roaring, which I can compare only to the purring of certain motors, emanated from every corner of the subterranean nave.

"I wondered for a long time what it could be.

"I finally figured out that this singular noise was nothing other than the droning of the Erloor who—the day having no doubt arrived—had come back to their den after their nocturnal hunt and were now sleeping, hanging by their talons from outcroppings in the wall.

"My suspicion was confirmed when I noticed that the monster that had struck me, had, like the others, yielded to sleep and was droning noisily behind me.

"My fatigue had virtually disappeared. I figured that, now that my enemies were asleep, it was a good time to renew my attempt to escape.

"Suddenly, wings beat, eyes flamed, and I felt myself roughly pulled by the mesh of the net. At the same time a hoarse voice said to me:

"'Come!'

"I recognized the Erloor whom I had tended, whom I had won over, and who had delivered me to his kind.

"I had managed to get him to speak a few words of the Martian tongue and to make him understand virtually all of it.

"'Where are you taking me?' I asked him.

"'Come,' he repeated, beating his wings impatiently.

"While speaking, he had freed my feet from the net in such a way that I was able to walk but without untying my arms.

"As I walked, I stumbled over old bones and animal carcasses; sometimes I sunk thigh-deep into a layer of guano that had been accumulating for centuries and could secure the fortune of several industrial enterprises.

"We followed a long corridor at the end of which appeared a spot of pale light that could only be daylight.

"Soon I could see that the glistening walls were, as I had deduced from their feel, volcanic in origin.

"My guide did not fly. He hopped along clumsily beside me, his wings dragging along the ground like a dirty coat, and I noticed that his movements became more hesitant as we advanced toward the light.

"However crazy it may seem, I supposed that he regretted his treason and wanted to furnish me with the means to escape.

"'Where are you taking me?' I asked, assuming the tone of authority that I employed in speaking to him when he was my prisoner in the Martian village.

"He raised his clawed hand in a frightened gesture to make me understand that he must not answer me.

"'Do you want to kill me?' I said as calmly as I could.

"He shook his head no.

"It was impossible to get anything out of him. He seemed intimidated by my resolute expression and yet quite determined not to give me any information. So, where was he taking me and why?

"I was furious.

"'I wish to leave!' I cried. 'I command you to lead me out of here.'

"And in a desperate gesture, I tensed my arms and succeeded in enlarging the hole in my net made the night before. He lunged at me. With my only free arm I struck him with a powerful punch to the chest; he stumbled, his feet tangled up in his wings.

"For a second I thought I had won. But as he fell he had deftly seized one of the stone balls that ballasted the base of the cast-net; he pulled hard and I found myself even more tightly bound.

"He snickered, which made his hideous face more hideous still.

"'Very well,' I said coldly, 'since you don't want to say where you are taking me, I'm not going any further.'

"I stood my ground: in spite of all his efforts, he couldn't make me take a single step.

"Then he pointed with his extended claw to the far end of the gallery where the light was coming in and said the word 'eat,' one of the first that I had taught him to pronounce.

"I finally understood that he was taking me to get some food; I was too hungry to continue my resistance any further, so I dutifully began to walk again.

"I must say, I never discovered whether my ex-prisoner was carrying out an order or acting on his own impulse.

"Twenty or so steps more and the light had increased considerably. I could make out the ground covered with a dust of bones and the detritus of animals of every species.

"The Erloor, whose eyes were painfully blinded by the light, moved forward more and more slowly, his eyes blinking. It was visibly taking an incredible effort for him to complete his task.

"For my part, I dragged him along, forcing him to walk as quickly as possible.

"As I had foreseen, there came a moment when he released me, half-blind, and, stopping in his tracks, hid his head under his membranous wing.

"I let out a cry of triumph and set off running at top speed, well aware that in full light he would not be able to pursue me.

"He made no effort; he remained crouched on the ground, his head tucked under his wings, completely immobile.

"I didn't stop to figure out what was wrong. My feet had wings; I felt that a beneficent energy was flowing into me from the light I dashed forward to meet.

"I hesitated for a moment, overcome with joy at the sight of a bit of blue sky in front of me, framed by basalt pilasters. Never had the soft and bright hues of a cathedral's rose window seemed more magnificent to me than this glimpse of sky.

"I set off again quickly and reached the radiant opening, already, in anticipation, breathing deeply of the invigorating air of liberty.

"But having arrived at the very threshold of the opening, I experienced the most bitter of disappointments.

"What I had taken for an exit to the outside was only a sort of window bored into the sheer rock; it must have served for the Erloor much as the holes of a dovecote for ordinary birds.

"Cautiously leaning out, I saw a thousand feet below me the brown water of a torrential river that lapped the base of the mountain.

"To escape that way, I would have needed wings. I was so dismayed, so despondent, that tears came to my eyes. I remained in this state for some time, completely unsure what to do.

"From where I stood, a sumptuous vista spread out before me. The forests, seen from this height, looked like a rich, multicolored tapestry in the most dazzling shades of yellow, orange, and incarnadine. The horizon offered the capricious folds and soft slopes of a negligently draped brocade.

"A multitude of resplendent birds were wheeling in the sky, like the living punctuation of this magnificent page of Martian nature.

"In the distance stood the eternal red and pink mountains, jagged as sierras.

"This vista helped to settle my thoughts.

"I pulled myself together. I reflected that I really had no choice but to return to the Erloor, whose conduct seemed to me harder and harder to explain.

"I had already taken, with much regret, a few steps back into the dark, fetid cave when I spotted a deep recess, to the left of the opening, that I hadn't noticed at first.

"A wooden dish had been placed there, filled with fruit, a slice of grilled meat, and several of the triangular bivalves that I had caught when I first arrived on the planet, in short a sampling of most of the foods that the Erloor had seen me eat in the Martian village.

"A bark bowl filled with water topped off this banquet to which my raging hunger rushed to do justice.

"After eating, I saw things in a very different light. I was disposed to be optimistic.

"It was evident that the Erloor didn't want to take my life and that they had some plan for me, but what, I couldn't guess.

"Consequently, I resolved to show all imaginable submissiveness for the time being, until I had worked out the details of an escape plan, the rough outline of which was coming into focus.

"I had neither the time nor the materials needed to plait a rope long enough to reach the surface of the river, but I was considering a parachute.

"The cast-net that held my arms fast would furnish the suspension lines, and for the fabric, my feather-lined cloak would provide enough material.

"I planned to attach this device to my shoulders and jump into the river, which I could easily swim across.

"I sat for a long time before the opening, stocking up, so to speak, on clean air and sunlight before returning to my foul prison.

"As I turned to take a last look at the radiant horizon, I caught sight of a thin column of blue smoke rising from the faraway trees.

"I can't express how moved I was, what preposterous hopes filled my mind at this sight.

"The slight plume, which rose straight into the still air, seemed to me like the symbol and sign of my impending deliverance.

"The use of fire, which caused the Erloor such great terror, was known only to the gentle Martians, my subjects.

"I assumed that they had come looking for me; my heart beat faster at the thought that only a few leagues separated me from these devoted friends.

"I couldn't tear myself away from this sight; I had to summon all my courage before I dared plunge back into the shadows of the gallery.

"I found the Erloor just where I had left him.

"Without a word, he led me back to the place from which he had taken me.

"I spent the remainder of the interminable day partly sleeping, partly daydreaming.

"As night fell, the Erloor emerged from their torpor; the cavern was filled, as before, with the beating of wings. Eyes of flame flashed, but I noticed that they paid much less attention to me.

"Although I was still watched over by the Erloor who had introduced me to his claw, I no longer excited general curiosity. This seemed to bode well for my escape plans.

"My life then became dreadfully monotonous.

"Each morning, my Erloor came to conduct me to the opening in the rock, where my food had always been scrupulously laid out.

"I was able to breathe and contemplate the countryside as much as I desired until I was brought back into the cave.

"I was greatly discouraged to find, on the second day, no trace of the plume of smoke that had awakened in me so much hope.

"So I decided it was time to carry out my parachute plan. I had taken care to set aside a few of the pointed bivalve shells, which I planned to use as blades to slice through the fibers of the net.

"In the end, I realized that, given the reduced weight of objects on the surface of Mars, I would need much less fabric than if I had to make a parachute on Earth.

"Unfortunately, in spite of the apparent liberty I enjoyed during the hour of my meal, I was so closely watched that an entire week slipped by without my being able to attempt anything.

"As my despair grew, my energy slowly dwindled, and I felt that I would soon succumb to the polluted air of that abominable cave.

"Now that I saw them up close, the Erloor, whom I had at first believed to have developed a sort of civilization, seemed little more than bloodthirsty brutes who directed all their faculties toward carnage.

"The only industry that I had seen was the weaving of bark nets similar to the one with which they had captured me and that they must have used in their nocturnal hunts; but this art seemed as instinctive, as unconscious to them as the fabrication of a web is for the spider.

"Their nets always had the same dimensions and the mesh the same proportions.

"It was the old Erloor incapable of flight who devoted themselves to this labor, for which they used the underbark of a tree reminiscent of birch.

"I always wondered why animals so formidably armed with wings and claws needed such nets, and I assumed that, in moments of famine, when terrestrial game was scarce, they must have used them to catch amphibious mammals and the fish that fill the Martian canals.

"My eyes had little by little adapted to the darkness of the cavern; while the Erloor slept, I ventured once or twice down its tortuous passages.

"It was even more vast than I could have imagined, branching off into depths I dared not explore.

"I hadn't been able to discover where that quantity of remains covering the ground had come from, but in the end I found the explanation.

"In one high recess, I found myself suddenly among a prodigious quantity of desiccated Erloor corpses; there were thousands of them, and it had no doubt taken centuries to produce this enormous accumulation.

"Nothing could be more hideous than this excuse for a cemetery with its grinning skulls, skeletons, and withered wings heaped in disarray.

"From the most recent corpses, I surmised that the Erloor, like certain savages, hastened to put to death and devour their elders who had become incapable of plaiting nets.

"All showed obvious marks of having been bled by their more robust fellow creatures.

"I stepped away in horror from this den of putrefaction that was largely responsible for the pestilential odor that poisoned the entire cave.

"Though the Erloor proved heartless toward the elderly, they showed much tenderness for the newborn.

"Until they were able to fly, they were sheltered in down-filled beds made of coils of strong and supple vines.

"I saw Erloor mothers suckling their young, generally two in number, gathered under their wings as under a coat, with hideous caresses.

"A section of the cave was filled with these nests scattered in the crevices of the rock.

"But these explorations taught me nothing of use for my escape.

"I did discover several other exits similar to the one I visited each day to eat and breathe, but all opening at an inaccessible height.

"Among the trials I have since had to bear, I don't believe I experienced a more lugubrious week.

"I felt hypochondria overcome me bit by bit. I began to despair that I might be destined to pass the remainder of my days in this sinister necropolis, where I had the impression I was being buried alive.

"Then a new concern joined my other torments.

"I couldn't help thinking of the sad fate that awaited my former subjects, the Martians of the lagoons, now that I was no longer there to defend and lead them.

"A new Prometheus, I had indeed given them fire, an invaluable gift; but I was sure that these naïve creatures would grow careless, would be emboldened by the appearance of safety and end up victim to their enemies' ferocity.

"I already imagined them torn apart by the claws of the Erloor, bled alive by the voracious monsters. It broke my heart to think of the sad fate reserved for these simple, guileless creatures.

"I then took stock of the Erloor's conduct toward me.

"Their intention was not, as I had at first vainly supposed, to advance themselves through my instruction, to gain for themselves the inventions with which I had endowed their adversaries and their victims.

"They merely kept me as a hostage who might prove valuable thereafter. With their innate cunning, they had correctly anticipated that, as soon as I was gone, the Martians would be at their mercy, would once again be the docile flock that they devoured at their leisure before my arrival.

"As I reflected on this I had a fit of anger. I was outraged at myself and at my fate, and this tore me away from the neurasthenic torpor that was taking hold of me.

"Could a man of such accomplishment become the plaything of these vile and ferocious creatures? That was something I could not allow.

"I swore to triumph or perish in the attempt, and I set to work without delay.

"One of the obstacles that had hindered the construction of my parachute was the lack of hoops or rings to support the edges of the chute and to maintain its shape.

"It suddenly occurred to me that the flexible creepers that the Erloor used to build their nests would work perfectly.

"I immediately went in search of some, being careful to strip only old, long abandoned nests.

"I forgot to mention that in the days prior to this I had cut away enough of the strands of the cast-net, with the help of the sharp shell I told you about, that it was hanging in tatters and no longer hindered my movement: I had rid myself in the same way of the stone balls that weighted it.

"I set to work in the evening, a little after sunset. I hoped to finish before the Erloor, all of whom had left in search of their nocturnal quarry, returned.

"The one that had served as my jailer the first few nights went away with the others, judging me no doubt sufficiently reconciled to my prison.

"I couldn't have hoped for a better opportunity.

"Unfortunately, I had no tools but my shells, and my wounded hand hurt dreadfully. It was with great difficulty that I made a sort of crude and handle-less parasol, with a hole in the center.

"This work, as rough as it was, took me all night, and dawn was approaching when it was finally finished.

"The Erloor were already starting to come back in bunches; the cavern was filling with the soft noise of their flaccid wings and the musky scent of their bodies, similar to the stench of a carnival menagerie.

"I now had to wait for day.

"I huddled in my crevice, burning with impatience.

"A half hour passed. The bulk of the flock had come back. Only isolated individuals now passed before my eyes, stragglers hurrying clumsily before the imminent break of day.

"Finally I saw no more of them; the thunderous snoring told me that the monsters had fallen back into their daily torpor.

It was that uncertain hour when shadows start to fade. I was still on edge after my night of anxious labor and didn't have the patience to wait until the sun had risen; I rushed toward the opening in the rock, dragging my contraption behind me.

"From my aerial observatory, I saw the dark sky crossed by a thin pale line that was the emerging dawn; a cool air rose from the river's tumultuous waters that I heard rolling at the foot of the mountain.

"I took a joyful, deep breath of pure, glacial air.

"The moment had come: I checked the straps of my parachute one last time, attached it to my shoulders, and jumped into the void, closing my eyes . . .

"I didn't fall even a third of the way.

"A dark mass flashed before my eyes: I felt myself seized in flight and carried into the air like a pigeon caught by a sparrow hawk.

"Misfortune had decreed that I be noticed by an Erloor who had remained behind the others, the last straggler of the band.

"I bitterly regretted my impatience then; the Erloor carried me under his arm, and I was half-smothered against the creature's fetid coat.

"It was an unbearable feeling. I sensed, from the labored beating of my abductor's wings and his hoarse panting that my weight, combined with that of my apparatus, was almost too heavy for him.

"With that lucidity that often accompanies imminent danger, I calculated that he was perhaps going to let me fall from high in the air.

"The next moment, he descended again, dragged down by my weight. I watched the white smudge of the day grow on the horizon. I might still survive; the water of the river would soften my fall.

"But the monster redoubled his efforts. His wings flapped furiously; with a final surge, breathless, half-dead, he dropped me on the edge of the opening I had left from.

"Next, to destroy all means and all hope for a new escape, he started to tear to shreds my poor apparatus that, as rudimentary as it was, had cost me so much effort.

"Then he dragged me roughly into the interior of the cave, while making a sort of high-pitched hissing, which must have been his own way of celebrating his victory.

"I was brought back to the same place where I had been tied up the first day.

"As we arrived, my vanquisher gave a strident shout that roused the multitude of Erloor from their slumber.

"Once again, thousands of burning eyes were fixed on me. The monsters swarmed all around me. But this time, it wasn't simple curiosity that animated them; their gestures, their hoarse growls were so many threats addressed to me.

"They shoved me, they placed their claws against my face. I was the target of their taunts and insults; like an Indian nailed to a torture post, I expected to be torn to bits, tortured in a thousand ways.

"At that very instant I experienced a momentary blackout, a sort of hallucination. Just as the fiercest of the Erloor was rushing at me with his claws outstretched, it seemed to me that my willpower, my consciousness, abandoned me.

"Everything grew hazy. I saw myself suddenly conveyed to Earth and into a strange room in an Indian pagoda where I confusedly made out the vague figure of Miss Alberte among people I did not recognize . . ."

"Good Lord," interrupted Ralph Pitcher exultantly. "That is without any doubt the very day that poor Captain Wad had you summoned by a yogi named Phara-Chibh.

"You quite simply materialized, as the occultists say, and we saw you distinctly—for I was there—you and the Erloor who threatened you."

"I don't dispute the fact," Robert Darvel continued, grown pensive again. "I am simply recounting what happened.

"In any case, this odd state lasted only a few seconds; in a flash I regained an awareness of my terrible situation.

"In the center of this circle of blazing eyes and sharp claws, I sensed that all was lost.

"Already they were no longer limiting themselves to threats. A few of them were lifting me into the air and making a game of letting me fall heavily on the bones that covered the floor of the cave; others pulled me by the arms and legs as if they wanted to tear me apart. There was one who lifted me by the hair, as if to mock my attempt to escape. I was like the legendary hermit tormented and teased by devils; but I felt certain that these wild games were only the prelude to my torture . . . The Erloor were playing with me as a cat plays with a mouse.

"Already a swipe of a claw had torn my shoulder. I was covered in blood, half blinded. I would have preferred to be dead, for it to be over with once and for all . . .

"I had just been knocked to the ground for perhaps the tenth time, half-stunned, surrounded by the monsters' high-pitched shouts and growls of joy, when a great clamor started from deep within the cave.

"At the same time, there was a growing reddish gleam.

"The Erloor withdrew hastily, emitting shrieks of terror . . . They whirled about like dead leaves in the wind, frantic, finding that the sole paths of escape from the unexpected menace ran through galleries that led only to the blinding light of day.

"This unexpected, inexplicable intervention gave me renewed energy and courage. I armed myself with a femur that was lying on the ground and marched toward the red light, striking with this improvised club at anything that blocked the way.

"But a shout of euphoric joy escaped from my lips when I recognized, in the gleam of the torches they brandished, twenty or so of my Martian subjects, led by the faithful Eeeoys.

"They had followed me, to save me in spite of myself. They had succeeded in discovering my hideaway and were coming to deliver me, which was, on the part of these timid creatures, an act of extraordinary courage.

"At the sight of me, they burst into cheers, but there was not a minute to lose. If the light, our most effective weapon, disappeared, we were doomed, and already several torches had been extinguished by the furiously beating wings of the Erloor.

"Following my orders, they rapidly piled the nests of woven vines in the middle of the cave and set them alight. A bright flame arose, illuminating the most secluded depths.

"Fire, the symbol of mind over matter, triumphed.

"The Erloor approached and fell unaided into the flame like a swarm of gigantic moths, and all those that fell were knocked senseless or had their throats cut by the pitiless Martians.

"It was a terrifying and magnificent spectacle, like a ghastly page from Revelation recreated by a sublime painter. Gilt by the flames, the tall columns of basalt formed a grim background fit for this gory scene. The blood flowed in a stream and reflected the glow of the blaze, and a haze of red and gold smoke enveloped the demonic whirlwind from which arose howls to freeze the marrow . . .

"At last we left. The putrid smoke made the place unbearable, and the blood threatened to extinguish the fire.

"On our way out, we followed a long tunnel that I didn't know about that seemed very recently dug . . ."

At this point in his account, Robert Darvel asked permission to rest for a few minutes; but the impression produced on his audience was such that nobody broke the silence.

After moistening his lips with a sorbet that Chérifa offered him, the explorer of the skies picked up where he had left off.

II

....

After the Victory

". . . Throughout my battle with the Erloor," he continued, "a feverish exultation had sustained me. I had experienced something like the Berserkers of Scandinavian legend, who, filled with sacred rage, would fight on, though riddled with mortal wounds, refusing to succumb before they were victorious.

"Safe and sound once more, I fainted from fatigue, tension, and the wounds that I had received and, despite the care the Martians lavished upon me, it was several hours before I awoke.

"When I opened my eyes again, Eeeoys was at my side, watching me with anxious devotion and splashing my forehead with cool water. Seeing me regain consciousness, her little delft-blue eyes beamed with simple pleasure. She cried with joy as she kissed me.

"I had often found the affectionate attentions that she lavished upon me tiresome — especially after she had gotten into her head the strange idea of marrying me — but I admit that I in turn heartily kissed her chubby, pink cheeks.

"'How you frightened us!' she murmured. 'We were afraid that you had been devoured. But, as you can see, we didn't forget you. Promise me that next time you won't be so reckless.'

"'I promise,' I said, quite moved by her naïve devotion.

"'You must never again venture without us into the accursed realms of the South! The Erloor are only some of the least of the dangers you will find there; but I hope that you have been cured of your curiosity. We are going to return to our land, where you will be able to relax, happy, at my side . . .'

"Among all these phrases she reeled off, one alone caught my attention:

"'Did you say that the Erloor are one of the least of the dangers in this region? What other perils might I find here?'

"'I don't know,' she stammered, as if she regretted having spoken.

"'What do you mean you don't know?'

"'I only know that it is a terrible land, from which our ancestors were driven long ago. My father said that one must never linger there.'

"I was unable to draw out anything else, but I couldn't stop thinking. Certainly, poor Eeeoys was wasting her time lecturing me. As wounded and bruised as I was, I had never been more eager to discover all the planet's secrets and I vowed to myself that I would succeed.

"Meanwhile, the Martians were making an awful racket all around me. They kissed my hands, dancing and laughing joyously.

"I was worshipped by these poor people, like the 'good king' in fairy tales and chivalric romances.

"Their adulation for my person was manifest in many ways.

"They had bandaged my wounds with a compress of geranium leaves, which are known to speed healing. They had replaced my robe of red and green feathers with another just as sumptuous, and they rushed to bring me grilled meat, fruit—all that they had been able to obtain.

"I certainly did justice to these refreshments, and my Martians watched me eat with an air of ecstatic rapture. Eeeoys cut up the joints on a wooden dish with a flint knife and made me drink between each mouthful, advising me to chew well and to take my time.

"We were on the bank of the torrential river I mentioned earlier. In front of me stood the mountain whose slopes harbored the Erloor's cavern. Swirls of black smoke with a fetid, atrocious odor of burnt flesh continued to escape from its openings.

"I had little doubt that the monsters had been exterminated, to the very last one.

"I was wrong. I suddenly saw an Erloor, then a second, leap hastily from that same opening through which I had rushed with my parachute; flames tore atrocious screams from them. They didn't get very far, in any case.

Blinded by the light of day they tumbled headfirst into the river, which carried them away to the cheers of the Martians.

"We had set up our camp in a delightful spot—a glade shaded by large trees, fronted by a strand of pink sand along the river. The foliage, as I had noted in all the regions of the planet that I crossed, had almost none of the green coloration of terrestrial foliation. It offered every register of yellow and orange, from the bright chromium of oranges and pumpkins to the brilliant yellow of bananas to the feverish green of limes.

"In place of the endless willows, red beeches, and hazels that covered the land to the north, here specimens of the palm and banana families shook their ample burnished-gold foliage in the wind; it was literally a golden forest of a richness almost too dazzling to behold.

"The ground was covered with a long violet moss, as gentle on the feet as the softest carpet of fine wool, and cacti the color of rusted iron, bristling with spines, lined the paths, like the fences of this natural park.

"The forest called to mind the capricious landscapes of Ariosto, of Atlantis, of Florida, all the magical places where, from time immemorial, the imagination of poets—bruised by the inexorable harshness of men and things—has found refuge. It had an ethereal quality; its colors were at once too muted and too dazzling, its copses arranged with too much splendor for all of it not to be an illusion that might disappear from one moment to the next.

"I tore myself away from these observations to ask the tender Eeeoys for the details of my deliverance; she hastened to share them, filled with pride and joy at a feat that, given the fearful nature of the Martians, seemed to me hardly believable.

"'After you left us,' she said, 'I was overwhelmed by despair. I shed many tears, fearing I would never see you again.

"'We remained for a long time around the large fire that we had lit, and it seemed to us that now that you were gone the fire would no longer have the same power to protect us.

"'We looked at each other in silent despair . . . I was the first to take courage . . . I declared that I would follow you by myself if necessary, but that we couldn't abandon you in this way.

"'It wasn't easy to persuade them . . . They were demoralized, it was dark, they would be devoured by the Erloor, which would be of no use to anyone.

"'Their main objection was the very interdiction that you had made.

"'I managed to persuade them by describing the misfortunes that would surely befall them if they were to let their benefactor and prince perish . . .

"'I even insinuated that your prohibition was perhaps only a means of testing their courage.

"'In the end I managed to persuade them to arm themselves with torches and set out to find you.

"'It was easy to follow the route that you had taken. It was a large sandy path flanked on either side by impenetrable thickets; we couldn't miss your footprints in the sand.

"'We walked for two hours as quickly as we could without making the torches go out. The forest was silent; we had up until then caught sight of no living being.

"'Suddenly, we heard familiar cries in the distance, cries we couldn't mistake: the cries of the Erloor.

"'We speeded up our pace, we ran.

"'A little farther, the ground carried the traces of a struggle, and I gathered several tufts of red and green feathers from your robe.

"'There could be no doubt: you had been taken by the Erloor . . .

"'At that moment, the clouds that hid Phobos and Deimos broke, revealing a steep mountain around which thousands of Erloor were fluttering like a flock of night birds.

"'My terrified companions refused to go any farther; they could see that before us lay one of the monsters' lairs and that they had taken you there.

"'Yet one thing reassured me; the Erloor, as you know, customarily devour their victims on the spot. Since they were content to take you prisoner, they didn't want to take your life.

"'Despite this reasoning, I passed the remainder of the night in terror. My companions had lit a large fire solidly protected by a roof of tree branches, but everyone trembled with fear, astonished at having ventured so close to the lair of their enemy.

"'In the meantime, the constantly swelling flocks of Erloor, which came and went in the sky like black clouds swept along by a rushing wind, didn't seem bothered that we were nearby. It may be that the satisfaction occasioned by your capture made them forget or disregard our presence.

"'We nonetheless were relieved when we saw the glorious light of dawn chase the Erloor into the cavities of the mountain until every last one of them had disappeared.

"'We took counsel.

"'Many were discouraged and wanted to start on the return march north. A selfish few even went so far as to say, in justification, that you were of a superior race and that you would extricate yourself from this problem perfectly well on your own.

"'Once again, I had to make them ashamed of their cowardice.

"'After a long discussion, it was decided that the camp would remain where it was, and I am sure that you must have been able to see our fire from high on the mountain.'

"I remembered then that column of smoke I had glimpsed from the opening in the rock, the sight of which comforted me so propitiously in my despair," stated Robert.

"'We spent that day,' continued Eeeoys, 'studying the mountain, but it was inaccessible on all sides; attempting to climb it was unthinkable.

"'Our discouragement and reluctance were growing.

"'An old man however made an interesting discovery. There was a place on the mountain where the hard basalt was seamed with layers of soil.[8]

"'He suggested that perhaps, by digging, we would be able to open a subterranean passage all the way to the Erloor who, surprised in their sleep, and thrown into a panic by our fire, would not be able to withstand us.

"'Bushes covered precisely this part of the base of the mountain, which permitted us to begin our work out of sight of the enemy.

"'Everyone rallied round this idea, although the construction of a subterranean passage in such conditions promised to be very difficult for us.

"'I anxiously wondered whether we would arrive in time to save you. That very evening, happily, one of us had the good fortune to discover a magnificent Roomboo caught in one of the traps that we had set along the riverbank just in case.

---

8   It is evident — as a note from the engineer himself proves — that the rudimentary sentences of the young Martian are explained and expanded upon here. A literal translation from the Martian would have been almost incomprehensible for the terrestrial reader.

"'We securely harnessed the gigantic burrowing beast, which had only been slightly wounded. Here was a collaborator readymade to assist us in our underground work.

"'The most difficult thing was to persuade the Roomboo to start working. It took an entire day of work to get it there; it struggled furiously in its bonds, frothing and bellowing in fury.

"'To reach our goal, we had to beat it and deprive it of food. In the end we only succeeded by menacing it with burning coals, the proximity of which, in spite of its blindness, caused it profound terror.

"'We finally had the satisfaction of seeing it begin to work in a sort of rage, advancing with disconcerting speed, its hard ivory claws making the earth and rocks fly around it.

"'Behind him, two of our most robust companions widened the opening, hastily propping up the ceiling with flat stones and the branches of trees.

"'In less than two days we reached the lair of the Erloor.

"'The rest you know, how we had the pleasure of wresting you from the claws of those demons . . .'

"Eeeoys had stopped, lowering her eyes with feigned modesty, but it was easy for me to see how proud she was of the operation's success, the greatest share of which she ascribed, quite rightly, to herself.

"For my part, I was astonished by the initiative and courage my Martians had demonstrated.

"I no longer recognized the pitiful savages, stultified by fear, of a few months earlier, and I was profoundly touched by what they had just done for me.

"I promised myself not to abandon them so thoughtlessly again, and to do all that I could to assist their material and moral progress.

"All the rest of that day and a part of the following night was spent recuperating and banqueting in my honor. We did not lack for provisions; the forest was extremely rich in game and my hunters had become quite skilled with a bow.

"Among the animals that I saw for the first time, I will make note of a variety of peacock with delicate pink plumage and wattles that dangle like a turkey's; and a type of canary-yellow ostrich, completely lacking wings that were called to mind only by two very short stumps; its feathers reduced to threads formed a sort of lustrous fleece of a very curious appearance that reminded me of no terrestrial bird, except perhaps—but very distantly—the kiwi of New Zealand. Flavored with aromatic berries, the flesh of this strange biped was moreover excellent.

"I should also mention a species of land tortoise with a shell of such beautiful orange that one might have said it was armored in burnished gold—but that wasn't its most remarkable characteristic. Its very long neck reached out from under its bright shell like a serpent, its legs were long, and its powerfully developed hindquarters permitted the animal to jump, to leap forward, in the manner of frogs.

"This tortoise lived in the damp undergrowth and ate insects and small mammals.

"In the same environs, the Martians had also killed a hideous beast whose like I have never seen in the prints of naturalists or in the most demented fancies of painters of the fantastic.

"Picture a biped, about a meter tall, with the long slender legs of a wading bird; a dreadful maw, reminiscent of a caiman with its elongated form and sharp teeth; and almost no body. Its backbone was reduced to two or three vertebrae, and its formidable jawbone was nearly directly joined to the greatly enlarged bones of the pelvis.

"This monster was so to speak nothing more than a mouth on two legs; its feet were webbed and its entire body covered in yellowish scales. Its very tiny eye expressed an incredible ferociousness; a blood-colored crest, capriciously jagged and fluted like the lace ruff of an Elizabethan gentleman, added to the horror of this extravagant being.

"I called this animal an 'eurygule,'" and I vowed to take one alive at the first opportunity.

"The Martians who had killed it told me that they had surprised it in a muddy spot, waddling on its long legs like a stork.

"I refused to try the colorless flesh of the eurygule, which the Martians, less fastidious than I, enjoyed thoroughly, declaring it very tender and savory.

"They were still busy skinning a few of these creatures, which keenly

9 Eurygule: large mouth

excited their curiosity, when night fell. I immediately ordered that a new stock of fuel be thrown on the fire and a supply of it reserved for the night, which my subjects hastened to do with remarkable swiftness.

"Their joy was evident when they saw that no Erloor came out of the rock, and I understood, from Eeeoys's explanations, that they imagined they had destroyed the entire race of these monsters.

"I was careful to not disabuse them, but I wasn't, personally, as reassured.

"I knew all in all only a minute portion of the planet, and it seemed likely that there existed, here or there, other Erloor caverns.

"If only one 'survivor' of the last massacre were to implore an allied flock, it would be enough to put us in terrible danger, all the more so since we knew very little of the region in which we found ourselves.

"Despite my weariness, I was unable to close my eyes all that night. My fears were for naught this time. Fortunately, no incident troubled the slumber of my companions.

"At dawn, the whole company was afoot and making enthusiastic preparations for departure.

"Despite their victory, my subjects were impatient to regain the safety of their marshland hamlets. Perhaps vanity as well played a part in their eagerness; they were impatient to show their relatives and friends the animals and unknown fruits they had found in the great forest.

"We started cheerfully on the march, down a large path whose reddened moss called to mind threadbare velvet.

"Eeeoys and I were the only ones to not carry any burden; the Martians were heavily laden with the paraphernalia of the camp and the yield of their hunt.

"A large number also carried clay vessels full of glowing coals, which I had had made a few weeks previously and which weren't so different from certain urns for holy water or Flemish smoking pots. This invention, as crude as it was, served in place of the chemical matches or tinderbox that I hadn't yet had an opportunity to make.

"At times I couldn't stop myself from smiling at the sight of this procession that, with its feathered miters and long down robes, its arrows and bows, had a vaguely Babylonian air.

"About midday we crossed a river of red water the color of unclouded blood; large reeds of the bamboo family growing in abundance on the banks made it easy to build a bridge that, as a precaution, I destroyed as soon as we had crossed.

"Speaking of which, you must have been struck, in all the descriptions that I have given you, by the predominance of the colors orange and red on the planet Mars. This fact can only be explained by the great abundance of iron, chromium, and other metals, or perhaps by the presence in their atmosphere of certain gases that are found only in low levels in our own.

"The countryside was now something to behold. Giant trees whose smooth trunks rose fifty or sixty meters without a branch formed an impenetrable vault above our heads. The profound silence prevailing under their shade reminded me of the caves of Ellora and Elephanta, which I had visited. The Martian forest offered all their mysterious horror.

"Now and then, a vast clearing formed a sort of bay of sunlight in these shadows, where we would stop for a bit before plunging back into the shade of the living pillars which, eventually, produced in me, as well as in the Martians, an overwhelming impression of gloom and malaise.

"Eeeoys, more than all her companions, was frightened and nervous. With each step, she looked back, as if she was afraid of being followed, and her arm, pressed against mine, was agitated at times by a violent shudder.

"'What's wrong, my child?' I asked her, softly caressing her red hair that I had taught her to braid as the young girls of Earth do.

"'I don't know,' she murmured, turning toward me, eyes shining with tears. 'I keep thinking I hear the noise of beating wings above us . . . at times, it seems like a fog passes before my eyes . . . I'm afraid. I sense some misfortune will befall us before the end of the day.'

"I did my best to reassure her.

"'I didn't think you were so easily frightened,' I said, laughing. 'Honestly, I no longer recognize you . . .

"'What do you have to fear? Am I not here beside you?'

"'Perhaps I am wrong,' she said all atremble, 'but I'm afraid, and a moment ago I felt an icy hand alight on my hair.'

"'It's your imagination . . . nerves . . . Reason your way through your fears a little, as I have taught you to do, and you will see that there is no cause for danger here. It is broad daylight, we are numerous and well armed, and I am here, by your side! . . . And the Erloor have been annihilated.'

"'It isn't the Erloor I am afraid of . . .'

"'What is it, then?'

"'I don't know . . . It's something I can't explain . . .'

"She was trembling like a leaf.

"'Wait, listen,' she added, pressing up against me. 'I hear very clearly the sound of wings now.'

"I lent an ear to humor what I called her whimsy and, to my great astonishment, it seemed to me that I heard right next to us an almost imperceptible noise, a very light beating of wings.

"'It's just some insect,' I said, desperate for an explanation.

"Inside, I was a little surprised but not unduly alarmed. I explained to the young Martian that under these vaults of branches, as in a genuine building, echoes reflected back with great clarity. What she had heard was the buzzing of some wood-wasp—perhaps quite far away—unless she'd simply been the victim of a mere hallucination, the result of the emotions of the preceding days.

"'But you just heard it too?'

"'Because you suggested it to me, no doubt . . .'

"I launched into a long explanation of suggestion and collective hallucinations. Poor Eeeoys doubtless understood very little of it, but it nevertheless seemed to reassure her a little.

"She forced herself to smile, but in spite of that she remained obstinately pressed against me, and I clearly saw that her fears were not allayed.

"She gave a sigh of relief when we came out of the dark cover of the great trees and entered a marshy plain, dotted with thickets and clumps of reeds, at the end of which a russet hill seemed to mark the horizon.

"At this moment, one of the Martians at the head of the column came back to me, his countenance troubled. While he insisted he was absolutely sure of the direction, he no longer recognized this countryside. He had never seen the hill that sprawled before us.

"I assumed that in spite of his assertions he was lost, and I told him to continue marching north. I was quite sure, whatever happened, that I could find my way thanks to the stars and also to certain canals that served as landmarks.

"We started walking again, but as we pushed forward, the russet hill took on a most surprising appearance.

"It appeared that the mass of which it was composed was agitated by a perpetual movement, and that the shape of its contours was continually shifting. Its summit seemed to rise or fall with the whims of the breeze.

"For a moment I believed I was dealing with a sandy mound such as I had seen in the Sahara whose appearance is constantly reshaped by the winds. But I soon saw that I was mistaken; there were none of those dusty wind-formed plumes that sometimes climb to great heights.

"As I approached it, this bizarre hill looked more and more like a prairie agitated by the breeze, like a capricious heap of greenery floating in the air just as certain aquatic plants float suspended in the water.

"We soon lost all uncertainty.

"An abrupt shift in the wind blew a verdant cloud over us and we were for a time half buried under thousands of tiny plants.

"In Central Africa I had already seen aerial plants, whose slender stems are similar to gossamer and that germinate and grow, flower and die, without ever touching the ground; but that was nothing like this prodigious mass of floating greenery.

"I was tremendously intrigued.

"While extricating myself as best I could from the host of plants in which I was tangled as if in a net, I took one of them and examined it carefully.

"It was hardly more than two decimeters long. The leaves on either side of a very slender stem were deeply serrated. By the grouping of their leaflets, they recalled the leaves of ash or acacia. Their color ranged from greenish-yellow to russet brown. The flower resembled a minuscule yellow lily, and the root formed a little tuft of fibers as fine as hair.

"After studying the plant for some time, I let it fall to ascertain how it was able to keep itself in the air.

"I then witnessed the most disconcerting phenomenon.

"Not only, as I anticipated, did the leaves on either side of the stem form a parachute, but they were shaken by a rapid movement of vibration, and they opened and closed like the leaves of the touch-me-not when it is abruptly approached.

"The root itself, a truly excitable tuft, participated in this movement as if it played the role of rudder for this vegetative airplane.

"I soon saw the plant lift slowly above my hand and lose itself in the moving torrent of its fellows.

"I carefully squeezed two examples of these curious aerophytes into the pockets of my feathered gown; imagining no doubt that I had just made some precious discovery, Eeeoys imitated me point for point.

"I was pleased to see that my Martians, now that they were able to account for the phenomenon, were no longer frightened. They laughed as they shook off masses of grass and teased one another to see themselves enmeshed in them.

"We were nonetheless blocked by the aerophytes, which formed in front of us a wall every bit as impassible as a craggy rock might have been.

"Night was coming and I didn't want us to risk being smothered by these accursed plants in our sleep.

"So we were obliged to retrace our footsteps and locate our camp on the border of the forest that had so frightened my little companion.

"The fires were lit and the sentinels positioned as usual.

"The sky was exceptionally clear, the air scented with the smell of water and fresh grass.

"I put off until the next day the problem of finding a path through the mass of aerophytes, and, after having one last time advised vigilance to the keepers of the fire, I allowed myself to sleep."

III

....

The Aerophytes

"I woke up several times during the night, in the grip of nightmares that I attributed to exhaustion and emotion, but which, strangely, recurred exactly the same every time I succeeded in closing my eyes.

"I dreamed that an Erloor was pressing his knee against my chest and strangling me or that I was being crushed in the coils of an enormous snake.

"I opened my eyes, anxious, my forehead clammy with sweat, but was soon reassured by the peaceful scene around me.

"The fire, carefully maintained by the watch, cast a peaceful light, and all around it the Martians were at rest, rolled up in their feather cloaks. On the horizon, the floating field of aerophytes formed a large brown cloud.

"I went back to sleep but awoke almost immediately, prey to the same persistent dread.

"Finally, the day dawned and I gave the signal to awaken to all the troops.

"Eeeoys, greeting me with a kiss me as she did each morning, told me that she had also been tormented by nightmares and, amazingly, they were exactly the same as my own.

"I tried not to make more of this fact than it deserved, but I was uneasy in spite of myself, prey to the nervousness that accompanies fatigue and insomnia.

"I was struck by my little friend's sad, pensive mien and tried in vain to distract her from her fears.

"'Say what you will,' she murmured, shaking her head, 'I sense some danger; something threatens us. I have a premonition that I will never see my father again. You shouldn't have come—one shouldn't try to fathom the secrets of the forbidden regions. Our fathers have always maintained that nothing but great misfortunes could come from this curiosity.'

"In spite of myself, I shared her misgivings, but I was careful to not let it show.

"'You're a scaredy-cat,' I said, forcing myself to smile. 'You have the grumpy face of a child who hasn't had enough sleep!

"'Once you are fully awake, you won't dwell any more on these inane tales.

"'Now we have serious matters to deal with.

"'We must cut a path through the aerial marsh.'

"'How are you thinking of doing it? I don't see a good way.'

"'The answer is plain as day. I am convinced that these little plants whose nervous sensitivity is so well developed must loathe smoke. With the help of a large fire of damp grass and green branches we shall triumphantly open a way through!'

"I wasn't as sure of the result as my boasting suggested, but I didn't see another stratagem to use against these infelicitous aerophytes.

"On my command, we struck camp and approached the aerial marsh.

"Clearly, the wind favored our plans, blowing the swirls of smoke toward the cloud of vegetation.

"At first my expectations were perfectly realized.

"As soon as the smoke reached them, the aerophytes quickly began to agitate the winglets of their leaves and beat a retreat.

"All this vegetation heaved like the sea in a gale.

"In less than a quarter of an hour, a large area in front of us was free.

"The Martians, amazed, shouted with joy and started into the channel we had cleared.

"I was surprised myself by the promptness and ease with which we had overcome this apparently insurmountable obstacle.

"I still bitterly regret my carelessness on that occasion.

"We had hardly taken a hundred steps between the two verdant ramparts the plants formed on either side when I heard behind me a sort of sputtering, similar to the sound produced when water is poured onto hot coals.

"I turned around. To my great consternation, the fire of damp grass had been extinguished and our supplies of fuel lay scattered in all directions.

"I was deeply stunned and apprehensive.

"The Erloor couldn't be guilty of this mischief. It was broad daylight and, in any case, fire inspired in them as much fear as light. The ground was solid rock, so it could not have been the Roomboo.

"I had at that moment only one thought.

"'Go back!' I shouted with all my might. 'Go back the way we came! . . .'

"It was already too late.

"The two walls of greenery were closing in. In less than a minute the route was blocked in front and behind.

"A minute later we were literally buried under the heavy mass of herbage.

"I was half-smothered, like a swimmer entangled in sea grass.

"I heard the cries of distress, the appeals of the unfortunate Martians, but these cries reached my ears more and more feebly.

"The grassy bundles, more dense with each passing moment, smothered their agony, and it was my name that they uttered, it was to me that they called for help, me whom they had saved from the claws of the Erloor!

"Their pleas broke my heart; I felt a surge of rage to see myself thus reduced to helplessness.

"But Eeeoys? From the first moment of the catastrophe, she had let go of my arm, in a movement of unguarded terror.

"I heard her voice, a few steps away.

"'Robert!' she pleaded. 'Help!'

"I struggled desperately against the floating jungle, attempting to head in the direction of my poor child's voice; my efforts succeeded only in making the treacherous web in which I was entangled thicker, like an object wrapped in hay.

"Each of my movements triggered the reflexes of the vibratile leaves of the aerophytes; if one of my gestures pushed them away, they immediately flowed back over me in greater numbers.

"Their mass weighed on my head and encircled me so tightly that I could no longer move a muscle.

"I was hardly able to breathe; at the same time, from this mountain of plants, each of which taken in isolation had no smell, came a dull and musky odor, which slowly went to my head and dulled my senses.

"I sensed that in the end this odor would be lethal, like the scent of tuberoses or mock oranges in a closed room.

"I could no longer see, deep darkness surrounded me, and a bitter pollen dust entered my eyes and caught in my throat.

"I had lost from the start any possibility of orienting myself. I no longer knew, as I tried to advance, whether I was penetrating more deeply into the floating greenery or heading toward open space.

"Courage and ingenuity were of no use against this blind and brutal phenomenon.

"I didn't even have the strength to fight anymore; one moment I had the idea that if I remained motionless the plants would move away, that it was my fighting that made them rush over me in greater numbers.

"I was mistaken. My immobility served only to tighten even further the mesh of the net holding me.

"I struggled only feebly now, convinced as I was of the uselessness of my efforts.

"Then I stumbled over a stone, lost my footing, and fell. I was convinced that I wouldn't be able to pick myself up again. I succeeded, however, by bracing myself with some effort, when Eeeoys's heartrending pleas reached my ears again:

"'Robert! Robert! . . .'

"Her voice seemed muffled, as if it came from far away. I saw that all my efforts to reach her had only served to increase the distance that separated us. I lunged forward in desperate rebellion . . . I tore, head lowered, through that elastic mass that bounced back like a mattress and resisted me just by its inert power. I crushed fistfuls of plants between my contorted fingers, I squashed them by the hundreds, but all of this only succeeded in opening a slight hollow in front of me that filled again almost immediately.

"My exasperation, augmented perhaps by the heady odor, became a sort of madness. I remember that I tore furiously at the tufts of the diabolical plants with my teeth.

"Suddenly my foot struck a sprawled body.

"I cried out in sorrow as I bent down, certain it was Eeeoys's body. I was mistaken: from the shaggy beard that my fingers encountered, I realized that it was one of the Martians of the retinue.

"I placed my hand on his chest. His heart was no longer beating, the limbs although warm were already rigid; finally, my fingers were wetted by something tepid that must have been blood. At the same instant, I felt a terrible burning sensation in my foot.

"I had stepped on one of the earthen fire pots that the Martian had dropped in his fall.

"I didn't linger to discover how and for what purpose this unfortunate man had been killed, while I was still alive; I seized the pot by its handle with a hand trembling with joy.

"I had just glimpsed a means of salvation.

"Fumbling around, and without worrying about burns, I gathered the coals that had rolled to the ground and started to blow over them, softly at first, to lift the thin layer of white ash with which they were coated, and then more strongly, until a small blue flame arose.

"Then, I threw two or three aerophytes onto the coals, and it was with real pleasure that I saw them writhe and shrivel on the blaze that I continued to feed with panting breaths.

"When the first were consumed, I threw on others; a slender swirl of smoke arose.

"I sneezed, I coughed, I was suffocated, but my hopes were realized.

"Stung by the smoke, the aerophytes moved away with all the speed of their vibratile leaves.

"I swung my fire pot at arm's length, like a censer, effusing the beneficial fumes in every direction. Soon I had enough space around me that I could breathe freely and I glimpsed, as if from the bottom of a pit, a round patch of blue sky above my head.

"I was drunk with joy, more pleased with the idea (albeit quite simple) that had come to me than with the most brilliant discovery. I already saw Eeeoys, and perhaps all my Martians, saved. I dashed straight ahead, the multitude of aerophytes dissipating like a cloud. A furious autumn whirl-wind raising thousands of yellowed leaves would be a pale reflection of this strange sight.

"But abruptly I retraced my steps. I felt a twinge of guilt about not first of all giving my attention to the unfortunate Martian whose clay brazier had brought me salvation.

"I had no trouble finding him. He was almost cold and there was nothing I could do to revive him, but I was terrified to see his body covered in blood and to find, close to his neck, marks similar to those the Erloor left, but smaller and more numerous.

At this point in the narrative, Ralph Pitcher and Mr. Frymcock exchanged glances, and the lord cook made an instinctive gesture toward his wrist still covered with bruises.

Robert Darvel continued, without having noticed this scene, which had not escaped Miss Alberte's piercing gaze.

"All my joy vanished in an instant. The Erloor couldn't be blamed. What then were the unknown monsters that lay hidden in the weeds? What new battles would I have to face? I anxiously wondered.

"I felt that cold in the marrow, that contraction of the larynx that accompanies great fear, and yet I could not afford to be afraid if I wished to escape this abyss of greenery with my life.

"I tried to pull myself together. I restocked my fire pot with fuel and walked without daring to turn around, afraid of seeing behind me some hideous face laughing in the shadow of the leaves.

"Despite my best efforts, it seemed to me that I made no progress. The narrow clearing formed by the whirl of smoke around me disappeared once I had passed; the eternal wall, green and quivering, seemed to have no end.

"Panic seized me. Twice, I carelessly scorched the feathers of my gown. Oh! To escape this ocean of moving leaves! I thought that I would never get out!

Robert Darvel had grown pale; his emaciated face was tensed in terror, as if he were still in the grip of this dreadful sensation.

After a moment of silence, he continued, with some effort.

"I did make it out, however. Suddenly, at the moment when I had given up hope, when I believed myself buried underneath the weeds, I emerged into full light. The immense horizon spread before my eyes.

"I breathed the invigorating air with delight while, behind me, the gap that my passage had made in the bank of aerophytes slowly closed, with a sort of eddy, like the sea after the passage of a ship.

"I was half dazed for a few minutes by this unexpected success, in which fortune had certainly played a big role, because I remembered having many times changed direction, and I might have walked for hours—for days perhaps—before escaping this vegetative cloud.

"Not far from where I stood, I suddenly perceived the remains of the fire that had been dispersed by unknown hands and it was then that I remembered Eeeoys.

"It would have been the vilest act of cowardice to abandon her, and I wondered how I had been able to forget her for a single second, even panicked as I was by fear.

"Without thinking, I threw myself anew into the weeds. But this time, I vowed to walk as much as possible in a straight line, so that it might be possible to get out again.

"I called, I shouted with all my strength; no voice answered mine.

"I hadn't taken ten steps when I stumbled on the corpse of one of my Martians; he had been bled from the neck like the first. I forged ahead, my mind tormented with the most grievous premonitions.

"Soon I found the body of Eeeoys. She was still breathing, weakly, but she bore the bloody stigmata of death.

"In the light of the fire that I blew on with all my strength, she recognized me and she took my hand with a desperate movement. She clung tightly to my feather gown, like a drowning man grasping the reeds on the shore. Her pale blue eyes expressed an endless plea and her strange red head of hair was standing on end from fear.

"'Save me,' she stammered. 'Robert, take me away! . . . They have killed me! . . .'

"Then I noticed her bloodless face, bleached as if all the blood in her veins had vanished in the short time we had been separated.

"I was overcome with pity, horror-stricken, beside myself.

"'Yes, I will save you,' I cried, 'I promise you.'

"I lifted her up and seated her on my left arm, her head on my shoulders like a child. Then I started walking again with this precious burden.

"Unfortunately, in my emotion, I had lost the composure I so desperately needed. I no longer knew which way to go. I took my chances, moving slowly, because I only had one hand left to wave the pot that held the fire.

"I was in agony. I felt that the little life that remained in the child I carried was fading with each minute. My trek through the weeds in these conditions was a veritable Calvary.

"Suddenly I felt a very weak kiss on my forehead; Eeeoys's body was agitated by a prolonged shudder. Her arms, knotted around my neck, stiffened into immobility.

"She was dead.

"I was mad with grief. I spoke to her, I embraced her, I tried to revive her. I would have liked, like the thaumaturges of old, to infuse her with my vital breath.

"But I saw clearly that it was all useless; the palpitations of life no longer lifted her chest.

"I was occupied with these cares and had set the fire pot down next to me, without worrying about the vegetation that again started to surround me, when I seemed to hear a sniggering in the depths of the herbarium.

"At the same time, my fire pot was sent rolling away, scattering its coals here and there, exactly as if someone had kicked it over.

"Laying on the ground the body of the little Martian who had been such a devoted friend, I dashed forward to retrieve my fire without even considering the bizarre way in which it had turned over, as it were, on its own.

"I threw myself flat on my stomach in the grass. But just as I was about to grab it, it inexplicably escaped from my hands, and as if this clay pot was gifted with a will of its own it did a little pirouette as if to taunt me and rolled a few more paces, emptying the last coals that had not been dispersed by the initial blow.

"At the same time, the ironic laugh that I had just heard resounded again, but this time nearby.

"I shuddered with horror. I was now in utter darkness, buried under the aerophytes and so discouraged that I lay down on the ground, alongside Eeeoys, so that death might take me as well.

"I felt I would not have long to wait. I no longer breathed except with difficulty, and darkness was closing in around me. Vanquished a moment earlier, the plants were returning in force, their dull, heady perfume seeping into my brain.

"At this moment, I saw, as if from the summit of a high mountain, the entire panorama of my past life, with its vain struggles, its tragic incidents and . . . its hopeless loves . . .

Robert Darvel's voice had become slightly troubled. He looked at Miss Alberte, who lowered her eyes, blushing.

"And after all of this," he continued, "to end in a death without glory, on an unknown planet. As I considered my strange fate, I felt a weight on my chest, just as something supple as a rat snake and nimble as a hand looped itself around my neck.

"'My dream from last night!' I cried. 'The snakes . . .'

"Later, I was able to convince myself that my nightmare had been perfectly real; but in this moment my imagination was aroused and my nocturnal vision seemed to me prophetic.

"I tried to get up, to stand, to struggle against the reptiles in the weeds—I believed they were reptiles and attributed to them the death of my companions. But I was unable to make the slightest movement.

"Half from fear, half from suffocation, I lost consciousness. . . ."

* * *

"When I came to, I was terribly fatigued, and my entire body ached. At the same time, I was so enfeebled that I experienced the greatest difficulty gathering my thoughts. The sense of my own existence, the notion of myself, had grown vague and hazy; I hardly knew who I was. Finally, after laborious efforts, I managed to remember. But a gap remained in my memory, like a great black hole.

I wasn't able to recall anything that had happened from the moment when the reptiles in the weeds had enveloped me until I awoke.

"I looked around. I found myself in a perfectly cubical cell, with no apparent doors or windows.

"The walls were made of a sort of semi-opaque glass or crystal, similar to that which is used as paving in buildings.

"I noticed that this glass had been bored with thousands of small holes, as fine as the finest needles, which allowed air to enter without permitting me to see outside. But what surprised me more than all the rest was that in the middle of my prison there was a large glass bowl, filled with blood.

"I wracked my brain but was unable to fathom what sort of place I found myself in."

IV

....

The Glass Tower

"Up to that point," continued the engineer, "all that I had seen on Mars had not diverged from what was likely or probable; all the beings that I had encountered had, very nearly, their equivalent on Earth.

"Although I had faced terrible risks, it had been possible for me to fight. I had, in short order, always been able to grasp my enemies' resources and their means of attack.

"This was no longer the case: I was entering the domain of the unknown; I was dumbfounded. I was crossing the threshold of a mysterious world I knew nothing about and I understood that the methods I had used up until then to defend myself might be of no use at all against these new enemies.

"The very appearance of my prison was proof of an advanced civilization; perforated glass plates of large size are rather complicated to manufacture, even with the present state of terrestrial industry.

"What intrigued me most of all was the goblet of freshly spilt blood that had been placed next to me. Did they hope to force me to drink it, or was it only a horrible symbol of the fate reserved for me?

"Finally, were they going to keep me captive for a long time in this cage of geometric lines where I would have certainly ended up going mad?

"I sat on the floor—there was no sort of seat in my cell—to try to think.

"I tried in vain to figure out how I had come to be there. As I have said, there was a gap in my memory. Since the death of Eeeoys, which I was unable to contemplate without a stab of anguish, all my memories seemed veiled in a fog that my best efforts failed to pierce.

"I forced myself not to dwell on the past but to consider straightaway a means of escape.

"This was all the more difficult, as I have already said, because I felt immense mental fatigue, a deep despondency like that which follows the singular inebriation caused by certain alkaloids, like haschischine or morphine. I attributed this state to the perfume of the aerophytes; but I felt my sluggishness dissipating little by little as I inhaled the invigorating air admitted by the perforated windows.

"I walked the perimeter of my cell several times. Its walls were approximately four feet long and formed a perfect cube. But however painstaking my examination, I couldn't discover any trace of an opening, no trapdoor, no skylights, no door or window of any sort.

"The walls were of a single piece and the semi-opaque glass left no uncertainty about the existence of any secret exit.

"Nevertheless I must have entered through some opening. I sounded the floor, which was of the same material as the walls; it rang equally hollow in all places.

"I felt like an insect enclosed in a cardboard box. I was just as helpless, but unlike the insect I had no mandibles—like a carpenter bee or wood borer—with which to dig through the walls.

"Eventually it occurred to me that I could perhaps break the glass by making use of the vessel, which was itself made of glass.

"The vessel was reduced to shards, but the walls, which were quite thick, were not even scratched; I managed only to skin my fingers and soak myself with blood.

"I was at once furious and humiliated. Nothing could be more frustrating to my self-esteem as an engineer than to be trapped by a simple sheet of glass. The hunger that I was starting to feel was another goad that should have stimulated my inventive genius, but I plumbed my brain in vain, finding nothing. I crouched in a corner for more than two hours, like a wild animal in its cage.

"Finally, after racking my brains, the inspiration so long in coming arrived. I remembered an old experiment with which our middle school teacher entertained our physical science class long ago that this fine man—an academic of the old school—pedantically entitled *An Excellent Method for Cutting Glass without a Diamond*.

"Here is how I proceeded: I rolled a part of my feathered gown into a pad and started to briskly rub a corner of the wall. After fifteen minutes of this work, the surface of the glass was burning hot and my pad threatened to catch fire.

"Then I suddenly flicked a few drops of blood onto the heated part.

"There was a slight creaking sound. The sudden contraction of the molecules had caused a partial fracture, and fine lines radiated out from it.

"I started the operation again in another place, then in a third and a fourth with equal success.

"I was sweating profusely, but a space large enough to pass through was held at no more than one or two points. It would only take a strong push to break off the entire piece and knock it out.

"I stopped for a moment, wondering whether it wouldn't be better to wait for nightfall before I left, as prudence dictated.

"The sound of breaking glass might attract my jailers.

"On the other hand, I determined that if they came to visit me they would doubtless notice my attempt to escape. I decided not to wait and to rely on my lucky star.

"I gave a vigorous knee-kick to the piece of glass encompassed by cracks. It fell without making as much noise as I had feared, which I attributed to the thickness of the glass.

"Light and air flooded in.

"I was quick to take advantage of this way out and, bending cautiously so as not to injure myself on the sharp edges, I found myself on a platform level with the floor of my prison cell.

"I was on top of a gigantic structure, a tower more than fifty meters in radius, constructed of the same opaque glass as the walls of my cell.

"When I say tower, I should rather say a circular structure, for the center was empty and formed an immense cavity whose bottom I could not perceive.

"A great number of cells similar to the one I had been in were uniformly positioned, forming as it were the crenellations of this giant rampart.

"I was eager to discover the mechanism that opened these prison cells. As

I should have suspected, each wall moved as a piece by sliding in a groove, and was kept in place by a simple bolt made of a red metal that shone like copper. To get an idea of this sliding door, picture those that animal tamers use to separate the cages of wild animals.

"I puerilely entertained myself by opening the cells neighboring my own; all were empty and bare, but in the middle of each I found the same goblet of blood.

"In a great number of them, the goblet was empty and the blood dried and brown, but I saw some in which the goblet was still half full, as if before its departure an absent occupant had sipped from it.

"Then I gladly stretched my legs. The glass tower was two or three times the size of the Coliseum and the circular platform on which I found myself, and which in addition had no balustrade, seemed to me infinitely vast.

"An ardent sun fired its piercing shafts into the depths of the central chasm, from which arose muffled voices.

"I leaned over this abyss streaming with light and counted thirty-nine levels of different colored columns. Each column was separated from its neighbor by a deep recess and a shadowy opening, and all of these niches were exactly the same size. The whole gave the astonishing impression of a colossal honeycomb with identical cells.

"The sun's rays did not penetrate below the thirty-ninth story; darkness engulfed the lower levels, suggesting the possibility of an infinite number of similar levels.

"I wondered with a sort of terror whether this tower in its appalling monotony reached as far as the bowels of the planet, and I struggled in vain to make out the purpose of these deep niches where one could house thousands, hundreds of thousands of statues.

"Every column had the same shape, a round, unadorned shaft with a ball for the base and the capital.

"The glass paste of which they were built was vividly colored and the balls and cylinders sparkled like enormous jewels.

"I never tired of gazing at them. The sparkling had a hypnotic effect that drew me to the dazzling abyss and I had to jump back, unsettled by a shudder of vertigo.

"I again wondered what use this infinity of niches could have. My most plausible hypothesis was that I must be looking at some aerial catacomb, in a vast vertical cemetery; each niche most likely concealed the cadaver of a Martian of olden times, embalmed or reduced to ashes.

"Yet many details seemed to contradict this hypothesis . . . The immense ring had none of the dilapidated appearance of a tomb, where plants, the constant companions of ruins, happily flourish; no parasitic tuft had anchored itself in the cracks. The glass was strikingly clean, as if brand new.

"I gave up trying to decipher this enigma that the future, no doubt, would resolve. I tore myself from the spellbinding charm of the abyss and surveyed the countryside, which I beheld from a dizzying height.

"My eyes were accustomed to wonders, but never had I seen a vista as awe-inspiring as I did then.

"A violet sea, its cresting waves the light pink of peach blossoms, rolled softly toward a strikingly jagged coastline, which from afar resembled a heap of viscid sponges, mixed with thickets of fantastically twisted coral.

"Fjords were carved and capes sculpted in the shapes of chimerical beasts or dreamlike plants, and this entire backdrop, as if in an exquisite jonquil-colored wash, was reflected in the violet ocean's scarcely troubled waves.

"Far in the distance, a high, round mountain with a tapered summit was crowned by a crest of red smoke: it was the first volcano I had spied on Mars.

"I turned my eyes to the foreground of this shimmering landscape: a dozen glass towers exactly like the one on top of which I found myself rose above the violet sea, forming a dappled archipelago of all the colors of the rainbow.

"I noticed then that the towers possessed no exterior openings; there were the same rows of pillars and arcades, but without the deep niches.

"Their design reminded me of the portraits of the tower of Babel, such as those found in the ancient bibles of Royaumont.

"I progressed from surprise to surprise, from wonder to wonder.

"The tower where I found myself rose like its neighbors from the bosom of the waves, and I couldn't begin to imagine by what miraculous means I had been transported there.

"I had to explore the entire platform. On the opposite side, there were more towers and the violet sea marked the horizon, where, far off, a bluish haze indicated, perhaps, the existence of a continent.

"I was spellbound by this supremely peaceful scene. Without the hunger pangs that I felt, I might have forgotten all about escaping. The most profound silence filled the calm of this beautiful afternoon: I had neither seen nor heard anyone, no jailer had started in pursuit of me, and I wondered whether it wasn't all a dream.

"It was with a sigh of regret that I tore myself away from contemplation of the beautiful and mysterious horizon to resume the struggle for life and for knowledge.

"I circled the platform a second time: logic told me that there must be some staircase, some ladder or perhaps some elevator by which one descended to the lower levels.

"In this, I was mistaken. The flat, smooth surface of the platform seemed cast of a single piece; if some secret trapdoor existed, the joins had been filled in with a subtlety that escaped ordinary human vision.

"I was disappointed, but not at all discouraged. I felt that I shouldn't wait until hunger and fatigue had drained my strength to try to save myself.

"I thought that if it were possible for me to reach one of those niches that opened directly below the platform, I would surely end up somewhere. These shadowy openings had to have an exit; the only trick was to reach it.

"It didn't take long to find a way.

"I lifted out of its groove one of the sliding doors from the cells and, breaking it, I removed the red metal bolt.

"I then had in my possession a bar a half foot in length, which I used to carve as deep a hole as possible in the vitrified paving.

"Once finished, I pushed the bar into the hole and secured it solidly.

"I then tore a large strip from my feathered robe, which, I have perhaps explained, was made from the skins of birds skillfully sewn together. I undid these skins, twisting and gathering them to make a fine cord about two meters in length, whose resilience I tested by pulling on it with all my strength.

"I attached this rope securely to the metal bar and lowered myself to the niche below.

"The descent was hardly perilous for a man like myself, accustomed to physical exertion. However I confess that, when I felt myself suspended above the shimmering abyss, I shut my eyes and needed all my willpower not to yield to the pull of vertigo.

"As soon as my feet brushed the edge of the ledge, I used it as a foothold and, a moment later, I stood safe and sound between two dazzling columns of azure glass. I took a few moments to rest after this feat, which I didn't feel I had the courage to repeat.

"To my right and left were two goblets like those that I had found in my cell, both full of blood.

"I didn't wish to tarry before this sinister omen. I was happy to note that these "niches" were indeed, as I had believed, entrances to so many hallways that ran through the main body of the tower.

"I walked boldly into the half-shadows down a gently sloping walkway that, after several steps, led me into another circular passage that followed the entire contour of the platform.

"I spoke just now of half-shadows. I was in fact bathed in a grayish and crepuscular light, the passages being lit only by the small amount of exterior light that filtered through the glass barrier. It was the ethereal light of limbo or dreams, in which the shadows of the transparent pillars stood out in soft shades.

The floor of the circular passage in which I found myself also sloped gently downward, winding around the building in an immense spiral connected, at each level, to the corridors leading from the niches.

"I descended endlessly, hour after hour. In spite of myself, Baudelaire's lines echoed in my head:

A lost, benighted soul descends
open stairs that never end . . .

"I must admit that my curiosity was so keenly aroused by this strange structure that I paid no mind to the fatigue or the hunger that tormented me.

"At long last, I reached a level where countless passages radiated out in all directions from the one that I followed.

"The eternal spiral continued on below and surely led to the bottom of the abyss whose depth I had been unable to measure.

"Despite my desire to clear up the mystery of the glass tower, I stopped here, for further down the passage plunged into thick darkness.

"Dare I mention it? I feared that that demonic spiral would never end; I saw myself condemned to descend in eternal circles like the Poet's 'lost soul.'

"'The lateral passages attracted me much more. I could see a very soft gleam, from their far end, glowing like a distant fire. But I was once again confounded by their very number. I didn't know which to choose, and I was tormented by the fear of getting lost in an unknown labyrinth.

"After a moment of indecision, I trusted my luck and took the first passage.

"It led steeply down, and after twenty or so steps my descent was blocked by a sliding glass door like the one in my cell.

"I opened it without difficulty and, passing through, found myself in a vaulted room. I gasped involuntarily at the sight of the wonders it contained:

"Through immense glass panels — this time as clear as crystal — framed by columns of red metal, an undersea landscape spread as far as the eye could see. Groves of white and pink coral alternated with golden fields of floating kelp, fucus, and an infinite variety of other seaweeds. Splendid sea flowers flourishing in sturdy bunches reminded me of the lush vegetation of Central Africa.

Several arborescent seaweeds bore strange fruit, similar to the pineapples and bananas of terrestrial agriculture.

"There were corollas as large as the *Victoria regia* of Australian marshes, whose flower measures nearly a meter in diameter.

"Charming crimson vines, incomparably delicate, threw their festoons here and there.

"Elsewhere, the deep purple trunks of a forest of giant fucus spread like banners their vast amber-colored foliage, which trembled at the slightest eddy of the waves.

"But what struck me the most, in this marvelous landscape, was the realization that this marine vegetation had been laid out in an order that could not be the result of chance.

"Geometrically traced paths and avenues cut across the landscape; I still remember a bed of seaweed with ribboned leaves and long yellow flowers, which almost had the look of a ripe field of wheat.

"Some bushes with azure berries seemed to still bear the marks of the pruner's sheers, and the paths of pink sand were maintained with the greatest care.

"This submarine landscape was animated with bustling life.

"Beautiful fish with blue and gold scales played in the seaweed or darted like flashes of mother-of-pearl between the clumps of coral; blue crustaceans, among whom I recognized several that were congenerous with those I had seen in the first days of my stay on Mars, scuttled soberly along the seabed; jellyfish swayed to and fro, mottled with all the colors of the rainbow.

"I even saw turtles, little different from the hawksbill and the green turtle that furnish us tortoiseshell, nibbling grasses with the serenity of sheep in the pasture.

"Conger eels emerged slowly from under the coral, with the insidious air of vipers; rays chased seahorses.

"I was standing before the most vast and impressive of aquariums.

"I was deeply affected.

"I knew then that I was truly on Mars. All that I saw bore the mark of very advanced progress.

"I forgot in an instant the wild beasts and savages with which I had dealt and my pulse quickened at the thought of being initiated into this unknown science.

"Those who had created this extraordinary undersea park, who had built the glass tower, had to be men of superior intelligence.

"I was no longer surprised that they had preserved my life.

"I was filled with enthusiasm, and my apprehension for the future vanished. With that serene confidence that the worship of an idea gives, I was certain I would be well received.

"I would learn their language.

"I would instruct them in all that I knew, I would teach them about Earth, I would recount the history of its human races and the destinies of its peoples.

"What was most surprising in this pageant of undersea life was that I saw no sharks, nor octopi, nor any of the voracious animals that are the pirates of the deep.

"I was avidly contemplating this magnificent panorama, feeling that this sight alone amply compensated for all my ordeals, when a being of roughly human form appeared coming around the bend of a meadow of fucus.

"He was of small size, with short and stocky limbs, but his stride exhibited a certain vigorous grace.

"His entire body was covered with dark fur like that of a sea otter or seal, except for his face and hands, which were covered with little shining scales that didn't obscure the lineaments of his features or the whiteness of his skin.

"Certain diseases produce similar scales.

"I remembered then the strange assertion of a Danish doctor in the Middle Ages, concerning a skin disease that affects fisherman of the north whose diet is composed exclusively of salted fish:

"*Leprosy*—he says—*is perhaps only an illness because it doesn't occur in an aquatic environment. It is simply a natural phenomenon that is not fully realized, and it indicates that under certain conditions the human face is called upon to cover itself with scales.*

"I was lost in thought for some time, for I too share this theory, that all illness is only the prelude to a new evolution of man toward another state that is more perfect or at the very least different.

"Never, in the course of the fascinating research to which I had consecrated my existence, had I felt a more keen interest.

"I never tired of watching the marine man, and I can still recall every detail of his external anatomy. His long fingers were tipped with short bluish claws and joined by a membrane that extended far enough to permit him to swim with ease and yet still maintain the agility of human fingers.

"His bright, brown eyes had nothing in common with the stupid, fixed expression that their lack of eyelids gives to fish; they reflected beauty and intelligence like the eyes of many amphibians, whose resemblance to man Michelet has noted, that it would take very little trouble to domesticate.

"The underwater creature had a small mouth topped by curling whiskers, which made him look a little like a lord from the time of Louis XIII; there was nothing brutish about his round forehead and short, finely shaped nose.

"I wondered straightaway by means of what physical conformation he was able to breathe and live under this expanse of water without possessing gills like fish and without rising to the surface to breathe, after the manner of amphibious mammals.

"I then remembered a fabled old theory very much in vogue among some doctors in the eighteenth century who still dabbled in alchemy.

"Before birth, venous and arterial blood is exchanged directly, without the intermediary of the lungs, through a hole pierced in the septum of the heart named Botal's hole.[10] This hole closes over a few hours after the child begins to breathe.

"In the past, some believed that a newborn, alternately plunged into warm water and into the air, would retain the ability to breathe underwater and in air, that its Botal's hole would remain open.

"There is moreover a historical example of this fact. The celebrated English architect Lightwater, who drew up the plans—only executed one hundred years after his death—for the drying of the Zuyderzee, had the ability to live underwater; a fact to which a number of his contemporaries attested.

"Recognized scholars, without taking the trouble of trying any of the experiments mentioned by these old authors, amply scoffed at this fantastic hypothesis.

"Only Berthelot, whose library was filled with more than thirty thousand volumes of alchemy and ancient medicine, had reserved judgment on this curious problem, which his death prevented him from elucidating.

"The great chemist knew from experience that the most incredible legends often conceal within them a measure of truth, and he never denied anything without a good reason.

"He liked to say that he had found the principles of hydrostatics and steam-powered machines in Hero of Alexandria, and of pyrotechnics in Marcus Graecus, and he never rejected any opinion without carefully examining it first.

"For my part, I am persuaded that the doctors of the eighteenth century were right and that nothing would be easier for man than to live under water.

"What's more, didn't I have a living example before my very eyes?

"While I was lost in these thoughts, the marine man moved slowly toward the wall of glass behind which I was crouching.

"I noticed then that he held a rod of red metal, lightly bowed in the middle, on which he leaned as if on a cane.

"With his slightly pointed face, the dark fur that covered his body, and

---

10 Botal, an anatomist born in Asti around the time of Henri III, wrote several highly esteemed works. It was he who discovered the passage between the right and left sides of the heart that bears his name.

his fine whiskers, he gave me the impression of an enormous cat with a human face.

"From time to time he would turn around, looking behind him as if he might have been waiting for someone.

"I soon learned the reason for his behavior: an animal that had something of an otter and a walrus to him and, at the same time, a bird's bill, like a platypus, caught up to him, leaping joyfully.

"A moment later the animal was creeping forward, as if stalking prey, and I realized that the undersea man was hunting and that his companion served in place of a dog.

"Suddenly, a large cartilaginous fish, of the same species as the common ray, came out from under a Sargasso bush. The otter dashed forward, but a second too late: the fish was fleeing as fast as its fins could carry it.

"Then the man threw the curved metal rod that he held in his hand.

"With no apparent effort on the part of the hunter, the weapon described an arc, hit its prey, and returned on its own, so to speak, to the hand that had launched it.

"The fatal blow felled the fish. The otter finished it off with two swipes of its claws and returned to lay it at the feet of its master, as the most docile and best trained of terrestrial spaniels might have done.

"The hunter picked up the fish and placed it in a net that he carried on his shoulder that appeared to be braided with the fibers of that sea byssus that is used in Sicily to make fabric.

"I was astounded by this scene of undersea life that I had caught, so to speak, unawares.

"I realized next that the metal weapon must be analogous, in its mode of operation, to the boomerang of the natives of Australia, a simple stick that returns to whoever threw it after having struck the chosen target.

"The man had taken several steps in my direction. I saw that his net already held other fish and large fruits similar to pineapples that were produced by a large plant with lilac foliage and stalks as stiff and prickly as a cactus.

"He was slowly approaching the window behind which I observed him; his face expressed a lively curiosity.

"Soon we were separated only by the thickness of the crystal.

"For a minute we looked at one another in silence, then all of a sudden, for no reason I was able to discern, the marine man seemed overcome by the most intense terror.

"He had undoubtedly never seen a being such as me. His entire body was convulsed with shudders and he didn't seem to understand the smiles and friendly gestures that I made to reassure him.

"Finally, he turned tail and fled.

"I soon lost sight of him in the groves of the undersea landscape.

"I remained for some time rooted to the spot, lost in thought.

"My astonishment was increasing with each bit of the planet's mystery that was revealed to me.

"At last, I resolved to continue exploring this passage lit periodically by the grand crystal bays that looked out to the bottom of the sea."

V

....

Arsenals and Catacombs

"The passage was endless, and I soon realized that it must serve as a means of communication between the tower that I had just left and those that I had seen from the top of the platform. I struggled in vain to discern the essential purpose these strange constructions served.

"I passed a succession of undersea landscapes of infinite variety.

"Here was a veritable forest with dark emerald foliage, veined with azure, and smooth gummy trunks, laden here and there with clusters of seashells that large, hairy-legged crabs crushed in their pincers before feeding on them.

"Farther on were gardens of dazzling flowers, above which, like a cloud of butterflies, wriggled thousands of small silvery fish.

"Still elsewhere, I saw deep grottos cut out of an underwater cliff, filled with a multitude of bustling humanoid creatures. I suspect it was a quarry or a working mine.

"Everywhere I saw proof that the bottom of the sea was cultivated with care and methodically farmed.

"I passed a sort of park divided into deep pens by little walls the height of a man; each held a crustacean resembling our lobsters, only much larger. Some reached five meters in length and their pincers must have been formidable weapons, capable of cutting a man in two with their saw-toothed edges.

"Each of these monsters was chained in its pit and I glimpsed a marine man, similar to the hunter I had seen, moving toward them, doubled up under the weight of a large basket filled with fish.

"He went to each ditch, throwing to each crustacean its share. No detail of this scene escaped my notice. I watched their antennae and pincers perk up in anticipation at the approach of their food. It was obviously a sort of farm where crustaceans were methodically fattened until they were fit for consumption.

Some distance from there, a beautiful myrtle-green meadow held several hundred large turtles guarded by a shepherd armed with a red metal boomerang and assisted, in place of dogs, by two otters with long whiskers.

"He carried a little basket that he was busily filling with shellfish, but, in spite of all my efforts to attract his attention, he didn't notice me.

"This was by no means my last surprise.

"After leaving behind the pasture where this underwater shepherd, who might have provided some Martian Theocritus with a subject for an idyll, watched over his peaceful flock, I found myself suddenly opposite a genuine village.

"A hundred or so dwellings with conical roofs were gracefully scattered among the blue and yellow copses of great seaweed. It was a wonder to behold.

"The cottages, whose pointed roofs reminded me of the shape of certain shells, were built of pink and white coral, and a great number among them were covered with glistening shells.

"One might have said a town of mother-of-pearl and alabaster asleep beneath the waves. Tame manatees and seals slept lazily on the thresholds of the houses.

"The narrow windows were fitted with rounded and bowed panes that seemed to me made of tortoise shells pounded thin. Beautiful trees of red coral placed here and there added to the charm.

"At regular intervals stood columns with a basin at the top, whose purpose I was unable to discover. I supposed, for want of a better idea, that they must have served for lighting, and I imagined, at night, the enchanting aspect of this hamlet asleep in the depths of the sea.

"Now, apart from the pets of which I spoke, I didn't see any living creature. The inhabitants must have been busy outside, hunting or attending to their crops and herds.

"Meanwhile, all these marvels that unfolded before my eyes did nothing to diminish my growing hunger, which I could see no way to appease.

"If only I were adapted to living and breathing underwater! I would have shattered the pane of glass that separated me from those rich underwater landscapes that beckoned to me. I would have begged for hospitality from the people of the beautiful village of mother-of-pearl and coral, and I am sure that I would not have been refused.

"I truly did not know where to turn; I was almost certain that at the other end of the passage I was following I would find another tower as deserted and as silent as the one I had just left.

"The inhabitants of these remarkable palaces had to show themselves eventually. I had tried not to dwell on this mystery, but it continued to haunt me; I could discover no explanation. The more I racked my brains, the farther I seemed to get from a solution to this thorny problem.

"I had sat down to rest and to ponder what I ought to do when I discovered a deep, low archway that appeared to lead to a level located beneath the underwater passage.

"As I hesitated to step into this shadowy vault, a piercing burst of laughter, which seemed just like the one I had heard in the aerial marsh, rose from the depths.

"At first this high-pitched, utterly inhuman laugh terrified me. My blood froze and my legs buckled at the thought of encountering a monster more terrible than any I had yet faced.

"But I quickly mastered my fear and urged myself to cross the threshold of the dark vault.

"Anything was better than the uncertainty into which I was plunged, and it was impossible that beings intelligent enough to erect the magnificent structures that I saw were savage brutes. I was convinced that I would come to an understanding with them.

"They had imprisoned me, but all in all they had done me no harm. To them I was perhaps only a curious, unknown animal that they proposed to study.

"Emboldened by these reflections, I crept cautiously into the shadowy passage and descended a very steep slope that, as in the other parts of the glass tower, took the place of a stairway.

"Due to the difficulty of finding my way in a darkness possibly bristling with pitfalls, I was about to abandon my plan when my feet struck small bumps, about the size of a nut, inlaid in the floor.

"At the same moment, by means of an unknown mechanism, the vault of the passage lit up with a very soft glow that was sufficiently bright for me to see where I was.

"For a few moments I didn't move a muscle out of surprise, almost convinced that I had entered an enchanted kingdom and that the fairy who guided my steps had just splendidly lit my way, at the very moment that I bemoaned the absence of light.

"The walls were of the same tinted glass that I had seen throughout the building, but the vault depicted animals and fantastic flowers, and a glow emanated from them that I can only compare to that given off by the fireflies of Central America.

"I took several steps forward. As I advanced, the ceiling grew dark behind me and the light moved in front of me, surrounding my entire person with a radiant halo.

"I saw straightaway that it was the weight of my body itself acting on the contacts protruding from the floor that produced the illumination that accompanied me.

"As for the nature of the light itself, I don't know whether it was produced by particular phosphorescent gases or due to some special luminosity of the planet.

"Carried along by the passage's downslope, I continued to descend, and two or three times I found myself at a subterranean crossroads, where different corridors met. I was careful not to yield to the temptation of turning off to the right or the left; the only way to avoid getting lost in this labyrinth was to walk in a straight line.

"Abruptly, I came out into a high room, where stiff, hieratic statues were aligned ad infinitum, some carved from red porphyry, others cast in a metal darker than bronze but flecked with spots of gold. The statues represented birds with a human face, winged crocodiles, spiny dragons, and a host of other beasts, of such capricious design that I wondered whether they were inventions of the artist's imagination or had really existed in nature.

"I settled for the latter option when I noticed the Roomboo and Erloor, executed with painstaking accuracy, among these effigies.

"There was something terrifyingly solemn about all these enormous statues stretching deep into the shadows that made me uneasy. They seemed to be fixing their pupils of precious stones, their implacable gaze, on my puny person, as if to say, 'We are the eternal guardians of a mystery you will never solve; you will never discover our secret.'

"I continued walking but with a more hesitant step.

"It seemed to me that beyond the circle of light that surrounded me as I walked, the monsters of stone and metal were closing ranks in the darkness as if to block my way back.

"I coughed; the sound returned after rolling from echo to echo, reverberating through the other rooms that I could sense in the distance. I feared that the being whose sniggering I had heard was going to suddenly appear from behind one of the pedestals and move toward me.

"I was mistaken. That grandiose room must have lain abandoned for centuries; a hazy layer of dust blurred the outlines of its contents and covered everything almost like frost.

"There was something oppressive about the very contemplation of this barbaric setting; I felt burdened by the ancient weight of the Martian civilizations that, no doubt, I would never know.

"I had meanwhile reached the far end of the row of giant statues, but there another room opened, still more vast than the first and peopled with the same hieratically stiff statues.

"I regretted having ventured that far and yet a secret force pushed me incessantly forward. I had walked quickly at first, in my haste to reach the end of these interminable rooms; now I ran.

"Surrounded by the nimbus that each one of my steps illumined in the vault, I must have resembled a meteor shooting through the darkness.

"I felt a rush of vertigo: after the two rooms I mentioned, I found others, then still others; I was traversing a veritable subterranean town, no doubt as vast as the gigantic palace of Angkor or some of the ruins of ancient Egypt.

"It must have taken centuries, surely, to excavate all these immense rooms underneath the sea.

"I stopped in the end, despairing to ever reach the final room.

"Tired and starving, I didn't know to what to do; I was as reluctant to retrace my steps as to push forward.

"The discovery of a portico that gave access to another subterranean level dispelled my uncertainty. Again I went down.

"The rooms in which I now found myself contained no statues; they seemed more like storehouses. The first that I entered held thousands of glass jars, hermetically sealed and stacked one upon another. The next was full of bundles, crudely tied with a material that seemed to be fish skin tanned by some special process.

"At the sight of the jars, I let out a cry of joy. The idea that I was in one of the stockrooms or storehouses of the unknown people whose prisoner I was revived my courage.

"I labored to shift one of the large glass vases, and having no other way to open it—the lid was secured by ropes and also sealed with a sort of asphalt—I let it fall from high enough to break it.

"Some elongated grains, shaped a little like kernels of corn, spilled onto the ground. I started eating without the least hesitation, and I was overjoyed to discover a starchy, slightly sweet flavor that was not at all disagreeable.

"I satisfied my hunger with this unhoped-for manna. At least I was sure not to suffer from hunger any more.

"I would have been able to survive for a year on the provisions in this single room, and I guessed that these vast caverns must contain other supplies.

"Once fortified, I continued my investigations, starting with the bundles tied with skins. They were made of dried fish, but forgotten there surely for years and years, they had grown so hard that an axe would have been needed to cut into them.

"I hurried to the neighboring room, which had an enormous pile of cylindrical trunks; I thought at first that I had discovered a stock of firewood, a gigantic woodpile. Examining the trunks more closely, I saw that they came from a plant similar in nature to bamboo and that they had been sawn through the nodes in order to form long barrels. I took one and managed, with my fingernails, to dig out the wax that sealed it. Then I spilled a few drops of liquid into the hollow of my hand.

"I sniffed warily: the liquid gave off an odor of ripe fruit. It smelled at once of pineapple and lemon, raspberry and guava. It would have been difficult for such reassuring fragrances to hide a fatal substance, and it was hardly plausible that someone might make such an ample supply of poison.

"This conclusion persuaded me. I tasted the unknown elixir; its flavor was close to that of the wine of Spain or Sicily, in which flowers and aromatic berries might have been steeped, yet it had an aftertaste of ether that warned of the danger there would surely be in abusing this drink.

"I limited myself to a few sips and felt almost immediately an incredible sense of well-being.

"My fatigue disappeared, my discouragement fled, and I was inclined to look at everything in a favorable light.

"No terrestrial beverage had had such a potent comforting effect on me, and what was odd about the tonic's influence is that I experienced neither excessive gaiety nor the flushed face and slight disorder of ideas that follow the tasting of noble wines.

"I was perfectly calm, perfectly lucid — so much so that I reviewed in my memory all the incidents that had marked the previous days, so as not to forget them.

"Then, all at once, I felt a pressing desire for open spaces and fresh air.

"Several times before, the atmosphere in this subterranean world had felt stifling and oppressively heavy. Now it seemed unbreathable, bereft of vital oxygen.

"Certain that, whenever I wished, I could find my back to the stock of supplies I had discovered, I climbed back up to the hall of statues, then to the undersea gallery.

"I was surprised to find it plunged into deep darkness. Without my being aware of it, night had fallen, probably much earlier, and the undersea gallery was not provided, like those that I had just traveled, with radiant vaults whose illumination was triggered by my feet.

"I was unsure what to do. I had not yet considered where I would spend the night; all in all, the undersea passage was too cold, the subterranean tunnels too unhealthy. I headed for the glass tower, determined to choose for my bedroom one of the deep niches I have mentioned. Despite the darkness, it was impossible to get lost, since I had only to walk in a straight line.

"A soft light emanated from the depths of the slumbering sea, and when

I passed by the coral village again, it seemed to me surrounded by a halo of yellow and blue phosphorus. It seemed almost sketched against the dark background in lines of pale fire. I paused to admire its soft magic for some time.

"The forests of seaweed and the fields that I passed next weren't, either, entirely enveloped in darkness. The animalcules and luminous plants created a kind of moonlight with soft blue shadows, and it was strange that this light shining from the plants and animals left the distance buried in darkness.

"And all this country lay silent and peaceful. The sea was deserted: the fish were asleep in the seaweed and the shellfish in holes in the rocks.

"Before reaching the glass tower, I caught just a glimpse of a huge black shape, with large eyes of liquid fire, rushing rapidly through the water.

"The vision promptly disappeared into the darkness. I couldn't tell whether it was a large shark or one of these mimics that had in the past caused me such great fear.

"I was now in the large spiral that led to the top of the tower. I would have been able to sleep just as well in one of the lower niches, but a childish curiosity led me back toward the top; I wanted to see whether the rope I had used to descend from the platform was still there.

"So I climbed the interminable circuit, but it was impossible to find the niche into which I had descended.

"After looking for it in vain for some time, I made up my mind to settle as comfortably as I could in the nearest of those identical crevices, each supplied with its bowl of blood.

"I leaned over the raised edge that stretched between the two columns of glass and separated the niches from the central abyss, and I discovered in a corner a heap of a substance that I at first took for cotton but that, after examination, appeared to be loose strands of asbestos or perhaps spun glass.

"I made a soft enough pillow out of it and settled down to sleep. My mind besieged by countless thoughts, I contemplated for a long time the infinite arcades of the tower over which Phobos and Deimos cast their magical glow, lending a diaphanous transparency to the iridescent columns. The stars twinkled in the clear sky and I wondered sometimes whether it wasn't all a hallucination, whether I hadn't gone crazy, whether while my soul wandered astrally on Mars my body wasn't lying in chains, in a hidden cell of some lunatic asylum or in the secret crypts of a Hindu temple.

"But when I looked up at the sky, I recognized the familiar geometry of the constellations, and eventually I caught sight of Earth, like a small speck of reluctant, timid light in the radiant harvest of the heavens . . . Earth, which held everything that I loved in the world! . . ."

Robert Darvel stopped, his voice changed. He exchanged with Alberte a look charged with the purest and most profound passion. It was with a slight tremble that the engineer continued:

"As I was deep in contemplation, I heard close by the brittle beating of insect wings and, almost immediately, before I had time to defend myself, I was grasped by sinuous undulating fingers like so many snakes — the same that had attacked me in the aerial swamp — and I was paralyzed with terror.

"The blood froze in my veins, and I believed, this time, that the hour of my death had come.

"But my adversary, whose form I couldn't distinguish in the darkness, merely propelled me rather brutally into the spiral hallway, where I sprawled more dead than alive.

"I didn't dare move a muscle and I felt my heart pounding dully in my chest. I lay there for a long time.

"Then I heard the same beating of wings, followed by the sound of sloshing liquid and a sort of slurping.

"I realized that my enemy must be quenching his thirst from the bowl of blood and lying down on the pillow of asbestos in the niche from which he had just driven me away.

"I reassured myself little by little. After recovering enough courage to stand, I frantically descended two or three levels.

"I was gasping for breath, terrified, frantic.

"I didn't dare risk sleeping in another niche, out of fear of a similar attack. I lay down in the spiral passage and closed my eyes. I eventually surrendered to sleep, but all through the night my rest was disturbed by alarming dreams.

"I awoke dozens of times, the cold sweat of anxiety on my forehead, thinking I heard, beneath the murmuring moan of the sea that beat against the base of the tower, rustlings, rapid flights, and the dreadful sound of snickering I had heard before and that I reproached myself for not having taken seriously.

"Day finally came. As soon as I could see clearly enough, I climbed back up to the higher floors, pushed by a sort of desperate and, this time, determined courage, to face these mysterious enemies.

"I visited a great number of niches; all were empty, but the fibers of asbestos held a rounded impression, and the majority of the bowls were dry.

"Nothing made sense. I faced a disconcerting enigma, like a prince of legend, a prisoner in some fairy castle, where he is served at will, without glimpsing any flesh and blood servant.

"I spent almost all of that day in the undersea gallery, enjoying its calm prospects, its soft, hazy scenery.

"I no longer dared enter the glass tower, and I still shuddered at the abominable memory of those long, warm fingers, supple yet strong, that had gripped me and thrown me out with such swift disdain.

"I passed a week in perpetual fear but without a moment of boredom. I had undertaken to explore the subterranean palace, and with each step I made surprising discoveries.

"An entire people had amassed the riches of lost centuries in those caverns. I visited arsenals whose spoils were forged of unknown metals; I remember some four-bladed axes, with beautiful emerald-colored blades that resembled green gold.

"I also saw copper, gold, and iron, but in very small quantities; on the other hand there was an abundance of a metal very rare in terrestrial mines: shimmering, magnificent iridium.

"It had been shaped into globes, made of two hemispheres, joined by a hinge, which were filled with sharp spikes on the inside; I was unable to figure out their use.

"There were also barbed shears, immense nets braided with wires of an azure metal, each link of which was filled with a curved hook like a fishhook.

"I wondered whether all these complicated, barbarous instruments were weapons, tools, or instruments of torture, and I sometimes spent hours trying to imagine who these beings were who had been able to make use of all this sparkling bric-a-brac and pile it into this crypt that was vaster than a city.

"I dared not even lay a hand on these objects except with caution. Once I found a silver disk pierced with holes about the diameter of a wrist, and I had carelessly put my finger in one of those holes.

"Abruptly, an interior spring was activated and a hidden blade slipped out; I very nearly lost my finger. This adventure had made me wary. However, I appropriated, for my personal defense, a gold axe that I slipped through my belt and a sort of iridium lance, with a silver point, whose heft and sharpness made it a formidable weapon.

"But I would need an entire day to describe, even summarily, the enormous stores of provisions, utensils, and objects of all sorts that filled the undersea catacombs . . .

"However, among the various details, one thing appeared evident: this had all been abandoned for centuries upon centuries. I concluded that long ago a whole civilization must have been exterminated by the present inhabitants of the glass tower, my still unknown jailers.

"One discovery gave me great pleasure: it was a room full of crates made of a red wood, similar to cedar, that contained carefully folded fabrics of every kind.

"They were woven with fibers of whose nature I was ignorant, but some had the suppleness of silk or the softness of cotton.

"When I wanted to unfold them, a certain number turned to dust like those fabrics of a specious quality that are found in the excavations of Herculaneum or Pompeii that crumble when touched.

"Others were perfectly conserved, including some fabrics made of brightly colored feathers, which I used to replace my clothes, which were in a rather pitiful state.

"I thought I had found a horde of clothes or a costume museum, but I soon realized my error. All the pieces of fabric that I saw were of a square or triangular shape, and they were embroidered or colored with designs representing different scenes. It was a library or cache of archives which would have delighted many an academy.

"Certainly, an important share of the planet's history was recorded there.

"I sorted through countless numbers of the precious cloths that all displayed on a dark blue or green background characters in louder colors—light yellow or bright red.

"These characters, like Egyptian hieroglyphs and ancient Chinese writings, were ideographic, which is to say that they represented, in cursory images, the objects that they designated. It would have taken years of work to decipher these signs; I understood that it would be madness to try.

"However, there were, in these woven pages that I removed one by one from perfumed coffers, scenes that seemed to me nearly intelligible and that gave me food for thought. I saw the representation, crude but exact, of an Erloor rushing at one of those men of the marshes who, only a few days earlier, had been my subjects. But another picture showed an Erloor himself devoured by a being that I had never seen on Mars that was formed solely of an enormous head and two wings. In a third image, this monster was in its turn snapped up by a shapeless mass of a scale out of proportion with the other figures.

"Thus, as on Earth, the creatures survived only at the price of bloodshed and by the destruction of some by the others.

"Meanwhile, time was passing and it seemed as though my situation would never change.

"Following the undersea gallery, I had reached another glass tower, but it was so much like the first that I didn't feel any need to explore a third.

"And the same empty silence reigned everywhere, now and then disturbed by the sensation of something brushing past or those high-pitched laughs that gave me such a fright.

"My hopes of seeing Earth again, or of simply being able to make my situation known to my friends there, were quickly fading; I was haunted by the fear of dying there, far from those who were dear to me, without even being able to share with them the results of my extraordinary expedition.

"Then an event occurred that was to have a decisive influence on my destiny.

"In my subterranean explorations, I had reached what I took to be the final row of crypts. Gouged out of the living rock itself, a type of fine-grained red granite, these had no glass panels, and the light of the vaults did not dispel the darkness. A metal door barred the entrance, but I managed to pry it open with the help of bars and other tools I had found in the armory.

"These circumstances had piqued my curiosity, but I couldn't dream of exploring these crypts by touch. I first needed to make a candle, a lamp, or something of the sort.

"It wasn't too difficult. I took some of the wax that sealed the barrels and kneaded it between my fingers to soften it. I then shaped it around a cotton wick pulled from a shred of fabric. All that remained was to light it, but I had trouble seeing how to do it.

"I first tried to make fire after the manner of savages by vigorously rubbing together two small boards taken from the crates, but I didn't know that for this exercise in patience to succeed it was necessary to use one soft piece of wood and one hard; or perhaps I wasn't persistent enough.

"Whatever the reason, the only result was that I began to perspire. I gave this up and eventually found another method.

"With a blow of my axe, I broke a shard of transparent glass off a wall and, by wearing it down and polishing it, I managed to give it roughly the shape of a lens.

"Stationing myself at the entrance to one of the niches, in a place well exposed to the sun, I lit one of my torches — I forgot to mention that I had made many — and, thrilled with my success, I descended straightaway to the subterranean rooms whose twists and turns I was coming to know well.

"In a quarter of an hour, I reached the granite crypt, eager for the marvels that I assumed it contained.

"I was greatly astonished to find in this catacomb nothing but a mass of voluminous, reddish brown spheres, regularly stacked in equal piles, like cannonballs in an artillery depot.

"I examined them more closely; they were speckled with green splotches like certain types of glazed stoneware."

At this moment the attention of Robert Darvel's listeners was so focused that they were hanging on his every word. The only sound in the silence came from the scratching of Frymcock's pen on the white page.

"With the blow of an axe, I cracked one of these spheres. The white interior was crisscrossed by tubes of red glass that, when broken, exuded a thick, pungent liquid . . . In short, these spheres were exactly like the one from which you extracted me . . ."

"But," interrupted Ralph Pitcher, no longer able to contain the feverish curiosity that consumed him, "what did it contain?"

"Guess! . . . An Erloor curled up like a mummy, as I was myself, which, given its rigidity, I took for a corpse.

"I was utterly stunned: hadn't I seen with my own eyes in the monsters' cave the mass grave that was more or less their cemetery?

"In the end I came to the conclusion that the ancient peoples who had dug this crypt had embalmed Erloor, just as, in times past, the Egyptians embalmed ibises, cats, and crocodiles.

"I continued on my way through the hallways of this new type of necropolis, pondering the uses of these liquid-filled tubes. I opted for the simplest explanation, supposing them filled with some antiseptic preparation destined to ensure the preservation of the body.

"As you have seen by my own example, I was wrong in every way.

"The liquid in the tubes is saturated with oxygen and also contains nitrogen, carbon, and the other substances essential to life. It's unfortunate I don't know its formula, for if I did, human life could be nearly infinitely prolonged.

"The liquid is absorbed through the skin and provides the organism the minimum refreshment it needs when plunged into a sort of cataleptic sleep and the beating of its heart is stilled.

"The pills that Phara-Chibh took before being buried alive must have a certain parallel to this liquid . . . But let's move on. That's a point that I want to save for later.

"The advantage of absorption through the skin is that the stomach is not forced to function, which would be impossible in a cataleptic state, and one can be very well nourished in this way. Do we not ease the hunger of some of the ailing by means of a bath in a special broth?

"The Erloor that I had removed from his repository was thus certainly still alive, but I wasn't able to work out the reason for this kind of embalming. Was he there, he and the others, simply as a supply of living food, easy to preserve in case of siege or famine? Or did they keep them to testify of extinct eras? I couldn't know.

"Deep in thought, I had reached a different section of the crypts, where the piles of spheres stretched as far as the eye could see, but this time, they were green and not as capacious.

"I broke one at random. The red tubes from the circumference to the center like the spines of a chestnut were indeed there, but to my growing astonishment the interior was empty. I broke a second sphere, it was similarly hollow, and it was the same for the third and the fourth.

"Just then, I heard the high-pitched and sinister snickering nearly in my ear. I turned around, but no one was there; I was alone in the gloomy crypt of living mummies."

VI

....

The Opal Helmet

Robert Darvel had stopped; it may be that he hesitated, that he was wrestling with something, that there were portions of his account that he might have wished to bury in oblivion.

"Are you tired?" asked Miss Alberte softly.

"Perhaps you would like to rest for a bit?"

"Not on your life," cried Pitcher, jumping on his chair with childish enthusiasm. "I certainly hope that Robert is not going to leave us hanging in the most thrilling part!"

"I am not at all tired," said Robert, smiling, "and I have no desire to frustrate your understandable curiosity; but what remains for me to tell you so exceeds conventional human hypotheses that, in spite of myself, I was hesitant to continue.

"All those who have written about the inhabitants of other planets have begun with terrestrial givens, which they have modified to a greater or lesser degree at the whim of their imagination and, sometimes, of their irony. What I have to recount—what I saw—is completely apart from and beyond even the most fanciful suppositions.

"It is an awe-inspiring and monstrous nightmare—like a dream of the Apocalypse, imagined by an Edgar Allan Poe . . ."

"Please carry on," murmured Miss Alberte, with a hint of supplication in her voice.

Eyelids half-closed, his gaze seemingly lost in otherworldly visions of the red planet, Robert Darvel continued, after taking a moment to gather himself:

"I have told you how this high-pitched laugh, whose intonation had something supernatural about it, produced in me a sensation of irrepressible terror.

"I myself believe that there is no such thing as the supernatural.

"That we use such a term shows our ignorance and our weakness; there are simply things that we don't know or that we don't understand.

"All that our senses and our intelligence can perceive must have an explanation, or our existence itself would be a ridiculous and monstrous absurdity!

"I slowly recovered from the irrepressible terror brought on by this snickering, the author of which I had never been able to discover, and I continued on my way after reassuring myself that I still had three of my wax torches.

"At the end of the gallery of green spheres, I was stopped by a massive gate. The bars were veritable columns, and they were so close together that it was impossible for me — even as thin as I had become — to pass through.

"The highly oxidized metal was a dark brown, but when I scraped it with the blade of my axe I could see that when it was new it must have been a dazzling ruby color.

"I brought a few axe blows to bear, more to set my mind at ease or just as a sort of mechanical gesture — setting one's mind at ease is often little else — than in any real hope of smashing the sturdy bars.

"I was surprised when the gate yielded with a creaking sound and completely fell to pieces, as if it had been made merely of crossbeams of rotted wood.

"I very quickly considered that the effect of the forge's work, which gives to metal a very resilient, fibrous interlacing, is promptly destroyed following repeated blows or simply at the end of a certain period of time.

"The metallic molecules forced together one moment by the hammer's violence don't take long to resume their crystalline state, and then they become very fragile.

"Aren't we obliged to replace, after a short period of time, the axles of locomotives, which would otherwise break sooner or later of their own accord? And it is the hardest metals that, in the end, become the most brittle.

"The bars that I had just destroyed, and whose debris I examined, were now nothing more than a crust oxidized by the moisture of centuries. Only their appearance had remained imposing.

Just beyond the gate gaped the mouth of a large shaft, from which rose nauseating drafts of air.

"Raised high, my torch revealed walls with rings, fitted at equal distances, as if to facilitate descent.

"I didn't hesitate. I attached my torch above my forehead with a headband improvised from a section of my robe, and, after testing the sturdiness of the rings, I started to descend.

"Several times the swampy stench from the depths turned my stomach to the point of nausea; I persisted.

"For a quarter of an hour I climbed down into the foul darkness without appearing to make any progress. Exhaustion started to set in and I wondered whether I would have the strength to climb back up and whether my torch would last long enough to light my way.

"After a half hour of these thankless gymnastics, I was thoroughly discouraged and I had almost made up my mind, grudgingly, to climb back to the upper galleries, when my feet no longer touched a ring in the expected place.

"I could see a muddy pool in front of me, which must have been the half-dry bed of a river or subterranean canal.

"Vast skeletons lay in the mud. With a quick glance I reconstructed saurians close to plesiosaurs, giant crocodiles—half snake and half toad—whose twenty-meter dorsal spine came to rest on short and stocky hindquarters.

"Fins of tiny bones, which must have been flippers, replaced the forelegs.

"I hurried to cross the muddy canal, caught up in a singular fever of discovery. I felt that I was on the trail of some priceless treasure. It had to be so for someone to have made such a succession of obstacles to guard it: the gate, the shaft, and this deep canal where the inquisitive must have been devoured by ravenous reptiles. But centuries had passed, oxidation had eaten away the metal of the gate, the canal was dried out, and the ferocious saurians had died of hunger or old age.

"It was I, having come from the most distant regions of the sky, who would harvest the fruit of these centuries-old precautions.

"I gained a foothold on a granite quay facing a portico completely eaten away by mold.

"On the other side, four immobile black figures, each the size of a man, were kneeling before a large plinth upon which sparkled an object that I took for a precious stone of uncommon size.

"Carved out of granite in a crude mixture of archaic styles, three of the figures represented an Erloor, an undersea man, and a Martian of the lagoons; the fourth was one of those half-octopus and half-bat creatures that I had seen embroidered on fabric.

"I suspected that the glistening stone had been the idol of all these races.

"I stepped forward trembling with impatience, but before I had taken two steps an enormous block dropped from the roof with a thunderous roar and came within a hair's breadth of crushing me.

"Without the initial cracking sound that had alerted me, so that I instinctively drew back, I would have been miserably crushed by the monolith, the enormous counterweight of the trap set for profaners. The idol was indeed well guarded.

"It was not without misgiving that I circled the mass that had almost crushed me and seized hold of the artfully defended idol.

"It was in reality a sort of helmet or mask — at once one and the other, because it fit onto the head just to the ears — cut of a stone similar to opal, flecked with green and pink.

"My torch was three-quarters gone; I rushed back up and not without extraordinary efforts scaled the shaft in which the descent — while easier than the ascent — had seemed to me so difficult.

"My underground journey had taken an entire afternoon; it was night when I reached the undersea gallery.

"After resting and fortifying myself, I had the quite natural idea of putting on the opal helmet for which I had taken such great risks. As soon as the translucid pupils of the mask were in place before my eyes, I sensed a strange transformation.

"The half-light of the gallery lit up, so to speak, with a new clarity. I saw bands of a phosphorescent light that I had never seen, of a deep green or a very dark violet.

"I have since learned that the helmet—I now knew why those ancient owners had seen it as so precious—had the property of permitting the retina to be acted on by the dark rays of the spectrum and by other radiances of the same order.

"It certainly would have allowed me to see the fatal emanations of radium or x-rays, and other, still more subtle luminous vibrations that will perhaps forever elude the human eye.

"I had hardly recovered from the surprise occasioned by this discovery when I saw pass, so close that it almost brushed me, a winged form that rapidly disappeared in the direction of the glass tower.

"I followed it, strangely moved, sensing that I was on the verge of solving the mystery of these silent palaces.

"Along the way, other shadows lightly brushed me, but so quickly that I was not able to distinguish them clearly.

"I rushed up the spiral and entered into the hallway of one of the niches.

"No words could possibly give you an idea of the terrifying vision that appeared before me; no phrase in any human language could convey the horror and the terror that seized me!

"Each niche of the colossal glass coliseum, over which at that moment Phobos and Deimos poured forth their radiant light, was occupied by a vaguely phosphorescent monster: an enormous, hideous head, between two dirty-white wings. They had no body and, in place of hands, only a jumble of palps or suckers that swarmed at the base like a tangle of serpents.

"Their eyes were huge and lidless, their noses missing, and their mouths thin-lipped and blood red."

At this particular description, all Robert Darvel's listeners had exchanged a look of mute terror. Frymcock's pen had ceased to run across the paper. Zarouk had turned livid gray, a sign of deep terror, and Chérifa herself was tightly pressed against Miss Alberte.

In thrall to the memory of his astounding adventures, Robert continued, without noticing the terrible effect that his words had just produced.

"This entire multitude turned their empty eyes on me and suddenly a piercing jeer rose up from the central abyss and climbed into the sky.

"I recognized, a thousand times repeated, that ironic and sharp burst of laughter that had stalked me over the previous days.

"There wasn't a drop of blood in my veins. I was nailed in place by a terror beyond what humans can bear, and the jeering rushed toward me, like the hissing of a storm.

"With desperate courage, or rather the instinctive reflex of a hunted beast, I bolted . . . I descended the endless gyre like a whirlwind. I had wings at my heels.

"I stopped only when I reached the end of the darkest of the galleries that housed the mummies, and I was well aware that, even there, I wasn't safe from these Vampires—from now on I won't call them anything else—compared to whom the Erloor were only inoffensive Chiropterae.

"If I had had the strength, I would have descended to the bottom of the pit from which I had recovered the opal mask. Oh! How I understood why this fateful talisman that enabled one to see the invisible had been so carefully concealed! How right they were to surround their possession with elaborate dangers!

"So, for days, I had lived side by side with these dreadful creatures! No doubt they had made a game of spying on me, of observing me, as one does with an animal that cannot run very far, that one always finds when the moment to sacrifice it has arrived.

"My odd adventures of those last days became perfectly clear.

"It was the Vampires who, waiting in the weeds of the aerial swamp, had exterminated my poor Martians and had taken me alone prisoner. I sensed again the embrace of their tentacles, and I trembled as I thought of the risk that I had run in settling in the niche of one of these monsters.

"The bowls of blood indicated only too well their customary food.

"It astounded me that there could exist invisible beings on this planet that I had believed inhabited solely by inoffensive savages and stupid Erloor. Turning to the explanations of science was of no use; I couldn't bear to think that I was at the mercy of these spectral creatures.

"Like a wild beast hiding in its hole and surrounded by hounds, I remained crouched between two piles of spheres for several hours, my throat dry with anxiety and my forehead damp with the sweat of agony.

"I was expecting from one moment to the next to hear the soft beating of the Vampires' wings and their snickers as they came to drag me from my refuge. The shrillness of the jeers with which they had greeted me still rang in my ears. This thought alone left me speechless and breathless, half dead from fear. It was surely the excess of this fear itself that prevented me from fainting.

"But the hours passed and no noise disturbed the silence of the subterranean gallery; the thought that my opal mask would enable me to avoid pitfalls from then on was a great comfort. I was still wearing this heavy headgear and I didn't dare remove it any more than I dared to sleep during that terrible night."

Robert Darvel had passed his hand over his forehead in a gesture of anxiety, as if reliving again those dreadful minutes.

Pitcher was fidgeting in his seat, ready to speak. He was about to blurt out everything, to shout at his friend that the Vampires had invaded Earth, that they were prowling about the villa, that they represented an imminent danger. But with an imperious gesture, Miss Alberte imposed silence on him, and even Georges and Frymcock supported the young woman with their glances. Wouldn't it be better to let Robert finish his story? There would still be time to inform him of the danger against which he must surely have some means of defense.

Pitcher nodded with a discontented air but remained silent, while Robert, who attributed the agitation and the terror that he saw painted on every face only to his own words, continued:

"You will probably be surprised to learn that two weeks passed after that day without anything untoward happening to me; on top of that, I had familiarized myself with my jailers and I lived — if one can venture such an expression — on good terms with them.

"I was convinced that they didn't wish me any harm — far from it — they had founded great hopes on me. The sharp cries that they had let out, the jeers and the snickers, were surely their way of expressing their immense astonishment at the sight of me wearing the opal mask, and I realized that my acquisition of this almost magical talisman had given them an elevated idea of my superiority.

"I rarely saw them during the day; unlike the Erloor, they left in the morning at daybreak and came home in the evening to resume their place, each one in the alcove that was assigned to him in the vast amphitheater.

"How they supplied their basins with fresh blood each day, that, they always carefully hid from me. Their invisibility surely facilitated the capture of all sorts of prey, but I always assumed that the Erloor and the Martians of the lagoons—I had experienced the sad proof of it—must make up their principal game.

"The Vampires had no articulate language. The kind of laughter that they let out to express their astonishment or their rage was the only cry they were able to utter.

"When they wanted to communicate between themselves, they placed themselves face to face and came to know one another's intentions by guessing them, in the way that mind readers penetrate the thoughts of their subjects.

"I learned all these details and many others in short order. At first, they fluttered timidly around me and, no doubt to prove their good intentions, one of them led me to a subterranean room that had escaped my explorations that contained in abundance all the provisions that he believed I might find to my taste.

"He was even so kind as to unseal for me the lid of a jar, by means of his long palps, whose soft, damp touch had given me such a horrible sensation.

"These organs, numbering five to each side, which I compared above to a tangle of snakes, had extraordinary strength and agility.

"They were at once fingers, tentacles, and legs, and the Vampires used them with exceptional dexterity: they plucked the tiniest objects from the ground; they tied knots and handled every tool and weapon with precision.

"Sometimes, they would walk on their stiffened palps, wings extended, like butterflies. Other times they would hang suspended from a ceiling—there were three suckers at the tip of each palp—attaching these suckers like suction cups."

At the word "suckers," Frymcock had been unable to stop himself from again bringing his hand to his wrist, but only Pitcher noticed this reaction and its accompanying grimace.

"On other occasions," continued Robert, "they hefted the heaviest burdens with them.

"As for their wings, which were slightly rounded, they were not articulated and membranous like those of the Erloor, true mammals; they were composed of a horny substance like those of insects, such as dragonflies.

"Yet I had great difficulty getting used to the hideous spectacle of those pale, gelatinous, larval faces, which one would have to classify between man and octopus. Those eyes without pupils, vague and empty like those of a skull, spawned an uneasiness that I was unable to dispel.

"I eventually overcame this disgust. I wanted to study these strange beings more closely.

"Not knowing how to converse with them, I took it into my head to draw with a piece of charcoal on a small board one of the fruits of the planet that I knew best, a water chestnut. I showed the drawing to the same Vampire who had seemed to take an interest in me by showing me provisions.

"He understood perfectly and answered me by repeating my drawing quite precisely; then he left in a flurry of wings and came back, in the blink of an eye, with several of the fruits that I had requested.

"I often used this method of communication, to which I soon added another: I led the Vampire into the room with embroidered fabric and made him understand that he might make sense of these images for me through his own drawings.

"But instead, he ordered me to stand in front of him and I saw that, by a sort of suggestion in reverse, he divined a part of my impressions of the moment, if not of my thoughts. I must say I always suffered a great distress from this sort of hypnotism.

"What's worse, I was often compelled to submit to the monster's orders; his will exercised over me a fascination from which I could not defend myself.

"He forced me for example to backtrack or to go, against my will, into a distant gallery where he wanted to make me see some interesting object.

"I should say however that the intentions of my strange instructor were honest. He went to great lengths to try to understand me, but in spite of his efforts and mine the abyss between us was impossible to bridge. Some of my ideas, even some of my sensations, had to remain a closed book for him.

"I gleaned, as you might expect, only a handful of details about the nation of the Vampires through these wordless conversations.

"I learned, thanks to the charcoal drawings traced by the monster's agile palps, that he and the other Invisibles knew all about my adventures on the planet.

"He retraced the first defeat of the Erloor, routed by fire, the death of the Roomboo, and a surprisingly good portrait of my former subjects.

"He gave me to understand that the Vampires could be skilled artisans in every sort of profession. It was their ancestors who had built the towers of glass linked by galleries in the middle of the sea and had hoarded all that I saw in the underground passages.

"The current Vampires themselves had simplified everything and no longer engaged in work other than to look for food.

"I asked them how long they lived, and it was not without difficulty that I managed to make my question understood.

"Then his hideous face expressed a heartrending sadness, his wings trembled with agitation.

"'You must also die,' the Vampire responded, by means of suggestion.

"And he raised and lowered his palps eight times to show me how much time remained for him to live.

"But was he speaking of weeks, of months, of years? I was unable to get him to specify.

"Several days passed before I began to see the truth. The Vampires were under the dominion of a terrible being, whose name they didn't even dare to pronounce and who, they asserted, had the ability to discern all their actions and all their thoughts.

"Like the ancient Minotaur, this Moloch, whom the embroidered allegories represented with a blazing half-circle, demanded every month a tribute of living Vampires that he devoured.

This formidable being lived in the hottest region of the planet, to the south, in a vast expanse of wilderness and sea, constantly battered by storms, that none but his designated victims dared enter.

"They had tried to please him with other holocausts, but the Vampires were the only prey that suited him, and even then he spurned contemptuously the wings and the palps, no doubt too difficult to digest.

"Long ago, the victims of this bloody tax had tried to resist, had flown off to the frozen regions of the Martian pole. The voracious god's vengeance had followed them wherever they went and exterminated them; glass towers had been reduced to dust by lightning, and the fugitive Vampires had been snatched by an irresistible force from the hiding places where they had found refuge, in the most secret caves of the mountains or the most tangled thickets of primeval forests.

"These bloody suppressions had borne fruit; no rebellion had taken place for a very long time; each month the prescribed number of docile victims took flight for the accursed regions of the South, never to return.

"The Invisible who served as my guide must have tried to make me understand that only eight months remained before his turn would arrive to offer himself in sacrifice to the Martian Moloch.

"These affirmations left me somewhat incredulous. The nearly divine omnipotence of the voracious monster seemed hardly believable, as did the tremendous size that the Vampires attributed to him, making him out to be as large as a mountain and crowned in flames.

"I surmised that it was perhaps a question only of a volcano or of some other natural phenomenon, of which the Vampires might have been victims in the past, under circumstances liable to strike their imagination. In truth I didn't know what to think. The Vampires were very reserved on this subject and betrayed the most striking terror each time I wanted to extract new information from them.

"However, there had to be some truth in what they had related, for I was witness, on the established date, to the departure of a convoy of Vampires to the south.

"It was a spectacle I will never forget.

"I neglected to tell you that, since discovering its marvelous qualities, I hardly ever removed my opal mask except to sleep for a few hours. I was just waking from one of these naps, a little before sunset, after a long excursion into the galleries, when my attention was drawn by the chorus of high-pitched cries similar to snickering that, for the Invisibles, expressed the height of emotion.

"I hurried to put on my mask and climb the inclined plane of the spiral. I was no longer afraid of approaching or entering the niches.

"The vast interior abyss was filled with a multitude of Vampires who were fluttering in circles, with a whining lament, not unlike a hive of bees in turmoil. I could not have imagined that these monsters, in appearance glacial and repulsive, would be able to feel such violent grief.

"In the meantime, they all eventually returned to their niches, but without ceasing their cries, and I saw that those who occupied the highest row of niches, just below the platform, were greedily emptying bowls filled to the rim with blood.

"At that moment, Phobos and Deimos emerged above the horizon, both sparkling in the pure stillness of the sky. At this sight, the bitter screams rose to a deafening pitch. Then, suddenly, the Vampires of the highest row rose as one, hurling a final guttural cry and gathered in a triangle, like wild geese or swallows leaving for their annual migration. Almost immediately, they sailed rapidly toward the south, accompanied by the universal lamentation of their companions.

"From the glass towers scattered far across the sea, other flocks of Vampires arose to fill the ranks of this troop on its death march.

"A heartrending clamor filled the air.

"These sharp jeers, so like ironic laughter, cut me to the quick.

"I could see now that behind the hideous faces of the Vampires were intelligent and suffering souls. I was profoundly moved and troubled. Dare I say, I pitied these strange creatures and wondered what I might do to save them.

"But already the united troops of Vampires formed a thick cloud on the southern horizon that was soon lost in the light mist.

"In the vast circle of the glass tower, the heartrending laughter had ceased.

"Then wings began to beat in the silence of the depths. From the interior abyss a troop of Vampires flew up and silently occupied the now empty niches of the upper row. These were the victims chosen for the next holocaust."

Robert Darvel, whose voice gave some signs of fatigue, had stopped. He drank a few sips of the iced beverage that Chérifa offered him.

Miss Alberte and her friends were lost in a world of thought. They impatiently awaited the rest of Robert's incredible adventures. Only the Negro, Zarouk, his eyes fixed on the veranda, seemed to contemplate with his empty gaze one of the monsters that the engineer had just described.

VII

....

The Isle of Death

Ralph Pitcher murmured something about the temperature, an insignificant statement that nobody picked up. The engineer, to the satisfaction of all, resumed after a few moments' rest:

"From that day on, I was tormented by the desire to see and meet the tyrant who wielded such despotic power over the Vampires. Well before the end of the month, when a new sacrifice was due to take place, my decision had been made. I would discover the monster's refuge and I would be present when he devoured his victims.

"I was convinced that much of what they told me was an exaggeration: the existence of a being such as had been portrayed to me seemed impossible.

"The Vampire to whom I confided this project appeared terrified by my audacity, yet he didn't refuse to obtain the objects I required for such an expedition or to provide the information I needed to reach the country that he called "the Isle of Death" that he couldn't mention without trembling.

"In a corner of the subterranean arsenal, he found a sturdy, lightweight skiff, as narrow as a dugout, and large enough to carry two people in comfort. It was made of sea turtle scales fused seamlessly into a single piece. I improvised oars and a rudder from some boards I salvaged from the cedar crates, and I soon had the satisfaction of seeing my craft, which the Vampires had launched and moored to the base of the tower, in the water.

"It was supplied with more than enough food for the length of the trip; but I had concluded there was no point equipping it with a sail. Besides the fact that I was a very inexperienced sailor, I knew that I would be carried both on the trip out and on the trip back by two currents flowing in opposite directions that were easy to distinguish by the color of their water.

"It was not without emotion that, three days before the fateful date of the sacrifice, I lowered myself one morning from the top of the tower to my turtle-shell skiff. I gave a few strokes with the oars and found myself almost immediately in the current, which flowed north to south and carried me along with great speed.

"I was supplied with a map, crudely drawn on a plank of wood with charcoal, and, according to the information that had been given to me, I knew that it was nearly impossible to err.

"The weather, which for that matter had remained beautiful during almost my entire stay with the Vampires, was splendid. Here and there the glass towers sparkled in the limpid sky above the sea as calm as a lake.

"Thanks to my opal mask, which I hadn't relinquished, I saw the Vampires watch me go by with horrified curiosity, lined up on the platforms like hideous birds.

"The journey passed without incident other than the arrival of large flying fish with pink wings, which dropped into my boat of their own accord. Just before nightfall, I landed on a sandy islet teeming with crustaceans and birds. I resumed my sailing at dawn, after a perfect night's sleep.

"The scenery changed as I left behind the region of the towers. The open sea, strewn with sinister red rocks, reflected a stormy sky streaked with clouds as black as pitch or the baleful color of lead. Large blood-colored sharks swam around my skiff and I shuddered to think that one of them might attack me on a whim; a single bite of its formidably armed jaws would have sufficed to reduce my skiff and me to bits.

"About midday, a large, pallid land mass appeared on the horizon and grew from hour to hour so that before evening its rounded summit appeared to disappear into the clouds.

"I recognized the dwelling place of the tyrant or god of the Vampires, and in spite of myself I felt moved to see at least a portion of what they had told me fulfilled. It felt as if the gigantic mountain that blocked the southern horizon weighed upon me with all its mass and that it was drawing my frail skiff on, like the magnetic mountain of Arab legend.

"I felt the first stabs of a strange apprehension. I found myself wondering why I had left the glass tower, where I was perfectly safe — and enjoyed ideal conditions for a study of the planet's history — to face certain danger. It took all my courage not to give in to the temptation to turn my prow around and go back to join the Vampires, to whom I felt a deep debt of gratitude.

"It was only with a great effort of self-mastery that I overcame this faintness of heart.

"I camped that night on a reef torn ragged by the waves but was unable to find a moment's rest. As soon as the sun went down, a dreadful storm broke out. Lightning appeared to split the sky across its entire breadth, the waves rose to splash me even on the crest of the rock, thunder rumbled all night, and a torrential rain drenched me to the bone.

"I knew that in many hot climes, for example certain regions of the Antilles, storms break nearly every evening and cool the earth that has been exhausted, during the day, by the heat of the sun.

"This reflection calmed my fears a little and gave an explanation for the Vampire having told me 'that the region of death was buffeted by a perpetual gale.' Here, already, was the explanation by natural laws of an initially marvelous event.

"In the morning, I took up my skiff, which I had sheltered in a crevice, and I put to sea again. The rain had happily ceased, but the sky remained covered and the heat was even more suffocating.

"The mountain now stood before me like a sheer rampart, and I noted that it had the exact shape of a half-sphere rising from the waves of the sea. I could see that the representations of this mountain I had seen in the embroidered portraits were perfectly faithful.

"I estimate the height of the mountain to be close to that of Mont Blanc, but about three times its breadth. As I approached, the enormous dome, perfectly smooth over its whole surface, took on a pale, washed out appearance, like a light with a whitish paper shade in full daylight.

"To the right and the left, I could see that the land was much lower and covered by a forest of immense size, with this peculiarity: its trees were shiny as if they had been rubbed in graphite or like some petrified wood found in coal mines. But all my attention was drawn to the accursed mountain that, through a well-known optical illusion, appeared very close, even though I was still quite some distance away.

"The sea there was sown with reefs and sandbanks and crisscrossed by currents, in the midst of which I had a good deal of trouble maintaining my craft; the cadavers of fish and birds floated belly up, as if the proximity of the accursed mountain might be deadly to all living things. A stench of carnage and corruption rose from the desolate waves.

"No terrestrial landscape can give an idea of the sinister and awe-inspiring effect of this prospect.

"Near midday, I passed an islet covered with greenery and flowers and I approached with the intention of stopping there for some time. I planned to rest a little there, awaiting the hour when I would witness the immolation of the Vampires.

"But when I neared those enchanted banks, I saw that they were planted with giant oleander and the breeze carried the bitter smell of prussic acid.

"I understood that it would have been deadly to set foot on this poisoned ground. The remains of insects, small mammals, and fish that littered the sand confirmed my fears only too well. I pulled away as fast as the oars could propel me.

"You understand now my deep aversion to anything that smells like bitter almonds.

"This discovery made a great impression on me. I saw that danger lurked on every side and from that moment I was persuaded that the Vampires had spoken the truth and that I was the plaything of an unknown and formidable power.

"I decided then to bear around and return, but I calculated that less than two hours of daylight remained. It would have been sheer madness to start my return voyage at night, and I was so unsettled that I don't know whether I would have been able to recognize the south-north current that was supposed to carry me back to the glass towers.

"I had wanted to see; I *would* see, in spite of myself if necessary. I trembled as I resigned myself to my fate, then I sailed cautiously toward the base of the mountain; I was now close enough to see that it was formed entirely of white quartz.

"This rounded cliff that rose perpendicularly in front of me was as abrupt, as straight up and down as if it had been cut from a single block or cast in a mold.

"I slowly sailed along the base obstructed by sandbars that I realized, with horror, were covered with an accumulation of Vampire palps and wings, which exhaled a suffocating stench.

"I then noticed that I had been able to see that hideous debris without the help of my mask.

"The power of invisibility that the Vampires possessed only functioned while they were alive and disappeared as soon as they died.

"I could have rowed for weeks around the giant dome without making any progress. I was about to make up my mind to drop the metal ingot that served as my anchor when I noticed, approximately in the center of the base of the mountain, a dark blotch that gave the impression of a door or something similar. I thought that it must give entry into the interior of the dome, into the very bosom of the monstrous block of quartz.

"I rowed hard in this direction and eventually reached a large shadowy bay that opened up at the water's edge.

"I didn't even for a moment consider venturing into this den, especially when I observed that the remains of the Vampires were more plentiful there than anywhere else and formed in the surroundings a sort of fetid swamp, full of slithering animals and raucous jaws.

"I pulled away from it, but not enough to lose sight of this frightening entryway. I anchored off a small rocky island situated to the left and I tried to eat, in spite of the anguish that gripped my throat and the nausea that turned my stomach. I hadn't yet eaten anything that day; but in spite of my efforts, I barely managed to swallow a sip of the fortifying liquid and a pinch of those starchy grains that I had found in the subterranean galleries.

"I watched the arrival of night with inexpressible anxiety. The sun had not yet disappeared when already the thunder started to rumble, and the daily gale burst.

"It was then that I observed a strange phenomenon. As the lightning grew in quantity and intensity, the forest of metallic trees that I just mentioned was surrounded by a bluish aura of electricity and the treetops were crowned with fire similar to that which sailors observe sometimes at the tip of the mast. The forest seemed to literally drink in the storm and feast on its mysterious power.

"None of this made sense; neither on Earth nor on Mars had I seen wood behave in a manner so contrary to the laws of conductivity.

"I was soon torn from this mute contemplation. Night had definitively fallen, and a furious wind had arisen, but, above its howling, a heartrending clamor was rising from beyond the horizon to the north and increasing from moment to moment.

"I felt the marrow in my bones freeze and my hair stand on end with horror as I recognized the high-pitched cry of the Vampires that, this time, was a cry of agony.

"They had left the towers, like those that I had seen the preceding month, and here their hideous and pitiful flock arrived, carried on the wings of the gale.

"Already their livid mass stained the sky striated with lightning bolts. I heard the rushing noise of their wings and those bitter cries that tore my heart.

"They seemed to be coming toward me, begging for help! It was dreadful . . . I had dropped, gasping for breath, on the sand; I would have preferred to close my eyes so I didn't have to see, and yet I watched, transfixed by the horror of the sight.

"The flock of pitiful monsters passed only a few meters above me and I saw the first disappear, with a speed of which only a waterspout or a whirlwind can give an idea, into the dark entranceway of which I spoke and that now was illuminated by a pale phosphorescence.

"Their swarm rushed toward it, drawn by an invincible force; they tumbled over each other like sheep at the narrow door of an abattoir. Slowly, the mountain swallowed the screeching and suppliant horde.

"The high-pitched cries were replaced by the dull sound of something being ground up and the sound of a belch that reached even to where I was. From time to time, the entryway — which I don't dare call a mouth — discharged in a flood of bloody foam the wings and the palps, which would pile up in a semicircular shoal the way filth forms at the entrance to sewers . . .

"Above this hideous drama, bolts of lightning slashed the black sky, illuminating the nightmarish landscape and the raging waves in great bursts . . .

"It was more than I could bear. I fainted.

"When I opened my eyes again, the swarm of Vampires had disappeared. All had vanished into the gaping maw. The solitary storm raged above the desolate horizon, but an inexplicable change had been wrought in the appearance of the mountain: its entire bulk now radiated a milky phosphorescence. Before me loomed a wall of livid light whose effect was terrible beyond belief.

"I couldn't help thinking of those tropical glowworms that shine only once they are sated; now, no doubt, the Leviathan[11] was digesting.

"I was shattered from exhaustion and fear, sick, nauseated. Even my curiosity had vanished. I had but one thought: to flee this accursed place forever.

"Ah! Why had I left Earth, the lovely maternal Earth, for this bloody planet where the law of survival of the fittest was applied in so atrocious and harsh a fashion!

"I now had but one idea, I repeat: to flee, to flee at any price, no matter where, no matter what the risks.

"I paid no attention even to the gale that was whipping the flock of wildly foaming waves with its lashes of lighting. I untied my skiff and seized my oars with a sort of madness, but I was hardly two cable-lengths from the shore when a groundswell lifted the vessel and sent it swirling about like a wisp of straw. I clung to the gunwales as I bounced along the crest of the waves at a stupefying speed.

"Thinking about it now, it must have been the exceptional lightness of my craft that prevented it from sinking to the bottom.

"I was tossed up and over sharp rocks, thrown brutally onto a beach of pebbles, then seized again by the flood and tossed all over again; a huge wave engulfed me, my arms went slack, and I sank to the bottom . . .

"By what miracle did I survive?

---

11 The Leviathan, like his equal the Behemoth, who devours in a single day all the vegetation of the planet, is an animal of fable who, according to Talmudic legend, will be served to the elect on the Day of Judgment in an immense banquet. Robert employs the term to designate the largest animal imaginable.

"When I opened my eyes again, to the hot rays of the noonday sun, I lay stretched on a pebbly shore, and as soon as I tried to move, I experienced intense pains all over my body.

"I felt like a man who had been soundly beaten with a club, the sharp edges of the rock had covered me with cuts and bruises, and I had violent stomach cramps from the seawater I had swallowed.

"I believed my last hour had come. Yet I had the strength to drag myself beyond the reach of the waves. I glimpsed, a few paces away, the remains of my tortoiseshell skiff, punctured and cracked, and also a few of the objects that had made up its load.

"I crawled that way, but I was so weakened that it took me certainly more than half an hour to cross the ten paces that separated me from the wreckage. Each movement wrung from me a moan of pain, and I was tortured by thirst.

"It was with a feeling of unutterable happiness that I recognized, more or less intact among the pebbles, the bamboo keg that contained my cordial. Slowly and with great effort, I managed again to drag myself to it and to undo the cover.

"I drank with rapture several gulps and almost immediately the effect of the noble elixir made itself felt; I felt better and, although my injuries caused me a lot of pain, I was able to stand and pull the debris of my skiff away from the beach, in the vague hope of repairing it later.

"I had trouble staying on my feet and — it was about midday — the blazing sun was beginning to get to me.

"It was only then that I thought to examine the shore where the gale had flung me. In front of me, a short distance from the sea, stretched the petrified forest with strange glints of graphite that I had seen crowned with glimmers of electricity the night before; far in the distance, the cone of a volcano was plumed with smoke; to my right, the vast white mass of the accursed mountain, with its rounded summit hidden by clouds, blocked my view.

"The terrible vision of the previous night's events rose in my memory.

"I trembled in terror. I believe that I would have felt more secure under the claw of a lion than in those awful surroundings. I knew that the monster hidden in that mountain could suck me in with a simple whim and devour me just as whales, at certain times, feed on microscopic animalcules.

"I wondered how it was that I was still alive. The same fervent desire to flee took hold of me; I thought that I owed my life only to the torpor that must have accompanied the mysterious Leviathan's digestion.

"To flee . . . But that was impossible; I glanced in despair at my blood-drenched legs and the remains of my skiff. I couldn't set to sea again without time to heal and rest and without mending, somehow or other, my skiff.

"I was absorbed in those sad reflections when it occurred to me that the cordial from my keg might be an excellent dressing for my wounds. Its balsam fragrance encouraged me and I experienced its beneficial effect almost immediately; the distressing sting of the cuts abated and, although I still limped a little, I felt sturdier on my feet.

"I used the rest of that day to rest and to recover what I could of my provisions. It was as I was carrying out this work that I noticed, half-buried in the sand, the opal mask that must have come off when I sank; this discovery gave me great joy.

"I placed it in a hole in the rock to keep it safe, along with the rest of what I had saved. With the lens I was able to light a fire, and I roasted a sea turtle with the neck of a snake I had captured in the sand.

"I won't mention the daily storm that arose as soon as the sun set, against which I sheltered myself as best I could. Exhaustion and, perhaps, the properties of my cordial helped me enjoy a profound slumber. Upon awakening I found myself nearly refreshed, in any case ready to set to work. The idea that the Leviathan's digestion should render it harmless for several days was very comforting.

"First of all, the embers of my fire, near which were scattered the remains of the sea turtle, made me think that with the aid of a certain number of similar shells, softened by heat, I would easily be able to repair my craft. But the shells grew hard and dry in the fire, and I remembered that, in comb-making, it was boiling water that was used to soften the material before working it, and I had nothing like a proper vessel to hold it.

"I was discouraged. I took my axe and headed in the direction of the crystallized forest, beyond which loomed the crater crowned with a plume of smoke.

"The proximity of the volcano gave me the hope, rather dubious I have to admit, of finding a hot spring.

"I entered the denuded space that lay between the mountain and the forest. I noticed then—I had given up noting every surprise and was blasé about the most extraordinary phenomena—that the trees were not, as I had believed, petrified fossils; they weren't trees at all, but rather metal masts with smaller bars branching off at right angles. These bars in turn branched into metallic sticks sharpened into very fine points.

"The whole had the appearance of a fir tree with a pointed top. The base of each mast, which served as a trunk, was securely fixed into a large plate of glass.

"I had before me a non-vegetal and completely artificial forest, a forest of lightning rods!

"I was no longer surprised now by the electric flames I had seen fluttering above these strange branches during the storm. But what became of the enormous quantity of current thus harnessed during each storm, that is to say each evening?

"I was at a complete loss.

"I continued alongside the forest until I arrived at a vast square, paved with large plates of transparent glass, below which I heard the murmur of running water. I knelt down and through the thickness of the paving, I made out a large metal beam, to which were connected a multitude of smaller cables, that was immersed in the water of a lake or of a subterranean canal.

"I had no doubt that each of the cables ran to the foot of one of the metal trees.

"So all the electrical energy harnessed by those thousands and thousands of lightning rods was absorbed and utilized—for what purpose?—by the unknown and formidable being that I had called Leviathan, for lack of a better word to describe it!

"I was so preoccupied with the discovery I had made that I didn't even notice I had left the glass-paved square and entered the metal forest, where the slightest breeze made the branches ring like Aeolian harps.

"'What on earth can this current be used for?' I cried aloud.

"And, while talking to myself, like all people who are under the sway of a fascinating idea, I continued walking, and quickly.

"I must have walked this way for a long time, because—I have calculated it since — the forest, at this spot, was around a league wide, with a length three times greater.

"I stopped in a bare, rocky spot only because a stream blocked the path; I had crossed the width of the electric wood and I could see, not far away, the first foothills of the volcano.

"The lava field was strewn with pumice-stones, ash, and scoria.

"I was preparing to step over the stream when I noticed that thick steam rose from its surface. I dipped my hand in: its water was boiling hot. By a strange bit of luck, my hypothesis had been proven right; I had before me one of those hot springs so common in volcanic regions, and I had to say that this discovery had taken very little effort.

I would be able to patch at my leisure the sides of my tortoiseshell skiff. I couldn't get over my good fortune and was about to set off to get it when I took it into my head to follow the course of the stream, which flowed toward the base of the mountain, along which it ran for a short distance.

"Along the way, it received the tribute of a small spring whose acrid, dirty yellowish water confirmed that it was a stream of acid, a phenomenon, by the way, as common in volcanic regions as a hot spring.

"I remembered that Humboldt reported in the Andes a 'natural' source of sulfuric acid that measured high on the scale of Baume's aerometer.

"But, judging from the way in which the vitrified lava of the banks had been hollowed out and, it appeared, dissolved, it wasn't this substance that I was dealing with: it had to be instead hydrofluoric acid, the most corrosive of all substances, since it eats away even the glass decanters that hold it.

"Mixing with the stream, the spring added its corrosive qualities to it and, when I arrived at the place where it reached the mountain, I perceived that the uninterrupted work of the waters had hollowed out of the quartz a recess of around a meter in height.

"The current entered into that minuscule grotto, from which it came out again a little farther along, to run into a swamp reeking of sulfur, which reminded me of the countryside around Etna, which I had visited in the past.

"I stopped before the grotto and examined the stone that I had taken to be quartz that covered the whole surface of the mountain. In the places where it had been corroded by the action of the acid, it looked exactly like the stone with hints of pink and green of which my mask was made, which I had taken to be opal.

"It was one more enigma to decipher, but I didn't attach any importance to it at first.

"Curiosity led me to enter the little grotto, to which a few stones strewn across the current permitted rather easy access. I forgot for a moment all my fears.

"I had to duck to enter the cave, and then I advanced a few steps, first in darkness, then surrounded by a faint light similar to moonlight. The grotto was no more than ten steps deep and ended in a rounded alcove from which emanated the lunar light.

"I moved closer for a look. At first it was like looking through a foggy windowpane and I saw only a heap of confused things: a series of regular undulations, troughs, and mounds.

"But suddenly the interior gleam grew. I could see clearly! In my wildest and most reckless hypotheses, I would never have imagined such a thing . . .

"The truth was more incredible and more marvelous than any fiction!

"Dare I say it? I had before me a gigantic, a monstrous brain, to which this mountain, as high as Mont Blanc, served as cranium!

"I distinctly perceived the different lobes as vast as hills and convolutions that seemed to me deep ravines . . .

"The giant organs were bathed in a phosphorescent liquid that made them visible to my eyes, and I saw the arteries and veins beat and leap with the powerful movement of a machine's pistons; it even seemed that a little heat came all the way to me, through the thick rampart of translucent stone!

"Never had a man experienced astonishment equal to mine. I wondered whether I wasn't the plaything of a diabolical hallucination. This creation, so colossal, so beyond the realm of possibility, crushed me with a horror that had no name; and, in spite of myself, I stayed there with my eyes glued to this window on the infinite, without the strength to flee.

"I was dazed, hypnotized by the staggering spectacle. I eventually pulled myself away from the grotto and took refuge in the metal forest. My head was pounding, my arteries threatened to burst; I felt madness taking hold of me.

"This living proof of the miraculous variety of shapes that life takes in the various creations of the worlds so overwhelmed me that I lost all power of reason.

"Men who have emerged from the depths of the Maelstrom, Dante after the dreams that led him each night into his Hell, experienced the same thing.

"I recovered little by little and ventured some explanations.

"Evidently, the electric current of the forest, transformed by some unknown process, provided nervous energy to that extraordinary cluster of cells, while the Vampires the monster devoured renewed its supply of phosphorus, once it was exhausted.

"I understood the formidable power of such a cerebral mass. What couldn't it accomplish, this enormous will, when focused on a single point?

"I was no longer surprised by Vampires blasted from a distance or drawn against their will all the way to the voracious chasm from within their glass tower.

"This Babel-like brain must embody, in a part of Mars, our idea of an all-powerful god. It must, at will, call forth storms or calm them and bring plants or animals to life at its whim. I no longer found any exaggeration in the Vampires' assertions that the terrible being could see all and hear all, when it made the effort.

"The stone dome — of the same nature as my mask — that served it for a skull obviously enabled it to perceive all the invisible radiances, without any need of pupils; its enormous optic lobe, I assumed, must be directly acted upon by light . . ."

Robert Darvel had stopped, distressed, eyes haggard, at the tremendous evocation of the giant brain. His friends, deeply shaken themselves, waited with poignant curiosity for him to continue.

"I read," he said, "a thousand questions in your eyes. You wonder how I, a scientist — and I could almost say a Martian scientist — can explain such an inconceivable creature, how I might link it to the chain of other beings! I wouldn't presume to furnish, for such a question, a finished theory; however, I believe that one might venture certain hypotheses."

Attention furrowed brows and gleamed more fervently in the eyes of the engineer's friends.

"I suspect," he resumed, "that the Vampires are only a sketch, a preliminary version of the unspeakable being I saw. They are already little more
than brains; if you were to take away the wings and the palps, which they
could do without in a pinch, they would be nearly identical to it.

"Remember what I told you about their strength of will, about their
power of suggestion, devoid as they are of claws and teeth.

"Imagine if you will, after a thousand centuries, these faculties multiplied
a hundred times. But that, you will object, does not explain the colossal
volume of this brain!

"I will answer that I believe it formed not of a single but of several thousand brains, juxtaposed, dissolved into only one according to an unknown
evolution.

"It isn't, upon reflection, as implausible as it initially seems.

"Let's imagine man stripped by science and time of his animal organs,
reduced to the only weighty matter, to the brain.

"Relieved of the organs of digestion and locomotion, nourished with a
drop of concentrated food, and no longer subjected to the same wear and
tear, its existence is almost infinite, and its will benefits from the diminution
of the burden that fell upon it in the past.

"Let's start with that. Now remember too that, already today, every
man engaged in an intellectual enterprise no longer needs to move as he
used to: a man who reads, writes, listens, or speaks is immobile; now in
a gathering of men whose imperfections—and, by consequence, whose
irregularities—have been done away with by science, it is inevitable that
all will share essentially the same thoughts.

"From there to envisaging that the material seat of this thinking might
also become common to all, that a thousand thinkers might no longer have
but a single brain between them, is not a big step to take.

"But it would take too long to fully explain my hypothesis. Let's return
to the rest of my adventures.

"I spent the remainder of that day, one of the most memorable in the
history of scientific discovery, absorbed in deep meditation.

"I imagined the existence of this multiple being, asleep in the dream that
it was creating for itself, according to its desires; attentive to the life of the
planet that it modified at will, and perhaps devising and realizing in that

very moment some new surge for itself toward a better and more beautiful future; it seemed to me like Buddha sitting in meditation on the lotus flower.

"It was no longer terror that I experienced but an overwhelming admiration. Who could list the unprecedented discoveries, the superhuman masterpieces of which the soul of the Martian god, ruminating under its stone cupola, was the author.

"I wondered whether its attention had dwelled upon my puny person, and I managed to convince myself that it had voluntarily spared me, that it had willingly permitted me to uncover a portion of the secrets of its nature.

"Then my daydreaming took another tack. I told myself that perhaps it had gotten lost in its own dream, that its powerful will had grown dull, that the centuries had blunted the acuity of its sensation, and that one day, after the passing of centuries, it would atrophy in its mountain like the brain of an old man who falls back into childhood . . .

"It was perhaps to a deterioration of this sort that I owed my existence . . .

"Immersed in this reverie, or, if you will, in this mental fog, I no longer thought of fixing my skiff, and I no longer noticed the passage of time. The night, which was falling, already white with lightning, reminded me abruptly of concerns of a material nature. I made my way back to the shore and distractedly munched a handful of my starchy grains.

"Suddenly, the first masts of the metallic forest were coursing with electric fires.

"I jumped to my feet as if I had been activated by a spring.

"I wanted to shout like Archimedes: Eureka! I had just glimpsed, suddenly, the possibility of communicating with Earth and perhaps of gaining dominion over the ineffable being, the Great Brain!

"I lay down drunk with pride beside the wreckage of my skiff, but I was unable to sleep.

"All night, my mind mulled over the idea that had unexpectedly presented itself; I perfected the details of my plan and resolved one by one every objection.

"When the sun rose into the still-tempestuous sky, my plan was ready and I was certain it would succeed."

VIII

....

The Road Home

"I hurriedly completed repairs on my skiff and put to sea again that very day, after finding the south-north current that I had been shown.

"I will spare you all the superfluous details. The plan that had made me pass the night in feverish elation consisted quite simply of depriving the Great Brain of the electric current that was, without any doubt, essential to its existence. Then it would be at my mercy.

"I myself would make use of the incredible energy amassed each evening by the metal trees to send signals to Earth. Once the means was at my disposal, the material installation would be a mere game for an electrician of my capabilities, especially when assisted — as I thought likely — by the Vampires.

"I made my return voyage without incident and disembarked at the glass tower, where the Vampires were surprised to see me again. They questioned me in their way, but I was very careful not to tell them of my plan. Meanwhile I hastily prepared all that I needed for a second expedition.

"I built a larger, sturdier boat, and the arsenal furnished all the materials I needed: metal wires, tubes, and provisions.

"A week later I set sail again. The only risk I ran — but it was tremendous — was that the Great Brain might notice my presence.

"Nothing of the sort happened; in all this expedition, I was favored by unimaginably good fortune.

"I arrived within sight of the metallic forest at nightfall, slept among the rocks, and set to work the next day. I had fabricated, with saltpeter from the tunnels, twenty or so kilograms of gunpowder, which I used to set a mine below the beam that conducted the current.

"I admit between us that my heart was pounding when I set fire to the fuse and while I calculated — on my fingers, in the absence of a chronometer — the time that should pass before the explosion.

"Finally, the detonation sounded, and it seemed to me that the mountain rocked on its base and the earth trembled beneath my feet, but that was all. I was surprised I wasn't struck down on the spot by the Great Brain's rage.

"When the cloud of dust and smoke had dissipated, I ventured to have a look. I had fully succeeded: the conductive beam — made of a very brittle metal — was broken in two places, and there was a hole in the glass paving through which flooded the water of the subterranean canal.

"Several trees of the forest had lost their branches, but this was the only unintentional damage I had done, and it was easily repairable.

"As I was gleefully surveying my handiwork, the landscape was abruptly enveloped in a fog as thick as the thickest darkness. It was, I imagined, one of the last manifestations of the power of a Great Brain that, struck in its most vulnerable spot, was hiding from its enemies and perhaps gathering itself to judge the gravity of the blow it had suffered.

"I waited impatiently for night to come. Until then I had everything to fear, but at night my terrible adversary's reserve of electrical energy would be exhausted and, since it would not be replenished, I would no longer have anything to fear.

"It was with a sigh of relief that I saw the first flashes of the storm shine at the peak of the denuded masts. I was saved.

"It was impossible to imagine that the colossal organism might perish suddenly from the lack of electricity — it had to be able to hold out for many months — but it would languish, it would be at my mercy.

"It would have to reveal its secrets to me.

"These thoughts swelled me with pride, and I lifted my head almost insolently to the majestic dome of the mountain.

"But I had achieved only a part — the most difficult part — of my plan. I needed the help of the Vampires to bring it to a wholly successful conclusion.

"They wouldn't believe the incredible news at first, and I had a lot of trouble persuading a few of them to accompany me all the way to the deadly mountain.

"But, once the first were convinced, they all rushed up, and the sky was filled with troops gathered from the farthest glass towers as fast as they could fly.

"I persuaded them without difficulty that if they wanted to be delivered from the bloody tax they paid each month to their tyrant they must obey my every command.

"I chose a long, deserted plain, a sort of Martian Sahara with sand the color of blood, in which to install a hundred of the masts, each fitted with a powerful arc lamp.

"Metals from the arsenal and a sort of very dense anthracite, to replace the coal of the retorts, furnished the necessary materials.

"The metal forest's conductive beam was connected to the lamps by means of a length of heavy wire, and I soon had the pleasure of seeing my signals function every night with perfect regularity.

"The Vampires had assisted me devotedly, and it was quite a sight to see a dozen of them lift an enormous beam into the air with their palps and put it in place with consummate skill.

"I was, however, anxious about what might transpire on the day assigned for the Vampires' fatal sacrifice. The apparent inertia of the Great Brain only half reassured me. Once, I had crept into the little grotto hollowed out by the spring of hydrofluoric acid, and I had seen the giant convolutions still lit with the phosphorus of life, and I had noticed that the pulsing of the blood vessels had not stopped but had only grown weaker.

"I feared some unexpected and incredible awakening of the Leviathan. I resolved to take every precaution in my power against a likely resurrection of the all-powerful will, still surprised that I had subdued it with such ease. On the day set for the monthly holocaust of the Vampires, I ordered that all those who were fated for death withdraw to the deepest of the subterranean galleries, whose doors were to be solidly shut after them.

"I hoped that they would be less susceptible there to the imperious attraction that forced them to fly to the mountain of death.

"At sunset, I heard loud cries and the tumult of beating wings; overpowered by the fatal suggestion, they tried to force the doors I had barricaded.

"They didn't succeed, and the uproar died down after a few moments. The Vampires were saved. The Great Brain, deprived of phosphorus, as it was already deprived of electrical energy, was now going to grow feeble, losing all willpower and all might.

"Three months passed. The Vampires bore me the deepest respect, the most subservient obedience. They anticipated and satisfied my every whim.

"They carried out all the labors I commanded of them, procured for me the rarest plants and animals of the planet, and carried me on their invisible wings wherever I wanted.

"In this way I made an appearance in the village of my former subjects, the Martians of the lagoons, whom I encouraged and showered with gifts. They surely must have considered me a being of an almost divine nature. As I left, I promised that I would not abandon them and that my protection would never stop watching over them from afar.

"I lived, for these few months, the enchanted and incredible existence of a sorcerer served by obedient demons.

"I would have enjoyed happiness beyond compare had it not been for my desire to see Earth again, which turned into an obsession and a haunting passion. How many nights did I spend on the platform of the glass towers, contemplating the home star, that distant little speck of light, seemingly lost in the swarms of the stellar worlds. In any case, I hadn't given up hope. After the incredible feats I had had the good fortune to accomplish, nothing seemed impossible.

"My signals, as I said, functioned flawlessly. A rudimentary keyboard with three keys allowed me to light and extinguish the three groups of electric lamps that, for the inhabitants of Earth, would constitute the dash and dot of Morse code. At first I took responsibility for this task, then I trained some Vampires to carry it out themselves. They acquitted themselves extremely well, with the help of a sort of notebook in which I had summarized my adventures in telegraphic symbols.[12]

---

12 As we go to press, we have learned that an American astronomer, a Mr. Pickering, of Boston, is in the process of constructing a system of signals designed to place Earth in communication with Mars. Let us not forget that it is a Frenchman, the poet Charles Cros, who first came up with the idea of these signals.

"I set these signals to repeat endlessly, persuaded that terrestrial astronomers would have to notice them sooner or later.

"Throughout the fourth month, there were frequent interruptions of the current. This was the result of a noticeable lessening of the violence of the storms over the metallic forest; in addition to this, the leaves of the trees had accumulated a covering of fine dust that made them much less conductive.

"I attributed these accidents to natural causes; I would soon learn how mistaken I was.

"But I am getting ahead of myself.

"Near the end of the fifth month, I was seated on the platform of one of the glass towers, peacefully contemplating the long line of signals that was beginning to light up in the growing shadows of dusk. A storm was brewing in the sky and the Vampires had nearly all withdrawn into their deep niches.

"Suddenly, with the abruptness of an unforeseeable cataclysm, a high-pitched cry, which was the monsters' manner of expressing their deepest distress, rose from the depths of the central pit. With jeers full of despair in which I thought I detected bloody reproaches and threats directed at me, a large flock arose and flew toward the accursed region of the south with frightening speed.

"I lost my head, crushed by this unexpected blow that I could not understand. I refused to believe that all that I had done was for naught, that the Great Brain had suddenly recovered its lost power, when I believed it to be slowly fading away.

"I stood up, frantic. Already, other flocks, from more distant towers, were on their way to join the first; the sky was filling with heartrending screams.

"Caught off guard, I searched desperately for some idea, some solution. The sense of my own helplessness overwhelmed me with despair and rage.

"At this moment, the thunder roared, and waves propelled by a sudden gale crashed against the towers, reaching as high as the platforms; in the midst of this maelstrom of nature-in-turmoil, I saw a blinding shower of lightning bolts above my signals. The luminous lines of the electric lamps disappeared. I understood that my work had been ruined by the vengeful rage of the Great Brain, awoken from its torpor, and by some unknown means recovered from the weakness in which I had sunk it through starvation.

"I had no time to recover from the despondency and consternation I felt; already the furious Vampires, believing that I had betrayed them—or perhaps obeying the all-powerful suggestion of my terrible adversary—were rushing from the depths of the tower and swooping down on me like vultures on a corpse.

"In an instant, I was surrounded; their high-pitched vociferations were deafening; they threw me to the ground and struck me with their palps. Some of them gripped my throat as if to strangle me; others dragged me to the edge of the platform and I thought that they were going to throw me into the sea.

"They fought over me as if I were their prey and wrenched me every which way; the least of the risks I ran was that of being torn apart.

"When they first assaulted me, I still had my opal mask. One of them took notice of this and tore it off.

"I was pulled this way and that, lacerated and bitten, and I couldn't see anything; it was horrible!

"I believed, this time, it was certain death, but I had been dealt such a blow by the destruction of my signals and the lightning-like awakening of the Great Brain that I was resigned to anything, as dazed as the man condemned to death, woken with a start and thrown gasping onto the plank of the guillotine.

"Suddenly, I felt the Vampires' palps knotting themselves like a rope around my limbs. I heard the beating of their wings as they took me away.

"They rushed me into the vast pit that formed the interior of the tower.

"I felt the vertiginous sensation of a vertical drop into darkness. I lost consciousness.

"From then on, I don't remember anything.

"It is here, in your midst, that my eyes opened again to the light . . ."

A feeling of astonishment was painted on every face at this abrupt and unexpected denouement. Robert Darvel couldn't stop himself from smiling.

"I believe," he said, "that what happened to me after I lost consciousness is self-explanatory. The Vampires, at the last minute, recoiled before the idea of putting me to death.

"Perhaps they remembered the services I had rendered them; perhaps they were afraid that my death might be avenged. Who knows what logic these at once complicated and simplistic minds obeyed?

"I guess that they must have been of two minds, that some of them stood up for me, tried to vindicate me; in the end, they bypassed the problem. They quite simply embalmed me in their way, perhaps to preserve the possibility, at a later date, of rousing me from this lethargic slumber.

"As to how my return was effected, I am limited to hypotheses.

"Here is the one I find the most plausible:

"The Great Brain, after the peril I had exposed him to, would no longer tolerate my presence on the planet—even as a mummy. He commanded the Vampires to send me back from whence I came.

"As for the means employed to launch me beyond the planet's sphere of attraction, the most natural assumption is that they made use of the easiest means at their disposal, namely, the eruptive force of a volcano.

"People are generally unaware of this force's great power.

"Father Martinet has written that Etna hurls rocks at a velocity of eight hundred meters per second. Vesuvius, Hekla, and Stromboli throw their projectiles at roughly twice that speed, between twelve and fifteen hundred meters per second. But Cotopaxi, Pichincha, and other South American volcanoes transmit, to the lava hurled from their craters, an initial speed that sometimes reaches four kilometers per second.

"On Mars I saw volcanoes as large as those I have just named. Their power of projection must be even greater still given the decreased gravitation and thinner atmosphere.

"Therefore it would by no means be surprising if the sphere from which you have pulled me had been loaded like an ordinary shell into the chimney of a volcano; in addition, perhaps the Vampires possess the secret—theoretically quite simple—of producing eruptions at will, and that of channeling the force of the gases' expansion.

"My journey from Mars to Earth must have been much like that of the numerous meteors that reach our globe every year.

"There is just one thing left to explain," concluded the engineer, suddenly contemplative. "How I came to land precisely on this villa. I don't believe it was simply chance, but this, perhaps, is a secret known only to the Great Brain . . ."

* * *

A deep silence greeted the conclusion of this fabulous tale. No idle questions, no banal congratulations entered anybody's head.

But Ralph Pitcher and Miss Alberte exchanged glances as if each was waiting for the other to speak.

It was the naturalist who, after a sign from the young woman, arose and stood in front of Robert Darvel.

"I have," he said, "something important to tell you. After hearing your story, I no longer have any doubt: the Vampires have followed you to Earth!"

"But that's impossible!" exclaimed the engineer, with great agitation. "Are you quite sure of this?"

"Absolutely sure. The Vampires are here; they prowl around the villa! Zarouk has seen them! Your brother Georges has seen them! . . ."

And in one breath, Pitcher related the incidents that had taken place at the Villa des Lentisques that we have recounted above.

Robert was dumbfounded.

"Why didn't you warn me earlier?" he murmured. "You have no idea what danger you are in . . ."

"To warn you," said Miss Alberte sharply, "was not possible.

"Only a few days ago, you were hovering between life and death.

"And, to tell the truth, we didn't know, we weren't sure.

"We needed your exact description of these monsters to fully comprehend the danger ourselves . . ."

"Have no fear," said Robert. "Now I am warned. I triumphed over the Vampires on their own ground, in their element. We would have to be very unlucky not to vanquish them on our planet, where all the odds are against them . . .

"I will go so far as to say that their presence is a happy event for science . . . Now it will be my turn to take them prisoner, to extract their secrets. I will surely find a way, with Ralph's help, to make them visible to our eyes, even though I no longer have my magic mask."

But, in spite of these assertions designed to reassure his friends, the engineer had become suddenly solemn and worried. His forehead was creased in reflection. He was frowning, and his efforts to conceal his preoccupation were in vain.

"You've suddenly grown very quiet," observed the young woman.

"Yes, I'm wondering why the Vampires followed me, whether they are numerous, whether they came in the same way as I. These are the questions I have, and I must find some answers.

"I don't believe that they came with harmful intentions. They had me at their mercy on the planet Mars. Nothing would have been easier for them than to kill me.

"Were they sent into exile after me by the Great Brain, in punishment for their rebellion?

"Is it, on the contrary, that they recognized that I alone was capable — as I showed them — of standing up to their tyrant?

"Finally, is it a calamity independent of their will that has landed them on our planet?

"I will have to figure all of this out . . ."

PART THREE

....

The Last of the Vampires

I

....

Nocturnal Phantasms

Robert Darvel was alone in his room. A little weary after recounting his adventures, he had left his hosts after agreeing to review, the following day, what measures to take to protect the villa.

While glancing over a few notes he had just taken, he thought about the strange state of affairs. He was profoundly surprised, he who shouldn't have been surprised by anything. He thought he had returned for good to his peaceful existence, and yet his fantastic odyssey continued, on the old planet where he had expected to find rest.

In reality he was, it should be said, more surprised than annoyed. Without being conscious of it, he felt a secret pleasure in being able to prove to everyone the truth of everything he had said. He would be able to show the Martian Vampires to scientists, to academies, and say, "See, they exist . . ."

He lay down absorbed in these thoughts to which were added the pre-occupation of finding the secret of his prized opal mask, an indispensable weapon in the battle he was preparing to fight.

"I said that it was opal," he murmured, "but if it was, it must have undergone some special preparation. Opal doesn't have that limpidity. It would be necessary to study the series of substances that receive impressions from these invisible rays . . ."

Sleep was overtaking him, and he finally gave in, after taking the precaution of shutting off the electric switch. Robert Darvel had been enjoying a deep sleep—the fortifier of convalescents—for about an hour, when he had a dream.

It seemed to him that the beating of wings filled his room, that fantastic, indistinct shapes were emerging from the shadows.

He recognized the Vampires.

They were swarming and whirling about him like moths, some were perched on his headboard, standing on their palps like pet birds.

Although the Martian Vampires did not possess the faculty of language, those in his dream spoke to him.

They related the Great Brain's terrible vengeance, the towers damaged by lightning, the earthquakes and the bloody massacres.

The Vampires had revolted again and had been crushed. So they had wanted to retrieve him, Robert Darvel, from the tomb where he had been buried in the depths of a crypt. They had bitterly regretted their ungracious conduct toward him.

But when they had tried to pull him from his tomb, the thunder rumbled and waves rose to the sky; the god of the mountain had given the imperious order to throw the sphere that contained the audacious organizer of the rebellions into the volcano.

They had no choice but to obey, seething with rage, and almost immediately an eruption had launched the sphere beyond the reach of the planet's gravity, in a giant column of liquid fire.

"It was then that fifteen or so desperate Vampires, sacrificing themselves for the common good, had decided to take the same path, to follow him and bring him back willingly or by force. He alone was able to save them, he alone was able to exterminate the Great Brain, and then take its place as their king, their god . . ."

In many dreams, the sleeper obeys a perfectly logical reasoning.

"If this is the case," objected Robert, pleased to learn that the number of monsters was not more significant, "how is it that some among you arrived before me, although you left after me?"

The Vampires answered, as seasoned astronomers might have done, that bodies abandoned to celestial space were subject to all sorts of hazards, that nothing more than the attraction of some other planet was enough to cause the bolide in which Robert found himself enclosed to deviate from its route . . .

Finally, they fervently begged Robert to follow them, and he heard those strange high-pitched cries that had no human equivalent intermixed with their entreaties.

Robert emphatically refused. He reminded them of their ingratitude and their stupidity, threatening them with his wrath if they didn't return to Mars.

Infuriated by his refusal, the Vampires passed from entreaties to threats. Robert defied them, pointing out that on Earth they didn't possess the same abilities as on their planet. They responded, squealing with rage, that they knew very well how to force him to obey them; they would seize, if necessary, all that was most dear to him in the world, his brother, his friends, his fiancée. Then, he would beg them to take him back to Mars and to search for a means of returning there.

The Vampires withdrew in an angry beating of wings and Robert Darvel again found himself alone in the shade of one of the blood-colored forests he had so often traversed on Mars.

Suddenly, he saw Miss Alberte's room, which he had visited a few days previously. The young woman was stretched out on her bed. A smile of mysterious candor illuminated her fresh face, and the gleam of the night-lights discreetly lit her beautiful dark gold hair.

But he discerned a fluttering of wings in the warm night air; from the other side of the Moorish window's stained glass panels, the large eyes of the Vampires glowed in the darkness.

The nightmare continued. One of the monsters infiltrated the room. Nudging open the window with his palps, he entered with a light, almost imperceptible flapping of his wings, searching the half-light with his vast pupils. Then he leaned over the young woman, his hideous face expressing astonishment and admiration, and he hesitantly placed one of his palps on the shoulder of the sleeping beauty, whose face froze with terror, though she did not wake up.

It seemed to Robert that he witnessed this entire scene from a great distance, unable to intervene; he wrung his hands in despair.

Meanwhile, the Vampires had entered one by one and there was now a whole swarm around the young woman's bed. They lifted her with infinite precautions, carrying her with their palps, but despite their skill and care, they couldn't prevent her from opening her eyes.

Miss Alberte let out a terrible scream, a heartrending appeal of terror and anguish . . .

* * *

Robert Darvel awoke, his heart beating wildly and his forehead drenched in sweat. Still in the grip of the hideous nightmare, he no longer knew whether he was asleep or awake when the same desperate scream that he thought he had heard in his dream pierced the silence of the night and was followed by jeering, high-pitched laughter.

Robert leapt from his bed, struck by a horrific thought.

He dashed out of the room. On the landing, he found his brother and the naturalist: they too had heard the scream and had rushed out of their rooms, without even taking time to dress.

"What's going on?" asked Ralph Pitcher. "I thought . . ."

"Can't you see," interrupted the engineer rudely. "The Vampires! . . . They are here . . . They have just kidnapped Miss Alberte . . . maybe killed her!"

He dashed toward the young woman's room, followed by Georges and Pitcher, and soon thereafter Zarouk, Chérifa, and Mr. Frymcock. When they caught up with the engineer, he had already forced the door with his shoulder.

The room was empty. The still-warm bed bore no trace of a struggle. In despair, Robert gestured to the open window.

"They carried her off through there," he cried, sobbing like a child. "Why didn't I watch over her?"

"We must find Miss Alberte," said Georges.

"You don't know these Vampires, Georges," replied the engineer despairingly. "They are already far away with their prey. Find Miss Alberte! So you imagine that it's an easy thing! Who knows how far the monsters have flown and which direction they took!

"There's nothing we can do! Nothing!"

And Robert sunk his nails into the palms of his clenched hands until they bled.

He had collapsed on a seat and was crying hot tears.

Ralph Pitcher, profoundly moved by his friend's grief, tried to console him, to question him.

In a few broken and gasping phrases, Robert told them about the nightmare that had haunted him and that was so closely linked to Miss Alberte's disappearance.

"Now I understand," he murmured. "My dream was generated by the Vampires' suggestions; perhaps I saw them even, I was in such a state of nervous tension . . . I no longer know . . . Was I the victim of a hallucination brought on by this exhausting evening, by my fears; was I, for a few moments, clairvoyant?

"But why did they attack Miss Alberte? Wouldn't it have been easy to capture me instead? My head's spinning. I am tortu ed by a horrible thought: could the Vampires be enamored of Alberte, as it is said that demons were enamored of angels in the first ages of the world?"

Robert had taken his temples in his hands. The unfortunate hero was a terrible sight to see. The intrepid scientist, the energetic explorer, had become as weak as a child.

"My dear friend," said Ralph, "we must not give way to discouragement. I myself believe that nothing is lost. Let's think. There are, you told me, only fifteen or so Vampires; whether you know this thanks to a hallucination or to a hypnotic suggestion, it doesn't matter!

"In these conditions, whatever the strength of their wings, they cannot go very far with the burden they are carrying.

"Didn't you also say that they usually slept at night?"

"Yes, I even added that in this they were absolutely different from the Erloor."

"Well, in that case, they should be sleeping now, in the hiding places where they are holding their captive, and this hideout cannot be very far. It should not be impossible to find it, and if we do, we have the opportunity to catch them asleep."

This sensible reasoning calmed and consoled Robert Darvel and rekindled his hope.

Dawn was breaking above the forest. This night, much of which had been filled by the engineer's account, had passed with disconcerting swiftness.

"We must set off this very instant," said Pitcher.

"May I come with you?" begged little Chérifa, whose large black eyes were blurred with tears.

"That will not be possible," said Pitcher softly. "You would slow us down, but Zarouk will accompany us. If we can discover the Vampires' trail, it will only be because of him. Was he not the first to sense their presence?"

The Negro turned the white globes of his expressionless eyes toward the naturalist. His face showed in this moment a singular mixture of terror and satisfaction.

"Do you have some idea of the place where your mistress might be hidden?" asked Georges.

Zarouk extended his arm toward the east.

"She is there!" he said gravely.

"But where over there?"

"In the ruins of Chehahia! She can only be there! It is there that the Vampires are hiding. Yesterday, and again tonight, I smelled them in the breath of the wind."

Pitcher and Georges looked at each other.

"Let's go!" the naturalist exclaimed impetuously.

"Let's hope," murmured the engineer in anguish, "that we don't arrive too late."

"Have hope. If Zarouk is so positive, he has his reasons.

"I explained to you already this Negro's exquisite sensitivity, which is equivalent to a sort of intuition.

"Many times, Miss Alberte has happened to get lost: each time Zarouk went directly and without hesitation to the place where she was. You can't begin to imagine how much the poor Negro's pronouncement has reassured me."

II

....

The Pursuit

As they talked, Robert and his friends had left the villa, leaving behind only Frymcock, who was to telephone Bizerta.

With Zarouk in the lead, they followed a path that left the forest route on the left and zigzagged through stands of wild olive, tamarind, and pomegranate.

They descended the steep slope of a ravine, at the bottom of which the clear water of a wadi rushed among the loose stones and tall oleanders.

The heat grew heavier and more oppressive as they walked; the sun, already high in the sky, was beating down on the roof of the forest, from which climbed the last mists of the morning dew. The trees, one might have said, were stewing in their own sap under their bark.

They had to stop for a few moments at the edge of a spring. When they set off again and Zarouk had resumed his place at the head of the little band, the Negro appeared to have forgotten his fear. Head upright, teeth clenched, nostrils agitated with a nervous tic, he took vast strides as if drawn by some unknown force.

Meanwhile, the ravines and woods, the hills and wadis, continued, and after nearly three hours no ruins had yet taken shape on the horizon. Exhausted and not yet himself, Robert Darvel struggled to keep up with his companions.

The country they crossed was deserted. They met no natives along the way; as this surprised Robert, Pitcher explained that since the bolide had fallen from the sky, terrifying stories had driven everyone away from the villa and its surroundings. The indiscretions of the servants had been enough for the lively Arab imagination to cut out of whole cloth the legend of the Vampires.

Which historian said that history is born from legends? In the brilliant fantasies of the Kroumir storytellers, facts had come to be added that nobody had witnessed, but which all declared to be true. They recounted that small children had been devoured by monsters, that lambs or goats had been bled to death.

Everyone had moved away from the villa, as if from an accursed place.

The pastures were deserted, and there was little but ruined shacks and piles of filth in the abandoned douars. The sorrowful, tuneless songs of shepherds and pig keepers no longer disturbed the solitude.

In spite of the vivid greenery and the bright sunlight sparkling on the slack and radiant sea, the landscape had a profoundly cheerless appearance.

Ralph Pitcher himself who, of the four, had best kept his composure, was more and more distressed by this desolate impression, when Zarouk, reaching the summit of a wooded hillock, stopped abruptly.

"We are there," he said, extending his hand. "They are over there!"

Robert made out a chaotic mass of collapsed arcades buried under dense brush, tumbled pillars, and broken archways, from which masses of creeping roots ran like grass snakes.

"These are the Roman ruins of Chehahia," said Ralph Pitcher.

"Miss Alberte is here, without any doubt. It is the only place within a ten-league radius that can serve as a hiding place for the Vampires.

"Used to sleeping each night, exhausted by the heavier atmosphere of Earth, and by the increased force of gravity, they must be worn out. We will have them cheap."

Robert said nothing, looking at his friend imploringly, as if to make him understand that his sole hope was to save Miss Alberte.

"Show some confidence, for heaven's sake!" muttered Pitcher in a gruff tone that hid his emotion poorly. "I swear to you that we will save her . . ."

Both of them looked for a moment at the majestic ruins, which comprised three levels of vaults leaning against the rock and engulfed by luxuriant vegetation. It looked almost like a cathedral bearing a forest on its roof. A hundred-year-old carob tree had attached itself to the highest terrace, teetering upon roots gripping whatever they could to fight against the fury of the winds, which are terrible in this region.

Slender laurels growing between the blocks of stone seemed still to stretch their noble branches to the passerby for the crown of emperors or poets. Wild vines, ivy, briars, and terebinth hung their garlands on the thresholds of the darkened rooms.

Georges Darvel, who had remained in the rear, moved forward.

"Before we venture inside," he murmured, lowering his voice as if he feared to arouse the attention of the Vampires, "we should study the layout of the structure."

"According to archaeologists," Pitcher gruffly responded, "this was a fortified storehouse, such as the decadent Romans constructed on every frontier for the provisioning of their legions.

"The layout of the interior is very simple; it is a succession of vast vaulted cellars of which only the lower floor is well preserved. There they packed wheat, oil, and wine in jars or amphorae, as the Arabs still do today.

"Zarouk, who, when the fancy takes him, has the custom common to many natives of looking for treasures in the ruins, has entered these cellars many times . . ."

"Enough of this!" exclaimed Georges fervidly. "The Negro will guide us and, if the Vampires are really housed in this hole, we shall see whether they are immune to armored bullets!"

Just in case, as he was leaving the villa, the young man had armed himself with a fine Colt revolver, some steel bullets, and a supply of cartridges. It isn't that he had a blind confidence in these rudimentary terrestrial weapons for fighting beings as strangely formed as the Vampires. Georges had reasoned that perhaps the monsters were unfamiliar with the effects of firearms, and he was impatient to test his theory. One can see that if he had searched his own feelings Georges Darvel would have discovered a sort of frustration and a feverish haste to come to blows with the Invisibles. He longed to enter into open combat with the mystery and to come to grips, so to speak, with the sphinx, man to man.

Zarouk, who had remained a little apart, had not missed a word of the conversation. He suddenly pulled the naturalist by the sleeve, and then, eyes uplifted and right hand extended, he made a peculiar nod.

For some time, the sky had been darkening, smeared with clouds the color of sulfur or soot, and the sun's rays had taken on a livid, leaden hue: lit in this way, the ruins acquired a dramatic, almost threatening aspect.

"You want to warn me that a storm is brewing," said Pitcher to the Negro. "I rather noticed it, but what does it matter to us? Lead us to the entrance of the cellars, that is all I ask of you. If you don't have enough courage to follow us, we will go in without you."

Without a word, Zarouk started off toward the ruins.

Following his lead, Pitcher and Robert Darvel were just passing between the first fallen columns of the fortress when Georges, who followed behind, stopped them with a gesture. His face was beaming; he had just made a discovery that Robert deemed of utmost importance.

It was a strip of green "liberty" silk caught on some brambles.

Robert was visibly moved as he examined it.

"It is a piece of the ribbon that Miss Alberte wore in her hair," he murmured in a changed voice. "This piece of silk can only have come from her. Zarouk spoke the truth! We are on the right track; Miss Alberte is here! . . ."

Georges Darvel was astounded: until then, he had had some doubts about the marvelous intuitive faculties of the blind Negro; now no objection was possible.

Robert tenderly stowed the piece of silk, and with renewed courage the little band passed through the curtain of vines that covered the entrance to the cellars. The Negro pulled a lantern from under his burnoose and lit it; Georges Darvel had his revolver in hand; they began their descent.

By a series of steps cut in the rock, they reached a long vaulted room without difficulty, scattering in alarm some night birds disturbed in their slumber.

Robert Darvel had insisted on going first. He couldn't help thinking, he who knew the Vampires, that their undertaking was sheer madness, but he reasoned that, if he were killed, his death would perhaps give his friends time to free Miss Alberte.

Georges, for his part, was brimming with confidence and enthusiasm; in spite of what his brother had told him of the Invisibles he was convinced that, however powerful they were, their brains would not withstand projectiles capable of passing straight through six inches of solid oak.

They advanced a dozen meters further, but more slowly. Zarouk appeared to be overcome by uncontrollable terror.

His whole body was racked with convulsive shudders and his face had acquired that livid gray hue that, with him—as we have mentioned on several occasions—characterized the pinnacle of fear.

He must have felt the presence of the Invisibles, and he truly deserved the utmost gratitude for this display of courage. Suddenly, he froze; his teeth were chattering like castanets, and in his hand the lantern was sketching fantastic zigzags.

"Give me that," said Pitcher. "It's plain to see that you have the shakes."

He didn't finish. A large indistinct shadow had passed between him and the wall, and Georges had been brushed in passing by a hairy wing. The young man felt his hair stand on end in horror.

"A Vampire!" he murmured.

But he was brave: as he spoke, he fired his weapon, aiming as best he could.

There was some stifled laugher, then nothing more. The bullet had fallen inert at Georges's feet. He thought it had ricocheted against a section of wall, but when he picked it up to examine it, it was intact; the sharp steel tip had not even been blunted.

Everyone grew silent, terrified.

Zarouk was an especially pitiful sight.

"You fired at a Vampire?" Pitcher finally asked in a low voice.

"I believe so," mumbled Georges . . . "But look!"

He showed him the undamaged bullet.

"I knew it," murmured Robert. "Do you remember what I told you yesterday evening?"

"Look, Georges," interrupted Ralph Pitcher, "have you ever seen English soldiers shoot at yogis for target practice?"

"No."

"Well! I have seen it more than once in the Indies. It is a diversion the unfortunate Captain Wad often provided for us.

"Even if you choose the best weapons and the most skillful marksmen, the Indian resists by the strength of his will, and the bullet falls without power at his feet . . . see, exactly like this one.

"Do you understand what incomparable power the Vampires with their enormous brains must possess next to those poor Indian jugglers!

"Your brother was right. It is awful, but I think that there is unfortunately nothing to be done against them . . . nothing."

It is plain that the naturalist, so enthusiastic and calm at the beginning of the expedition, was giving way little by little to discouragement.

But at his words Georges felt a surge of noble rage.

"We shall see about that!" he exclaimed, clenching his teeth. "I will not give up! We shall see! . . ."

And three times in quick succession, before his brother and his friends were able to stop him, he fired his weapon again in the direction where the monster had disappeared.

Three times the bullets fell inert at his feet as the first had . . . But at the sound of the last shot a heartrending cry arose from the depths of the cellar.

"Alberte! It's Alberte," exclaimed Robert with a mad gesture. "She has heard us! She is calling to us! . . ."

He dashed forward and then, suddenly, recoiled inexplicably, with a strangled shout.

To the profound astonishment of his companions, he headed off, gesticulating as he went, toward the exit of the tunnel, but *backward*.

"Where are you going, Robert?" exclaimed the naturalist.

"Are you abandoning us? . . ."

Pitcher fell silent, seized with horror, as he realized that the engineer's feet *were not touching the ground*.

At the very moment that he made this terrifying observation, he felt himself seized by the hair and dragged outside by an irresistible force.

When he recovered his wits, after this infernal sensation, he found himself at the entrance of the stairs, in the midst of his three companions, who were white and trembling as he was. All four were at a complete loss for words.

"You see," Robert Darvel finally stammered in a very weak voice, hoarse from fear. "They didn't even deign to kill us. They threw us out of their lair with contempt . . . They are going to keep Miss Alberte! What can we do? My God, what can we do?"

"Yes, what can we do? . . ." Georges repeated, deeply demoralized.

"They gave us a warning," uttered Zarouk with difficulty. "If we attack them again, they will kill us, that much is certain. By Allah, I am greatly afraid."

"We are all afraid," said Georges Darvel sadly. "There is no shame in that. We are dealing with no ordinary enemy here."

"Yet," grumbled Pitcher, whose anger was awakening, "we must gain the upper hand. I will succeed or my name isn't Ralph Pitcher!"

The naturalist had sat down on the shaft of a fallen column to think, his head in his hands like a schoolboy single-mindedly searching for the solution to a difficult problem.

Suddenly he stood up, his face aglow.

"My friends," he said, "let's not let ourselves be controlled by phenomena that, after all, are already in part classified and known to science. First there were x-rays, now there are x-beings—nothing is more logical. This has the advantage of explaining the nature of the many ghosts that terrified the Middle Ages! But even if the Vampires are invisible, that is no reason to be afraid of them, and I shall show them that they are no match for this Scotsman."

The naturalist had delivered this speech, animated by national pride, with typically British aplomb.

"But for heaven's sake," asked Georges with impatience, "what do you intend to do?"

Pitcher took Zarouk's heavy club from him and pointed to an overhanging slab of masonry above the entrance to the cavern, which seemed held in place only by a miracle.

"I am quite simply going to trap the Invisibles in their lair. They will not be able to carry off Miss Alberte without us seeing them. We will remain here, as sentries. During this time one of us, Georges for example, will go to Ain Draham to ask the commander of the fort to place the soldiers of the penal battalion at our disposal. He will certainly not refuse.

"The ruins will be surrounded by a cordon of troops, and we will clear away the rubble only after we have placed a net of iron mesh over the entrance. The cellars have no exit but this. No Vampire will escape, I'll make sure of it!"

"Wonderful!" Georges objected, "And where would we find such a net? In the time it would take, Miss Alberte might perish a hundred times over.

"I have thought of that," replied Pitcher. "There is, at this very moment, a destroyer harbored at Tabarka: the anti-torpedo nets with which it is supplied are exactly what we need! We will pay whatever compensation the Royal Navy requires, if need be!"

Robert and Georges were surprised by the naturalist's display of quick thinking and common sense.

"Take care," objected the engineer, "that your cave-in doesn't entirely cut off the cavern's supply of breathable air. Remember that Miss Alberte . . ."

Pitcher shrugged his shoulders.

"This is of no concern. There are enough cracks in the old walls," he murmured.

And cutting the discussion short, he climbed over the broken stones and, using Zarouk's club as a lever, he thrust it into a fissure and set about prying loose the enormous block.

At that moment, a hail of large stones, launched with the force and accuracy of a catapult, flew out of the gaping entrance to the cellar. The Vampires, after having expelled their enemies, were pursuing their victory.

Robert Darvel, who had immediately thrown himself flat on the ground, wasn't hit; Zarouk suffered a glancing blow to his leg; but Georges, who was hit on the side of the head, collapsed, severely injured.

At that very moment, Pitcher's efforts managed to dislodge the few stones that held the unsteady block: torn from its resting place, it crashed with a thunderous roar, blocking the entrance to the cellar with its bulk and raising a thick cloud of dust.

Robert Darvel dashed toward the unconscious body of his brother.

"My brother! My dear Georges!" he repeated, frantically.

Pitcher and Zarouk helped him transport the wounded man to the shade of a carob tree; he no longer showed any sign of life. Devastated by this latest misfortune, Robert babbled incoherently. Pitcher feared for a moment that this terrible shock might have made him lose his mind.

"Come," he said roughly, "show some courage and above all self-control! Moaning will get us nowhere—we have to act. The wound doesn't appear as serious as I thought at first, but the most urgent thing is to take care of

Georges. There is a spring a hundred meters from here. We will carry him there. The cool water will bring him around . . . Yet I hesitate to let these devils of Vampires out of my sight! . . . They must not profit from our absence to remove the barricade that holds them prisoner! . . ."

After hasty deliberation, it was decided that Zarouk would remain as a sentry before the ruins. Georges was laid on a stretcher hastily improvised from branches; Pitcher and Robert Darvel each took one end and headed toward the spring.

They were slowed as much by the muggy heat of the storm, threatening since the morning, as by exhaustion. A stale odor rose from the ground, and the motionless foliage was bowing sadly as if it too was faltering in the sweltering heat of a burning sky.

Suddenly, the clouds burst in a cluster of lightning. The downpour fell with a violence unknown in our temperate climates. The rain flowed continuously, gouging holes in the ground, uprooting plants, laying bare the roots of trees, and carrying off rocks and dead wood in quick, suddenly swollen cascades.

Soaked from head to toe, Ralph and Robert had to stop, taking shelter under the cover of a large tree.

But the cool, torrential rain had been beneficial for the injured man: he opened his eyes, let out a deep sigh, and sat up.

Pitcher was pleased to see him regain consciousness more easily than he had expected when Zarouk appeared between the trees, his face distressed, streaming with water.

Pitcher sensed some new catastrophe.

"Quick!" cried the Negro in a strangled voice, "You must come. Fire . . . fire in the ruins!"

"You're mad," Pitcher answered back. "How can the ruins have caught on fire in this rain?"

"It doesn't matter!" said Robert. "Let's go. I'm afraid I understand all too well! . . ."

The two friends dashed off behind the Negro, hurdling streams and leaping puddles.

Robert wasn't wrong: when he arrived in front of the ruins, eddies of noxious smoke were escaping from every crack in the ancient building.

"Miss Alberte is in this blaze," stammered Robert, pale with shock . . .

"And I blocked off the only entrance!" cried Pitcher in despair.

Without a word, all three set to work, shifting the blocks with mad fury, their fingernails bleeding from the roughness of the stone.

"What a terrible idea you had, my poor friend!" the engineer couldn't stop himself from saying.

Pitcher didn't answer, but he continued to clear a path through the rubble with silent fury. He moved slabs of masonry nearly as large as he; his arms were covered with blood and mud up to the elbow.

Soon, an opening large enough for a man to pass through had been cleared; a cloud of smoke streamed over the workers through this new exit.

Pitcher was already halfway into the opening when Robert Darvel violently pulled him back.

"I'm the one who will save my fiancée!" he said roughly, and before anyone could stop him he slipped into the dark hole.

"He'll die for sure!" Pitcher complained. "He's exhausted, still recuperating. It would have made much more sense for me to take my chances."

But even as he spoke he had slipped in turn into the hole.

Zarouk didn't have the heart to follow them into the blaze, but he continued to work with all his strength to widen the opening.

A few minutes passed. Great swirls of smoke mixed with sparks still escaped from the abyss, but the two courageous rescuers had not yet reappeared.

Zarouk was suffering, as it were, every sort of anxiety; finally he seemed to hear calls for help from the cavern.

This time, devotion prevailed over fear and he too dashed into the smoke. He had only taken a few steps when he collided with Robert in the darkness.

"Quick," murmured the engineer in a fading voice, "I have Miss Alberte, take her, save her! . . ."

The Negro took the inert body of the young woman and carried her outside, where he laid her on the ground; then he courageously returned to look for Robert.

He had great difficulty finding him: during this short interval, the engineer, at the end of his strength, had fainted; he eventually discovered him by groping about and laid him next to Miss Alberte.

Robert, fortunately, regained consciousness immediately once he was out in the open air and cooled by the now dying storm.

"Alberte is safe!" were his first words.

Then, not catching sight of the naturalist:

"But Pitcher? Where is Pitcher?"

"Present!" responded a hoarse voice.

And Pitcher, black with soot and smoke, burst from the hole, coughing and sneezing loudly.

"Is she alive?" asked the naturalist with great concern.

"Yes," murmured Robert, anxiously leaning toward the face of the young woman, "she is still breathing, but very weakly!"

"There is only one thing to do: carry her to the spring where we took your brother.

"I will bathe her brow in cool water while one of us goes to seek help at the villa."

He lifted Miss Alberte in his brawny arms and started walking as buoy- antly as if he carried no burden at all.

But suddenly he stopped, like someone remembering something impor- tant he has forgotten.

"Zarouk," he said, with his customary composure, "you will do me the pleasure of staying here and not leaving before this hole is hermetically and solidly sealed. It is an indispensable precaution if you no longer wish to be tormented by the Vampires."

Zarouk didn't need to be told twice; he set about the task with an ardor made greater by the hope of shutting the monsters into their lair and of being forever delivered from them.

Arriving near the spring where they had left Georges, Robert and his friend, who was carrying the still-unconscious young woman, were sur- prised to find the wounded man almost recovered: he was erect, leaning against the trunk of the tree, and he had bandaged his injury himself with his handkerchief.

He moved forward to meet Pitcher when the sounds of an automobile horn rang out not far away.

"Frymcock!" exclaimed Georges. "It's Frymcock — he had the good sense to take the car by the forest road to join us . . . I'll run to tell him not to go any farther."

While the young man dashed through the woods to reach the road, Miss Alberte was laid down on the moss-covered slope. Her friends had the pleasure of seeing her come to, thanks to large streams of cool water. The first thing she saw was Robert's face; a fragile smile took shape on her pale lips, and she closed her eyes again; but her face had regained its typical rosy glow and her pulse beat steadily. She was going to be fine.

She was promptly seated in the car, which set off for the villa at a moderate speed. She was still in no state to speak, but she had taken one of Robert's hands in her own and made him understand, by a soft pressure, all the happiness that she felt to find herself safe and sound by his side.

As for the lord cook, who held the steering wheel with all the panache of a consummate chauffeur, he itched to question Pitcher. His sad clown's face expressed the most lively curiosity, but Pitcher made him understand, with an expressive gesture, that no idle talk must trouble the young woman's rest. Her recovery might be compromised by the slightest negligence.

Pitcher's concerns were well founded.

Miss Alberte was so weakened, so enervated by her terrible jolt, that at the moment the car stopped before the front steps of the villa, she again lost consciousness.

Robert seized her in his arms and insisted he carry her himself to her room.

III

....

Explanations

In the end, Miss Alberte — apart from the asphyxiation that had nearly killed her — had experienced more fear than pain.

The devoted attention lavished on her, and above all the presence of Robert, who made himself her nurse, had quickly restored her. The only signs of this extraordinary adventure were a strange pallor and some slight burns that would soon disappear, without leaving scars capable of marring her beauty.

That very evening, she was able to stand and go down to the dining room.

After the meal, the same figures as the previous evening gathered in the same room where Robert had given the account of his marvelous expedition.

"Today," said Miss Alberte, laughing, "I am the one who will take the floor; I will, in turn, recount my adventures with the Vampires. They will surely not be as varied or as fascinating as Robert's, but I am nonetheless persuaded that you will find them interesting."

This opening drew an appreciative murmur from the audience: the young woman had been rather coy in not sharing with anyone — not even Robert — a single detail of her captivity among the Invisibles. Everyone was impatient to hear the tale of her experiences.

"I must have been asleep for about an hour," she began, "and my imagination was no doubt still occupied with the strange inhabitants of Mars, when I dreamed that the Vampires of the glass tower threw themselves on me as they had thrown themselves on Robert when they believed he had betrayed them.

"The enormous bulk of one of the monsters weighed on my bosom and I felt the supple embrace of their undulating palps. I would soon realize that I was not dreaming.

"I opened my eyes at the moment when they carried me from my bed; that is when I screamed, when I called out . . .

"I cannot believe I avoided being driven mad by fear.

"Certainly that would have happened to me if I hadn't been in some measure alerted by the account I had just heard.

"I had not the slightest uncertainty about the nature of the danger that I faced.

"I was being kidnapped by the Vampires! This idea came into my mind with terrible certainty. In an instant, I understood that this was the end for me; that was when I cried out a second time for help, a cry that surely must have echoed in every corner of the villa.

"All of that happened in a few seconds; but already I was no longer able to call out—the swiftness with which I was carried off took my breath away.

"I can't remember a feeling more appalling than what I experienced then.

"The hideous contact of those bands around my wrists, my ankles, and my neck was sickening, but the steady beating of the Invisibles' wings fanned, so to speak, my face.

"At the instant when, brutally torn from my bed, I saw myself suspended, without visible support, above the terraces of the villa, I had instinctively shut my eyes.

"A minute later, when I opened them again, I was being carried away in a dizzying ride above the treetops of the forest, under a sky veiled with heavy clouds.

"My head spun, my heart failed me, and I tell you that at that moment it didn't occur to me how much my situation resembled that of the Valkyries carried away into the clouds or that of the saints of legend carried into ecstasies by angels.

"I was dying of fear and tormented by the horrible idea that the Vampires were going to throw me into the sea or drop me into some abyss.

"I fainted. I don't know exactly how long my blackout lasted.

"When I came to, I was still being carried by the Invisibles on the same rapid flight.

"Parenthetically, I guarantee that I will never be tempted to travel by airplane . . .

"I was however a little reassured concerning the possibility of a fall; the Vampires always held me very tight. But I observed that their flight was a lot less rapid than at the beginning. They must have been tired of carrying me like this on the wing.

"I didn't have to wait for proof of this. Suddenly the vice that imprisoned one of my arms loosened.

"I closed my eyes, already convinced that the monsters were going to drop me from high in the sky as I had been fearing; but my arm had just, in almost the same instant, been vigorously seized again. This merry-go-round was repeated several times. I concluded that the Vampires were taking turns.

"They were now flying slowly enough that I was able to recognize the familiar countryside over which we were passing. I was anxiously wondering what they were going to do to me when we descended toward the ruins where you found me.

"Dawn was starting to lighten the sky to the east. I watched those first gleams of dawn with despair, wondering whether I would ever again see the light of day.

"The Vampires surely brought me into that rubble only to devour me at their leisure. I recalled the bowls full of blood in the glass tower and I trembled in every limb.

"They set me down gently enough, but without letting go of me. As they pushed me toward the entrance to the vault, I appealed again for help. But my voice was lost in this desert, and my jailers, no doubt irritated by my rebellious gesture, dragged me deep underground with brutal haste.

"There, they released me. I recovered my freedom of movement with an inexpressible pleasure. You cannot possibly imagine the disgust that the caresses of their palps inspired in me; I think that if snakes, instead of being icy, were warm-blooded animals, they would be even more loathsome to us.

"I seated myself on a large stone, quite astonished that the Vampires had not yet thrown themselves on me, waiting for death from one moment to the next.

"To my great surprise, they didn't bother me in the slightest, but a ray of light that filtered through a crack in the roof showed me that the vault was entirely empty. It felt like I was all alone; I didn't hear the slightest sound, and yet I knew very well that they must still be there.

"Emboldened by the silence, I stood up and headed very quietly toward the exit; but before I had taken three steps my wrist was grasped by a hideous palp and squeezed so hard that tears of pain came to my eyes.

"It was a warning. They didn't want to harm me, at least not for the moment, but they would punish very severely even the smallest attempts at escape. At least that is how I understood it, and I'm certain I was right.

"I spent hours in an indescribable daze and eventually gave in to exhaustion. Resting against the old mossy wall, I closed my eyes for a moment.

"I was awakened by the noise of an explosion that, after it scared me half to death, brought me inexpressible joy.

"I was sure that it was you who were coming to my rescue.

"I recognized Mr. Georges's voice, and the gleam of a lantern revealed your silhouettes in the distance.

"That's when I screamed with all my strength to let you know that I was there and where to find me.

"My appeals and the gunshots produced great confusion among the Vampires. They let out high-pitched cries, they beat their wings, and I believed it was a good time to try to reach you.

"I dashed forward and I could already make out the entrance of the vault when I was roughly shoved and forced to beat a retreat.

"It is then that I felt an angular object under my feet, which I picked up. It was nothing other than a little metal box full of wax matches.

"I have since learned that Zarouk dropped it when he gave his lantern to Mr. Pitcher.

"I returned to my place against the rock. I still held the matches but did not yet know how I might use them.

"Suddenly, the idea came to me to set fire to the dried leaves and undergrowth that covered the floor of the vault and in which I was sunk to my knees. The smoke would force the Vampires to leave and I would take the opportunity to flee. I preferred risking asphyxiation to putting up with this frightening captivity any longer; and the fact that you were all there, close by, gave me a courage that I would surely not have otherwise had.

"This idea had just come to me when a strange phenomenon occurred.

"Probably from the influence of the storm that was about to break, the shapes of the Vampires became discernible to me, as if they had been lightly rubbed with phosphorus.

"Mr. Robert explained to me that bodies rich in phosphorus are very sensitive to the influence of the electricity in thunderstorms; on stormy nights — every fisherman will tell you — certain fish, certain crustaceans become luminous.

"The brain, like sea creatures, contains a heavy proportion of phosphorus: the Vampires, who are so to speak all brain, must be subject to this influence more than others.

"But I had overcome my initial fears. Without making a noise, I gathered at my feet a mound of dried leaves and, straightaway, I set it on fire.

"The flame rose with amazing speed, stimulated by the drafts of air from the cracks, which functioned like chimneys, and a thick smoke flooded the vault.

"I rushed forward; at the very moment I approached the outside opening, a muffled crash boomed out, and the rubble brought down by Mr. Pitcher closed my only exit to light and liberty.

Pitcher blushed like a schoolboy caught in the act and bowed his head.

"I don't blame you," continued Miss Alberte, smiling at the naturalist. "You acted with the best of intentions — you couldn't know that I had just started the fire — but at the time I was filled with dismay. To be trapped in that inferno with the Vampires! I spent several dreadful minutes.

"The monsters, suffocating, leapt about in the smoke, emitting high-pitched and piercing cries. I shuddered to think that they might tear me to pieces in revenge for what I had done. The smoke was blinding, and my coughing was so violent that I began to bring up blood. Soon I lost consciousness, believing that, this time, it really was the end.

"When I reopened my eyes, Mr. Ralph and Mr. Robert were splashing me with water.

"This is the true account of my excursion with the Vampires.

"I would very much like to know, however, whether any of them escaped the flames. If so, the survivors must hold it against me terribly!"

"Let me reassure you in that regard," said Pitcher. "I went to the ruins before we dined. I had the entrance to the cellars cleared away and went in myself.

"The vault is filled with the half-charred bodies of the monsters, a dreadful mush of brains, which it will not even be possible to dissect."

"You can sleep peacefully from now on. There are no more Invisibles!"

* * *

Miss Alberte has been, for a month, the happy wife of Robert Darvel, following splendid celebrations, thanks to which Mr. Frymcock's renown has spread throughout Europe. The lord cook has just refused to enter the Emperor of Russia's service at two hundred thousand rubles a year.

Robert Darvel, whose happiness is complete, is preparing an authoritative work on the planet Mars; in scientific milieus, his theory of the Great Brain is already the object of impassioned debate.

As for Ralph Pitcher, he rarely leaves the rebuilt laboratory: actively assisted by Zarouk and Georges, he is searching for a scientific means of becoming invisible. He has obtained surprising results and already boasts of having made small objects invisible — at the risk of being labeled a pickpocket by wags.

Finally, the Arabs, who avoid the Roman ruins of Chehahia like the plague, are making fabulous tales from the events that we have recounted.

A legend has grown up among them: they maintain that one of the Vampires escaped the massacre and that he wanders mournfully in the great forest of Kroumiria.

They attribute the deaths of their sheep, the illnesses of their children, and in general all unexplainable events to him. Many swear they have heard his forlorn snickers echoing in the emptiness, when the country is threatened with some misfortune.

END

IN THE BISON FRONTIERS OF IMAGINATION SERIES

Gulliver of Mars
By Edwin L. Arnold
Introduced by Richard A. Lupoff
Afterword by Gary Hoppenstand

*A Journey in Other Worlds: A
Romance of the Future*
By John Jacob Astor
Introduced by S. M. Stirling

Queen of Atlantis
By Pierre Benoit
Afterword by Hugo Frey

The Wonder
By J. D. Beresford
Introduced by Jack L. Chalker

*Voices of Vision: Creators of Science
Fiction and Fantasy Speak*
By Jayme Lynn Blaschke

*The Man with the Strange Head and
Other Early Science Fiction Stories*
By Miles J. Breuer
Edited and introduced by Michael R. Page

At the Earth's Core
By Edgar Rice Burroughs
Introduced by Gregory A. Benford
Afterword by Phillip R. Burger

Back to the Stone Age
By Edgar Rice Burroughs
Introduced by Gary Dunham

Beyond Thirty
By Edgar Rice Burroughs
Introduced by David Brin
Essays by Phillip R. Burger
and Richard A. Lupoff

The Eternal Savage: Nu of the Niocene
By Edgar Rice Burroughs
Introduced by Tom Deitz

Land of Terror
By Edgar Rice Burroughs
Introduced by Anne Harris

The Land That Time Forgot
By Edgar Rice Burroughs
Introduced by Mike Resnick

Lost on Venus
By Edgar Rice Burroughs
Introduced by Kevin J. Anderson

The Moon Maid: Complete and Restored
By Edgar Rice Burroughs
Introduced by Terry Bisson

Pellucidar
By Edgar Rice Burroughs
Introduced by Jack McDevitt
Afterword by Phillip R. Burger

Pirates of Venus
By Edgar Rice Burroughs
Introduced by F. Paul Wilson
Afterword by Phillip R. Burger

Savage Pellucidar
By Edgar Rice Burroughs
Introduced by Harry Turtledove

Tanar of Pellucidar
By Edgar Rice Burroughs
Introduced by Paul Cook

Tarzan at the Earth's Core
By Edgar Rice Burroughs
Introduced by Sean McMullen

Under the Moons of Mars
By Edgar Rice Burroughs
Introduced by James P. Hogan

The Absolute at Large
By Karel Čapek
Introduced by Stephen Baxter

The Girl in the Golden Atom
By Ray Cummings
Introduced by Jack Williamson

*The Poison Belt: Being an Account
of Another Amazing Adventure
of Professor Challenger*
By Sir Arthur Conan Doyle
Introduced by Katya Reimann

Tarzan Alive
By Philip José Farmer
New foreword by Win Scott Eckert
Introduced by Mike Resnick

The Circus of Dr. Lao
By Charles G. Finney
Foreword by John Marco
Introduced by Michael Martone

Omega: The Last Days of the World
By Camille Flammarion
Introduced by Robert Silverberg

Ralph 124C 41+
By Hugo Gernsback
Introduced by Jack Williamson

Perfect Murders
By Horace L. Gold
Introduced by E. J. Gold

*The Journey of Niels Klim to
the World Underground*
By Ludvig Holberg
Introduced and edited by
James I. McNelis Jr.
Preface by Peter Fitting

The Lost Continent: The Story of Atlantis
By C. J. Cutcliffe Hyne
Introduced by Harry Turtledove
Afterword by Gary Hoppenstand

*The Great Romance: A Rediscovered
Utopian Adventure*
By The Inhabitant
Edited by Dominic Alessio

Mizora: A World of Women
By Mary E. Bradley Lane
Introduced by Joan Saberhagen

Prisoner of the Vampires of Mars
By Gustave Le Rouge
Translated by David Beus
and Brian Evenson
Introduced by William Ambler

A Voyage to Arcturus
By David Lindsay
Introduced by John Clute

Before Adam
By Jack London
Introduced by Dennis L. McKiernan

Fantastic Tales
By Jack London
Edited by Dale L. Walker

*Master of Adventure: The Worlds
of Edgar Rice Burroughs*
By Richard A. Lupoff
With an introduction to the Bison
Books edition by the author
Foreword by Michael Moorcock
Preface by Henry Hardy Heins
With an essay by Phillip R. Burger

The Year 3000: A Dream
By Paolo Mantegazza
Edited and introduced by
Nicoletta Pireddu
Translated by David Jacobson

The Moon Pool
By A. Merritt
Introduced by Robert Silverberg

The Purple Cloud
By M. P. Shiel
Introduced by John Clute

Shadrach in the Furnace
By Robert Silverberg

Lost Worlds
By Clark Ashton Smith
Introduced by Jeff VanderMeer

Out of Space and Time
By Clark Ashton Smith
Introduced by Jeff VanderMeer

The Skylark of Space
By E. E. "Doc" Smith
Introduced by Vernor Vinge

Skylark Three
By E. E. "Doc" Smith
Introduced by Jack Williamson

*The Nightmare and Other
Tales of Dark Fantasy*
By Francis Stevens
Edited and introduced by
Gary Hoppenstand

Tales of Wonder
By Mark Twain
Edited, introduced, and with
notes by David Ketterer

The Chase of the Golden Meteor
By Jules Verne
Introduced by Gregory A. Benford

*The Golden Volcano: The First English
Translation of Verne's Original Manuscript*
By Jules Verne
Translated and edited by Edward Baxter

*Lighthouse at the End of the World:
The First English Translation of
Verne's Original Manuscript*
By Jules Verne
Translated and edited by William Butcher

Magellania
By Jules Verne
Translated by Benjamin Ivry
Introduced by Olivier Dumas

*The Meteor Hunt: The First English
Translation of Verne's Original Manuscript*
By Jules Verne
Translated and edited by Frederick
Paul Walter and Walter James Miller

The Secret of Wilhelm Storitz
By Jules Verne
Translated and edited by Peter Schulman

The Self-Propelled Island
By Jules Verne
Translated by Marie-Thérèse Noiset
Introduced by Volker Dehs

The Croquet Player
By H. G. Wells
Afterword by John Huntington

In the Days of the Comet
By H. G. Wells
Introduced by Ben Bova

The Last War: A World Set Free
By H. G. Wells
Introduced by Greg Bear

The Sleeper Awakes
By H. G. Wells
Introduced by J. Gregory Keyes
Afterword by Gareth Davies-Morris

The War in the Air
By H. G. Wells
Introduced by Dave Duncan

The Disappearance
By Philip Wylie
Introduced by Robert Silverberg

Gladiator
By Philip Wylie
Introduced by Janny Wurts

The Savage Gentleman
By Philip Wylie
Introduced by Richard A. Lupoff

When Worlds Collide
By Philip Wylie and Edwin Balmer
Introduced by John Varley

To order or obtain more information on these or other University of Nebraska Press titles, visit nebraskapress.unl.edu.